Kings of B'more

R. ERIC THOMAS

Kokila

Kokila
An imprint of Penguin Random House LLC, New York

First published in the United States of America by Kokila,
an imprint of Penguin Random House LLC, 2022

Copyright © 2022 by R. Eric Thomas

Visit us online at penguinrandomhouse.com.

Library of Congress Cataloging-in-Publication Data is available.

Book Manufactured in Canada

ISBN 9780593326183

1 3 5 7 9 10 8 6 4 2
FRI

Design by Jasmin Rubero
Text set in Tibere OT

For Electra

I have come to believe over and over again that what is most important to me must be spoken, made verbal and shared, even at the risk of having it bruised or misunderstood.

—AUDRE LORDE

The Truth must dazzle gradually.

—EMILY DICKINSON

Wednesday

2:00 p.m.

"Now, *this* is living," Linus said, standing in the middle of the empty cemetery.

Harrison ignored him.

Linus swooped into Harrison's eyeline. His height made his animated face unavoidable even though Harrison had developed a sudden intense interest in a cloud. Harrison stared back as if to say *You're really trying it.*

Linus wiggled his eyebrows. *Do you get it?*

Yeah, Harrison got it. *Hilarious. Gets more hilarious every time we visit.*

"Now, this is living!" Linus repeated, this time calling out triumphantly into the endless June sky. His voice carried over sprawling green hills and into the city beneath them, startling a couple of nearby crows into flight.

Baltimore Cemetery was a huge, old-timey hillside burial ground packed to bursting with elaborate historical grave markers and, tucked among them, two sixteen-year-olds pretending to be annoyed with each other. Their trip, as always, was Linus's idea. The main purpose of the space aside, Linus's affinity for this cemetery wasn't morbid. They always came

3

in daylight, and Linus was primarily interested in the space between the dates on each marker and what had happened within it. To Harrison's mind, the thing that kept them coming back was the fact that it didn't feel creepy or forbidding, but rather that it was one of the most wide-open, awe-inspiring spaces they'd ever encountered. Here amongst the stone and the crows and those who belonged only to history, they felt like they'd stumbled into a dazzling new perspective on a city they'd always called home.

Now, this was living.

"There's no place like this," Harrison conceded, still refusing to acknowledge that he was in the presence of a comedy genius. Linus thrust his arms out now and spun in a slow circle. Very *Sound of Music*, except these hills were not alive. If the hills were alive, he and his friend would be in some trouble, and the next bus wasn't coming for another twenty-five minutes. Linus plopped himself down onto a patch of grass and gazed up at a twelve-foot blue-gray angel standing on top of a gravestone. Harrison stepped over Linus's legs, wandered around the base of the gravestone, and made his way to the asphalt driveway. He cast a look back; Linus was the one staring up at the clouds now, not a care in the world, it seemed.

"You going somewhere?" Linus called.

"Just—Nowhere. I'm still here." He couldn't stop moving, fidgeting, futzing with his glasses. He didn't know why. He wasn't going anywhere, but he sure was in a hurry to get there.

Harrison turned and faced the horizon. The cemetery rose up at the end of flat North Avenue like it was built upon the back of a poorly disguised dragon. From the top, you could see all the way downtown to the Harbor south of them, all the way to the tall, narrow houses of West Baltimore, where Linus lived, north to the slightly nearer neighborhood with the wider, shorter homes, where Harrison lived, and out to the docks and highways in the East, through which the city dribbled out into the water in rivulets. If it weren't, you know, a final resting place, Harrison would have thought it rather serene, like a statue garden. Or maybe that was why it was serene. He didn't know. It unnerved him, but the fact that it didn't unnerve Linus gave him license to see it in a different way.

No shade to all the souls gathered there, but they did have a favorite amongst all the statuelike gravestones. It was the one against which Linus was leaning—a tall angel atop a grave from 1860. She had a bowed head, and from one raised hand she pointed her index finger skyward. The first time they'd seen it, Harrison had said, "She looks like she's at a party, going, 'Yes! They're playing my song!'" Linus had laughed so hard, he fell over. They dubbed her "DJ, Turn It Up!"

Though the cemetery was open to the public, that summer it felt like it belonged only to them. An old station wagon sat by the gate most days, and initially the boys held their breath, waiting to be chased away, as if their mere presence were evidence of a crime. But no one ever came. A rarity, a respite. And so they would take the bus from the middle of the city to trek up the hill more and more frequently. They came to wander and to talk and to gaze into the horizon from the only place where they could find it in every direction.

Now Harrison gnawed on the corner of his thumb as he leaned over to look at the name carved on a squat rectangular stone. It seemed everyone in the past had a fanciful name, like something out of a folktale. He wondered when names got so boring. He wanted to live in a world that was just a bit more eccentric. Not the past, he'd correct himself quickly. The past was not exactly ideal for two Black queer boys. But a version of the present that had a bit more magical potential.

This particular stone left a little something to be desired in the name department. It was just a block that bore the word FATHER. Simply FATHER. Father to us all. Next to it was a block of the same size and shape that read MOTHER. So, that's the family. Linus came over and sat next to FATHER. Family meeting. Harrison forced himself to sit down, too. They were surrounded on all sides by statues—many ten or twelve feet high—columns, and figures, and vases, and plinths carved to look like they were shrouded in cloth. Some stones had become discolored—brown, black, gray, with a splash of mustard-yellow moss on a few. Often the graves were slightly tilted, leaning forward or to the side, as if the dragon had stirred in its sleep ages ago. Harrison looked over at Linus and decided that he was uncharacteristically quiet today. Or maybe it was just that Harrison was full of internal chatter. There were times, Harrison thought, that they were totally in sync, like when they communicated without bothering to use words. But there were still times when Harrison wondered about the mystery of his friend and the mystery of himself. Linus always had a lot to say—more questions, more ideas, more grand plans, more jokes. This was the way Harrison preferred it. Most of the time in life, Harrison felt like he could never find the right words despite everything going on inside. He realized that the moving, the fidgeting, was the same feeling he got right before going onstage in a play at school—like there was a motor sputtering somewhere between his chest and his stomach. Like there was more energy inside than scientists recommend. Like, well, like he was anxious. More than usual. He stopped gnawing on his thumb. That was it—Harrison was anxious, and if there was ever a person not to be anxious around, it was Linus.

Harrison's strategy for avoiding being anxious mostly consisted of declining to have outside thoughts, only inside thoughts. During rehearsal at school once, it had been explained to him that the reason there are songs in musicals is because when characters can't find the words to express themselves, they sing. The songs aren't happening in real life. They're the interior life, the better life, the bigger self. That was Harrison. He was a song, he thought. He would never say as much, of course. Or sing it, as it were. Judging by the parts in which he was cast, his musical talents were something of an open question. But it was a fact he carried inside himself, like the fact of his and Linus's friendship, that had finally felt cemented that summer.

"I've been thinking about it, and I have an idea," Harrison said, at last giving voice to the thing he'd been hemming and hawing and gnawing about all day. The motor in his chest was still rumbling. *This is what happens,* he reminded himself, *when you move inside thoughts outside.* "What would you think about us going to the same college?"

They were entering the eleventh grade and were on the precipice of, well, everything. The horizon of standardized testing and college and, beyond that, adulthood was filled with terrifying unknowns and looming pressures, and every time they talked about it, they got overwhelmed. The future wanted to eat them alive. Which is why they had to face it together.

"I've been thinking about it, too," Linus replied.

Now the motor in Harrison's chest revved to life. He felt a burst of energy, like the times he went buck wild and had a soda at lunch. "Oh, good! My mother sent me a website where you fill out a survey and it tells you what colleges you might want to go to, so I've been filling one out for me and also one for you, and then I'm going to compare the lists and we can pick," Harrison continued.

"What are you filling out for me?" Linus asked.

To be honest, the whole survey had been a real pickle right from the start. Harrison had gone in with the idea that he'd study

8

musical theater, but then he started thinking about the process of auditioning (not a strength) and also the whole singing and dancing of it all (a challenge) and he'd gotten stressed out. Could you go to college for musical theater enthusiasm alone? The survey was inconclusive. Then when he'd filled it out for Linus, he'd checked off premed even though that was clearly a lie to everyone but Linus's father.

"Obviously, your dad is only going to pay for a premed program," Harrison said, "but you can do whatever you want."

"Boy, my dad isn't paying for a thing," Linus said.

This was news. "Then what's your plan?"

"Scholarships. Where you been? There was never one question in my mind about that. I have a whole spreadsheet."

Of course he had a spreadsheet. "Well, yeah, I need to get scholarships, too," Harrison said, pretending that he had in any way thought this through. "But our parents have to help. It's not like we're geniuses."

Linus arched an eyebrow. *Speak for yourself.* Then aloud, he said, "My dad is going to do what my dad is going to do." He flicked at a fuzzy dandelion head. The motor inside Harrison started to sputter.

"Well, we'll figure out the whole college part of college. Not important. The point is that we should have a plan. Together." Linus didn't respond. "Eleventh grade isn't too early." Still nothing from Linus. Harrison tried a joke. "So far in the plan, I have: Step one—decide where to go to college. Step two—

money???" Linus laughed. "Step three—literally forget about the existence of everyone we've ever met." Linus laughed again.

"Oh, you're doing the Corrine plan," Linus said.

"Yeah. My sister went to school and was like 'Harrison who?' 'Baltimore where?'"

Linus was still chuckling, but Harrison felt himself getting anxious again. What was the problem?

"Anyway," Harrison said, "that's what I've been thinking."

Linus lay back on the grass next to FATHER. He had features that, in some lights, looked like one of the stone statues that dotted the hill. His nose, broad and strong, an expressive brow, full lips that were always talking or smirking or curled up in thought. *It's a shame statues only come in white,* Harrison thought. Linus's dark skin wouldn't fit in at the cemetery, but everything about his look, even the way his purposefully oversized clothes seemed to hang off his wiry frame, seemed like art.

Harrison tried a different tactic. "If you *were* going to go for premed, what kind of doctor would you be?"

"I don't want to be a doctor."

"Okay, but if you had to. Like, if it was required by law."

Linus hitched himself up. *There's no law,* his side-eye said. He lay back down. "Podiatrist."

This made sense. Sister Dale was the richest Black person at their church—well, at what used to be their church—and she was a podiatrist. Linus and his father didn't go to church anymore. It was unclear if the church kept being theirs even if they weren't in the building. In any case, Sister Dale went to Iceland every summer and had a big house, where she'd just hosted a Juneteenth party, so what other evidence did you need?

"You really want to look at feet all day?" Harrison asked. He wriggled his foot out of his sandal and poked Linus in the side with it.

"Boy, if you don't get your grody hoof out of my face!"

"This is the medical school entrance interview."

"If they come at me with some bare feet, I'm out." Linus only wore low, flat, old-school tennis shoes. Every day, all year.

"I'm on the interview committee. You have to take this seriously."

"You're a doctor now?"

"Well, they asked me to help out."

"Who all is on this committee with you?"

"It's . . ." Harrison struggled to think of any doctor. "Dr. Okeke." (His pediatrician.) "Sister Dale." (Her house has four bathrooms.) "Dr. Frank-N-Furter." (From *Rocky Horror*; Linus hadn't been allowed to go.) "And Dr. Jill Biden."

Linus laughed. "Not Dr. Biden! She's an education doctor. She's the only one I'm trying to talk to, actually."

"Well, you have to go through the foot."

"You're gross and I hate you."

"That's fine. Hate me while we make a plan. Your idea that we should get the same job this summer was, like, in the top-ten best ideas ever. We'll keep working together when school starts, we'll go to the same college, then I'll go to Broadway, and if you don't become a doctor, you'll become a . . . wait, what do you do with a history degree?"

"Now you sound like my dad." Linus looked at him askance. "The point is: What you start out doing doesn't need to be what you end up doing. Mr. Mirepoix went to college for gender studies."

Oh, Mr. Mirepoix, *Mr. Mirepoix*. In ninth grade, Linus had taken AP World History with Mr. Mirepoix, and it was all he wanted to talk about for months. Linus went to Harper, a public magnet school, and Harrison went to Plowshares, a private school out in Baltimore County. Prior to Mr. Mirepoix, Linus and Harrison's regular afternoon phone calls had mostly consisted of Harrison filling Linus in on the drama from the Plowshares drama department. But with the advent of AP World History, suddenly Linus had urgent daily updates. It was clear that Linus idolized Mr. Mirepoix. He said that when Mr. Mirepoix talked about world events, all the trivia and little-known facts and ideas in Linus's head organized themselves in a way that felt revelatory.

After class one day, Linus had told Mr. Mirepoix about how he'd recently become obsessed with the *Titanic*. How he wanted to find everything out about the ship and the sinking, and the second ship, the *Britannic*, that had also sunk. "There's just so many stories from the past," Linus had said, "and I'm like, is everyone just walking around knowing this?"

Mr. Mirepoix had offered that there was a point when he was young when the *Titanic* was literally all anyone talked about. Linus was agog. "Everybody saw the movie multiple times, of course," Mr. Mirepoix said. "And that song! Well, you know I'm a Celine Dion–head anyway." Mr. Mirepoix found the oddest ways of working stories about the many times he'd seen Celine Dion in concert into his lessons. One minute you're learning about rebuilding Europe after World War II, and the next minute Mr. Mirepoix is casually dropping an anecdote about the merchandise counter at London's O2 Arena. It was so much. The next week, Mr. Mirepoix had brought in a souvenir book about the movie *Titanic* and lent it to Linus. Linus was annoyed it was about a movie and not, like, real life, but it did have incredible research.

"You can go to college to be like Mr. Mirepoix," Harrison offered, hitching himself up next to FATHER. "You can do whatever you want. All I know is that everybody is going to have an opinion about what we need to be doing, and I feel like eleventh grade was when Corrine started making her plans, and it just seems like the best idea if we do . . . whatever it is we need to do, together." Corrine was Harrison's older sister. She'd blasted off from high school, a rocket of promise, and then, midway through her sophomore year of college, came plummeting back to their parents' house, a strange and surly version of herself. Whatever transformation she'd undergone was a mystery that hovered ghostlike in their home, a warning to Harrison.

Things would be different for him, though, because he would not be doing it alone.

Linus pulled himself up slowly from the grass around the grave, like a vampire starting their day. The sun sketched shallow shadows on the sides of his features. And for just a moment, Harrison released his thoughts from judgment. The thought in question, one that had never occurred to him before but which now seemed as natural and long-standing as if it were part of his molecular structure, was simple. He observed Linus, a few short locks falling across his face, his eyes searching the air above him for answers about the future, and the thought presented itself to Harrison: He is beautiful. It showed up like a fact. The color-of-the-sky kind of fact. And for a moment, Harrison let his thought be true and untroubled and free.

Was it unusual to think one's friend was beautiful? Uh, maybe. *Depends on who your friend is,* Harrison surmised. But didn't knowing a friend, really knowing them, mean that you got to hang out in the light of the best parts of them? Maybe no one else had friendships like this. Maybe Harrison and Linus had wandered into some new way of being friends. That was fine, too.

The slight breeze wrapped them in June's warmth. The day, like his friend and their friendship, was beautiful.

Did Harrison feel the same way about himself? Well, physically, the two boys had different looks. Linus was partial to boxy shirts and long-sleeved tees and thrifted finds that he dubbed "dadcore" (FATHER would approve, Harrison guessed). Harrison didn't put much thought into his "look." He wore what fit, sometimes perplexed by his rounder face, his spiky twists that refused to grow, his softer frame, the different way that he moved through the world. Today he'd chosen a plain T-shirt plucked from a pile on the floor, a pair of jean shorts, and sliders, all in the interest of staying as cool as possible. What was his look? "Lukewarmcore."

Harrison pulled out his phone to take a picture. Linus waved him off. "You look cool! Pose!" Harrison insisted. Linus sucked his teeth and flashed a begrudging V-sign with two fingers.

"Okay, model!" Harrison said.

Linus shook his head. "You're corny."

Yeah, Harrison's eye roll said. *I'm the corny one. Okay.*

Harrison slipped his phone back into his pocket, lay back on the grass, and lost himself in the sky, so vivid that the cloudless blue seemed to take on dimension. It went on forever, a space he could inhabit.

"I have something to tell you," Linus said at last. His voice floated over Harrison.

The motor inside Harrison started up again. He hoped it was something about college, something about their plan, something good. Or nothing, which would be even better. But he got the feeling he should sit up for what would come next. He searched Linus's face for clues, but for once his face had nothing to say.

Harrison tried his words. "Yeah?"

"So the thing is . . . I'm moving away."

Though they'd known each other basically all their lives, Harrison and Linus's friendship had taken the scenic route. Harrison's family, the Merediths, and Linus's, the Munros, had gone to the same church when they were little, and they'd see each other around and sometimes play at each other's houses when their parents were having dinner. But back then, all their friendships were basically dictated by whoever their parents were hanging out with or whoever could babysit. Still, because they went to different schools and lived in different neighborhoods, it sometimes felt like they were worlds apart. Then when Linus's parents split up, he went to live with his mom. She'd bring him to church, but the visits with Harrison stopped.

They were in middle school at that point, and when the pandemic hit, their lives collapsed into their respective homes and whatever they could find online. Harrison hadn't seen Linus for months, and although he wouldn't have said they were friends, he thought of Linus a lot during that period. He just kept coming to mind. Linus didn't have any social media or, apparently, any way to be reached. Harrison himself didn't have a phone yet, but he had a laptop that he could use for school and keeping up with people. And so when he logged on to a Zoom hosted by the church, advertised as "Youth Rap with Brother Aldo," and Harrison saw Linus's face in one of the small, fuzzy squares, his heart did a little leap.

Hello, Harrison typed in a private chat to Linus that afternoon. Brother Aldo was yelling at people to mute themselves.

Do you remember me? Harrison followed up.

Duh. Linus wrote back. Your mom is a good singer.

Okay, that was nice, but it wasn't technically about Harrison; he'd let it slide. He was feeling generous.

They messaged back and forth during the youth rap, both a little perplexed that the chat feature hadn't been disabled like it was in school. As the session came to a close, Linus wrote, I just got email. Do you?

What did that mean? Everybody had email. Harrison sent back his Plowshares email address, and Linus sent him an email right away. Hi this is Linus. The city sent my mom a Chromebook for me to do school and I got this email address but I don't know what I'm supposed to do with it. So we can just talk.

They emailed back and forth every day, sometimes multiple times a day. They bonded over the strict controls their parents put on their lives, which had only gotten stricter in quarantine. Linus would go on and on about the random historical events he was learning about, about the Wikipedia wormholes he'd treated himself to, about the little-known facts he'd discovered. He'd always ask Harrison, Did you know this? And Harrison would always write, You know I did not. And Linus would write back, Baby boy, what are they teaching you at that fancy school? He had a point, but Harrison always wondered exactly how many middle schoolers were learning about the Bay of Pigs invasion, for instance.

They moved from trivia to fact and from fact to feeling. Linus wrote, I feel bad for my mom because it's hard having me here. Harrison felt a door to his friend open up, but he didn't know how to walk through or show that he understood, because the truth was that he didn't understand. Harrison wrote, I think my sister likes her friend Keshona, who is a girl, and when Linus wrote, That's cool, Harrison followed up with By the way, did you know I'm gay? As if this was knowledge that anyone had. As if he was talking about a weather-related rumor. *By the way, did you hear we might get a snow day?* Casual, casual.

Of course it hadn't seemed so ridiculous when, a month later, Linus had been writing about his latest online find and then closed the mini lecture with By the way, did you know I'm gay? He stole Harrison's entire line! No credit given! Grand larceny!

Their back-and-forth went on for the rest of the school year. Linus talked about his excitement for heading to high school at Harper. Harrison talked about how, since Plowshares was a K—12, he'd just be going to different classrooms but it still made him feel anxious because everything made him feel anxious. Linus confessed that he was nervous, too, but that high school felt like the beginning of anything, everything. He wrote something Harrison thought about all the time: "There's been so much ending, I just want something to begin."

A few weeks later, Harrison said that making a friend, a real friend, felt like a beginning, too. Linus replied, "We've known each other forever." They decided they were both right. They both wondered sometimes whether the other had a bunch of other email friendships going on with people all over the city. To Harrison's surprise, Linus actually asked it. An outside thought, loose in the world. Harrison couldn't imagine emailing anyone else.

And then, when the school year ended, it was over. Linus moved in with his dad and, without internet access, seemingly dropped off the face of the earth for a year. They started having church in person again, but neither Linus nor his parents were there. And then a few months later, when Linus's mother came back to church, sitting in her usual pew, which had been reclaimed by another family in the absence of the Munros, she was there alone.

▦▦ ▦▦ ▦▧◣

"You're moving away? To where?" Harrison asked now. His voice was like an old-school fade: high and tight. Linus was pacing around FATHER.

"Charleston."

Harrison suddenly forgot all geography. "Where is that?"

"South Carolina."

The motor inside him was going berserk. "I don't understand."

"My dad says he can't keep doing the rideshare and the bar; it's not working. My aunt Bird got him a job down there."

"He can't commute?"

"Harrison, will you be serious?"

He *was* being serious. He did not understand what was happening to him.

"My dad says he needs to take this job. He says it's for both of us. The school down there is good and we can live with Aunt Bird for free, and he said he'd even be able to save a little to help me with college." Linus wouldn't meet Harrison's gaze.

"When? When is this happening?"

"Sunday."

"Why are you just now telling me?" Harrison cried.

A couple crows startled and took off before landing nearby. "Dad has to start work Monday," Linus said.

"This is ..." Harrison, again, was at a loss for words.

"This is awful," Linus said. "I can't believe he would do this to me. I mean, I know it's important and it's been hard on him since the divorce, but ..."

"We'll figure something out."

"Like what? Like ... there's no option here."

"Your mom ...?"

"No," Linus said quietly. "I'm just so—" He stopped himself. Harrison could see he was getting worked up. "Thanks for listening."

"Always."

Then they both ran out of words.

This is not how life is supposed to be, Harrison thought. An inside thought that, powered by the motor running wild inside him, rushed up to his mouth and burst into the air. "We are going to make a plan."

"A plan for what?" Linus asked.

"A plan to fix this. Or . . ." He was thinking too fast; he couldn't keep up with himself. He couldn't find words to say what he was actually trying to communicate. "We can still do all the things we've been talking about. We can still have, like, everything. We just need a plan."

"I don't know."

"Linus, this isn't bigger than us. We just need a big plan."

Linus shook his head. "Trust—grand gestures aren't going to change the facts. This is what it is."

Harrison deflated. They just looked at each other. After a moment, his phone pinged with a message coming in over the family location-tracking app called Check In, from Harrison's dad: Heading home? It was 3:45. The cemetery would be closing soon. They wordlessly got up and started walking to the exit. Linus paused at DJ, Turn It Up! and considered her sadly.

"Do you want me to take a picture of you with her?" Harrison asked. Linus shook his head and kept walking.

As they waited for the bus, Harrison made one more attempt. "I'll throw a party for you. Not a going-away party. But we can invite our friends. If you want to invite people from school, that would be nice."

"I don't know about all that," Linus said. He rubbed the back of his neck. "I think . . . I think today is enough, you know? I just need to make a clean break."

Harrison felt his chest constrict.

Linus continued, "I been through enough messy breaks, my mom and everything. I just want to close the door. I don't have another choice. My dad says we both need a clean break and to start over."

Harrison looked at him. *Even from me?* Linus's gaze wasn't focused, and Harrison couldn't tell if he was just not responding or if he was simply saying the thing Harrison most feared. Linus was, for a second time, unreachable. They rode together in their separate worlds until they reached the stop nearest Harrison's house. Linus said he wasn't feeling up to hanging out longer. Harrison watched his profile, so striking, in the window as the bus pulled off. Linus didn't even wave.

4:30 p.m.

As Linus rode the twenty minutes from Harrison's bus stop to his own, he kept asking himself why he hadn't waved. He didn't have an answer. It was as if every moment of life was an emotional SAT that he hadn't studied for. Which was ridiculous because Linus always studied. Linus studied for tests he didn't have to take. A fun night at home? Flash cards. So why was he coming up short here? Why hadn't he waved to his best friend? Why was he failing this test? He'd have to petition his grade.

Despite his concern, Linus couldn't help but chuckle as he got off the bus—he was being so dramatic. Normally that was Harrison's domain. It was one of his favorite aspects of his friend, who had a reservoir of thoughts, and feelings, and, yes, drama inside. Linus had no patience for dramatics—life was dramatic enough—but from Harrison, they were a delight. Every time they hung out, Linus felt like he understood life differently. Everything felt more expansive. More possible.

He waved to a neighbor sitting on the worn marble steps of the house next door and let himself into the two-story brick-row home he shared with his father. The door didn't open all the way, bumping on the corner of a half-packed box just inside.

The living room was basically gone. His father had stayed up the night before, taking care of it. Linus had declined the invitation to help, instead lying in his bed and staring at the ceiling as the sound of the tape gun and his father's random sighs and grunts occasionally pierced through the door. This, too, was dramatic and unlike Linus. But he didn't know what else to do. His life was disappearing into boxes, and one of the first things to get taken off the shelf and boxed up was any say he had over what was happening to him.

"We have to move," his father had said abruptly one night. When Linus had come home, Dad had been making a crawfish boil. Linus thought it was just a fun rare treat, but it turned out to be some kind of bribe. "This is what they eat in South Carolina!" he'd said after he broke the news. "You love this stuff." Not anymore. A whole lot of trouble to go through just to ruin your son's appetite. His dad was always Doing Too Much to make up for all the small things that didn't go right for the two of them. Linus hated it. Why did everything have to be a big production? He tried to be good, to make things easier for his dad; he didn't ask for much. He didn't want big plans. All he wanted was to stay.

Linus and his father had argued that night and every day since, and each time, Linus had found himself less and less able to say the thing that he wanted to say, which was "If we leave, I might lose my friend. And I don't want to lose my friend." The only person he could tell the things he really wanted to say was

Harrison. It wasn't that he didn't understand his father's explanations about money and savings and work and life. But didn't Linus have a say?

Harrison had been the only constant through the storm of Linus's parents' divorce, and the unsettled, hard period when he'd lived with his mom. He'd been desperate, in that year after he'd moved out of his mom's, to reestablish that easy friendship he'd had with Harrison. All Linus had wanted for so long was just to be able to be with the people he cared about, and . . . well, it hadn't worked out with anyone. Almost anyone. So, of course, he figured out a way that they could spend their summers together. He'd felt so lucky—he was sure Harrison would already have plans for wild and fun adventures with his group of school friends. But Harrison had said yes immediately. And their summer together had been amazing. So amazing, in fact, that when he found out about the move weeks earlier, Linus had refused to allow himself to break the news to Harrison until the very last minute. It was as if he might prove it was all just a dream. That was not looking likely.

The shifting reality of distance had always been the thing that complicated things for them. But it was rarely geographical. Harper was one of the better schools in the city, but it seemed to exist on a totally different world from Plowshares, the intimate private school in the suburban county that Harrison's parents drove him to every day. Linus decided that that was why Harrison had such a different experience with school friends than he did.

It wasn't that he didn't know people at school, but for Harrison, school friends extended to a whole social group. Linus got to hang around with them, but he sometimes felt like he was missing something.

Linus wasn't envious. Envy was dramatic. Well, maybe he was a little envious. Or, more than that, just sad. But mostly he understood that sometimes people forget about you if you're not there. And Linus couldn't let that happen again.

Before his dad had made a complete mess of Linus's life, Linus had decided he was going to try to hang out with some of the people he liked the most at his own school, invite them to hang with him and Harrison. Phil Truong, Fab Figueroa, Mazz Reber. A whole group. Now Fab was even texting him to see if he was hanging out that weekend.

"I don't really understand why we're talking right now, but this is cute, I guess." Fab's warm, laugh-filled voice was coming through Linus's cell. He hadn't had the energy to keep the phone to his ear, so he'd put it on speaker and was now lying back on his bed, staring at the ceiling again, and yelling into the air like Alexander Graham Bell testing out his first prototype.

"Oh!" he shouted into his empty bedroom and in the general direction of his phone. "I thought it would be easier if I called to answer your question."

"Uh. Okay. Great," said Fab. "Well, I'm glad to hear your voice. And I'm excited to get a live answer to my text question, which was: Are you going to Pride?"

"No."

There was a long pause, and then Fab said, "Is there more to that answer?"

"No," Linus replied.

"So glad we are speaking on the phone about it. What's the deal? Your dad won't let you?"

"I'm moving away!"

"What?! But it's Pride!"

Linus could only moan in response.

"Oh, Linus. I'm going to miss you. I like you a lot. Where are you moving?"

"South Carolina."

"Lucky for you, I have this girl that I was kind of dating who lives in North Carolina, so if you're looking for local lesbians, I can hook you up," Fab said. At the same time, a text came through, also from Fab, with a photo of a girl with braids piled high on her head. Linus presumed this was the girl from North Carolina, but really she could have been anyone.

"Did she use to live here?" Linus asked.

"No. We met because we just started commenting on each other's fanfics, and you know how that is."

"I don't think I do."

"Linus, shut up! Yes, you do. You read the one fic I wrote. Remember when Mr. Mirepoix was doing that unit on the forties and he let me turn in that story about two women falling in love while working at an airplane factory during World War II instead of, like, writing a paper? I put it up on my site and then she liked it and then I liked her thing about Storm from *X-Men* and Okoye from *Black Panther* falling in love. And it went on like that."

"Have you met her? In person?" Linus asked.

"No! How am I supposed to get to North Carolina? That's kind of why we broke up, to be honest. Long distance is hard. But it's very much not a big deal, so don't say anything about it when you meet her."

Linus sighed loudly and sat up. He could hear his father boxing and taping again; he smelled dinner. Tonight's Doing Too Much feast was shrimp and grits, another South Carolina staple. And another bribe. Maybe if he spent less money buying seafood for these big elaborate schemes, they could afford to stay.

"That's the problem," he told Fab. "I just want to keep Harrison in my life. People talk about long-distance relationships, but what is a long-distance friendship? Is that a thing? Friendship is kind of, like, whatever. What is there to hold on to with all this distance?"

"It's not like you're moving to Mars. I feel like it should be easier than trying to long-distance date because you're not thinking about when you're going to make out or whatever."

"He's got a whole life. And he's going to go off to college. And he's got all these friends at his school. And . . . he's my best friend. But maybe he has a bunch of best friends. I don't know."

"Linus, this is so dramatic."

"I know! It's exhausting!"

"What does your friend say about it?"

"We ain't talked about it."

"Why?"

More questions Linus couldn't answer. Or rather, he wouldn't. He couldn't bring himself to say the truth. Fabiola sighed.

"Well, I gotta admit," she said, "this seems chaotic. Just tell him what you're thinking."

"I don't do deep feelings, is the thing," Linus said.

"I don't mean to upset you, but literally everything we've talked about on the phone has been the deepest possible feelings. Like, I never talk on the phone. You called me. On the phone! And jumped into the deep end. And I want to say thank you for trusting me and I def understand. But let's be real now. Phil and I are best friends and if she ever moved away, I'd call her up and be like, 'Yo, as you are aware, we're going to be in each other's lives forever.' We're like you guys: We don't want to date; we don't like each other like that, yet we want to talk to each other every day forever. Just tell him. Text him if you don't want to call."

"I don't like texting."

"Then call."

"He doesn't really talk on the phone."

"You got a real star-crossed friendship here, Linus."

Thursday

10:30 a.m.

Sunlight invaded Harrison's room, which was rude. He woke up late—what was there to get out of bed for?—and kicked at his comforter savagely, sending a pile of clothes flying off the bed. He briefly considered that he might not be handling this whole thing about Linus leaving very well. But what did handling well mean at a time like this? Everything everywhere was, objectively, terrible and would be terrible for, pretty much, ever. Harrison slammed his head against his pillow and squeezed his eyes shut. He knew he was veering dangerously close to the point where he started to annoy himself with how bad a mood he was in. It happened often. He'd be really digging into a sulk, basically bathing in an internal tantrum, when the whole thing would dive off a cliff and it suddenly wouldn't be satisfying to be upset anymore, but rather just frustrating.

He knew that if he stayed in bed much longer, he would have no hope of rescuing his mood. He had no idea where his phone was, but judging from the context clues of the sun shining in his window and the absence of the sounds of his parents getting ready, he knew it was after 8:30. He didn't have to work at BaltiTours—the place where he and Linus worked together but mostly just talked to each other all day. This made things even worse, since it meant he wouldn't have an excuse to lobby Linus in the ticket office between customers. They usually hung out on their days off, but Linus's words "a clean break" floated back up to the top of Harrison's mind, and he wondered if that break had already started. If Linus had wanted to hang out today, why wasn't he already there? What was he doing? Packing? Practicing his southern accent? Forgetting? Anything was possible.

He supposed he could invite Linus over to the Meredith family's "mandatory fun" movie night, as he usually did on Thursdays, but something in him resisted this thought. Was it possible he was angry at Linus? He was hungry. The crises were mounting, obviously. The night before, he had considered dramatically refusing to eat until Linus agreed to stay. Now his stomach growled, and he decided that the hunger strike could start maybe after breakfast. And lunch. He'd skip dinner. Well, he'd pick at it, perhaps. He wouldn't enjoy it. No act was too bold if it meant saving his friendship. Wait, movie night meant they were ordering pizza. He'd start the hunger strike tomorrow at the latest.

Should he cry about it? Would that help? Maybe! He scrunched up his face and tried. Nope. How did actors cry? He'd watched roughly six hundred bootleg YouTube videos of people performing "She Used to Be Mine" from *Waitress* onstage, and like 90 percent of them seemed to be crying. It wasn't easy to see, though, because a lot of times the video quality wasn't good or the camera was far from the stage. But Harrison felt pretty confident that most of the actresses were crying as they sang. Shoshana Bean? Absolutely bawling.

He fished around in the tangled mess of his comforter until he found his phone. Left uncharged the night before, it had only 8 percent battery, and his charger was . . . maybe in the sheets, too? He didn't know. Ah, the desperateness of this time. There was a text from Linus: Hello. What was that supposed to mean? In person, Linus never shut up, but over text he was basically a mime. Harrison decided he couldn't handle the terseness at the moment. It was all too much. He did the only thing left for him to do in the moment: He cued up "She Used to Be Mine" and played it over and over again until his phone died.

After a breakfast of a slightly under-toasted waffle, eaten standing up, by hand, with no syrup, Harrison decided that his next healthy coping mechanism would be to sit in the backyard and be miserable in public. Or semipublic, since his neighbors never used their yards and the only person he ever saw when sitting miserably in public was the junkman pushing a shopping cart up the alley.

But, of course, because nothing could go right for him, he discovered Corrine already sitting out there, sunbathing next to a bowl of rocks. Harrison's trials, it seemed, were unending.

Corrine had come back from college "woo-woo." Harrison's sister had always marched to the beat of her own drum. Or, as

Harrison might have put it during some of their more contentious battles, Corrine always did exactly what she wanted. But when she'd suddenly returned home a year and a half earlier than expected and taken up residence again in the bedroom next to Harrison's, something had changed. The posters of Cardi and FKA and Meg came down; a new paint color—purple—went up on the bare walls, and with it an abstract silver mural she'd created herself. She started talking about an app that told her her horoscope every single day, something that neither of their decidedly non-woo-woo parents seemed to take issue with, surprisingly. And, perhaps most vexingly, Corrine had gotten really into rocks. Harrison knew there was another name for the rocks, or a series of names, a whole dictionary of rock words, but he didn't learn them and he wasn't trying to. So when he found his sister sitting in their tiny patch of backyard and cement, leaning back in a plastic chair, untwisting her hair, with a kitchen mixing bowl full of rocks sitting on the ground between her feet, that's what he called them.

"You tanning your rocks?" he said, shutting the screen door behind him. Corrine didn't respond. He wasn't sure she heard him or was even aware of his presence, as her eyes were shielded by a huge pair of amber sunglasses. She continued dutifully unwrapping her hair, bundled in tight knots from the night before and soon to be coaxed out and released again into the curly twist-out halo she usually sported. Harrison stepped in front of her, accidentally kicking the bowl. Nothing too hard, but Corrine snapped forward and pulled the bowl back.

"They're crystals, dummy."

"Oh, so you *did* hear me."

Harrison paused, expecting Corrine to explain why she had a bowl of rocks—excuse me, crystals—hanging out in the backyard with her like it was some old breakfast oatmeal. Corrine's hands had returned to her hair, searching around her head in a well-practiced order, like she knew every strand by heart. Her shaded eyes, however, had made a brief jaunt to appraise Harrison before returning to a spot on the chain-link fence or maybe some bit of errant grass in the alley or maybe something far beyond that. Harrison rolled his eyes with his whole body and tried again.

"Why are you tanning your crystals?"

Corrine didn't stop staring into the middle distance, but she did pause her untwisting. "Last night was a full moon," she said. As if that was illuminating. *Thanks for the astronomy lesson. All questions answered. Very thorough. Please get up from the lawn chair now; I need it to sulk.* Harrison was so consumed by his own annoyance that he almost missed the fact that Corrine had started speaking again. "I set them out to charge in the moonlight, and now they're sunbathing for a bit before I take them back inside." See? That? Woo-woo.

"Woo-woo" was not a phrase that got thrown around all too often in the Meredith household. It was old-timey, like something senior Black folks would say. Which is why Harrison liked

37

it. He'd first heard it from his grandfather on his father's side, who they called Pop. Pop was always talking about his roommate, Phyllis, who liked incense and said she was a little psychic. There was nothing especially weird about that—Phyllis had predicted that Harrison would not get cast as Tevye in *Fiddler*, after all. But to be honest, that was clear to everyone. Nevertheless, sometimes her habits got on Pop's nerves. It was mostly the incense. "I have sensitive sinuses," he'd explain. And then he'd go on to say that he had no idea why he chose to let someone as woo-woo as Phyllis move in to his house and how he didn't even need the money, it was just the company, and on and on and on. "Woo-woo," it seemed, could mean something as simple as accurately casting a high-school play or as complex as casting a spell. Or whatever it was that charging crystals in the moonlight was meant to accomplish. Harrison had no idea.

"What happens after they recharge?" he asked.

Corrine sighed and looked at him. "Do you really care?"

"I mean, I did, but if you're going to be a jerk about it, never mind."

Corrine shook out her hair, all finished. "They push out bad energy. And they bring in good energy. And I need as much of that stuff as I can get. It's like anything—praying or yoga or setting an intention. But it doesn't just come from inside you. You're tapping into something powerful in the universe. We're all so small; why wouldn't we want to do that?"

Sometimes Corrine actually made sense to Harrison. They

had always seen the world differently, their whole lives, but since she'd come back, that had been a problem. She might say they had different energies. He might agree. But when she talked about connecting to something larger in the universe, something pricked up in him and he remembered the thing that hadn't been far from his mind since he heard Linus's news. Would that Harrison had a way to harness some power in the universe to stop this move. Would that he had any power at all. The world of adulthood and adult decisions swirled around them, moving them like chess pieces. Everyone said that he had big choices to make coming up—classes, tests, college, literally the rest of his life—but all of it seemed so removed from his current life, where other people made choices around him and he just had to react. He just had to deal with it. He just had to accept it and move on. He hated that. He needed a plan. Maybe he should get a crystal!

"Can I hold one?" he asked, already reaching down.

Corrine swatted his hand away. "Harrison, you have atrocious energy! Absolutely not." She looked at him in the face now. "Wait, what's wrong?"

"What do you mean?"

"There's something going on with you."

"Oh God, who are you? Phyllis?" he said. Corrine laughed at that, big and loud. A burst of energy.

"Next thing you know, Pop is going to start calling me woo-woo," she said. Nobody tell her that Harrison had already

39

gotten there first. "No, seriously, though. You look miserable. What's wrong?"

Harrison kicked a pebble into the alley behind the house. "Linus is moving away. To South Carolina."

"Oh no! That sucks. I'm sorry." She sounded genuinely sad for him. "When is he moving?"

"Sunday."

"God, that sucks even more. Aww. I know y'all are close. I see you two huddled up all the time in the living room, clucking. It's nice to have a best friend." She shrugged. "He is your best friend, right? I can never tell. The Phalanx of Sad Boys has so many rotating cast members."

The Phalanx of Sad Boys was Corrine's nickname for Harrison's general group of friends. He wasn't even sure who was supposedly in the Phalanx (whatever a phalanx was). Definitely Linus. And Dario Lushovsky. Dario, one of Harrison's classmates, was the king of Sad Boys—handsome like the White Boy of the Month on a cable-TV show about morose teenagers, Dario was full to the brim with abs and emotion. He would often send text messages that were just the entire lyrics of a particularly emo song, including all the choruses. He loved crying. The world was not big enough for Dario's feelings, but he didn't seem to notice. One of Harrison's favorite facts about Dario was that Dario had a fainting couch in his bedroom at his mom's house. Harrison had seen it. It was, to be honest, just a regular couch, but Dario had collapsed on it in a flurry of limbs and groans one afternoon after one of the lacrosse players he was in love with took too long to text back.

To be honest, Harrison actually did like Dario. It was nice to be with someone who was prone to drama but not formally involved in the theater department. Dario was real-world dramatic. They'd hung out a lot freshman year and the summer after, but then Linus had met Dario and quickly developed a crush on him. Harrison got tired of hearing Linus casually (but not casually) asking about Dario when Harrison and Linus would call each other after school, and he certainly had had enough of Dario daydreaming about Linus every minute he was in school. Why didn't they just text each other and leave him out of it? Annoying! By sophomore year, Linus had stopped asking, which was a relief. But the last time Harrison had seen Dario before the school year ended, Dario cornered Harrison by the Meditation Room and declared, "I am desperate to see your handsome melancholic friend with the bird body. I think Linus may be my husband!"

"Okay," Harrison had said.

Who else was a Sad Boy? Possibly Aparna Aiyar. She was not a boy, but she was who Harrison hung out with the most besides Linus, so it's possible that Corrine was just lumping her in with the rest. She had a lot of dark clothes, and Harrison's dad had once called her Lydia Deetz, so that was a clue. Harrison was fairly certain that Aparna wasn't sad, though, despite her sometimes intense way of seeing the world. She was "realistic," she said, which was kind of true, except that her reality always seemed to swan-dive into hijinks. She would definitely have objected to this characterization—"Things just happen around me, Harrison! I am literally just trying to have a normal life." Still, he lived for stories about how her attempts to beat her work nemesis at the lotion and soap store where she worked after school somehow spiraled into all-out battles that left the break room covered in glittery bath-bomb dust. As their school's best stage manager, Aparna always had some manner of backstage farce to disentangle. And, as the child of two consummate do-gooders who had jobs Harrison didn't quite understand, Aparna was always getting herself caught up in social-justice drama involving petitions and invisible fences and some app that half the neighborhood used for snitching on others that, according to Aparna, was rife with terrible punctuation. Harrison thought Aparna was too busy to be sad.

The only other possible member of the Phalanx was Mondale Berz, who, to Harrison, wasn't so much Sad as he was On Another Planet. Mondale, a lanky Black and Filipino boy, was built like a collapsing Jenga tower, all angles and collarbones. He went everywhere with his enormous pink headphones resting just above his ears, like the eraser on one of those weirdly shaped pencils. Mondale got straight As even though he never had any idea what anybody was talking about in class or in casual conversation—probably because of the headphones. He didn't really seem to need to be friends with the rest of the group; he kept his own company. But he always accepted an invitation when offered, he always invited the Sad Boys to his house to watch anime, and he always gave the best gifts—for birthdays, the one year they randomly decided to do Secret Santa, or just because he was thinking about one of them. Mondale was thoughtful; he was, it seemed, constructed completely out of thoughts. And that made him seem sad sometimes, Harrison guessed.

Harrison didn't think of himself as Sad, present circumstances excluded. Everybody said he was quiet, but that's just because he didn't talk much. It wasn't the same thing. Sure, he felt insecure; sure, he worried that he wasn't going to be popular, ever; sure, he was anxious about the future. But he wasn't sad about it. Everybody got down sometimes. Best not to think too hard about it. Maybe a crystal!

Linus was Sad, though. Harrison knew that.

Sometimes it snuck up on him; sometimes it hung just over his head; sometimes it felt a part of his body, like the hunch of his shoulders around his ears or the way he sort of leaned when standing, his hip jutting out like it was searching for a wall to crumble on.

Linus was sad. And sometimes they were sad together. Harrison didn't know what they'd do when they had to be sad apart.

Harrison realized he'd never answered Corrine's question. And she'd let him stand there, moping in silence. He replied now. "It does suck." He hesitated and looked away. "I don't know what to do."

"Well, what are you going to do?"

"I just told you I don't know what to do!"

"First of all, take that bass out your voice. I didn't realize you meant you actually didn't know. Linus is always plotting and you stay going along with any harebrained scheme." She swept her head wrap from around her neck and stuffed it in the pocket of her jeans as she stood up. She leaned down and picked up the bowl of crystals, cradling it in her arm as if it were a baby. A baby that held the power of the universe. "So come up with some harebrained scheme." She turned and started up the back stairs.

"You're leaving?" Harrison called.

"You obviously came out here to be sad, and I think you have that right."

"You could stay, though."

Corrine curled her lip and growled like a gunslinger from a Western. "This yard's not big enough fer the both uv us." She laughed at herself. "Enjoy the sun!"

"Wait."

"What?"

Harrison looked down the alley. A half-empty carton of what looked like fried rice was sitting on the ground just beyond their yard. The fork was still in it.

"What?" Corrine said, this time in italics.

"Why are you being nice to me?"

Corrine didn't respond right away. Harrison regretted even saying anything.

"You're sad. Why wouldn't I be nice to you?"

"Just surprised you care is all."

"Your energy is truly awful. You need to get some help."

"Okay!"

"That was easy." Corrine could see that Harrison was in no mood for needling. She set the bowl on the railing. It looked precarious, but maybe it was being balanced by space power. "You're my brother."

"And?"

"And . . . and what?"

"And when did you start caring about any of us?"

Corrine cocked her head curiously. "I've always cared."

"I don't believe that," Harrison said.

"I don't care what you believe." Corrine threw her hands up, jostling her bowl. The crystals teetered and she caught them. She scowled at Harrison. "Any other questions?"

"Thanks for the pep talk. You're a great sister."

"You're an asshole," Corrine said quietly. She swept into the house and let the screen door slam behind her—a huge transgression if their parents were home.

Harrison slumped into the newly empty chair and glared at the world around him: the chain-link fence, the alley, the tiny herb garden, the bird feeder that had been lying on its side since a squirrel knocked it down, the fried rice container, and the little patch of grass that nobody cared about but which, for some reason, Harrison still had to mow with a Weedwhacker every

45

other week. The sounds of a summer afternoon in his neighborhood came to life around him. Kids shrieking and giggling in the street, the hungry growl of revving motorbikes, the exhausted grumble of buses sighing to a stop and then heaving themselves forward again like old men hoisting themselves off the couch, the ever-present horror-movie soundtrack of the ice cream truck, and the white noise of cars driving by or idling on the corner with their stereos turned up. Everyone was having a great damn day.

And to make matters worse, it seemed that every car, every radio station, every playlist had "Press the Sky Higher" on it. Harrison heard it so many times wafting through the air over the scuttle of the neighborhood that he knew all the lyrics by midafternoon. He finally gave up and retreated to the air-conditioning. He could put up with the oppressive heat, but the ubiquitous song of the summer was a bridge too far.

What did the lyrics even mean? *"We been down and we been broken, but we're pushing up and over / hard times ain't coming back no more"*? Up and over where? Hard times ain't coming back? Says who?! Ridiculous. And also, shouldn't it be "push the sky," not "press the sky"? Everyone loved the new song, but no one was talking about the fact that it was completely inaccurate. Even before the recent development with Linus, Harrison had had his doubts about the victory anthem's message: that we have the power to lift the sky, to change the world. It was a song about hope in the future, and for Harrison, the sky had never seemed so low.

7:00 p.m.

"PIZZA TRACKER IS ON AND POPPING!" Harrison's dad called through the door.

"Yeah. Okay! I got it," Harrison said. Under his breath, he muttered, "You need to chill out, Obed." Lately, he'd experimented with calling his parents—Sheree and Obed—by their first names like he was some kind of wealthy white child of divorce. He only did this in his head, of course, because he was none of those things, and Sheree and Obed didn't play those kinds of games. When he'd come home from Plowshares one day in third grade and asked his parents when he could call them by their real names, they'd looked at him like he'd just revealed he knew they were in a witness protection program and living double lives.

"When . . . what?" Obed, or rather, *Dad*, had asked.

Harrison had explained that Dario called his parents by their real names, and he was just curious about whether he'd missed a cue.

"Oh!" Sheree had said. "Um, I think . . . I think Mom and Dad is fine for now."

"Are you sure?" Harrison asked. The whole thing was very

anxiety-producing. New identities at this late age?

"Yeah, Dario's folks—Don't worry about it. When you're grown, you can call us by our first names. If you need to."

Well, he wasn't all the way grown, but he'd found that he liked the way their names sounded when he tossed them about in his head; he liked the feeling of saying them under his breath. It felt like power.

He sat up in his bed and pulled up Linus's text from hours earlier. Normally Harrison would respond to one of Linus's oblique messages by just calling, which was what Linus wanted anyway. Linus had a janky bare-bones phone that didn't do much more than make calls and text, so it was basically useless. It might as well have been a telegraph machine. But it connected them. When Linus texted one word, it was the same as his raised eyebrow or his hunched shoulder or the electric space that hung in the gaze between the two of them. It said everything. It said *Let's talk forever.* And Harrison always responded.

But . . . Harrison didn't have anything to say now. He swung his feet out of the bed, pretending that was true. He ignored, for once, the pull of the tether that connected the two of them. He didn't have time to work through it at the moment. It was almost MANDATORY FUN O'CLOCK.

What the Meredith family needed, he decided, was an excused-absence policy. He surveyed the rumpled mass of his clothes from earlier in the day, furiously whipped off and thrown to the corner. They bore the brunt of a resentment that was really aimed at the sun, and the heat, and the summer, and also the state of South Carolina, and the ghost of his junior- and senior-year plans with Linus and, most of all, Linus's dad, Wallingford Munro (yes, Harrison was using his full government name now; it was that serious). He went to another pile of clothes, picked up a shirt, sniffed it, and put it on. It was snug and uncomfortable and clung to the parts of his body that he, honestly, felt ambivalent about but which seemed to be a point of commentary for everyone else. He tugged the sides of the shirt down over the curve of his stomach, found a pair of shorts, and left his room, closing the door carefully behind him (but slamming it in his mind).

Sheree and Obed were already posted up on one of the couches when Harrison got to the living room. Corrine had assumed her usual place, draped at odd angles in an overstuffed chair. That left Harrison alone on the other couch, where he lay down.

"Finally!" Corrine said. She reached forward and snagged a slice of pizza from one of the boxes on the table.

"Grace?" their mom warned.

Corrine closed her eyes and moved her lips as she held the pizza aloft. It looked like praying, but what she was saying was only known to her and God and the rocks.

Harrison buried his head in one of the throw pillows on the couch.

"You're going to love this one, boy-o," Obed called.

49

"*Nnnff,*" he replied into the pillow.

"It stars Matthew Broderick," said Sheree. "He was in *The Producers*. On Broadway." She pulled a slice of pizza for herself and paused to say grace over it silently.

Harrison turned his head slightly and looked at the TV, where a baby-faced teenager in a bathrobe was frozen on the launch screen. He held an absolutely gargantuan phone in his hand. It was, indeed, the guy from *The Producers*.

"What movie is this?" he asked.

"*Ferris Bueller's Day Off*, an absolute classic," his dad said, shifting giddily on the couch. "It's about—"

"He's going to find out what it's about in a minute, baby," Sheree interjected.

Harrison had already read the description on the screen: *A clever teenager and his friends play hooky, enjoying the day with the principal in hot pursuit.* What was "hooky"? Harrison figured without video games and normal-sized phones, back then teenagers had to find other things to play.

He skimmed down the screen and looked at who was in it. Mia Sara. Alan Ruck. Jennifer Grey. Wait a minute . . . Harrison pulled out his phone and googled.

"No phones at movie night," Obed warned.

"Joel Grey!" Harrison crowed. "You should have led with that!"

Everyone looked at him as if he was going to explain, when they all should have known damn well by now that he wasn't going to. Jennifer Grey was Joel Grey's daughter; Joel Grey was the emcee in *Cabaret*. Now *that* was a classic. He shrugged at his family. He was so misunderstood, and he was in no mood to watch a couple of teenage friends from the Dark Ages playing "hooky." He hated sports. He sent his head flying back into the pillow.

He felt someone shifting his legs over and sitting next to him on the couch. Harrison looked up and came face-to-face with Linus holding a soda.

"Hello," Linus said.

"What are you doing here?" Harrison scooted over to give Linus room and then scooted back to bump his shoulder against Linus's.

"Come on, now. It's movie night. My dad dropped me off like always."

"Oh. Nice." Harrison leaned forward and grabbed a slice of pizza.

"You ain't text me back."

"I was sleeping."

"Are you okay?" Linus asked.

"Ummmmmmmmmm."

Linus let out a sound that was half groan, half whine and threw his head back into the couch. Harrison collapsed back into the pillow. They were dead; leave them behind.

"What's going on over there?" Obed asked.

"They're sad," Corrine said.

"Baby girl! We are more than sad!" Linus confirmed. "Mr.

and Mrs. Meredith, no lie, I feel as if these movie nights opened up a whole universe for me. You all have some real interesting taste, I gotta say. Did I like it all? No, I did not. But I liked coming here every time. I don't think I ever would have heard of any of these movies if not for your movie nights, so it was like a class, which was nice."

"Is he giving a speech?" Corrine asked.

"Just some remarks," Linus replied, setting his soda down on a coaster. "When my dad was laying out his reasons for moving, he said that my aunt Bird is our people, and since we don't have other people up here, that's why we're going to live with her. But I feel as if you all are my people, too. I hope you don't mind."

"What do you mean, you're going to live with her?" Obed asked.

"We're moving. To South Carolina."

"Oh, Linus! No! When?" Sheree asked.

"Sunday."

Harrison's dad let out a sound like he was in pain. Obed pulled out his cell.

"No phones at movie night!" Corrine said. Obed hushed her.

As usual, Linus's speech was not finished. "I don't know what kind of entertainment they have down in Charleston. Do they have movies? I don't know. Like, for all I know, it's cotillions and Jack and Jill dancing or some such. So, obviously, I'm pressed. But I appreciate you all."

"You can Zoom in with us on movie nights," Sheree said.

"That's ridiculous." Harrison sniffed.

"Excuse me?" Sheree leaned back and looked at him askance.

"You can't watch a movie over Zoom," he said.

"I think I understand how Zoom works," said his mother. "What I'm struggling with understanding, however, is this tone."

Obed tapped Sheree on the arm and showed her his phone. She read it and they talked to each other with just their expressions for a moment. Harrison couldn't make sense of it. Now he knew how other people felt when he and Linus had silent conversations. He nudged Linus: *What are they talking about?*

They're your parents. How should I know?

They're weird.

A whole room full of people talking with their eyes. A Zoom call on mute.

"Oh-*kay*. Can we—?" Corrine acted like she had someplace to go.

Harrison's dad turned down the TV, which had started cycling between previews on the streaming platform. "What was your favorite movie, Linus?"

"I feel like I have to say one of your picks," Linus said, laughing.

Every member of the family got one week a month to choose the movie for the mandatory fun night. When there were five weeks in the month, Linus got to choose, but since he wasn't a movie person, he always gave it to Harrison. Corrine always demanded a recount.

Linus thought for a second and then answered the question. "I really did like everything. I especially liked that documentary on James Baldwin that Corrine chose last winter."

Internally, Harrison rolled his eyes. Linus must have sensed it, because he turned to Harrison and exclaimed, "I *did*!"

"I didn't say anything!" Harrison shrieked, cutting his eyes at Corrine and then back to Linus.

You stay so mad, Linus's eyebrows said.

How dare you choose one of Corrine's homework assignments disguised as family bonding? Harrison retorted.

Just hold on! You're so annoying, Linus replied. He turned back to the family and continued the conversation out loud.

"Anyways, I think my favorite was *Hamilton*."

Harrison let out a whoop like he'd actually won something. Family bragging rights were one step below a Tony, honestly. Corrine threw her hands up in frustration.

"*Hamilton* isn't even a movie!"

"You're just mad," Harrison shot back.

"I'm just stating the facts of the situation." She turned to their father. "Dad!"

"It's true," Obed said. "It's a filmed stage musical."

"Thank you!" Corrine sat back heavily, as if she'd achieved some great moral victory. "So, Linus, your favorite movie was my pick and your favorite filmed staged musical was *Hamilton*. Just. So. We're. Clear."

Much to Harrison's surprise, he liked *Ferris Bueller's Day Off.*
It was usually really hit-and-miss with his dad's choices. He was
always saying things were "essential" and "classics," but to be
honest, a lot of them were boring. His job at the radio station kept
him more up to date on music trends than Harrison cared to be,
but when it came to movies, Harrison thought his dad must have
stopped paying attention sometime in 1991. His mom had good
movie taste, if a touch dramatic. Someone was always giving a
speech in a courtroom or slamming a cardboard box full of papers
on a desk. At the end, she'd always say the same thing: "That was
very good, but I don't see why there couldn't be more Black people
in it." This was usually a valid point, but Harrison couldn't help
but wonder why she didn't just choose movies with Black people.
Everyone in the family had such different movie taste, and while
Harrison was certain that his taste was the only good one in the
bunch, movie night always provoked conversation afterward.

When Linus started coming, Corrine had really latched on to
his habit of fact-checking in real time, even for movies that weren't
based on real events. He was a welcome addition, particularly
since Harrison never had anything to say if the movie didn't have
singing. And if the movie did have singing, he didn't let anyone
else talk during it.

After *Ferris Bueller's Day Off* ended, Linus and Harrison's dad
got lost in a side conversation about Chicago, where the movie
took place, and the first Black mayor of that city, who was not
a plot point in the film. Corrine and Sheree, meanwhile, were

chatting about some event Corrine was thinking about going to. The movie didn't have any courtrooms and it wasn't a three-hour documentary, so they were both out.

"Who all is going to be there?" Sheree asked.

"Just some people," Corrine replied. As if that answer ever got either of them anywhere. Corrine may have been twenty-one, but she still lived in their parents' house, and that meant conducting an entire census any time she wanted to attend a social engagement.

"Lady, you act like you're the first person whose entire friend group was 'just some people.'" Sheree chuckled and shook her head. "I spent my entire teenage years not having a single friend with a name. Just fifteen folks all named Some People. But go on. Have fun. It's none of my business."

"What?" Harrison cried. Suddenly she was hands off?

Corrine cut her eyes at Harrison, having caught him ear hustling, and moved the conversation into the kitchen. Rude.

Even though the difference in treatment between himself and Corrine was unjust (he made a mental note to fill a cardboard box of papers about it), Harrison couldn't muster true annoyance. Instead, his mind kept wandering back to the movie, which, like the description said, followed a high school kid named Ferris who skips school and convinces his best friend, Cameron, and girlfriend, Sloane, to come with him. They have adventures all over Chicago—going to lunch, driving around in Cameron's dad's convertible, visiting a museum, lounging by a pool, going to a baseball game (Harrison assumed this was the hooky part). Ferris takes the day because he's going to college and he and Cameron are going to be apart and he and Sloane are going to be long-distance and he doesn't want everything to change. And instead, the day changes them; it brings them together in a new way. It hit Harrison like a crystal launched from Jupiter. This wasn't just a movie; this was a message. Ferris made a plan. A big plan. Ferris says that life moves fast and you have to stop every once in a while or you'll miss it. And though he was talking to a bunch of people back in the eighties, it was clear that this was a manifesto aimed right at Harrison here in the present. He couldn't stop Linus from moving, but if he could stop time for just a day, he could stitch together whatever was in the process of clean-breaking with Linus. The solution to all his problems was to have a Ferris Day.

10:13 p.m.

If Harrison and Linus had a day of adventure, then everything would change for them, too. Or, more precisely, nothing would change—they'd remain friends, their bond wouldn't break, and Harrison wouldn't have to face a future alone. He couldn't just announce this plan to Linus, though. In the movie, Cameron hadn't wanted to go. Cameron had said no. Linus would say no, too. Cameron didn't understand the beauty of Ferris Day until the end. Harrison would have to win Linus over.

Harrison opened the family calendar app on his phone. Ideally, they could do Ferris Day the next day, Friday, because Harrison and Linus were off work, but Sheree was working from home, which would mean she'd be paying attention to what they were doing. He wasn't sure what Ferris Day would entail, but he was certain his parents wouldn't approve of any activities that were actually fun. The point of Ferris Day was that the parents didn't know, after all. Would he have to pretend to be sick? Ah! An acting challenge! This was already amazing. However he finagled it, he had to be sure his parents and Linus's dad didn't catch on. Obed and Sheree got nervous if he went anywhere besides school, work, and the houses of the Phalanx of Sad Boys, all of which were labeled on Check In. And Linus's dad, Wally, was even worse, because he wanted a full schedule in advance. There was no "We're going up to Aparna's house" for him. If it wasn't on the little index card that Linus had to write out, which Wally kept on his dashboard as he drove around for the rideshare, Linus didn't get to do it. They'd learned that lesson, a couple of times, the hard way. Wally would freak out, he'd call, they'd explain, and the minute he had the chance, Wally would use his own family-tracker app to show up and ferry Linus back home, where nothing could harm him. It was all so much.

So, Harrison figured, in the context of the movie, Wally was Cameron's dad, which made sense. Or maybe he was the principal trying to catch Ferris? Hmm. Possibilities. Maybe he should make a cast list?

First he wrote FERRIS: ME. That seemed obvious. This was his plan, and he was an impish delight.

CAMERON: LINUS.

There was Ferris's girlfriend, Sloane. That was tricky because Harrison, of course, was famously single. Over the course of the day, Sloane and Ferris fall deeper in love. The point of the day was Ferris and Cameron's friendship, but Sloane and Ferris had something different. Suddenly, it all became clear to Harrison, and he thought in quick succession *Oh yes!* and then *Oh no!* He grimaced and picked up his pen.

SLOANE: DARIO.

Linus had never kissed a boy. And now Linus was going

to have to pick up and start over at a new high school. What if there were no gay people there? What if Linus ended up in some heterosexual dystopia? It could happen; Harrison had seen stories on the news. The world was full of surprising horrors. So the good friend thing to do would be to set up a Ferris Day, making it possible for Linus and Dario to kiss like they both obviously wanted to. And maybe fall in love or whatever, but only if it wasn't annoying.

Harrison thought for a second and then crossed out FERRIS: ME and wrote FERRIS: LINUS? Harrison was impressed by his selflessness, both in allowing Dario to crash their Ferris Day and by recasting Linus as Ferris, despite the fact that it was Harrison's part. Was this growth?!

He decided that continuing to fill out the cast list would be too complicated. He had to figure out what they were actually going to do on Ferris Day and when. He woke his phone up and looked at the calendar app again. On Saturday, his dad's schedule was blocked off for work all day, and his mom had choir practice in the morning and had blocked off her afternoon with an event that read *"Mom: busy."* Corrine, meanwhile, was getting her hair braided at 2:00, which would take at least six hours. Linus and Harrison also had to work, but that seemed less of a concern as Harrison stared at a full day of colored boxes on a calendar, all indicating that his nosy family would be otherwise engaged.

FERRIS DAY: SATURDAY!

Wow, Harrison was on fire. But he wasn't really sure what

the next step was. He thought for a second and then realized that the next step was a snack. Your brain needs food for thinking—everyone knows that. The calories and et cetera make the thing do the thing. It's science. Mondale could explain it when he got back from space camp, which is actually where he was spending his summer and not just a snarky remark Harrison would have texted to Aparna. Mondale was spending his summer in the desert in Arizona, looking at the sky, trying to find something. Aliens or something. It was a shame because if anyone could figure out something meaningful to do with Linus, it was Mondale, master gift-giver. Mondale was just better at noticing things, which probably made him really good at looking at Mars or whatever he was up to. Harrison would have to figure this out on his own, though, and soon, because the Merediths had a strict "no calls after 10 p.m." rule and it was already 10:15.

The rule about calls and texts was so dumb, he decided. He was not a child. He stayed up until midnight or 1:00 a.m. most nights, googling "Audra McDonald Tony Awards performance videos," so what good did it do his parents to forbid communication with the outside world just because the sun was down? It's not like it was the old days, when some phone was going to ring in someone's house and wake up their weird dad. Linus never even turned his ringer on. No one did. Except Mondale, actually, but he never heard his phone ringing over his headphones.

Wait! Mondale was in Arizona, where it was not 10:21

p.m. at the moment, but rather 8:21. A perfectly legal time for telephonic correspondence! He could call Mondale and make a plan, and at the end of the month, when Harrison's mother rolled through, holding her laptop with the phone bill pulled up, Harrison would simply point out that he couldn't possibly have broken the rule thanks to a little loophole called time zones. He was not necessarily following the spirit of the law, but he was following the letter of the law. Well, he wasn't following the letter of the law, either. But he had an excuse locked and loaded, and that was all that mattered. Maybe he'd go to school to be a lawyer. After Broadway, of course. He got his phone out and called Mondale.

"Hold on. I don't understand. Why didn't they just do all that stuff on the weekend?" Mondale was getting really caught up in the plot points of *Ferris Bueller's Day Off*, and Harrison was stressed. They'd been talking about the movie for twenty minutes. This was already a disaster.

"Because he wanted to take a day off from school!"

"I don't understand why. Was he a bad student?"

"Mondale, it doesn't matter. He just wanted to do something else."

Mondale paused, and Harrison knew he was pondering it. This was not a moment to ponder! Finally, Mondale spoke again. "I think it does matter. Maybe he wasn't taking the right subjects."

"Okay, sure. Yes, that was it, Mondale. He wasn't being

challenged by his academic program. Can we move on now?"

"I guess . . ." Oh, great, now Mondale was sad about Ferris Bueller's intellectual stimulation.

"So . . ." Harrison felt himself running out of steam. Was this a bad idea? Would Mondale get it?

"Are you going to go to Chicago?"

"Of course not. We're doing a Ferris Day in Baltimore."

"What does that mean?"

Harrison whimpered. He didn't know what it meant. That was why he'd called Mondale. All he knew was that he wanted to make it special.

"I just want . . ." Harrison started. "What about if we do what they do in the movie?"

"Drive a convertible and go swimming?"

"Well, Linus can't swim, so not that. But a convertible. That's something."

He wrote it down, but the spelling looked funny, so he crossed it out and wrote *CAR WITHOUT ROOF*. He continued: "What do you think Linus would like to do?"

"Well . . . he'd probably just want to hang out with you," Mondale replied. Harrison couldn't believe he was risking getting in trouble for this brilliant advice.

"But what should we *do* when we hang out?"

"Like, whatever you usually do. Oh! What about—You remember that one time we went hiking in the park near Johns Hopkins?"

"That was terrible."

"I thought it was really fun! We discovered that creek! Linus made you take a bunch of pictures of him on top of that place where there used to be a Confederate monument."

"All I know is that I was sweaty and tired the whole time."

"You're always sweaty and tired, though."

Ouch. Mondale said careless things like this all the time, and Harrison knew enough to know he didn't mean it as an insult—it was objectively true that Harrison often got sweaty and tired. News flash: He was a human being on a planet that was getting hotter by the minute. Whomst amongst us is not tired? But the facts of a thing can come at you sideways sometimes. This was something that Linus knew well and treated with care, and which Mondale, sadly, did not.

Mondale was quiet on the other end of the line.

"What are you doing?" Harrison asked.

"I'm lying on the front lawn of the lodge we're staying in. Well, it's not a lawn; it's mostly just dirt. It's so dark here that even with my phone on the darkest setting, it still hurts my eyes a little."

"Are there a lot of stars?"

Mondale inhaled sharply and then exhaled, like he was experiencing the first gasp of love. "Harrison, it's *all* stars. I wish I could send you a picture. But you'd never see it. On the phone, you'd never see it like it is here. The first night I got here and saw the sky, I got dizzy—it was like I've never seen the night sky before. It was like the lid of the world had gotten ripped off and suddenly I got to see where we are. All this stuff I've read about and studied and . . . it was all just there. The sky is full of stars. It's crowded, Harrison. They're in there bumping into one another."

Harrison laughed.

Mondale sighed again. "I wish you could see it. I thought of you. You're somebody who really gets amazed. When you feel wonder, it shows everywhere. And I thought this would amaze you, and that would be a cool sight. You know how you can see more stars at Plowshares than you can in the city? Cuz of all the lights in the city?"

"Yeah."

"Plowshares ain't got nothing on this. It looks like an Oreo milkshake up there. There's more stars than sky. You know what I'm saying? We go around thinking that the night sky is darkness with a couple of dots of light. But the reality is that we're covered by light. It goes on forever."

The thought made Harrison nervous, and Mondale had lulled him into such a state of wonder that he actually said it out loud.

"Why?" Mondale asked.

"I don't know." Harrison was silent, hoping Mondale would just move on. Mondale was silent because, well, when did Mondale ever move on? "I'm afraid of everything," Harrison said with a small laugh, which perished in the air in front of his mouth. "Life is big enough. It's overwhelming." Linus always talked about how long time was. He'd invite Harrison to try to imagine everyone who ever died. Harrison would politely decline out loud. But the thought still hung around his head. Linus saw it as a comfort—*Everything that feels too big for us is just a small dot in a time line*, he'd marvel. But that didn't make any of the things that Harrison faced—the anxieties about the future, about the present, about who and what he was supposed to be—feel any more manageable. He spoke up on the phone. "I think if I saw the sky like that, I'd feel like it was going to crush me," he said.

Mondale went quiet again. Harrison could hear him rolling over on the ground. He must have been so dusty. Mondale really was on some other plane.

Finally, he spoke up again. "I've been trying to figure out what it feels like to be on Earth. Like, we're on the ground, we're in a building, we're in a place, wherever. But how much do you think about the fact that you're on a planet in space? Sometimes, lying here, looking at the stars, I get a little hint of the feeling. I think. I don't know." He laughed. "I guess I won't know if I know. I just feel like . . . I came out here to be face-to-face with these immense things. So I probably should keep my eyes open when they show up."

Harrison mulled that over. He wagered he understood roughly 73 percent of what Mondale said most of the time.

"Anyway," Mondale said with a sheepish chuckle, "we should have a stargazing night at Plowshares when I get back. I think that's what my point was."

"Oh, that was your point," Harrison said with a laugh.

"Yeah, you got it."

"I'd like that," Harrison said. "The stargazing." He wondered why he didn't call Mondale more often.

"But, as far as the Ferris Day—" Mondale began.

"Yes. Right."

"It seems to me that what they were trying to do in the movie was dare themselves. Like, to see what they were capable of. School was too small for Ferris Bueller. If you're gonna skip school, there's no sense in just having a regular old day of your regular life, right?"

"Right."

"So, what are y'all scared to do? What's big enough to hold you together?"

Friday

1:10 p.m.

It was one thing to write down an agenda for Ferris Day. But, fun fact: Writing a thing down and doing it are completely different undertakings. Harrison realized that he simply could not do it alone. There was the matter of their job schedule and the matter of their parents—both seemingly insurmountable. Harrison needed outside help. First stop: Aparna Aiyar, part of the Phalanx of Sad Boys (possibly), but, more important, the key to their freedom.

The Aiyars were only a ten-minute drive away from Harrison's house—walkable in a pinch—but felt a world away. Like many of Harrison's classmates, Aparna lived in a big, bright house with a giant green lawn, but hers was technically within the city limits, not in the suburb that surrounded Baltimore, where Plowshares's campus was. Still, the houses, trees, and lawns were all larger and fancier. And the people inside were mostly whiter and richer. Harrison's parents, for reasons that were unclear but which he assumed had to do with how different the respective neighborhoods were, usually asked Harrison not to walk over. They'd give him a ride, or, in their absence, he was to ask Corrine. God forbid. Today, with both of his parents occupied at work and the heat too high for any physical activity whatsoever, he was left with no other option. His sister had listened to a podcast about white supremacy the whole ride and didn't speak to him once. Was this adult fun? Anyway, he'd gotten there, on a mission.

Set up in Aparna's bedroom, Harrison flipped open her laptop and airdropped a file to it. He had made a PowerPoint presentation, a fact that was not good news for anyone, as it was universally acknowledged that Harrison was *terrible* at PowerPoint. But you don't show up to Aparna Aiyar's house with a bunch of jumbled emotions and a scattershot agenda. You bring a plan. Aparna was the most talented and competent stage manager at Plowshares and the school paper's most eagle-eyed copy editor; she could do anything, but she needed a script.

"You can just tell me what you're thinking," she said, warily eyeing his title screen, which had a pixelated photo of Harrison and Linus and the title "FERRIS DAY" across their faces.

Harrison hit the arrow key, and a blank screen appeared. *Hmm.* He hit it again, and the words "Kiss Today Goodbye" unfurled on the screen at a deathly slow pace. He hit the key again. A still image from *Ferris Bueller's Day Off* spun onto the screen. Harrison wished he had a laser pointer. "So, Joel Grey's daughter plays the sister of a high school student named—"

"Harrison, I've seen *Ferris Bueller's Day Off.*"

"Oh. Okay! I hadn't. I'd never heard of it."

Aparna pulled off the tie holding her black hair in a neat ponytail and deftly started braiding. "The guy who plays Cameron is on *Succession*, and I got really obsessed with that show last year and decided I wanted to be a completist."

"So you watched everything everyone on that show has been in?"

"It was a light semester."

Aparna sighed, leaned over, and took the presentation out of presenter mode with a couple keystrokes. She scanned the slides, which seemed to wither under her gaze, and finally pulled up Slide 47: The Agenda.

"Linus is moving away on Sunday, so I'm taking him on a Ferris Day." Harrison tried his best to sound breezy and not what he was inside—breaking. Otherwise, Aparna would get all caught up in being his friend and helping him process, and that was not what he needed right now. He did not need to accept this. He did not need a listening ear. He needed a stage manager. He needed an accomplice.

"We're going to skip work and we're going to spend the day doing stuff that is . . . memorable. I want to make a memory for him."

Aparna scanned the agenda Harrison had prepared, which read:

☐ SOLO TRAIN TO DC
☐ DARIO
☐ BACK TO BALTIMORE

- [ ] PRIDE
- [ ] ATM MACHINE?
- [ ] FERRIS WHEEL
- [ ] CAR WITHOUT ROOF

"What does any of this mean?" Aparna said.

"Well, I'm glad you asked!" Harrison moved to the next slide. "Linus's dad never lets him do anything, and my parents never let me do anything. And that's fine, mostly, cuz what is there to do besides hang out here or at my house or at school or at the library or—"

"I get it."

"Right. So we have a lot to do, but I think we both want to experience more. Linus has never even kissed a boy. I can't drive! Meanwhile, everybody around us is growing up and living life."

"I don't think that's true."

"Cressida González said that after we got picked up from the *Fiddler* cast party, everything turned really sexy."

"I don't think that's true."

"She said Cool Aparna jumped in the pool in her bra and panties."

"I don't think that's true."

"She said all three Shawns triple-kissed."

"How is that even possible, logistically?"

"I don't know! That's what I'm saying! I have no idea."

"So this day is going to help you figure it out?" she asked, thankfully ignoring the fact that Harrison had slipped and called *the other* Aparna, Aparna Ramamurthy, by the unfortunate nickname given to her at school: Cool Aparna. Unfortunate, that is, for Aparna Aiyar, who, the nickname would infer, was not cool. Or, at least, not *as* cool. Harrison wasn't sure that he agreed with everyone else's assessment of the two Aparnas, but he had to admit (privately) that Cool Aparna's Fruma Sarah in *Fiddler* had been iconic. And the rumor was that their theater teacher had told Cool Aparna that she'd cast her as Mother in next fall's production of *Ragtime* if Cool Aparna promised to stop vaping and messing with her voice. Everyone agreed that this was an incredible development.

"Look, I thought we were going to have all of junior and senior years to figure life out and do new things, but we're not. So I have to do it all in one day. Which is what Cameron and Ferris do in the movie. But, you know, we're different from them, so we have a different plan."

"I'm shocked that two Black queer boys from Baltimore don't have the same agenda as two white straight boys from the suburbs of Chicago in the eighties," Aparna said facetiously.

"I kind of feel like Cameron is a little gay."

"I think that's wishful thinking." Aparna closed the laptop. "Okay, walk me through the day. As I recall, it's: 'Solo Train to DC, Dario, Back to Baltimore, Pride, ATM Machine Question Mark, Ferris Wheel, and Car Without Roof,' right?" Harrison knew he'd come to the right person.

"So, neither one of us has ridden the commuter train that runs to DC, but Coo—" he caught himself and quickly corrected. Aparna raised an eyebrow. "Aparna R. told me once that she'd taken it to a march when she was young and that it was really easy. Linus and I are a little sketched out by public transportation, and our parents do *not* let us ride the light rail, so I figured this might be a fun way into the day."

"Okay, got it." Aparna reopened her laptop and started typing quickly. She glanced up at Harrison like, *Go on.*

"In DC we're going to meet up with Dario Lushovsky. Dario is staying with his dad down there for the summer, so maybe he can show us around for a bit."

Aparna cast a sidelong glance at Harrison over her laptop.

"What?" he said.

"I thought you and Dario weren't really friends anymore."

"Oh, no. Our class schedule was just really different, and . . ."

"Uh-huh."

"And, okay—actually, I think Linus has a crush on Dario. And Dario def has a crush on Linus. Or at least he did last year."

"And so you're taking Linus down to DC so that he can . . ."

"I don't know. Hang out, have lunch, smooch." Harrison shrugged elaborately.

"I absolutely cannot handle when you say the word 'smooch.' Say 'kiss.'"

"Blech! 'Kiss' sounds gross; 'smooch' sounds romantic. I only say 'kiss' for your benefit, and I can't suffer any longer."

"And your plan," Aparna said, "is for Dario and Linus to have a romantic day in DC?"

"A smooch day! I mean. If they want!"

"Hmm." Aparna was tapping her computer absentmindedly, her eyes never leaving Harrison's. "Why?"

What a question. Why does anybody do anything? Why does Earth orbit the sun? Harrison, it had to be said, was . . . ambivalent about Dario. But he and Linus seemed to have a connection, and he *thought* that the good friend thing to do would be to make that happen, and yet every time he tried to be selfless and do that, everybody got all weird.

Why? Harrison huffed internally even as he turned the question over in his mind. He was sure that there was a Power-Point slide in there that said something like "How else is a friend supposed to make sure his friend doesn't forget him, other than arranging for him to go on a daytime date with a classmate at a Panera or something like that?" But he couldn't pull the slide up because Aparna was still on the computer and she was typing again.

"What are you typing? Are you typing about the Dario thing?"

"No! You're so paranoid. Do whatever matchmaking you want. I'm just asking a question."

"Do you not think they're good together?"

"I have other things to think about," Aparna replied without looking up.

"Fine, but what are you typing, though?!"

"I'm finding the cost of the commuter train so I can add it to the itinerary I'm putting together. *Is that okay?*"

"Oh. Yeah." Harrison, chastened, flopped back on Aparna's bed. On the nightstand, he spied a bottle of Mint Chocolate Dream lotion from her weird summer job at a bath and body store called Potions. He flipped the cap open and took a sniff. It smelled like something you want to eat, which gave him pause about putting it on his skin. But his elbows were a little ashy, so he took a dollop. If he got eaten, he got eaten. "So after we hang out with Dario and they smooch or whatever, then we're all three of us coming back to Baltimore to go to the Pride festival," Harrison said. He took another little dollop of lotion and rubbed it between his fingers. It felt like an injustice that he got ashy even in the summertime. "It's Pride weekend, but we've never been to any of the stuff that they do. It'll be fun to just walk around, I think."

"Do you want to prepurchase a wristband?" Aparna asked, head back down in her computer.

"A what? For Pride?"

"Yeah. It says here that you can . . . Oh, I see. No, never mind. That's for if you want to drink. But the festival is all-ages, so you should have no trouble getting in. You can't bring any bottled beverages, though. Even water. I'll put that in the itinerary."

"Thanks." Harrison wondered if he'd thought this plan

through sufficiently. Wasn't it enough to just set the intention of having a good day? Now he was sounding like Corrine, with her affirmations and intentions and whatever. But he found himself stuck between the feeling that he needed to present Linus with a foolproof plan for a lasting friendship, one that would convince Linus that they were actually best friends despite the distance, and the feeling that he should just go with the flow. It wasn't like the two of them ever had a plan when they hung out anyway. But Saturday would be different. Saturday would set the course for the rest of their lives.

"There's a couple things I still want to check out," Aparna said, "but let's move on. What is this ATM thing?"

Harrison laughed. "Linus is afraid of ATM machines, so I'm going to help him use one."

"As in afraid of having his identity stolen?"

"No! He's afraid they're going to eat him or suddenly start beeping and call the cops. He is actually afraid of them. I don't think he's ever used one. It's super strange. So that's just a thing. *But!* I figure if I can help him overcome his ATM machine fear, then every time he uses one in South Carolina and for the rest of his life, he'll think of me."

"Do you want me to search for ATM locations, or do you just want to wing it?" Aparna asked.

"I'll just wing it. It's not a big deal. Just put 'At some point, find an ATM' or something."

"I'm going to be more detailed than that. I'm running this itinerary, and it won't be an embarrassment to my good name. Also, 'ATM' stands for 'automated teller machine.'"

"Okay."

"So when you say 'ATM Machine,' you're saying 'automated teller machine machine,'" Aparna said.

"Okay."

"So you can just say 'ATM.'"

Harrison grinned and winked. "Why are you telling me?" he cried, quoting *You're a Good Man, Charlie Brown*.

Aparna rolled her eyes, but every time she wrote "ATM" in the itinerary, she added an extra "machine" just for Harrison. "What's next?" she asked.

"I thought it would be cute to ride on a Ferris wheel to end the day."

"Like in *Love, Simon*?" Aparna asked, and yes, the thought had occurred to Harrison that a Ferris wheel ride was exactly how two characters end up at the end of that movie and the book, and yes, it was very romantic, and yes, Harrison found clips of that scene online and watched it obsessively. But the crucial difference was that he wasn't trying to create a romantic moment. Not between himself and Linus. Linus had appeared out of the blankness of the internet and then reappeared on his doorstep, and somehow they'd become the kind of friends who, it was true, felt like they'd always been in each other's lives. That was important to Harrison—the friendship, the magic of having found it. So he wasn't interested in a romantic moment; he was trying to create a magical moment. Magic and romance are cousins. That's a fact.

"Not because of *Love, Simon*," he said. "Because it's Ferris Day."

"But Ferris doesn't ride a Ferris wheel."

"But his *name* is Ferris."

"He rides on a parade float."

"I just want to ride the Ferris wheel," Harrison said.

"Okay, I don't know how to break it to you, but we live in Baltimore," Aparna said. "And the state fair isn't until August. But there is a Pride parade on Saturday morning, before the street festival. You'd have to bump the Dario meeting down to the afternoon, but it's doable."

"Aparna, I love you, but this is too much. I don't want to get on a parade float. I've never even been to Pride and I own zero pieces of rainbow attire and no one is trying to wave to me from the crowd. We're just going to ride on a Ferris wheel and then through the magic of the day, we're going to happen upon a car with a convertible roof and we're going to ride in it and we're going to yell at the top of our lungs and we'll be friends forever."

"Whose car is it?"

"Aparna! It's magic! I don't know yet! But it will happen!" Harrison admitted to himself that he was definitely setting an intention. Maybe he'd come back from college woo-woo, too. Great, more things to worry about. "There's one more piece to the day."

Aparna was, as always, ten steps ahead of him. "How to keep your parents off your trail, since you're doing a bunch of stuff they probably would be weird about for no reason."

"Exactly. I kind of thought that . . . maybe . . . somebody could hold on to my phone and Linus's phone and take them to all the places we're supposed to be that day so that when our parents look at the location apps, the GPS doesn't give it away. "

Aparna smiled. "Someone, for instance, who knows the run of the show and is used to calling cues."

"Yeah. I wonder what kind of person, who is smart and wonderful and one of my dearest friends in the whole world and who I will owe forever, would do that. Maybe I can text Tully?" he said, name-checking Plowshares's *other* competent stage manager.

"Don't you dare," Aparna laughed. "I'm obsessed with this. This phone thing is very CIA superspy."

"I'll give you a list of all the places we're supposed to be on Saturday and when you can leave the phones there or whatever."

"I'll figure it out," Aparna said. "Have you thought about what to do if someone texts you or Linus? Or what if I need to reach you? You might need a burner phone."

"What's a burner phone?"

"Like in movies when somebody gets a disposable phone for doing crimes."

"But I'm not doing crimes."

"I think Sheree and Obed might beg to differ."

"Well, where do I get a burner phone?"

"I have no idea, Harrison. I am sixteen years old and I do not do crimes." She checked the clock on the wall, which had the face of a different member of a K-Pop boy band at every hour. "And I am due at work in half an hour, so let's put a pin in this."

While Aparna disappeared into her closet to change clothes, Harrison wandered down to the kitchen for a drink. Linus had once said to Harrison that Aparna had the kind of house where you could tell the parents were obsessed with the kid, and Harrison was never able to get that out of his head. Now every time he looked at the staircase lined with pictures of Aparna slowly getting older and winning more awards for various activities, he couldn't help but laugh. He had asked Linus if he thought Sheree and Obed were obsessed with him, and Linus had succinctly replied, "No." He wasn't saying they didn't like him or didn't love him, Linus had quickly added. "They just got other things going on. Your parents' aesthetic is not 'We have a sixteen-year-old son.' That's all I'm saying."

As Aparna aged into herself through photos on the wall beside him again, Harris pulled his phone out and, almost without thinking, texted Linus. What are you doing?

Linus, of course, called. "Packing," he said before Harrison could say "Hello." Not that Harrison would have said anything, because he knew that when Linus called after a text, he just jumped into the conversation in midstream. "What are you doing?"

"I'm running errands," Harrison said.

"Oh! Where?" Linus said. Shoot. Harrison had forgotten—Linus loved errands. They assumed errands were adult trips to do serious things, like pick up a prescription or withdraw $20,000 from a bank teller, but Linus liked to amuse himself by referring to even the simplest of tasks as an errand. He ran an errand to get himself a glass of water; he ran an errand to pick up takeout from the delivery driver; he ran an errand to get out of bed. He really cracked himself up with it. Harrison, not so much.

"Just . . . boring stuff," Harrison replied. He slipped back into Aparna's room and sat on her bed. His stomach was rumbling; he hated lying, and he was sure that this was going to become some elaborate improv piece and he really didn't have the creative energy for all that today.

"Sorry," Linus interjected. "My dad wants me to help him move some furniture. Can I call you back?"

"Def."

"If you want to come over tonight, he's making fried green tomatoes." Harrison thought that sounded amazing, but Linus sounded annoyed. A mystery. He hung up as Aparna emerged from her closet far more frazzled than when she'd gone in.

"Did I tell you they made me buy new clothes?" She stood with a light pink cowl-neck blouse draped across her chest. The price tag still dangled from the armpit. "The new manager said, 'Your look doesn't really fit the brand. The all-black is a little creepy.' Creepy? It's chic, it's sleek, it's effortless! Also, I frequently wear gray."

Harrison started to speak, but Aparna was apparently in full-story mode. She continued, "I have worked at Potions since the beginning of sophomore year. I have sold more than almost anyone else at that location. When I transferred to the Potions location at the Gallery, I immediately outsold everyone there, too. The customers don't care what I'm wearing; they care what the product can do for them. And that's what I tell them. It's called sales!" She'd arranged herself into a perch on her bed, shoving to the side her laptop, a headlamp, a few rolls of gaffer's tape, a stack of books, an apple, three fancy candles still wrapped in plastic, and a home speaker system. She drew her knees up to her chest, looking, Harrison thought, like some kind of forlorn figure in a painting you'd see at an art museum. It didn't hurt that the wall behind her was covered with pictures of K-Pop stars, every one more gorgeous than the last. The guys stared down like angels on poor Aparna as she lamented having to go shopping. "My mother got so excited. She came home with four bags of 'work clothes' for me." She kicked a foot in the direction of the blouse on the chair. "Every single one a costume piece from her middle-aged lady store. I look like a teller at a bank. I told her, 'Mom, I'm at a mall selling lotions that do not smell like anything that can be found in nature. This aesthetic is very Millie Dillmount on the first day of work.'"

"Did she get the *Thoroughly Modern Millie* reference?"

Harrison asked. Aparna glowered at him. Of course not. Dr. Aiyar was very nice, she always checked in with Harrison's parents on his behalf so that he and Aparna could come and go as they pleased, and she faithfully bought twenty tickets to every Plowshares theater performance for friends, family, and clients despite the fact that Aparna never once appeared onstage. But the minute the lights came back up, it was like every single thing that had happened in the musical she'd just seen left her head. Nevertheless, ever since the spring production, Harrison had taken to greeting her by saying, in a singsong voice, "A blessing on your house!" to which Dr. Aiyar would respond in her own throaty singsong voice, "Mazel tov! Mazel tov!" It was a line from *Fiddler on the Roof,* but Harrison wagered he could tell her it was from *Legally Blonde* and she'd still respond, "Oh, you all were magnificent in that! And the set! Better than Broadway!"

"Are you going to quit your job?" Harrison asked.

Aparna unfolded into a shrug like human origami. "Uh, no. I like the money, and I'm good at it. I just don't think it's necessary to be dressed like a lighthearted divorcée."

Harrison had once made the mistake of labeling Aparna's propensity for wearing all-black all the time as goth. The two had been friends since Harrison had first started at Plowshares in second grade, and although she was sometimes annoyed by him and his dramatics, Aparna had never looked at him with any expression more scornful than light confusion. Bemusement, one might say if one recently spent months learning new words for a test that purported to affect the rest of your life. But when he called her goth, he saw something new in her face. It was possible that Aparna had actually been disappointed in him.

"There's more to being goth than just dressing in black, Harrison," Aparna had said. "It's not a costume. It's an outlook. What I wear is a uniform."

The pink cowl-neck she'd finally convinced herself to put on did not, to Harrison's mind, look as much like a uniform as her regular clothing, but Aparna seemed undeterred.

"Okay, to recap," she said, handing Harrison his laptop back and leading him out of the room, "I am going to break a sales record today out of spite, and I'm going to email you the itinerary for Ferris Day tonight. It's all handled."

2:35 p.m.

Harrison took the bus from Aparna's house south, across North Avenue, en route to the Harbor and his second destination: the office of BaltiTours, where he would have to somehow convince his boss to give him and Linus the day off with almost no notice. Perhaps he could plead his case by really emphasizing that this was a Big Plan. He considered showing her the PowerPoint. He wondered if she'd let him use the flat-screen TV in the front window.

Out of habit, again, he pulled out his phone. His ongoing text conversation with Linus lately made it looked like Harrison was getting left on "read." It had been all one-sided for the past two days—questions and statements from Harrison sent at various times that seemingly never got answered. Of course, Linus always answered; he more than answered. Linus was hitting the CALL button before the text even finished going through. But would it always be like that? The motor in his chest hadn't quieted down any since he'd been at Aparna's. What if it didn't work?

No. There was no "what if." It *had* to work.

The bus turned on to Franklin Street, passing the huge display windows in front of the public library. Besides the cemetery, this was the place where they spent the most time together. Harrison had actually never been until Linus showed up and invited him. Now it felt like another limitless secret space that belonged to them. Or, at least, it *had* felt like that.

He was back on his phone. He scrolled up until he got to the last text from Linus. *Hello.* This was better somehow.

Before Linus, Harrison's primary texting audience had been Corrine, of all people. Though they'd always feigned annoyance with each other, before she'd gone to college, the wall between them hadn't been there. There were times, he thought, that they'd actually been friends. And so, delighted by the freedom that a phone brought, he'd text her pictures and GIFs and random messages throughout the day. And she'd always write back. When they were in their separate classes at Plowshares and he missed her, he'd text a question that they both knew he could answer on his own. And she'd answer it. When their parents were getting on their nerves, she'd text him a selfie of her rolling her eyes or a paparazzi shot of Sheree or Obed doing something weird.

They talked at home, but it was in those texts that their relationship flourished.

And then she'd left for college, enthusiastic and eager, he knew, but also anxious and fearful. For a while, she updated him on her dorm, her roommate, the misadventures of getting around campus. And he'd text her about how much their parents talked about her in her absence and the neighborhood drama and the reappearance of Linus, the boy from church.

And then suddenly it had stopped. If he'd scrolled back through their messages, which he would never let himself do, he would have seen that it trickled down slowly. One message here or there left with no reply, then a few more. Corrine's messages becoming shorter and stranger. He'd been nervous then because it felt like the thing that connected them was getting frayed and he couldn't tell why.

Eventually, when he opened his phone to text Corrine, he saw only a wall of his own unanswered queries.

How are you?
Is it fun?
U there?
Are you okay?

Something was happening. He could tell because the conversations his parents had about her during her sophomore year got quieter and more serious. But no one—not them, not her—would tell him anything. Something was wrong. He even struggled to talk to Linus about it.

He wasn't able to get to sleep anymore. He'd lie awake thinking about Corrine. And during those nights, he'd hear his mother's cell phone ring and then a door close and then his parents' hushed voices, talking. Talking to her. He wanted so badly to go inside and find out what was wrong at school, even if it scared him. He wanted for someone to just tell him the truth. He was in ninth grade; he didn't know everything, but he knew a lot. And he knew that whatever Corrine had expected to find at college had not been there. And, for some reason, what she had at home hadn't been enough to hold her together.

Then one night, the phone rang early, Harrison's parents had conferred quietly, and then Obed had left the house. Harrison was still awake at one in the morning when Obed returned. Harrison heard a third hushed voice, Corrine's. He heard her come up the stairs and close the door of the room next to his. He texted again. What's wrong? No response.

He stuck his head into the hallway, catching his father by surprise.

"Nothing happened," Obed said. "It's okay. Corrine's just going to take some time off. Go back to sleep."

Harrison retreated to his room but was no more settled than he had been before. When he couldn't take it anymore, he opened another text message and wrote to Linus. Hello. Linus called back right away. With tears burning hot across his face, Harrison whispered into the phone all his fears about his sister and the strange air that had taken over his house. Linus listened. He kept listening. Harrison told Linus everything. He didn't know why he'd thought to call him, but he knew, from the way that Linus had shared the hard spaces and questions in his own life, that Linus would understand.

"She's my sister, but she *was* my friend." Harrison whispered. "She was my best friend. I don't know why she won't answer."

They stayed on the phone until Harrison ran out of words. They stayed on the phone until the tears dried on his face. They stayed on the phone until they fell asleep.

The next morning, Linus had showed up at Harrison's front door unannounced. He'd never come without his dad before.

"Hello," he'd said.

"Hi," Harrison replied.

"Do you want to go to the library with me? I need to look something up. I thought we could go together. If you feel like hanging out."

The bus pulled up to Harrison's stop at Harborplace, and he got out. His phone vibrated with an email from Aparna: She had apparently typed up . . . minutes? From their meeting? While in the car? She was a wonder.

STAGE MANAGER'S REPORT:
DESIGN TEAM MEETING

SM: Aparna Aiyar

DIRECTOR: Harrison Meredith

DRAMATURGICAL NOTES: I looked it up, and actually

there is some evidence to the theory that Cameron is gay in *Ferris Bueller's Day Off*.

STAGE MANAGER'S NOTES:

Team met to discuss Ferris Day. I will be leading point, providing diversion on the location-tracking apps while Harrison and Linus do all the things on the itinerary.

We still have to figure out where Harrison can get a burner phone so that we can communicate. (We will. Don't freak out. —AA)

3:25 p.m.

Ferris Bueller hadn't asked anyone permission to take the day, but as Aparna succinctly pointed out, there were some key differences between Harrison and Ferris. Harrison could, and would have to, fool his parents, but he knew that just not showing up at work would definitely get him fired. He'd do anything for Linus, but his allowance was a pittance. A pittance! This meant that he would somehow have to convince his manager at BaltiTours to do him a favor, something most adults seemed completely uninterested in doing. And he still hadn't figured out what his plan was when he encountered said manager, Sweet Baby Cashman, standing next to the dumpster behind Harborplace, snapping a rubber band against her wrist.

"Hey, hey!" Harrison called, so casual, so cool. Just a person saying hello at a dumpster.

Sweet Baby, a woman whose bright tuft of blonde hair always seemed on the verge of flying away, caught sight of Harrison. "You're not on the schedule today, bub."

"Oh, I know. I just came to—I was just in the neighborhood and I figured I'd stop by. I have a—Chaz said you were out here smoking."

"I'm not smoking! Do you not see that I am actively not smoking?"

Oh God. Red alert. Retreat. Now that he recalled it, Sweet Baby's quit-smoking plan had sort of been a thing around the office, but as a nonsmoker and someone who only went to work to hang out with Linus, he hadn't paid attention to it. One of the college students who worked at BaltiTours had told her to try "the gum," but then a week later, Sweet Baby had come in looking absolutely wrecked, talking about how the gum made her go jogging in her sleep and she had to barricade herself in her apartment. Honestly, Harrison was shocked by how much time these people were willing to devote to discussing the various ways they were in crisis. Now, if he recalled the latest news from the front, Sweet Baby was back off the gum and going cold turkey. He didn't understand why this method involved her going to the dumpster, the place where everyone smoked, and just standing there looking miserable, but he knew better than to ask.

A waiter came out of a restaurant in the building and lit up an actual cigarette, apparently free from strife. Sweet Baby ran her hands through her luminescent hair and exhaled slowly.

"Can I ask you something?" Harrison said. "Maybe over there by the doors?"

Sweet Baby nodded tensely as they left the dumpster area. "If you need off, don't even think about it," she said. "This schedule has been a nightmare ever since Marlie and Brian started dating.

I cannot deal with y'all and all your little personal dramas." She snapped her rubber band.

"I'm not asking off!" Harrison said. "Also, when did Marlie and Brian start dating?"

"They hooked up at a Memorial Day party."

"Oh my god!"

"That's not even half of it. Then they spent a week being weird to each other at work. Brian actually asked Chaz for advice, and you know that dude don't have advice about nothing except the apocalypse."

"I mentioned to him that I was planning on applying to colleges, and he told me that there would be no higher education after the Reckoning."

"I mean, that's probably true, but I think you got time," Sweet Baby said. "Anyway, I finally had to take Brian and Marlie aside, *at work*, and tell them to either get it on or end it, because I can't handle all kinds of tomfoolery in a professional environment. We are trying to sell land and sea tours of the downtown Baltimore area, Fort McHenry, and Fells Point. You can't convince people to pay cold, hard American dollars for the chance to see the birthplace of "The Star-Spangled Banner" if you're too busy arguing about who did what, where, and when, and on whose roof-deck."

"That's wild," Harrison said. "So they're together now? And they want to work together?"

"Every shift. It's bananas! I do not want to work with my

husband. When we were both working from home, every day I was like, 'If you don't get *out* of my *face* . . .'" And I love him! Couples need space! You and Linus better learn from this."

"Linus isn't my boyfriend," he said.

"Harrison, I do not give a *flamin' hot damn.*"

"I'm just saying. So we don't need space."

"No skin off my nose. All the better for my scheduling."

"You know he's leaving, right?"

Sweet Baby let out a noise of disgust. "Yes. He came down here and gave me a speech about it. Tomorrow is his last day."

"Actually, that's what I'm here to discuss," Harrison said.

"I'm not discussing a thing with you."

"We're both scheduled for the morning shift, and I was wondering if you could give us off so that I can say goodbye to him."

"You said you weren't here to talk about the schedule!" Sweet Baby roared.

"I lied!"

Sweet Baby gasped.

"I'm sorry! I'll let you schedule me whenever! I'll work with Chaz every day."

Sweet Baby looked at Harrison, straight-up pissed, and he tried to look pitiful and adorable, like Cosette from *Les Mis.*

"I was going to bring cupcakes for his last day," she said. She snapped her wrist again. "All right, whatever. You two can be off. I'll put Marlie and Brian on because they owe me. Now *you* owe me, too. And I will collect!"

5:10 p.m.

Harrison returned to an empty house, full of determination. He got a glass of water from the kitchen and drank it all at once. He was raring to go.

Aparna texted him: 1) Already smashed the sales record.

Harrison texted back: Must be the pink blouse.

Aparna: 2) Do you have an old phone?

Aparna: Rude.

Harrison: Congrats!

Harrison: don't think so

Harrison: I've dropped every phone I own

Aparna: I'll keep thinking.

Harrison set his glass down in the sink even though the sign on the dishwasher clearly said DIRTY and he could have put it in there. He didn't have time for small things when he was on the cusp of such greatness. Against all odds, he'd accomplished so much already. He thought he ought to celebrate—maybe he could find a way to get over to Linus's for fried green tomatoes. He hoped the Munros hadn't packed their TV yet; he was having such a successful day, he was pretty sure he could convince Linus to watch *Hamilton* with him again for the ninth time.

Linus was not a musicals person, or really a theater person at all, although he always came to see Harrison's performances with the rest of the Merediths and he'd even brought flowers one time, even though Harrison had not had a big part and had flubbed the one line he had. Of all the musicals Linus had seen Harrison in, the only one that he seemed to have taken any interest in was *Fiddler.* He'd gone with Harrison and the cast to the diner after the opening-night performance and then curled up in the booth with Harrison's phone, googling "Jewish life in Ukraine," "the history of pogroms," and "the painter Marc Chagall." This was Linus really connecting with the magic of theater.

Years earlier, Harrison's aunt Bella had taken him and Corrine to New York one summer to visit the American Museum of Natural History and to see *Hamilton* on Broadway. Before he and Linus had reunited, before everything. Harrison had quickly become obsessed, learning the lyrics, drawing fan art, spending a semester with Aparna designing and lobbying the school to let them paint a "Who Lives, Who Dies, Who Tells Your Story" mural. (They were not successful in this pursuit.)

When Linus came back into his life and their friendship was cemented, Harrison cycled through a number of onstage friendships before figuring out who he thought they were. Elphaba and Glinda? *No, they didn't hate each other at the beginning.* Elle and Paulette from *Legally Blonde? Oh my god, but who was who?* Finally it came to him: they were Revolutionary War besties Alexander Hamilton and John Laurens from the musical *Hamilton* about

Hamilton. *Yay,* Hamilton! He couldn't wait to tell Linus, who of course did not get it. Harrison told him to just listen to the album. Linus said, "Thanks, but no thanks, baby boy!" Harrison sent him links to scholarly articles he didn't understand and a conversation between Ron Chernow and Lin-Manuel Miranda. Linus wrote back, "Interesting!" And then Harrison gave up. He would just know it was true in his own heart, without the validation.

And so it wasn't until the movie night when Harrison had chosen *Hamilton* that Linus finally saw what Harrison was talking about and with it the intensity of feeling—the rarity of being seen by someone else, the way they were total badasses. (Harrison had conceded that this last bit was not necessarily true to the friendship he and Linus had, but it was important to have goals.) Harrison remembered now the moment when Hamilton and Laurens say goodbye that is not included on the cast album. When it happened onscreen, Linus had gasped and grabbed Harrison's arm. "They mean so much to each other!" he cried.

Corrine snorted.

Linus said, "This part isn't on the album."

Harrison shot back gently, "You said you didn't listen to it."

Linus shushed him and went back to watching the film. It had been a perfect moment. Harrison had everything he needed in that room.

Yes, they would watch *Hamilton* again today. And Linus, who was still not a musicals person and had gone deep on the fact versus fiction of it all, would love it just as much. Harrison wouldn't say anything about Ferris Day, in case Linus's dad was listening. He was so close. It could all go so wrong. But what if it all went right?

He checked the time on the kitchen iPad. They had all evening. They had the rest of their lives. They had—Wait, the kitchen iPad. This was the last piece for the plan. No one ever used it, it didn't have a lock code, and, most important, it was not connected to Check In. Harrison could borrow it and use it to communicate with Aparna on Ferris Day. He'd found his burner phone, he'd cleared all his obstacles, and he still had enough time for a two-act musical. Harrison was killing it. *"Nothing's gonna stop! Me! Now!"* he thought happily, quoting *Dreamgirls*. Then he revised himself, scanning his brain for a more on-theme lyric. He found it in *Hamilton*, of course. *"Tomorrow they'll be more of us,"* he sang to himself. More of him and Linus, more of life, more. Tomorrow.

Saturday

7:00 a.m.

Ferris Day was beginning, bright and beautiful and top-secret, and Harrison was a mass of nerves. It certainly didn't help that Corrine was taking roughly nineteen hours to prepare her power bowl. He needed the iPad for his plan with Aparna, and to get it, he need Corrine to finish making her breakfast.

Oblivious to the torture she was inflicting, Corrine hummed to herself as she pulled out the quinoa she'd left soaking in yogurt overnight. She felt him watching her and looked up.

"What?" she said.

"Is that good?"

"Obviously," she said.

Harrison thought it wasn't so obvious, considering it had the appearance of regurgitated baby food.

Corrine smirked. "You don't have to approve, bighead. You can try it if you'd like, but you don't need to stand here and judge me while you put a bunch of chemicals and complex carbohydrates in your body."

"I didn't say anything!"

"You never say anything, Harrison. But what you don't seem to understand is that your face gives you away left, right, and center." Harrison suddenly felt exposed by every benign thought he'd ever had and implicated by the less-benign plan that he was desperately anxious to enact.

"We have plenty of time," Corrine said, now methodically picking the best raspberries out of a container.

"Huh?" Harrison said.

"We've got plenty of time to get you to work and me to boxing. You keep checking the clock." She pointed at the kitchen iPad. Caught again! That settled it: He had to get rid of his face.

"Stop stressing out," Corrine said, slivering almonds and cutting into Harrison's fragile mental state. "And take your hands off your cheeks. You're going to irritate your skin." She sprinkled the almonds on top of the truly unwieldy mound of grains, fruits, seeds, and mush in her bowl, and headed out back. "I'll be ready to go in twenty minutes," she said.

As soon as she closed the screen door, Harrison grabbed a grocery tote from under the sink and slid the kitchen iPad into it. He started to pull open drawers in search of a charger cable.

"What are you looking for?" Harrison's mom had come in at some point without him hearing her. His eyes flitted from her face—currently not suspicious, but one never knows—to the tote bag on the counter—not necessarily iPad-shaped but not *not* iPad-shaped. This actually settled it: He would have to meticulously go over every interaction he'd had with his family during the past week and ask himself what they knew and how they knew it.

"I'm not looking for anything," Harrison replied.

"Just taking a tour?" Sheree raised her eyebrows. Good, she was amused by him. This was a positive sign. Unless it was a trap. She put the kettle on and pulled out a tea bag. "You know," she said, not facing him, "that when an emergency vehicle comes down the road behind you, you need to pull the car over to the side to let them pass, right?"

What . . . was this? Was this code? Was this some kind of a test? Harrison stared at his mother's back as she unwrapped the tea bag. He pondered for so long that Sheree got tense and turned around to look at him. One of her micro braids slipped out of the bun on top of her head, and she caught it and started fiddling with it to set it right.

"Did you know that?" she asked.

Did he know that? Frankly, it sounded like a good idea, but the truth was that Harrison really didn't know what he knew when it came to the rules of the road. In the spring semester, he'd endured six tension-filled driving lessons with Brother Aldo from church. He ran a side business called Jesus Is Lord Driving School. Brother Aldo had taught Sheree to drive years before, and then had taught Corrine to drive, and the plan was for him to teach Harrison as well, but what ended up happening was they spent a few weekend mornings together, with Brother Aldo pounding the dashboard and yelling, "Hands at ten and two!" and Harrison screaming into the windshield. It had not been a success.

"I did know that," he said.

"Oh, good," she said. She turned back to the counter and grabbed a bottle of honey. What was this mind game? "I couldn't remember if Brother Aldo included that in the lessons or not. You know it's been a minute for me. But it's important."

"Uh-huh." Harrison had failed the driver's test twice and hence had decided that vehicular movement, like other forms of choreography, was not one of his talents.

"When he taught me to drive, Brother Aldo swore, *swore* that the police have a way of knowing how loud the volume in your car is. I said, 'Brother Aldo, are you talking about ears?' He got so mad." The muscles in Sheree's shoulders shook as she chuckled. "He was insistent that they had some kind of radar. 'But they only use it on Black folks,' he said. I mean, he was probably right. Anyway, when you drive, don't listen to the radio. I know how you do."

The teakettle started to fuss.

"What do you mean, how I do?" Harrison asked.

"I'm not saying anything mean. You like music. It's going to be hard to resist the temptation to blast *My Evan Hansel* or what-have-you when you're in the car on your own." *My Evan Hansel?!* What world did his parents live in? This was why he didn't speak: Nobody listened. "You're off early today, right?" Sheree asked.

Harrison was brought back down to Earth. "Yes," he said quickly, "but Linus and I are going to the library afterward."

The teakettle had worked itself up to a low whine.

"That's fine," Sheree said. "I've got a breakfast meeting and then choir rehearsal, but after that I thought it might be nice for you and me to practice your driving."

The teakettle started screaming.

"It's Linus's last day," Harrison said.

"I know. That's why I'm suggesting it. I've seen how down you've been this week. I thought that working on getting your license might be a nice thing to take your mind off it."

"We're going to hang out, though!" Harrison cried. Sheree turned at the sound of his voice. The kettle kept hitting key changes like it was performing "Love on Top."

"Linus can come! We'll just be in a parking lot. It won't be illegal for him to be in the car with me there, I think. Oh! Look at you. Baby, I know you're scared, but you can absolutely do this. Brother Aldo has a very particular style, and maybe that was a mistake, to pair you two. But I know we can figure this out."

Harrison dove forward, turned off the stove, and moved the kettle to another burner. "I had to stop the screaming," he said to his mother.

"Oh, sorry!" she said.

She poured hot water into a mug that read DIDN'T YOU HAVE BIG FUN IN BALTIMORE? (Harrison had no clue what this meant, but when his father had given it to her mother for her fortieth birthday and said, "This is you now," she'd laughed so hard, she'd cried. Okay.)

"So, whatcha think?" Sheree said.

Harrison was panicking. He tried to tell his face to stop panicking, but he felt like maybe that was only making his face panic more.

"I was just hoping we could have our last day together just . . . to hang out," he said, finally.

"You don't want to say goodbye with a fun and educational driving lesson?" She winked at him.

Corrine came back in and put her empty bowl in the sink even though the dishwasher sign said DIRTY. She sat down behind Harrison at the counter.

"Suit yourself," Sheree said. "We'll do the driving lesson some other time." She looked past Harrison to speak to Corrine. "You saving this dish for later?" She pointed at the sign.

"Oh my goodness." Corrine sighed as she got up from the counter. "Harrison, are you ready to go?"

"I gotta get my backpack," he said. He eyed the tote on the counter between himself and Corrine. If he took it, there'd be questions; if he left it, they might notice it, or they might not. What was the move?! Should he text Aparna for guidance?

"Well?" Corrine said.

"I . . . don't know where it is."

"I'll be in the car. Get it together, if you please."

As she left, Harrison heard his father play a few notes on his keyboard in the living room.

"That's my cue," Sheree said. She kissed him on the forehead. "Have a wonderful day. Feel better."

"What are you doing in there?"

"We're just going to run through my solo before your dad goes to work."

"Okay, so I thought the point of choir practice was to practice," Harrison said playfully.

"My beautiful boy, the way you get the solo is talent. The way you keep the solo is showing up prepared." She raised her mug to him in salute and walked into the living room.

Harrison stared after her for a moment before realizing that the kitchen was finally empty. He snatched the tote bag bearing the iPad off the counter, plucked his backpack from under a chair, and rushed to the front door. He couldn't say for certain that he had the talent to pull off Ferris Day, but he was a Meredith and he was going to show up to Linus's house prepared.

7:31 a.m.

Linus heard Harrison before he saw him. Well, technically, he heard a car blasting a song from the musical *Newsies* outside his house. He didn't know most of the people in his neighborhood, but Linus was willing to bet that folks on this Baltimore street had never had their windows rattled by the sounds of "The World Will Know." At least not before noon. Linus pulled his uniform shirt over his head and then stopped midway through. He'd actually identified the musical *and* the song? Harrison's movie nights had been a real education. Maybe he'd take a theater class in South Carolina. No. No, that was doing too much. Maybe he'd just listen to the songs when he missed Harrison. Linus heard the car door shut and the music immediately switch to a talk radio interview. He pulled his head through his shirt the rest of the way and peered out his bedroom window in time to see Corrine's car pulling away and Harrison watching it go before surreptitiously peeking into the two bags he was carrying.

Harrison looked up suddenly, seemingly aware of Linus's gaze. He smiled brightly and waved. Linus waved back.

"Baby boy, what are you up to?" Linus muttered.

He wove his way through the mess of mostly full boxes on his floor. He hadn't cared enough to fold, label, or tape anything shut. If he had to go to Charleston, he was going to get there a hot mess. He closed his bedroom door and went downstairs.

"Don't act suspicious," Harrison said when Linus opened the front door. "Oh, wow, everything's packed up." Harrison craned his head to look around Linus, who came out onto his marble steps and pulled the door shut behind him.

"Why would I be acting suspicious?" Linus said.

"You're not. Just don't!" Harrison grinned in a way that can only be described as deranged, though Linus was sure that Harrison would have described it as "triumphant." This much he knew. What was he triumphing over?

"You trying to come in first?" Linus asked.

"No. Maybe. Do you have a change of clothes for after work?"

"Nah. I don't care."

"Can you grab some? Just in case?"

"Why?"

Linus felt the door tug open behind him. His father put his hand on his shoulder. "What's up, Harrison?"

"Hey, Mr. Munro. It's cool if we go to the library after work today and then to my house, right?"

Linus's dad turned to Linus. "Is that on the notecard?" Really with this? Of course Linus had filled out the notecard—**WORK, LUNCH, LIBRARY**—and left it on the kitchen table for Dad *even though* he did the same thing every day and today would be no different and then after tomorrow his schedule would only have one entry: "nothing." Linus thought about filling out a bunch of notecards in advance as protest. Instead he just answered the question. Sometimes that was easier.

"Yeah. Except the thing about going to Harrison's house. I didn't know about that."

"You know the rule—"

"All right!" Linus rolled his eyes and brushed past his dad into the house. They didn't have the easiest relationship, but even he had to admit that this here was on some other level. What other option did he have, though? He'd complained about the move; he'd said he didn't want to go. He'd even called Aunt Bird, who'd told him, "You'll have a TV in your room; you like video games? I'll get Cedrick to give you his old system." He didn't want his cousin's hand-me-downs. Why was everyone doing everything except the thing he wanted? *This is the problem with the Munros,* he thought as he grabbed the note-card and scrawled **HARRISON'S HOUSE AS USUAL**—*they all have these big plans, they do too much, and it never works out.* At least, it never worked out for Linus.

He bounded up the stairs and back into his room. He had no idea why Harrison wanted him to bring a change of clothes to just sit around his living room, but the two bags he was carrying were peculiar. Maybe Linus was being kidnapped. What should he take? He had a new shirt, white with silhouettes of birds on it, draped on the back of a chair. That was definitely coming. What else? He grabbed his MP3 player and headphones from the desk. He opened a random box, which held his old gym uniform, a stack of books, a plant that had seen better days, and a box of cookies. Things weren't looking so hot.

From outside, he heard his dad talking to Harrison. "Old boy is pissed at me today," Dad said. Linus knew that Harrison got extremely nervous any time an adult spoke to him or acknowledged his presence. He had to hurry. He pulled a plastic bag out from under his bed, grabbed the gym shorts, stuffed them and the white shirt in, and ran back down the steps.

Linus's dad was folding himself into his car when Linus stomped out of the house. He handed the notecard through the open passenger window. Dad plucked it out of Linus's hands and reviewed the amended schedule. "Thank you kindly! What time are you coming back from Harrison's?" Mr. Munro asked.

Harrison piped up. "Can it be late? We might watch a movie. My parents can make us dinner."

"That's fine," Mr. Munro said, making a note on the index card. "Eight o'clock."

"Eight o'clock?" Linus said. "The sun will still be out."

Mr. Munro rolled up the window and turned on his rideshare app. This guy was trying it.

"Let's go," Linus said. He walked back to the front door, locked it, and started down the street to the bus stop.

"Wait. Wave goodbye to your father," Harrison said.

"Why? Are you kidnapping me?"

"No! Do you want to be kidnapped?"

"For real, though, I did think about it. I was like, 'What if I just refuse to leave, and live at Harrison's?'" Linus said. They turned the corner.

"It's a perfect plan," Harrison said.

"It would have been a disaster," Linus said.

"No, we could have made it work. You should have mentioned it earlier, like when you called me after I got home yesterday to explain the deeply interesting story about how Baltimore's old football team moved to Indianapolis in the middle of the night and the whole city boycotted the moving company that took them."

"I thought it was cool! This is my way of coping."

"Well, my way of coping is that I came up with a new plan. We're not going to work."

This sounded like Doing Too Much.

"We're on the schedule," Linus said. "It may be my last day, but Sweet Baby don't play."

"No, I got permission. We're going to meet Aparna at work and then we're going on a day of adventure like in *Ferris Bueller's Day Off*."

Linus stopped. This was definitely Doing Too Much. "What are you talking about?"

"I have a way of keeping your dad off your tail."

Boy, what is this? Linus asked Harrison silently.

Harrison grabbed Linus's shoulders: *The best day of our continued and enduring friendship.*

"I ain't trying to hear my dad's mouth all the way down to Charleston. Like, we cannot be doing some kind of last hurrah–type nonsense like we don't have a care in the world."

"This is *not* the last hurrah," Harrison said. "That's the point. Look, we're just going to have a day. We get to be living some other kind of life. We get to hang out. We can do anything you want!"

"For real?"

"I mean, Aparna made a very tightly organized schedule, but if there's room, you can do anything you want."

"Whatever, boy." He sucked his teeth. "So what's on this schedule?"

"I'm glad you asked. You're going to love Ferris Day."

Linus's dad chose this moment to pull up next to them and roll down the window. "Come on, I'll give you a ride."

Linus looked at Harrison, who of course looked panicked. *Ferris Day ain't on the notecard.* Linus climbed into the back seat and pulled his headphones out of his pocket.

7:50 a.m.

Linus had put on his headphones as soon as they'd climbed into the back seat of Mr. Munro's car, leaving Harrison to try to make small talk and monitor his own face for revelations of the plan. Harrison wondered if he could have one of the tiny water bottles in the back seat. He was already parched.

"Harrison!" Mr. Munro called as if he could tell Harrison was weighing the pros and cons of asking for water. "You're going to have to write to Linus when we move."

"Yes, sir! Absolutely!" He'd write, but would Linus write back? He'd dropped off the face of the Earth once before, and from the way he'd talked, he was back on the edge with a parachute strapped to his back.

"Who you going to talk with at work after he's gone, you think?" Mr. Munro asked. Sheesh! He was really rubbing it in. *This is why,* Harrison thought, *talking to adults never turns out well.* They never had anything to say and would instead ask questions about all the terrible things that waited in the future. *You excited about college or worried that you will be the same person you are here? What field are you trying to get into and do you think that will lock you in a cycle of poverty? Are you kept awake by thoughts of the collapse of democracy?*

"I'll probably end up talking to Sweet Baby most of the time," Harrison offered, by way of a joke. Mr. Munro met his eyes in the rearview mirror. Harrison looked away instinctively.

"Who's that?"

"Our manager. She's always got a story."

"You're not talking about Sweet Baby Bailey, are you?"

"No, her last name is Cashman." Could there really be two people in Baltimore named Sweet Baby?

"Cashman!" Mr. Munro said, slapping the wheel. "That's it! She got married, I forgot. We went to high school together. Small-timore." Mr. Munro chuckled. "Everybody in this city knows everybody else, and everybody in this city up in everybody else's business. Can't do *nothing* secret in this town, boy." He laughed. "Tell Sweet Baby I say hello."

"Oh. Yes. I . . . I will." How was this happening? What if Mr. Munro came inside and talked to Sweet Baby and found out that they were off? Why was everything always on the edge of falling apart? Ferris Bueller did not live his life with this much chaos. Sure, Ferris had tricked his parents into believing that he was home sleeping in bed by hooking up some complicated computer program and playing snoring sounds on the stereo and putting a mannequin in his bed, so, you know, Ferris also had a lot going on. But in a slightly less frantic way, it seemed.

The radio started playing "Press the Sky Higher" and Harrison was so lost in thought that he audibly groaned.

"Don't like this song?" Mr. Munro asked.

"I hate it! I think they just made it so people would watch that one singing competition, but now everyone's acting like it's a victory song and the song of the summer at once. I don't even like the tune, and—"

Mr. Munro was laughing out loud. "I opened up a can of worms with that one, didn't I? You haven't put more than two words together the whole time I've known you, but this song got you out here lecturing like Linus."

Harrison smiled sheepishly. "I just don't—It's everywhere, and I think I'm a little tired of it."

"Fair, fair." Mr. Munro said. He reached back and tapped Linus on the leg. Linus pulled his headphones off. "Your song is on."

Linus scowled at his dad and then brightened upon hearing the song. He started to sing along quietly.

"You *like* 'Press the Sky Higher'?!" Harrison asked.

"I have never heard a better song in my entire life," Linus said. What a monster. "Did you know that the chorus is inspired by a song from the Civil War?"

"It's inspired by a TV show trying to get people to watch and then stream," Harrison replied.

"You're too cynical."

"*I'm* cynical? Your favorite song is from the deadliest war on American soil."

"Deadliest so far," Linus said.

"Cut that out," Mr. Munro called. "Always taking it too far." He flicked his eyes up to the rearview and fixed Linus in his gaze.

"There's been some real bad times here. I don't know why you'd want to invite that energy into your life."

"I'm just talking about a song I like and also the real fact that *throughout history*, those folks are liable to pop off any time they don't get what they want. I didn't invite that. I'm just trying to live my life as best I can with the circumstances I've been put in, and you're taking me down south to the heart of the action!"

"Charleston is no different from Baltimore. And your school will be better! Stop acting like I'm selling you down the river. Don't make no sense!"

They pulled up outside of Harborplace. Mr. Munro punched in his phone's access code and turned on his rideshare app again. "All right, man," he said to Linus, closing their contentious conversation.

"All right." Linus got out and closed the door, a little harder than Harrison ever would have dared.

Harrison slipped out the other side. He really wanted a tiny water. He ducked his head back in the car. "Sweet Baby is off today, so she is not inside and you would not be able to see her, but I will tell her that you said hello tomorrow, which is when I will see her again."

Mr. Munro looked at him with a mix of confusion and annoyance. Harrison smiled weakly and closed the door. Mr. Munro drove away. Harrison turned to face the building. Aparna and Linus were standing under the awning, already talking. It was 8:01 a.m. Ferris Day had begun.

8:02 a.m.

I'm wearing your shirt. Linus stood in the empty bathroom of Harborplace and stared at the text on his phone, which would be the first in a conversation if he sent it. That was a big If. He didn't really know what he thought he was doing starting a conversation with Mazz Reber on his last day in Baltimore. But when he'd been sent inside by Aparna to change out of his work polo and boxy brown shorts to prepare for Ferris Day, it was Mazz he'd thought of. Why was he nervous about this? Was it too late to send a first text to Mazz? Well, not time-wise. Time-wise, it was probably too early to be texting someone. But was it too late in the course of their—what would he call it?—friendship? Classmate-ship? Knowing-each-other-ship? Fabiola would have called it a ship-ship because according to her, she "shipped" Linus and Mazz. Okay. Good to know. He wished he were a character in one of her fanfics, just being moved around the beautiful, strange world by someone else, occasionally having a conversation with Black Panther.

He should just send the text, right? When he'd told Harrison about Mazz, Harrison had gotten all hype and jumped up on the bed and shouted, "Call them right now! Do you want to smooch them?" And it had been so much that Linus had said, "No, it's not that deep. I just like their vibe." And then, for some reason, Linus had brought up Dario, even though he wasn't even interested in Dario anymore. How was it possible that he had no love life at all and yet still had relationship stress?

See, this? This is why he hated texting.

He looked down at his brilliant opening greeting. I'm wearing your shirt. Real smooth.

Linus only owned the shirt in question, an oversized white bowling shirt with a flock of embroidered black birds flying up one side, because Mazz had suggested—no, insisted—that he get it. Linus wasn't really all about other people telling him how to spend his money, but Mazz had been right. It did look good. And you could almost see through it, which Mazz had pointed out as a plus, though Linus wasn't so sure. He looked again now. The dim bathroom lighting wasn't exactly doing wonders for his 'fit, but he decided to believe that he looked good, the shirt wasn't too wrinkled even after being shoved in a grocery bag at the last minute, and it was translucent but not see-through.

He hadn't been thinking of Mazz when he grabbed the shirt. At least not consciously. But now that he was wearing it and had an open schedule . . . well, now he was thinking of Mazz. He hit SEND. Whatever. It was his last day.

Linus had had Mazz's number for months, since the beginning of winter break, when they'd finally had an extended conversation after weeks of "hi" and "what's up" in the halls. They'd stood at the bus stop waiting for a bus that, it turned out, would never arrive, and just talked about nothing. Mazz had complimented Linus's short locks. Mazz said they were thinking of locking their hair, or maybe just twists. Linus suggested an undercut based on Mazz's head shape. Mazz said they were impressed, and then Linus got nervous that he'd actually steered Mazz wrong about the haircut. What did Linus know about hair or heads or anything?

"Don't take it from me," Linus said. "I just feel as if I've seen people who look like you and they looked good with the undercut and twists."

Mazz had said, "Now I want to know who it is that looks like me."

Linus laughed. "Well, no one looks as good as you. But they try." It had just come out—the truth. But a truth that sounded a little dazzling. Mazz broke out into a grin. Linus felt his face get hot. Embarrassing. But also a relief—it was actually very cold out there, and the bus was very late.

In retrospect, Linus thought talking with Mazz had been as easy as talking with Harrison, which Linus knew was a rare thing to find. And there was something else there, another energy. It was interesting to meet someone and know that person was not going to be your best friend—that position was filled—but they were someone you wanted to spend more time with. Mazz offered Linus their phone number; they traded. And then . . . Linus didn't know what happened. He dropped the ball. He never actually texted. Mazz never texted, either, but Linus decided it was his fault somehow. They went back to "hi" and "what's up" in the halls.

But they kept running into each other. Once at Harborplace, once at the farmer's market, and once in the thrift store, which Linus hadn't even planned on going into until he saw Mazz through the window. And, as a result, now he had this shirt.

Send me a pic! Mazz texted back. Linus's Achilles heel! No one seemed to understand how or why he had a phone that did not take photos. It had never worked, and the phone had been a hand-me-down, so there was no taking it back to the store to get it fixed. And he could not figure out how to impress upon people that he didn't care.

"Why didn't your dad get you an old iPhone?" Harrison had asked when they had the phone discussion, which shouldn't have even been a discussion, yet they had ended up discussing it. "There's plenty of cheap iPhones, I'm sure."

"I think this was free," Linus said. "And the data is affordable. Also, what am I supposed to be taking pictures of?"

Harrison asked the same question again in multiple ways. Linus did not have a different answer. This was always the way with them around some topics. A few. Linus knew what most of those topics were, and he'd learned to avoid them for his own sake and for the sake of their friendship. Harrison never meant anything by the questions that felt a little too pointed, the answers that should have been obvious but somehow weren't. The thing that Linus knew to be true was that the little details that made their lives different didn't determine who they really were. And they shared the parts that really mattered. Harrison could obsess over anything he didn't understand—Linus supposed in the same way that he could obsess over things he did, but at the end of the day, it was trivia. Historical facts. Despite the fact that Harrison sometimes didn't quite catch on to all the ways that his parents' jobs made life easier for him. Harrison was the person who Linus trusted with his ideas and feelings and fears. Harrison didn't really care what kind of phone Linus had; Harrison was just asking questions. Harrison always picked up the phone when Linus called. That's what mattered most.

My phone doesn't take pictures, Linus texted back to Mazz. But I'm off today and hanging out. Maybe we'll run into each other again and you can see the shirt.

Too much? He'd said "maybe." How was "maybe" too much? And yet . . .

See, this? This right here? This was why he didn't play that flirty "pick me" game. He had too much going on, he was too stressed, and he certainly wasn't about to go asking Wallingford Munro to let him go on a date. Did he even like Mazz like that? All this over a shirt. You really hate to see it.

I'm working but I'll text you when I'm off, Mazz texted back.

Then another text: What are you pairing the shirt with?

Linus texted back: Just brown khaki shorts. Kinda baggy.

A beat. Maybe not? The other shorts he'd grabbed were

gray sweat-shorts, which were fine for whatever, but not if he was going to have a whole day of adventures.

I can see it. Nice! Mazz wrote.

Nice! His heart sped up. The most amazing text ever sent! He read it again. Nice! Unbelievable!

Baby boy, Linus said to himself, *you need to get out of this bathroom.*

🚃🚃🚃

Harrison whooped upon seeing Linus emerge from Harbor-place. Linus smiled despite himself. Sometimes Doing Too Much wasn't so bad.

"I like your shirt," Aparna said.

"Thanks," Linus replied. "I was visiting my friend from school at their job at a thrift store, and—"

"His friend who he's obsessed with."

"Stop," Linus said. "I just like their vibe."

"That's what being obsessed is."

Aparna piped up. "You guys should get to the train, not that this isn't a great show."

"Wait," Linus said to Aparna, "since we don't have to work, why don't we all just hang out here? I mean, it's the Harbor. We can just walk around or whatever."

"Harrison has a whole day of activities," Aparna said. "I think you're going to have fun. Plus, I'm very excited about my big acting break." Linus didn't know what that meant, and apparently his face showed it, because Aparna clarified. "I'm going to be pretending to be you two. On the app, at least."

Oh, right. They'd convinced him that for everything to work, he had to give up his phone, which had been really annoying, actually, because he was supposed to be getting a text from Mazz. Not that it was a big deal. It was just a text. And he hated texts anyway. And of course Linus couldn't explain his reasons for wanting to keep his phone, because it would seem like it was a big deal. Which it wasn't.

That's it, he thought. *I'm Doing Too Much, too.*

"Text me what you get up to," Harrison was saying to Aparna.

"Why?" Aparna asked.

"Uh, because you literally always have an adventure and I'm actually mad I can't be in two places at once." He handed his backpack to her.

Linus piped up, "Which is why we should hang out together! Adventure! Adventure!"

Harrison pulled Linus in the direction of the train station.

"I promise you, I am going to have the most unremarkable day!" Aparna exclaimed.

STAGE MANAGER'S REPORT #1

SM: Aparna Aiyar

CAST: Harrison Meredith, Linus Munro (no callouts)

WEATHER FORECAST: 73 degrees, sunny

PROP NOTES: Harrison's phone screen is so cracked, it's barely legible.

STAGE MANAGER'S NOTES:

As planned, I met Harrison at the west entrance of the Light Street Pavilion at Harborplace at 8:00 a.m. I took Linus's phone, Harrison's phone, and Harrison's backpack; I downloaded a new messaging app onto my phone to communicate with Harrison's parents' iPad. I suggested we synchronize watches, but Harrison didn't know what that meant, and as it turns out, none of us were wearing watches.

The tour company home base is nestled into one of two long, bi-level buildings called Harborplace. Go out one of the long sides and you'll find the water of the Inner Harbor ringed with a brick boardwalk and dotted with ferries, historical ships, and paddleboats. If you go out the other side of Harborplace, you encounter a street, and beyond it, a few blocks of tourist attractions, like hotels, restaurants, and a mall called the Gallery. The Gallery is where the Harbor location of Potions is located. I briefly transferred to the Gallery store last Christmas to help out, and so I'm familiar with the harbor and therefore well-suited to this day of walking around the area being someone else.

Cool Aparna once told me that I was a good stage

manager because I'm good at being invisible. I don't think being good at stage management is about being invisible. Everything I do is about visibility. All the work I do makes what you see onstage, in front of an audience, possible. Who do you think tells them to raise the curtain? Plus, the show is visible because I took notes during rehearsal, and marked places on the stage with gaffer's tape, and called cues, and launched Cool Aparna out of the closet so she could launch into her song as Fruma Sarah, a ghost woman who doesn't want Tevye's daughter marrying her still-living husband, Lazar Wolf, in *Fiddler on the Roof.*

The same is true of copyediting for the school paper. The evidence of my work is clean copy. When a word is misspelled or the grammar is wrong or the meaning of a sentence isn't clear, the reader gets tripped up, they get confused, or they stop reading altogether.

My work is always visible, even if my hand in it isn't. Being inconspicuous is a superpower in stage management and in copyediting. Maybe in life, in general. TBD. What I know now is that if I do my job right, what's conspicuous is the quality, the story, the spectacle, the copy that helps you understand the world in a new way. None of that is invisible work.

But today, I am invisible.

8:40 a.m.

"How much do I owe you?" Linus asked as Harrison made a guess at which door they should take to get to the train platform. They made their way down a staircase. The silver two-level regional train, the MARC, idled on one side, and two conductors waited at the bottom. A good guess! Harrison produced their tickets, handed them to the conductors to be torn, and then handed Linus his stub.

"Don't worry about it," Harrison said. "They were cheap. Plus, I'm dragging you along."

"We work the same job; I can pay my own way, though," Linus said.

Harrison looked at Linus. *I know that*, he said silently.

Linus responded out loud, "So, how much?"

"I don't know—we'll figure it out later."

They boarded the train and climbed the stairs to the upper level. Half of the seats faced them and half of the seats faced away from them. The different sets of seats met in the middle, facing each other.

"Which way is forward, do you think?" Harrison said.

A man, previously unseen, leaned his head out of a row in

front of them and turned around. "They're both forward," he said, never pausing the aggressive manner in which he gnawed on a plastic straw.

"Sir," Linus said, "that can't possibly be true!"

Linus looked at Harrison: *Here?*

Harrison: *Sure.*

They slid into a seat. They heard someone jog up the stairs behind them. The doors on the train closed. They felt themselves start to move backward. Linus stood up and looked at the man.

"Yo! I told you!" Linus said. The man didn't feel the need to acknowledge this.

Baltimore slipped away in reverse.

"So what's the plan? What time do you think we'll be back? Just out of curiosity," Linus asked, watching the row homes turn into dark tunnels and then into trees as the train moved.

"Don't you want to be surprised?"

"Never that," Linus said. "So?"

"Okay, so the first thing we're going to do is meet up with Dario."

"DARIO?" Linus said, a little louder than he intended. Harrison got antsy. What was the volume situation on this train? He glanced around but didn't see any conductors charging down the aisles to kick them off for noise violations. All clear.

Out of the corner of his eye, Harrison caught the top of a woman's head a few rows back. She had a twist out, and his first thought was *Oh, there's Corrine.* He turned around, realized what a weird thought it was, and turned back. He couldn't see the woman's face. He thought about getting up and looking, but he honestly could not justify standing up, scooting past Linus, being seen by the straw-gnawer and everyone, and going to look this stranger in the face. It couldn't be her. He saw three little curls and decided that all Black people look alike. Ridiculous. He turned back around.

"What's wrong?" Linus asked.

"I thought I saw my sister," Harrison said with a laugh.

"Smalltimore," said Linus.

"Exactly."

"Okay, hold up. What's the deal with Dario?"

"He's staying at his dad's place in DC, and we're going to meet up with him so you two can hang out." Harrison giggled despite himself. Mess. Linus's eyes got wide.

"Harrison. What did you do?"

"You guys get along. Dario's been pestering me about hanging out again. That's all."

"Say more."

"There's not more to say, Linus! I just thought it would be fun."

"Did you really think it would be fun, though?" Linus said. Normally this would've been one of their unspoken comments, a raised eyebrow or a grimace. Linus must have really wanted to know.

"It's Ferris Day!" Harrison cried, his voice ticking up an octave. "You know how in the movie they do things that are new and scary? That's this."

"So we're going straight to the part where they kick a car out of the window?" Linus said.

"Seeing Dario is not the same as kicking a car out of a window. He likes you."

"Now it can be said!" Linus crowed. "You *are* setting us up."

"I'm providing an opportunity."

"An opportunity to what?" Linus asked. Harrison shrugged. "You're so corny." Over the course of their friendship, Harrison had been characteristically less than talkative about boys. His crushes were numerous, but he thought he wasn't being obvious about them. He was wrong. Linus would ask him why he never acted on them, and Harrison would wave him off any time he tried to broach the subject. "I'm a virgin who can't drive!" Harrison would say, paraphrasing a quote from one of the movie night selections.

It's from Clue, Linus thought.

"You're not Mrs. Clue," Linus had said once, over Harrison's objections. "You need to cut that nonsense out. First of all, you can technically drive. You just can't pass a test."

"That claim is disputed," Harrison said.

"And didn't you hook up on vacation?"

Harrison waved his hands in front of his face. "It's not the same thing! We basically just smooched." Harrison refused to use un-ridiculous words when talking about boys. Making it into some kind of joke robbed the whole subject of its bite, its ability to wound, its way of finding that place inside you that hopes.

When Linus had declared to Harrison back in May, "This summer, I'm gonna smooch," who else could he have been thinking about if not Dario? Now it occurred to Harrison that maybe Linus had been thinking of someone else, though. Or maybe he hadn't been thinking of anyone at all. He'd just been feeling himself, feeling the big open sky of the Harbor on a break from work, feeling free or something like it. Feeling carefree, at least. Feeling silly. He was just being silly. Perhaps the fact that he used the word "smooch" at all was a clue. Harrison had missed another one of Linus's hilarious jokes.

"I wouldn't hate hanging out with Dario," Linus said.

"Okay, good," said Harrison. "I mean, duh."

"Stop it. What's after that? Lemme see your agenda."

"It won't make any sense to you."

"I want to make sure you don't got me doing something I don't want to do."

Harrison's feelings were a little bruised by that. Why would he ever set up Linus to do something he didn't want to do? The whole point of this day was to prove that to him, but frankly, Harrison thought Linus already knew. He thought Ferris Day would be a reminder. Maybe a wake-up call that they weren't just two guys who knew each other when. Maybe Linus didn't know it after all.

"I just made a list of things that we can do that will be memorable," Harrison said.

"Coming out the gate with Dario is a strong play," Linus said with a laugh. "What are we building to? Dancing naked on a Pride Parade float?"

Oh God no. Wait, did Linus actually want to dance on a Pride float? Was it too late for Aparna to work her magic? *We definitely couldn't be naked, but we could dance,* he thought.

No, this plan couldn't withstand last-minute adjustments. Everything had to go exactly the way he'd envisioned it, or there would be total disaster.

"Lower your expectations," Harrison tried to say. What he actually said, by accident, was "Lower your respectations."

"Did you say 'lower your respectations'?'"

"No. Why would I say that?"

"That's what I want to know. That's what everyone wants to know. The whole train is asking."

Harrison looked behind him again for the woman with the twist out, but now the rest of the train appeared to be empty.

"I got flustered," Harrison said. "I *meant* 'expectations.'"

"Are you nervous about this?" Linus asked.

"Don't ask me that."

"Why?"

"Because if you ask me if I'm nervous, I'm going to have to tell you that yes, I am nervous, since you can always tell when I'm lying."

Linus paused for a beat and then said, "Well, I definitely won't be asking that, then."

Harrison wondered what Linus was thinking. It wasn't

like them to be at crossed purposes. He didn't understand why Linus wouldn't just trust him. What was Linus's plan for the day? Go to work, go to the library, say goodbye forever. Absolutely not. Harrison decided that whatever weirdness there was between himself and Linus was just a by-product of their circumstances and the change of plans and the general uncertainty of being alive. But he had a plan, and he had to focus on that with the plucky determination of a musical theater leading lady, usually played by Cool Aparna. He fished his notebook out of his tote bag, flipped it open, and showed his list of agenda items to Linus.

Linus read the page and blinked a few times. "Okay."

"Wow. So excited."

Linus couldn't help but laugh. "I mean . . . it's going to be great."

9:50 a.m.

Harrison called Aparna in a panic. Called. On the kitchen iPad. He stood outside Union Station in Washington, DC, with an entire iPad pressed against the side of his face. He did not even care.

"Dario is not in this state and now we are here and everything is ruined and I don't know what I'm supposed to do," he said all in one breath before launching into the full crisis. He'd texted Dario as they were pulling into the station, as they had previously agreed would happen. Dario had even downloaded the messaging app they'd agreed on the night before, and they'd tested it out. Harrison had thought of everything. There was a small-to-medium flaw in the plan, and that was that Dario hadn't been sure if his dad would be home or not. But now Harrison and Linus had exited the train station and waited in the area in front of it, which Linus had informed him was called a portico. No response from Dario. Harrison had texted again. He did not know where he was supposed to be heading. They'd decided they could wing it. Harrison had not wanted to wing anything. HE WAS NOT A BIRD.

Dario finally responded. Everything in my life is falling apart at the same time, darling, he wrote. My father and his ogre of a brother woke me at 5 a.m. so that we could go fishing! Male bonding. What a nightmare! I am so exhausted and I am in Virginia! HELP!

Harrison sent a barrage of texts, asking all the very pressing questions that came to mind: *when would he be back, what were they supposed to do until then, how far was Virginia from there, what kind of fish, and what about Ferris Day?* Dario did not respond. He was sleeping with the fishes. Wait, Harrison was certain that didn't mean what he thought it meant. In any case, there was no Dario and they were in DC for no reason and he had failed, utterly, already. The sun hadn't even fully committed to the day yet and he was already done for.

"Harrison," Aparna said, "let's pull back and figure out what to do. You're coming back for Pride; that's still on. But the next train back to Baltimore is, unfortunately, not for two hours."

Harrison moaned. They were actually trapped in the nation's capital like a bunch of British soldiers.

"What is Linus doing now?" Aparna asked.

"He's inside, reading the information panel about Union Station, of course. He has said six times how he wished that he had his phone with him so he could google questions he has. He's mad and this sucks and I've ruined it."

"The upside is that you get to hang out now, just the two of you," Aparna said. "You should . . . you should be tourists."

"Like, see the Lincoln Memorial?"

"If you want. What does Linus like?"

"Graveyards."

"Arlington Cemetery is a little far, I think . . . hold on." Aparna put him on speaker and went silent for a moment. "You could do it. The Metro will get you there and back, but it's really going to be a tight turnaround. . . ."

"I cannot handle navigating any more public transportation. I took one train; that's enough for the day. I should get an award."

"Scratch that, then," Aparna said. "Look, if I know Linus, and I think I do, the most exciting thing for him would be going someplace where he could read every word of an informational panel."

"You think I should take him to a museum like we're on a field trip?" Harrison asked. He was starting to sweat. He vaguely remembered a teacher on a field trip once commenting that DC was built on a swamp. Or was that just something that problematic politicians said? Was it literal or was it figurative? He needed answers. All he knew was that he was very interested in finding air-conditioning relatively soon.

"I mean, would he hate going to the Smithsonian?"

"But it's not a thing that scares us. That's the point of Ferris Day. It's new adventures and lifelong memories and conquering our fears."

"You sound like a brochure for a cult. There's plenty of day left. I've got you tickets to the National Museum of African American History and Culture."

"What's that?"

"The Black Smithsonian."

"Oh! Oh, that's a good idea."

"I know. I just texted them to you. Go get some history. Or some culture!"

Linus emerged from the train station, fanning himself. Harrison hung up the iPad.

"Did you know that before this place got built, this neighborhood was called Swampoodle?" Linus said.

The plot thickens, Harrison thought.

Linus continued, "That sign was really interesting, but I wanted to know more about the architecture, actually."

"You have so many interests."

Linus laughed. "I literally have two interests. So—no pressure—but what's the plan?"

"I don't think we're going to see Dario today."

"Man, that boy is too much. I know you had your heart set on us making out."

"I did not!"

"You did. Sorry, Charlie," Linus said.

"Imagine being Charlie," Harrison said. "Constant disappointment."

"Wouldn't be me."

STAGE MANAGER'S REPORT #2

SM: Aparna Aiyar

CAST: Harrison Meredith, Linus Munro, ~~Dario Lushovsky~~

PROPS: Digital Smithsonian passes (2)

STAGE MANAGER'S NOTES:

We had a little bit of a rocky first scene, but fortunately I was able to help Harrison avoid a premature end to Ferris Day. He called me, freaking out, and to hear him better, I crossed the street from the Harborplace boardwalk and ducked into the Gallery. I got them set up with tickets to the National Museum of African American History and Culture. I waited for a moment to see if there'd be another crisis. I don't expect crises, but I do anticipate them. That's the difference.

Out of habit, I rode the escalator up to the second floor and wandered into the Potions location, which was teeming with tourists. Every tourist at the Harbor is looking to be wowed by something enormous and historical and close to a gift shop and a bathroom while on vacation from themselves. You would think that the presence of Potions, the same lotion and soap store as they have at home, might be jarring.

But I think the ability to buy a pear-yuzu hand sanitizer from a familiar place is crucial to the adventure.

You never see regular people at the Gallery location of Potions. Think about it: It's not near anything that a regular person would go to except some office buildings. The hotels, the convention center, the restaurants, the museums—they're all for tourists. It's a part of a city constructed solely for them to pass through without affecting or changing it in any way. My mother assures me that plenty of the people around here are actually Baltimoreans. But I don't know. Once you enter the tourist kingdom, you become anonymous.

This fact, I think chief among a bunch of other strange facts, was what made it so remarkable when I rounded a floor display in Potions and saw, across the store, the very non-anonymous face of Aparna Ramamurthy. Otherwise known as Cool Aparna.

10:03 a.m.

Linus believed there were places in the world where the sky was higher, and Washington, DC, was such a place. On the block where he lived, the two- and three-story row homes crowded against one another and against the sky and pulled the ceiling down to Earth. There was no place, he felt, to look up and out. In the corner of your eye you'd always catch the edge of a house, the spire of a church, a peeling billboard, a looming apartment building. It was never just sky. Even though the aspects of Harrison's neighborhood were nicer—more trees, no billboards, carved stone on the top corners of the buildings—the piece of the sky was even smaller and lower. Linus believed that in a city, the sky was full and heavy and if you stood up too fast, you'd bump your head on it.

He thought maybe everywhere was like this. The houses in his mother's neighborhood were squatter, but he didn't feel anything more expansive. He imagined if he went someplace like the Grand Canyon or Niagara Falls, then he'd feel it—that sense of liberty that he wasn't sure existed but which glimmered in his mind like a lodestar anyway. He'd never been to those places, though, and he had no idea how to get there. He wondered about the ceiling of the world in South Carolina. How low would it seem? How small would he have to make himself?

Washington, DC, however, had no ceiling—at least where he stood, in that great expanse of open space between the Capitol and the Lincoln Memorial that was dotted with flags and monuments and trees but which somehow opens up bigger, wider, higher than anywhere else Linus had ever been. Maybe it was because there was nothing else there but flags, monuments, and trees. No houses, no billboards—nothing but sky and history.

He had his faced turned all the way up, taking in the blue and the clouds and the warmth of the sun on his face. *This is better,* he thought. *This is nice.* He stood on the sidewalk outside the National Museum of African American History and Culture while Harrison paid the cabdriver. Linus made a mental note to pay him back half of the fare. He slowly lowered his gaze, and the building, a dark stack of trapezoids, slowly came into view. It looked black at first, but then it revealed itself—its facade was made up of copper-colored screens with intricate designs. Like lace made of metal. Light poured through from above. He imagined the museum as a stained-glass window in a church. He imagined the museum as a twist out catching the light. He imagined the museum as a thousand screen doors.

If you shifted to the side a little, you could see the shocking white of the Washington Monument beside the museum. They looked like a set of salt and pepper shakers. Linus shifted back. The salt disappeared.

"You're going to love this," Harrison said, joining Linus on the pavement.

"Did you know that George Washington's dentures were made from Black people's teeth?" Linus said.

Harrison looked stricken.

"I thought they were wooden."

Linus shook his head.

"Were they from people he enslaved?" Harrison asked.

"I don't know."

"How do you know these things?"

"I dunno. The regular way. I was curious."

"I have never been curious about George Washington's teeth," Harrison said.

Linus didn't know why he'd brought up George Washington's teeth, but also, he'd never thought to himself *This is not a time to discuss the teeth of the first president.* Why was he feeling weird? He was nervous—he'd said as much. And then he regretted saying anything. Was it acknowledging nervousness that threw Linus off or was it the feeling that Harrison was trying to do too much and that maybe it would all go wrong? Linus couldn't say for sure, but the vibe of the whole thing was strange, and that made him sad. This was all supposed to be silly, wasn't it? The movie that Harrison was taking life advice from wasn't exactly a drama. What was going on?

He knew that the coming distance between himself and Harrison would only bring out the ways in which they were different. And he knew that maybe, unless they just looked it in its face at the beginning, they'd pretend for a while that they had stayed exactly the same. He'd seen his parents playacting as their old selves for a long time, for years, just to avoid the inevitable truth: that they'd grown apart. He'd seen them try to playact, for him, that nothing was different. He'd seen that fail. Was this how it started?

They wound their way through a maze of stanchions, the crowd still relatively sparse. A cluster of crows called out from a patch of grass nearby. Harrison presented his iPad to be scanned for entry. Linus strained but couldn't see the price on the tickets. He'd ask at Information, he decided. They passed through the metal detectors and placed their belongings on an X-ray conveyor belt. Linus wondered if they'd be stopped for not having phones. Who doesn't have phones? If it were up to him, he'd find it suspicious. But they were let through with no questions.

Harrison plucked a map from a display and unfurled it noisily. He had been here before, Linus knew, on a field trip. Linus's school, Frances Ellen Watkins Harper High School, had field trips, of course, but they weren't as frequent and usually weren't as elaborate as the ones Harrison got to go on. Linus had never been to this museum, though he'd twice gone on field trips to the National Great Blacks in Wax Museum on North Avenue and once to the Reginald F. Lewis Museum downtown. He wondered sometimes what the field trips his friend went on must have been like, whether the museums and the stories they told seemed different in front of an audience of mostly white teenagers versus the audience at Harper, which was largely Black, Asian, and Latinx. A museum was a place where every part of a story was happening at once. All of time rushed at them, broken up into pieces but moving in concert, like a flock of migratory birds shifting direction. It was amazing. It was overwhelming. But also, wasn't existing within arm's reach of everything that has happened to your people—every good thing, every horror, every fight, every trauma—just what it was to be Black?

Was he—a living, breathing Black boy—a museum?

"Upstairs, there's a bunch of galleries," Harrison said, his face in the map. "There's an amazing room about theater and TV and movies. Obviously, I loved it. But there's other stuff, too. A music room. An art gallery. And then underneath us, there's— Oh, wow. I didn't realize it was this big. The history galleries are downstairs, and it's forty-four-thousand square feet. That's huge. There's three floors underground that track the history of Black people in America from the 1400s to today. You follow one path all the way through."

Harrison started toward an escalator, and Linus followed behind him. They descended from the lobby to the concourse, an area where another serpentine set of stanchions would lead, it seemed, to all of history.

Linus imagined the museum as an iceberg. Linus imagined the museum as a root vegetable. Linus imagined the museum as a ship, sitting low in the water, its belly full of cargo.

He pushed down a wave of anxiety. "Do you want to see the theater stuff?" he asked as they got in line. A swooping black staircase curled above their heads. A man got in line behind them and was standing too close for Linus's liking. Like he was eavesdropping.

"No, it's fine," Harrison said. "I don't mind."

A docent in a black blazer stood in front of a glass door. She spoke to the small crowd at the end of the line. "Good morning. Once you go through these doors, you'll take the elevator down to the lowest level of the History Galleries. Please be advised that there is one way in and one way out. To exit the gallery, you have to go up through all the levels."

The line shifted forward, but Linus paused where he was. He kept hearing "one way out." He was stuck on it.

"Can you—?" the man behind him said irritably.

Linus imagined the museum as a graveyard. Linus imagined the museum as a tour of the underworld. Linus imagined the museum, with its solitary path, as a fun house of time. Linus imagined his face reflected back in a distorted mirror of his story. Linus imagined himself with no way out.

"I don't think I want to go," he said finally.

"Boys!" The man behind them was really trying it. "The line is moving."

"Yo, just go around. Damn!" Linus snarled at the man. The man opened his mouth to speak, but Linus turned around, erasing him from his mind.

"I thought you'd want to see the gallery," Harrison said.

Linus felt beads of sweat spring up all over him. He imagined the museum as a trapdoor swinging open and shut. He wasn't in the right headspace. He needed to reset. He had to get this day right.

"I'm going to go upstairs and see the other galleries. But you go ahead. I'll meet you back down here."

"What?" Harrison said, eyes wide.

Linus looked him in the face so that Harrison could see the truth. "It's fine. I just need to take a walk."

"Do you want me to—"

"It's fine. Just . . . give me a second."

Linus ducked under the stanchion and walked quickly down the concourse, around the corner to the escalator, and rode into the air.

10:19 a.m.

The line kept moving, and Harrison, not knowing what else to do, moved with it. He was swept through the glass doors and into the waiting area for the elevator. Harrison had been sure that Linus would love the history gallery, so sure, he felt like he didn't even need to make the case. That was his thing. But sometimes this was his thing, too—begging off for a second, taking a minute. Harrison decided he would fill Linus in on all the details later. They'd compare notes. Over lunch! They'd eat before they went back to the train.

The waiting area had a glass partition on one wall and over-looked the part of the history gallery that covered the early Civil Rights Movement. Harrison stepped forward and looked out over a recreated lunch counter and an entire segregated train car. Talk about set design! Harrison wondered how you got an entire train inside a museum in DC. He remembered there was also an entire cabin that a formerly enslaved person had lived in. How did you transport an entire cabin from the 1800s all the way to DC? This museum was a marvel. Harrison stepped back into line.

"Uh-uh, buddy," a man called sternly over his shoulder. "We're not butting in line today. I was here."

Oh, good, Harrison thought, *a nightmare person.* Harrison realized that he'd stepped back into line ahead of the guy from earlier. The white guy he had originally been in front of. Harrison apologized instinctively and immediately felt annoyed at himself about it. He stepped to the side to let the guy pass. They were both ushered into the elevator at the same time.

A docent was positioned in the corner. As the doors closed, she started speaking. This was Harrison's favorite part. When he'd come with his Plowshares class, he'd remarked to Aparna that the elevator speech was "very Grover's Corner's." A high compliment.

"Good afternoon," the docent said. "My name is Ms. Doreen. What we're about to do is go way back in time. You can see on the wall here that the years are going to start peeling back. We're going all the way back to the year 1400."

The carriage shuddered into motion. A couple of the kids giggled in surprise. All the walls were made of glass, and as the world slipped away, Harrison noticed that one side faced a cement wall. Outside the glass, the wall had the word "today" painted on it and then years going backward underneath. The years rose up and slipped away as they descended.

Ms. Doreen continued, "What you're going to do is you're going to walk every step of the way through our history, start-ing at the beginning and ending up back here, where we got to today. It's a lot. It might seem like too much. But it's important. That's why y'all are here. Once you get back to the surface, you can go into the Contemplative Court. There's a waterfall there and benches and you can just sit and let it all settle." The carriage slowed and stopped. "If it's too much, the water will put peace in your soul."

The doors opened to a dark exhibit with low ceilings. Everyone filed out dutifully. Harrison flashed Ms. Doreen a huge smile as he passed her. He was living for her monologue.

The guy from the line stepped in front of Harrison.

"Are you here with a group?" the guy demanded.

"Just my friend."

"Okay, well, you need to understand that this is not a place to play around," the guy said. Harrison noticed that he'd missed a couple of loops on his pants with his belt, and it bunched in a weird way that looked liked curtains. "Do you understand?" the guy asked.

Harrison did not answer.

"You can't run around down here. No yelling." He leaned in closer and pointed his finger in Harrison's face. "No horsing around, understand?"

The white guy pushed past him and beelined for a display called "The Paradox of Liberty."

It seemed to Harrison that if there was any place on Earth where he could butt in line in front of a white person—accidentally or otherwise—it was the Black Smithsonian. But whatever. People really will talk to you any old kind of way.

Harrison found himself preoccupied with a series of displays on slavery in the Low Country, a place in South Carolina. He looked at a painted mural of Black people toiling in a field of white. He knew that a long time had passed between then and now—and here was a handy time line to prove it—but he couldn't help but feel as if his friend were moving to some distant land, out of time and space, even if it was wrong. He lingered at the display and then made himself move on, out of the section, passing over a display about slavery in the mid-Atlantic states, like Maryland. Why had the Low Country display freaked him out so much? And what was he searching for? Evidence to present to Mr. Munro about why they shouldn't move?

The past was a done thing.

Harrison stepped out of the squat dark passageway and into a soaring room with words from the Declaration of Independence installed in gold letters on the walls. He came face-to-face with a statue of Thomas Jefferson. Better known to Harrison as Fake Daveed Diggs, an actor from *Hamilton*. He drifted past other statues—of Phyllis Wheatley and Elizabeth Freeman—and then turned to discover the whole cabin that had been magic'd to the inside of the museum. He just didn't get it. It was so old. It was made of wood and, what, gumption? Some old-timey thing. How did it survive the trip from . . . where? He leaned down to read the informational plaque. Like he was Fake Linus. It was called Point of Pines Cabin, and it was from a plantation on

Edisto Island, which was in . . . South Carolina. Harrison promised himself that he was not going around looking for this stuff. He peered inside. You couldn't get in because there was a bar at shin level meant to restrict entry, but there was no door and he could see a brick fireplace and a bare wood floor and not much else. He tried to imagine living in a place made just of wood. But then he stopped. He'd been down this road before.

It was one thing to imagine, but he often felt the pull to conjure some deeper knowledge that he didn't have. To turn his imagination into suffering. When he was in fourth grade, for instance, his class had toured a historical church downtown. The tour guide had told them about how different families owned different pews, which definitely sounded like the way his family's church operated now, except without the formal ownership. But literally God help you if you sat in someone else's row. The guide had looked at Harrison, who was the only Black kid in his class at the time, and said, "It would be different for you, of course. Black people, even free ones, were only allowed in the balcony." Everyone had looked at him like he needed to issue a press release on where people sat in a church he'd never been to before. He'd thought, *Why are you telling* me? He wondered if history was always going to be instances of one story told to everyone and then another, crueler story told to him. A story he didn't know what to do with.

He'd come here to experience something new. He would pass by the cabin, he would keep traveling upward, he would get peace in his soul. Then he'd find Linus. He tripped over the barrier bar as he turned the corner around the cabin, and caught himself on a display case. He felt a hand grip his arm and lift him off the case. He jerked away and saw—ugh, Jesus—the guy from the line.

"You can't go around putting your hands all over things," he said.

"I fell!"

"If you can't be more careful, you shouldn't be here!"

Before Harrison could respond, the guy charged away and vanished into a side room named "Antebellum Politics."

Okay, so Harrison was a little shaken, he would admit that. He knew that eventually he wouldn't so obviously be a teenager, but he wondered if that would change the way that people responded to him, for the better or for the worse. He definitely didn't see himself being the kind of adult who would go to fisticuffs in the Black Smithsonian. So what now?

Behind the cabin, a long ramp led up to a wall and then doubled back and emptied out to the next level. The future was coming. On a wall beside the ramp, gold letters spelled out an Ida B. Wells quote: THE WAY TO RIGHT WRONGS IS TO TURN THE LIGHT OF TRUTH UPON THEM. That was the big idea here. That was why they'd put a slave cabin in a truck and drove it up from South Carolina. That was why they'd built this museum deep into the Earth—to shine the light of truth. Harrison started up the ramp. Mural-sized photos of cotton covered each side, behind the railings. They reminded him of the poppy field scene in *The Wiz*. He started to do the little skipping dance from "Ease on Down the Road" and sing to himself. What else were ramps for other than light choreography?

He reached the landing and did a turn. He liked museums in the mornings—so much space.

"Hey!" a voice rang out. Guess who. At the bottom of the ramp, the white guy from the line was pointing at him like Effie White doing "And I Am Telling You I'm Not Going." He came barreling up the ramp toward Harrison. "I TOLD YOU NO RUNNING."

Harrison hesitated. No, he did not want to see how this played out. He took off up the ramp to the next level. The guy rounded the corner behind him and yelled, "HEY!" again. A few people nearby looked at him and then looked away. Nothing to see here; just a teenager receiving unconstructive criticism about his *Wiz* choreo.

Harrison speed-walked through Reconstruction. He'd try to lose the man by Jim Crow. The ceilings were low again, and the lighting was dark, moody, with shocks of brightness on certain displays. Harrison slid past a woman and a man in wheelchairs reading a panel on lynching. He rounded a corner and encountered a wedding dress hovering like a ghost; across from it was a disembodied World War I helmet. Behind a pane of glass: a Klan hood, lit ominously from above. Farther down, he passed a floor-to-ceiling video of people dancing during the Harlem

Renaissance, arms and legs and hands and teeth all moving. As alive now as they once had been.

The guy from the line spotted him through the wedding dress display case. "YOU NEED TO COME WITH ME!" he shouted. His breath fogged the glass.

Oh, honey, absolutely not. Harrison kept going, through a hallway dedicated to the Black church—gospel piped in from video screens—and stumbled out into a bright yellow-and-white room focused on the Civil Rights Movement. He looked behind him. The guy from the line did not seem to have followed.

Harrison peered into the cases: a red Black Panther Party button, a rifle owned by a group called the Deacons, a hat pin that the sign said was worn by women in Civil Rights marches and protests to be used in self-defense. So many different ways of protecting oneself, claiming one's space. The display was called Black Power.

He turned to a large installation with a life-size photo of Bayard Rustin, a lanky man with glasses and curly salt-and-pepper hair. The sign next to the photo said that he had been one of the organizers of the March on Washington and the Freedom Rides and he'd been an advisor to Dr. King. It also said that he was a gay man who was out in the fifties and sixties. Harrison had literally never heard of this before. He looked at Bayard's face: a thin mustache, an analytical expression, that same determination you saw in a lot of the photos of Civil Rights leaders. Why hadn't he ever known this man's name?

What was his life like back then? What had he made possible for Harrison and for Linus? He wondered if Linus knew about him. Out of habit, he reached for his phone to text Linus before remembering. He missed him already. That was the exact opposite of the point of this day. They didn't need to be separated a minute longer.

Harrison turned to find the way out and ran right into the guy from the line, who grunted before grabbing Harrison's arm again.

"YOU'RE OUT OF CONTROL!" the guy bellowed into Harrison's face. His breath smelled like old coffee and onions.

"Get your hands off of me!" Harrison yelled back. The couple in wheelchairs drew near and stopped behind the guy.

"Everything all right here?" the woman asked.

The guy turned to them sharply. "It's fine; I'm taking care of this."

"He's harassing me!" Harrison cried. He couldn't tell if he was in trouble, but he was certain he had done nothing wrong.

"You need to stay *right here*," the guy said gruffly. "I'm going to go get a docent to escort you out. You have NO RESPECT." He glanced at the couple as if deputizing them and then hustled back down the corridor they had all come from, back in time.

Harrison looked at the couple.

"Chiiild . . ." the man said dismissively.

Harrison wanted to stay in that moment and share whatever was happening with the couple—some strange connection that felt deep and complex but also simple and instinctual. He also really wanted to get the hell out of there before the guy came back. He flashed a quick smile at the couple, who were now reading about Bayard Rustin, and walked quickly out of the room, up the next ramp, past Oprah's studio and the Black Panther tote and Michelle Obama's dress from the night President Obama was first elected and an audio clip of President Obama saying "If I had a son, he'd look like Trayvon" and a wall of video screens playing BLM protests and Black Trans Lives Matter protests. Up, up, up he scrambled, climbing out of the well of history and into his time. He deposited himself, panting, into the next room: the Contemplative Court.

There was a circle of water falling from an impossibly high ceiling, landing in a square pool lit by glowing lights and surrounded by dark stone benches. The room was empty. The water echoed. His thoughts raced. He felt he was letting Ms. Doreen down because he did not feel peace in his soul. The room smelled faintly of chlorine, and he had the sudden memory of being submerged, of struggle, of panic. Staring into the circle of lights in the water, he was again eight years old at a pool party, playing too enthusiastically and then finding himself too far down in an instant, straining for balance, reaching for air. He stared up at the falling stream and he was nine again, the following summer, facing the placid surface of a community pool in the lessons his parents enrolled him and Corrine in every year thereafter. The disorientation of being underneath, the way that his senses all started lying to him in the water, came rushing back as the instructor informed them that the only way out of the class was to jump in. He circled the room and he was fourteen now, having signed up for after-school access to the pool at Plowshares, dropping himself into a lane and making the slow journey back and forth, the terror of the first time always at his heels, his mother's voice before swim lessons rushing past his ears: "We just don't ever want to lose you." At the tips of his fingers, unreachable no matter how fast or how far or how long he swam, was always the promise inherent in water: of lightness, of buoyancy, that he could float away. He heard Linus's voice in a memory, happy and free, calling, "Now, *this* is living." The dark rectangle of the exit door appeared behind the falling water. He needed to find Linus. He rounded the pool, left the room, and caught the escalator up into the daylight.

10:20 a.m.

Linus did not stop moving when he boarded the escalator from the concourse, heading away from Harrison; he did not stop moving as he crossed the main level, slipping through tour groups and families and docents; he did not stop when he boarded an escalator to the second floor, then the third floor, then the top floor, watching the Washington Monument lower itself to eye level as he headed skyward; he did not stop until he reached the end of the last floor, pressing himself against the railing, facing the inside of the shell of the building, which looked like iron lace. His body was working independently from his mind. Or maybe his mind had given his body one instruction—GO—and his body had obeyed.

He'd never felt himself so overwhelmed by the prospect of history before. He'd never seen the fact of the past rise up like a zombie. He'd never thought of the present as so different from the past, but suddenly it seemed to him that the here and now was just a fun house reflection of yesterday. It seemed a hopeless feeling from which he wanted to get as far away as possible.

So he moved until he couldn't anymore. He had reached the

farthest corner of the museum. There was nowhere else to go. He turned now and investigated his surroundings. There was one gallery on this floor. He walked through the entrance and was greeted by a 360-degree video screen playing images and videos of cultural touchstones—sitcoms blended into gospel songs, which blended into food demonstrations and more. He felt like he'd stepped into mission control in the Blackest spaceship in the galaxy. To the right, he spied the entrance to the area that Harrison had mentioned, the one focused on theater, TV, and film. In front of him was a music gallery. A giant car was on display up front. And to his left, less flashy but nonetheless intriguing, was a curved white wall with a dark blue sign on it that read VISUAL ART. Linus went to the left.

Linus had seen a movie once where a character went to a museum every day and sat in front of the same painting in an attempt to understand it. This was wild as hell to him. He had definitely liked paintings before. But he wasn't sure how you could come back day after day, looking for some new meaning. What was the fact of the painting? That was what he wanted to know. It seemed like, beyond the basic idea, anything else you were pulling out was coming from you. And that was fine. It was, he guessed, like Harrison's plays, some of which he didn't really get but which were supposedly classics. This was especially true of the ones that weren't musicals. Linus went to see them because he went to see everything Harrison did, but he wasn't sure he got what the big deal was.

Harrison was in this play last school year about a family whose father had died and they were all gathered around to read the will. All the actors playing the family were different races because it was a school play and not Broadway or something. But for some reason, Linus wouldn't let it go. He couldn't decide if it was the best thing in the world that the girl Harrison called Cool Aparna was his mom even though she was a sixteen-year-old Indian girl with baby powder in her hair to make it gray and that Harrison, then fifteen, was playing some kind of sad former jock character, who, Linus thought, was definitely white in the mind of the playwright. Everybody was white in the mind of the playwright, it seemed, and yet here we were.

They'd outfitted Harrison in a pair of little shorts because it was the fifties or something, and back then, men showed leg, apparently. And he'd worn a sweater with numbers on it. Linus had spent the whole play wondering exactly what time of year it was to be dressed like this, out in the yard arguing with this multiracial family. Theater was sometimes a real chore, actually. But the thing was, something had switched on in Harrison onstage. He was supposed to be playing drunk—the old jock had "buried all his sports dreams in the bottom of a bottle." That was an actual line from the play. Harrison threw himself into it, and it seemed to Linus, from the audience at the Plowshares black box theater, like Harrison had forgotten about any limitations anyone else might put on him. At least for that performance. And it was a beautiful thing. He moved like light moves across the room, like he knew every angle and every ledge; he was powerful and magnetic; he was brilliant. He was capital-A acting, Linus had thought then. He was doing real art. And Linus had to admit that it was a surprise to him—because, well, Harrison was not exactly Zendaya in the acting department usually. But it was like the character, or the play, or something gave him permission to throw all the parts of himself that he held back right out to the lip of the stage, like he was laying his burdens down on the altar at church.

Linus didn't remember who got the inheritance in the play—he didn't know what deep lesson the play was trying to teach him—but he did learn something new about his friend that night.

🚃🚃🚃

Linus stood in front of a canvas that was probably eight feet tall, maybe ten. The background was all gold. It glinted when he moved around. The image on top was of a boy leaping; you could only see him from the waist down. He looked like he was blasting off into the top left corner of the painting. He was Black—you could see his balled-up fists. He had on nice tennis shoes—expensive, maybe. And he had on jeans, which were slung low, exposing another pair of pants, which were also slung low, exposing a pair of boxers. Linus didn't know that these kinds of things got painted. It felt silly for him to think it—of course he knew that people painted Black boys. But did he really know it? Did they paint them like this? Surrounded in gold and heading skyward? Linus looked at the card beside the painting. It was by an artist named Dr. Fahamu Pecou. The card had a quote from the artist: "What if we believed in the abilities of our Black boys more than we lamented their identity?" Linus reached for his phone to write that down . . . but realized that his phone was having its own adventure somewhere in Baltimore.

There were so many programs and websites and speakers and teachers who told Linus that they were empowering him. He wondered all the time whether he would know when he was finally empowered, what it would feel like. He was constantly reminded that he was "at risk" and also "underserved," and although he understood what the meaning was behind it—he didn't have as much as some other kids, often including Harrison—he had trouble connecting that to who he was. How many people were approaching Linus like he was encased in gold, heading skyward? How many people saw him as a work of art? Linus fished his MP3 player out of his pocket and slid his earbuds into his ears. He pulled up the only song he ever listened to. He'd found the player at a thrift store, and he'd used his Dad's computer to turn a song from an old CD into a digital file. For the past couple of years, he'd listened to the song every day. It was the only song on the MP3 player. The organ came on first. Then the voices of people in the audience. Yelling. Cheering. Crying. One long, loud wail. The choir came in next. He knew this gospel song by heart. He kept walking. When it ended, he played it again. The organ. The murmur. The yelling in the crowd. The cheering. The people, scattered throughout the audience, crying. Then that one long, loud wail. It was his mother's voice. The wailing woman was his mother. He knew because he had been standing next to her. He'd been holding her hand. He'd been staring up at her while the organ played, and the crowd cheered, and the church choir sang, and the mics crackled, and in the back of the church an engineer recorded, and his mother cried out.

▦▦ ▦▦ ▦▦▧

A woman with a teacup was staring him down from across the room. Linus had been startled at first because she seemed to hold him directly in her gaze. Then he realized she wasn't there. The painting, by Amy Sherald, was of a dark-skinned Black woman against a midnight-blue background. She wore a bright yellow bow around her neck, a bright red shirt, and black-and-white-striped pants. *Honestly,* Linus thought, *the look is a serve.* He wished he could drip like that. She held a teacup in her hands, with one pinkie up like they did in British movies. And she stared at him. He stared back. What was he supposed to understand here? He fought the idea that there was something that he wasn't getting yet. He pushed down the idea that he should come back tomorrow to try again. There was no tomorrow. This time tomorrow, he and his dad would be halfway through Virginia in a rented truck stacked with boxes. He'd never see this painting again.

The woman with the teacup was in a corner. On the opposite wall, up higher than normal, was a cluster of three paintings.

One was a sort of impressionistic painting of a Black man in muted colors; he was holding a paintbrush and looking at the viewer. Below it was a larger painting of another Black man in bolder colors and wearing an emerald-green hat. It had a style that seemed more like old paintings, like from the Renaissance. Above that, to the right of the first painting, was a totally abstract painting with 3D elements. It was mostly gray, with a swath of blue on one side. It looked to Linus like an aerial map, like looking at the Harbor from above.

He read the cards near the cluster. The artists were James A. Porter, Frederick Flemister, and Jack Whitten. The strange thing was, based on the titles, they were all supposed to be self-portraits. They all looked so different; one of them didn't even have a person in it. Were there rules about how a painter could present themself? Linus stood back and considered them again. He looked at the frames as if they held mirrors, and didn't understand what he saw. Something in his head mixed up "self-portrait" with the idea that these were all portraits of him. It wasn't the fun house reflections that he was expecting downstairs. It was, quite simply but still confusingly, different versions of the truth of himself. He could paint a hundred canvases of possible Linuses right now, and the truth was he had no idea which one of them would be real. He knew who he was here, now. But the fear that he and Harrison shared—that the future was an oblique place with challenges they weren't up to—was only made worse by the fact that everything he knew for sure was being taken away. What of him remained? What of him was coming with him to Charleston? Who waited for him down the road?

"There you are!" Harrison was out of breath and sweaty. He looked like he'd taken the escalator stairs two at a time. He slung an arm around Linus and checked his friend's face for an update.

Was Harrison worried about Linus? Linus remembered how he'd left so abruptly, startled and shaken. It wasn't so different from how he felt now, but at least the thing that was startling him now—his own self—was familiar.

Harrison was insisting that they eat before they left. He swept Linus out of the gallery, having no response beyond "Oh!" when Linus showed him the self-portraits. They rode the escalators down three floors, and then Harrison led them to the black spiral staircase that had wound its way skyward above them when they were in line for the history galleries. Linus stopped a few steps down. He shifted to the side so a family could walk around him.

"I'm not really hungry yet," he said.

"No, you don't understand, we have to eat here. When we came on a trip with Plowshares, my dad was like, "You *have* to get lunch there!" But apparently the field trip–planning committee did not consult Obed Meredith on their itinerary. Cuz they told us to pack a lunch and we ate on the bus."

"Is this on your agenda?"

"No. None of this was on the agenda, though."

"Then I say we skip it. What's next?"

"Well, Pride, but—"

"Okay," said Linus as he started walking back to the top, "we can eat at Pride, then."

Harrison laughed. "Not to be homophobic, but I don't think the food at Pride will be as good as the food here."

"Yeah, but it'll be cheaper," Linus said. "I didn't leave the house today thinking I was going to be dropping twenty dollars on lunch. I *thought* we were just going to eat at your house like normal."

"Oh!" said Harrison. "Oh, sorry—it's my treat. I should have said that."

"I don't want you to treat me."

"It's fine! I planned for it. You know how I don't ever spend my allowance anyway."

Linus felt a wave of heat roll over him. He gripped the handrail and went back down to meet Harrison.

"I know you think you're being nice," Linus said. "But it's not what I want. It smells real good; it looks amazing. I don't want it."

"But—"

"Why are you treating me like I don't know what I want? You paid for the train, you paid for the cab, you paid for the tickets to the museum—now you're paying for lunch. I didn't ask for this!"

"Linus, oh my god. The tickets to the museum were free."

"That's not the point!" Linus yelled. A couple coming up the staircase looked at them.

"We have to go," Harrison said quickly. He hustled up, past

170

Linus. Linus didn't follow. Harrison turned around at the top. "Come on. Please."

Harrison walked briskly through the lobby and pushed his way out the glass doors. When the outside air hit him, he inhaled sharply. Linus noticed he was shaking.

"What's wrong?" Linus asked.

"This isn't working, is it?"

"Maaannn . . ." Linus said. He kicked at a patch of grass and then wandered over to a round black structure sticking up out of the ground, in contrast to the flatness of everything else around it besides the museum. Another mission control. It had a row of windows all the way around it, and Linus leaned in to look and found that it gave a glimpse into a room that seemed to extend deep underground. There was a circle of water falling from someplace high up, landing in a pool. People walked around it. Some sat. Linus wished he was in the water. Right in the middle of the circle, blocked from everything else. Because, this? Baby, this was not it.

Harrison appeared next to him. He held up the iPad, which bore a text from Aparna:

MARC train back to Baltimore leaving in 30.

Silently, the two boys walked to the curb.

STAGE MANAGER'S REPORT #3

SM: Aparna Aiyar

CAST: Harrison Meredith, Linus Munro, Cool Aparna?

PROPS: One bottle of Gold Maxx Daily-Use Bronzer (don't ask)

STAGE MANAGER'S NOTES:

My only task this hour was to remind Harrison of the train schedule, which I almost forgot to do because I was so surprised to see the last person I ever expected to run into here. Or anywhere. But especially here, a sightseeing-adjacent shop where tourists come, arms loaded with bags, and totes, and flyers, and souvenirs. Cool Aparna, seventeen-year-old Baltimore County resident and Plowshares rising senior, held nothing except her cell in one hand and a chunky key ring—with multiple metal keys, a car key, a carabiner, a gym tag, a Panera tag, and mace—in the other.

She dropped her Mom Keys, and they made the kind of clatter that I would have thought she'd be embarrassed by. But she laughed instead, loudly and to no one in particular. Then she knelt down, knocking a bottle of Gold Maxx Daily-Use Bronzer off the shelf, caught it with her cell phone hand, picked up the keys with her other hand, plucked open the neckline of her sweatshirt, and dropped the Gold Maxx into it. She stood up, did a little jump—I think to make sure the bronzer wouldn't fall out—and then bought a Moon Sounds Aromatherapy packaged gift set. The Moon Sounds box cost $45.50. The bronzer in her shirt would have cost $7.99 if she had paid for it, which she did not.

If she was nervous about the Gold Maxx setting off an alarm on her way out, she didn't show it. Instead, she paused to sniff a pomegranate-basil scrub that everyone thinks they want until they smell it. Then she put it back on the shelf.

She started moving again and that's when the voice of Toinette, a store manager I'd worked with frequently, cut through the chorus of "Press the Sky Higher" on the speaker system.

"Excuse me, miss!"

Cool Aparna turned around, and for the first time, she saw me. Confusion washed over her face.

"I think you forgot to pay for something, miss," Toinette said, walking past me.

"Um. No, thank you," Cool Aparna said. "I don't think so."

Loss Prevention is really just an improv exercise in which managers pretend they believe the thief was forgetful and encourage them to "yes and" themselves into paying for whatever they've stuffed into their backpack, pants, coat, or stroller. But when the thief doesn't play along, then it becomes a problem. Cool Aparna had clearly not been through our Loss Prevention training, because she froze as Toinette approached, whereas were she to just step outside the store, Toinette wouldn't have been able to do anything and Cool Aparna would have gotten away with it.

Toinette smoothly stepped in between Cool Aparna and the exit. She was about to try tactic two: restocking. If Cool Aparna wouldn't pay, Toinette needed to get the merch back.

"Miss, I'm going to have to ask you to give me the product in your shirt."

"I absolutely don't know what you're talking about," Cool Aparna said, her voice getting high and loud. Two men with big shopping bags from the VR arcade and tall souvenir glasses from the tiki bar turned to watch.

Toinette sighed and shifted her gaze from Cool Aparna to the cashier behind me. It was time for tactic three: call Gallery security. At this point, I did something I hadn't been expecting to do. I stuck my hand up, into Toinette's field of vision, and I waved.

"Toinette! Hi. Can you hold on a second?"

"Aparna?" Toinette said.

"I don't know if you remember me, but I was transferred from Towson during the holidays, and—"

"I just called you by your name, so clearly I remember you. Also, you still hold two floor-sales records, so any time you're trying to come back . . ."

She looked between me and Cool Aparna. "You know this young lady?"

"Um. I do. This is my cousin. Cool—Coolleen. She's going through something. I was supposed to be watching her, but I got distracted and I'm sorry. I was wondering if you'd let me pay the cost of a bottle of Gold Maxx Daily-Use Bronzer and get a receipt, and that way nobody has to fill out any paperwork or make any calls."

After the new Loss Prevention strategy was released, managers were required to fill out six different forms for any day there was an incident and encounter. It was half an hour's worth of work, at least. Toinette knew that. I knew that. Cool Aparna didn't.

"I like the way you think," Toinette told me.

She led us back to the counter, scanned another bottle of Gold Maxx from the shelf, and put it back. I handed her my card; she handed me a receipt. And any crimes that had allegedly been committed suddenly didn't exist anymore.

"Thank you so much," I said.

"No problem. And, Aparna," Toinette said to me. "I meant what I said. Come back anytime."

"Sure thing," Cool Aparna said. "That's very sweet. I will."

Toinette looked perplexed and then decided

it wasn't worth thinking about. I watched her put Cool Aparna completely out of her mind. I smiled at Toinette, turned to go, and tugged Cool Aparna's sleeve so she'd follow me. We didn't speak until we were all the way out of the Gallery and standing outside near the water.

"That was so awkward," Cool Aparna said. She peeled her sweatshirt off, revealing a strappy camisole tucked into her shorts. She caught the Gold Maxx as it fell out.

"You were almost in a lot of trouble."

"Oh! Mmm. Not really," she said. "Thanks for your help, though. You're so useful." She didn't offer to pay me back.

"Do you want this?" She held out the Gold Maxx. "I don't use bronzer."

"Oh . . ." I said. "Do you use skin lighteners?"

"Ugh, no. I get not-so-subtle hints about it from some aunties, but, like, no. I'm good."

Cool Aparna searched the street around us. Her eyes came to rest on a person sitting by a mailbox, holding a cardboard sign.

"Should we donate the bronzer, do you think?" she asked.

I didn't know how to answer that. "It isn't really a thing you donate, is it?"

Cool Aparna looked at me with what seemed like benevolence. "I think everyone deserves to feel good." She shrugged.

"What are you doing here?" I asked.

"I've never been here before. I wanted to feel like a tourist."

"Okay," I said. "Well, have fun. The VR arcade is kind of cool."

"VR gives me vertigo." She waved her hand to dismiss the idea. "What else?"

"Oh. Um . . . you could go to the aquarium?" I felt like I was failing her.

"What are you doing here?" she asked.

"I'm running an errand for a friend. I have to stay here for another ten minutes and then I have to go to the library and then I have to drop my bag off at my friend's house."

She paused for a second and then said, "Ten minutes?"

I nodded.

"Okay," she said. "Let's do that." Then she sat on the curb, placed the Gold Maxx next to her, and lost herself in her phone. We didn't speak again for ten minutes.

11:50 a.m.

How to fix this . . .

Harrison could hear the same old gospel song blasting from Linus's earbuds. Linus had chosen the window seat on the train and curled himself up in his music and the disappearing view almost as soon as he sat down. They were silent with each other all the time. But he couldn't help but feel like this was one person being silent and the other person just fidgeting with his tote bag and cleaning his glasses repeatedly. He was going to have superhero vision by the end of this train ride. Either that or his lenses would be worn down to sand. Only time would tell.

Linus flicked on his MP3 player and started the song over again. The gospel thing was weird, Harrison had to admit. Was it as weird as Linus liking "Press the Sky Higher"? No. No, that was outrageous. If Linus hadn't been pissed at him, Harrison would have spent the train ride asking the same question: How? How could he like that song? Explain. Apologize for your bad taste!

Harrison thought the gospel, though, was odd.

"You think there's a bathroom on the train?" Linus asked.

Harrison said he thought so, and Linus pushed past him to

go look. "Save my seat," he said to Harrison. Okay, so Linus didn't totally hate him. A good sign. Linus disappeared down the stairwell.

The train sped by a tiny cemetery with brown grass and a rusted gate. Harrison was shocked to find himself actually missing their cemetery. Then he was shocked to realize he'd thought of Baltimore Cemetery as theirs. But it was true—it was their domain, it and all they surveyed. And inside it they'd shared secrets and questions and provided each other with answers and solace. He missed it; he couldn't believe it.

His first impression had not been so rosy. They'd initially ventured up while still vibrating with excitement about getting the job at BaltiTours. They had applied on what Linus had described as the first nice day of spring, but which Harrison privately felt was already too warm and offensively so. Both boys had been dropped off and left to their own devices by their parents, who were all too busy to keep tabs. This wasn't typical, but maybe, just maybe, it was an indication of the kind of freedom that the job could provide.

Harrison had thought, since they'd been allowed to take the bus home that day, they could grab ice cream nearby without arousing the suspicions of their parents by setting off an alert on Check In. But Linus had other plans and informed Harrison that he had an errand to run. Harrison assumed Linus was being silly. *Let's run an errand to that ice cream shop!* Instead, Linus had whispered eagerly, "Let's go to the cemetery."

Um, what? Harrison's eyebrows said, but Linus could see it because he was already heading for the bus stop.

"What's at the cemetery?" Harrison called to Linus's back.

"Everyone who ever lived!" Linus said. Technically, Harrison thought, it was everyone who had ever died. The living were, you know, doing other things. Running errands, having ice cream, not going on creepy field trips.

Linus stopped and turned back to Harrison suddenly, and his eyes lit up. "It's just, this place is so full of history—I saw it online when I was doing research for a project. And I've been wanting to go forever. And, boy, it is so dramatic. I just feel like today's the perfect day to go look at it. We got nothing we need to do and we can just hang out all day and—I don't know—maybe every day can be like this." Linus seemed to lose confidence in what he was saying.

"A summer of errands!" Harrison said quickly, hoping he'd found the words to express the part of him that was enthused about something that belonged only to them.

"I thought it would be fun to hang out. I wanted to show you," Linus had said.

"Definitely. I'm into it."

"Really?" Linus had grinned then, turned on his heel, and charged toward the street corner.

Harrison hustled to catch up, as Linus's legs were longer.

"Why are you moving so fast? The cemetery's not going anywhere," Harrison said. The CityLink, the bus they were waiting for, was stopped at the red light a block away. Linus already had his pass out. Harrison felt a lone drop of sweat wind its way from his armpit down the side of his torso and then fuse itself with the elastic band of his drawers.

"We have our whole day ahead of us!" Linus had said. "I want to get it started as soon as possible."

The bus sighed to a stop in front of them. Two older women climbed onboard, followed by Linus. At the top of the stairs, Linus turned around expectantly and looked down at Harrison, who was still on the sidewalk, sweating down to his birth weight. "What are you doing?" Linus called.

Harrison froze (which was a relief even in the metaphorical). He surveyed the faces framed by the scratched-up windows of the bus and then looked back at Linus, whose boldness at boarding the bus was not typical. Their respective parents' worry about the world had trickled down to them—they didn't want Harrison and Linus riding around Baltimore on public transportation, preferring that they wait to be picked up or dropped off—and now Harrison and Linus were all weird about the bus. It was silly, they knew, but it always seemed to them that everyone else knew what to do and were annoyed at them for mysterious reasons.

From behind Linus, the bus driver called out, "Y'all stop playing around. Are you getting on, young man?" Oh, god. Everyone was mad at Harrison already. He caught a smile flit across Linus's lips. Linus raised his eyebrows, daring, and mouthed,

Are you getting on or not, young man? Okay, everyone was mad at Harrison except Linus. That he could handle. He climbed the steps and had started to follow Linus to an available pair of seats when he was stopped by the driver's voice over his shoulder. "Do you plan on paying, young man?" It's amazing how some people's tones can make even your demographic truths into a read. He turned around and swiped his pass.

They hadn't gone a full block before a message came in over Check In. Check in, please. From Mom.

Running an errand, he texted back. Linus needs to see something at Baltimore Cemetery.

He waited anxiously. Surely his mother would have follow-up questions or, more likely, other ideas. The typing bubble popped up on the screen, which Harrison usually thought was ironic because it always meant that his bubble was about to be popped.

But that day, something was different. The text came through: Don't get in trouble. Call me if there's a problem.

This was a surprise, but a happy one. And a confusing one. If there was trouble at a cemetery, his first call should probably be to their pastor.

The bus exited the Harbor and turned up Broadway. Harrison heard the revving engine of motorbikes from someplace behind them. Out of his window, he saw a Black boy, probably his age, maybe younger, speed by on a growling bike. He looked across the bus, and another Black boy sped by on the other side. They outpaced the bus and zigzagged in front of it, switching places.

One boy did a wheelie and then landed back on the street with a *thunk*. He sped up. He waved to the other boy to match his pace, and they both raced down Broadway, the sound of their engines cutting through the noise of a spring city afternoon.

"Would you ever want to ride one of those?" Harrison asked. He wondered if he'd done something wrong to miss the invitation.

"Come on, now," Linus said. "I'd be scared to death."

"Of getting hurt or getting in trouble?"

"Yes."

The bus dropped them off at the bottom of the hill that led up to the castlelike stone gates of the cemetery.

"Is this the scariest thing you've ever done?" Linus asked as they walked.

"I'm not scared of ghosts." Harrison asserted.

"I'm just asking, is going to the cemetery the scariest thing you've ever done?"

"Probably. That or the first time I took swimming lessons."

"Is it even legal to go to a cemetery if you're alive?" In response, Linus pointed to the rusted sign on the entryway that read CEM-ETERY HOURS 8 A.M.——4 P.M. Apparently the dead liked their evenings to themselves.

"If you're going to freak out, you let me know. I'll leave right away," Linus said, his voice echoing off the stone as they passed underneath the entry arch.

"I'm good," Harrison said. And then he looked Linus in the eye so he could see that what he'd said was the truth.

They stepped onto the grass; the hill and its statues towered above them. "Think about all the stories," Linus marveled.

That first day, they'd spent hours wandering around before settling in at the base of the grave marker they'd soon dub "DJ, Turn It Up!" They'd stared out at the city, and the sky, and the horizon, and they'd talked about everything and nothing, as they always did. They talked about school and their futures. Harrison asked about Linus's parents. Linus asked about Harrison's sister. Neither had the answers, but they fumbled through their thoughts. Harrison pressed Linus about his crush on Dario, which made Linus laugh uproariously. "I don't believe you," Harrison said. "You have a crush."

"Man, whatever," Linus said. "Dario is whatever. Do you like this shirt? I just got it thrifting." Harrison thought he was changing the subject, but he wasn't, really.

Flushed with the freedom of the open space and their new job and the rest of life unfolding, free to try on new versions of themselves with each other. They didn't have to pretend or withhold, and they didn't have to worry. They were safe together.

Just before the cemetery closed, they took a picture together under the statue. From the angle below, it looked like she was zooming down from heaven with a hand outstretched to bless them both.

🚃🚃🚃

There was a noise coming from the stairwell of the MARC train to Baltimore. It sounded like yelling. It sounded like Linus's voice.

"If you don't back up!" Harrison heard Linus warn. Linus stomped up the stairs and met Harrison's gaze.

What? Harrison asked.

I have no idea! Linus shook his head. He arrived back at their seat and stood in the aisle. Linus opened his mouth to speak, and that's when Harrison saw him, rising from the stairwell: the guy from the line at the museum. He was red-faced, pointing at them.

"I remember you!" the guy said, reaching the top step.

Harrison grabbed his tote and scrambled out of the seat. He squeezed in front of Linus and pushed him backward.

"We have to go," Harrison whispered. Linus started backing up and then turned and started jogging down the aisle. The guy from the museum charged after them. Harrison pressed into Linus, stepping on his heels.

"What is happening?" Linus asked, still moving.

"I actually don't know," Harrison responded.

People on the train around them were watching, but no one was doing anything to stop the guy from pursuing them. He was getting closer. They clambered down the staircase, coming to a connection between two train cars. They had a choice: They could double back, slipping into the lower level of the car they were just in, or they could go forward, either up or down.

Back? Harrison nodded. Linus nodded. *Back.*

They turned and scooted down the stairs underneath the flight they had just come down. Over their heads, they heard the guy crashing down the steps. Then there was silence. Harrison stole a glance; they were midway through the train car. He could only see the man's legs and torso framed in the open doorway. He seemed to be looking around, twisting his body to weigh his options. Harrison paused. Suddenly, the torso bent and compressed and the guy's head jerked into view.

"Go, go!" Harrison started moving again and pushed Linus along. They rushed down the aisle, up another set of stairs, through a doorway, and into the next car. A conductor was coming up the stairs as Linus crossed over into the car and the two collided. The conductor caught himself on the railing.

"Sorry," Linus said, huffing and out of breath.

"STOP THEM!" the man called from the train car behind them.

The conductor looked over their heads and then looked back down at the boys.

"STOP THEM RIGHT NOW!" the guy called. He neared the staircase. The conductor tapped Linus on the shoulder and moved him to the side. Harrison followed behind. The guy from the museum tumbled down the stairs and came careening through the connection between the cars. The conductor scanned his badge, and the door of the car slid closed just as the man was about to cross in. The man grabbed the handle and jostled it brusquely, to no avail. He banged on the glass with an open palm, leaving a ghostly handprint.

The conductor turned back and faced the boys. "Everything okay?"

"He's chasing us!" Linus cried.

"He yelled at me at the slave cabin!" Harrison added.

The conductor drew back. "Okay, I don't know what that means, but . . . okay." He turned back to the door and spoke through the glass. "Sir, go back to your seat."

The guy started to protest, but the conductor held up a hand. "Back to your seat, sir."

The conductor turned to Linus and Harrison as the guy continued to fuss behind the door.

"Explain it to me again. You know this guy?"

"No!" said Harrison. "He was rude to us in the National Museum of African American History and Culture. And now he's here. We didn't do anything to him."

"He's following you?"

"I don't think so," Linus said. "He just got mad at me cuz he said he saw me putting graffiti in the bathroom. Which I didn't do."

"That's been here since last Monday," the conductor said, casting a glance at the door. Then he shrugged. "Weirdo. Next train's not till this evening, so it could just be a coincidence you ended up here together."

"I promise we didn't do anything," Harrison said.

"Oh, I believe you. I was wondering if he followed you without you knowing. I don't like his energy at all. But this isn't even the strangest thing I've seen today. You just need to be careful. Y'all might want to move to the next car."

Linus and Harrison nodded and started walking the length of the car. "Boys?" the conductor called. "Where are you getting off?"

"Baltimore," they said in unison.

"Okay, just take a seat at the end of the car. I'm going to deal with this, and then I'll come back and walk you out when you get there. Wait for me. I just want to make sure you're okay." The conductor turned, scanned his badge, opened the door, stepped through, closed it behind him, and then disappeared from view.

▄▄▄▄ ▄▄▄▄ ▄▄▄◣

Baltimore grew larger as they approached. Linus and Harrison sat squeezed together even though there was plenty of room in the seats. They pressed into each other—shoulders, legs, arms, as if any point on their bodies that wasn't connected could be snatched away.

"Let's start over," Linus said finally.

Harrison nodded eagerly.

"I'm excited for Pride," Linus said. "I'm glad you thought of it. But let's not do an agenda. Let's just do whatever we want. Let's be free."

12:45 p.m.

At the same time, Harrison and Linus had the realization of how quiet the train had been, and how quiet they'd been on the train, and now, how the noise of Baltimore, and a Saturday, and at a distance the Pride street festival, ushered them into a new world. They couldn't see it yet; it was a few blocks over, in the middle of a large street now hidden from view by buildings. But the sounds that carried up and over houses and around corners pulled them in like a date grabbing your arm and rushing to the dance floor when the DJ drops the needle. They could make out at least two different songs playing at different volumes, the electric murmur of a crowd—yelling, laughing, talking—the *brrrapp!* that Linus thought was produced by the opening of handheld fans and Harrison decided was firecrackers. They bickered about it as they walked, bumping each other playfully as they attempted trash talk (which Harrison had to admit neither of them was any good at whatsoever).

"How big would the fan need to be to make all that noise? I swear it's firecrackers." Harrison said.

"In the middle of the day? In public? What world you living in?"

"Uh, Baltimore," Harrison said, laughing. "I bet you a dollar it's firecrackers."

Linus's eyes lit up. "All right. Bet."

Harrison didn't actually care who was right about the sound—although he was sure he was; he knew firecrackers when he heard them—he just wanted to stay in this place for as long as possible. They were finally back on track, back in Baltimore, and back to their old selves.

They approached the entrance to the Pride festival through a side street. They could glimpse, in the intersection ahead, food carts and booths, balloon arches and painted signs, and a crowd milling up and down the block. As they neared, the buildings on either side of the street framed the glimpse of the festival like archways leading to a castle. And, like a modern castle in a mythic urban land, there were two guards stationed in front of it at a metal fence, blocking the way in until they could check people's backpacks.

"No outside liquids inside!" one of the guards called to the crowd as Harrison and Linus joined a line of people. "No bottles, no cans, no flasks, none of those Nalgenes, no Tupperware full of juice, no casks."

"No goblets!" the other security guard called. "No sippy cups!"

"No SOLO cups!"

"No teacups!" The guards cracked each other up as people filed in between them, occasionally stopping to pour out a water bottle into a giant trash can that was already overflowing. Harrison had thought the Nalgene thing was a joke, but then he noticed a small mound of abandoned reusable plastic bottles, most of them covered in stickers, on the ground by the gate.

"Oh, and no guns, knives, or weapons," the first security guard added.

"And don't come in here with no drinking gourd!" the other called. They laughed again.

"Hold up," Linus said to Harrison, pulling him out of the line. "Now I'm thirsty."

"They just explicitly said that it is illegal to be thirsty at Pride."

"I'll drink fast. I promise."

He walked back up the block and ducked into a convenience store, followed close behind by Harrison. Linus swung the refrigerator case open and luxuriated in the cold air for a moment before plucking two water bottles from the shelf and tossing one to Harrison.

Linus approached the counter and pulled his wallet out faster than Harrison did. Harrison had learned not to make a thing of it.

"Oh, can you do cash back?" he asked the cashier. The cashier pointed to a sign that read NO. Not "no cash back," just "No." Useful.

"There's an ATM over there."

Linus looked. He seemed to be weighing his options.

"What do you need cash for?" Harrison asked, immediately

regretting breaking the decision-making process that seemed to be happening. Linus was terrified of ATM machines. "ATM Machine" was *on the list*. This could be happening . . .

"We made a bet," Linus said.

"Okay, but were you planning on losing the bet?" *WHY AM I TALKING HIM OUT OF THIS?* Harrison quickly made up for it. "Because you should plan on it. And I need my dollar."

"You better send that bill elsewhere," Linus said. But he still approached the ATM. Harrison held his breath. Linus pulled out his debit card.

OH YES, BABY! The ATM machine was a go. Ferris Day, back on track. Part two: ATM PIN and Pride.

Linus positioned himself at dueling distance from the ATM. He held his card out like a treat a wild-animal tamer used to placate a lion. It did not appear that he had any intention of moving closer. If it had been possible for him to throw the card into the machine like a big-top juggler doing the ring toss, Linus probably would have done it. The process of extracting cash had become a circus act.

"Do you want some help?" Harrison asked, not smugly but also *not*-not smugly.

"What you gonna do, wrestle the machine?" Linus countered.

"What do you think is going to happen?"

"What if I do it wrong and it starts beeping?"

"The sound is broken," the cashier said.

"See?" said Harrison.

"What if something happens and I get my identity stolen and the account gets hacked? My dad will be pissed."

"That is a possibility," the cashier said.

"No, it's not," said Harrison.

"Don't you watch the news?" the cashier said.

"Uh, no," said Harrison.

"How are you going to find out what's happening in the real world?" the cashier exclaimed. "You're going to be caught out here unawares. You need to stay vigilant. Things are crazy." A cat that definitely hadn't been there before but definitely seemed to run the place hopped up on the counter. It stared Harrison in the eye as if backing up the admonition of the cashier. The cat was wearing a rainbow collar in the shape of a necktie. An ally. A professional.

Linus took a step forward and plunged his debit card into the machine. It did not explode, nor did it lead to the utter financial ruin of his family, his ancestors, and all his descendants. It asked him to choose a language. He did, then he withdrew twenty dollars and bought two bottles of water. The cashier told them "Happy Pride"; the cat did not. Ferris Day's first success was in the books.

"Are you excited?" Harrison asked outside the store. Linus was chugging an entire bottle of water.

"What?" Linus said, gulping in air.

"You used an ATM machine!"

"I don't know about 'excited.' I was going to have to do it eventually."

"But eventually turned out to be today! Now you can use any ATM machine in South Carolina any time you want and remember how easy this was."

"The cashier was right, though. The world is crazy."

"What are you going to do, just keep your money in a box under your bed?" Harrison asked.

"Well, first I gotta get money. But after that, yes. Did you see the cat in there?"

"I did. I was wondering if that was allowed."

"The cat had a lot of attitude."

"Cat-itude," said Harrison.

"The cat was the manager," Linus said.

"The cat wrote the 'No' sign."

"The cat was trying to follow us around the store like, 'You boys need to empty your pockets.'"

Harrison laughed. "The cat is going to steal your PIN."

"Yo, that's not funny," Linus said. But he was smiling. He was looking at Harrison with delight again.

They rejoined the line. The security guards were still calling out all kinds of drinking equipment that was not allowed within the confines of the Pride festival. Harrison wondered if they'd stayed up the night before, making a list. He got so caught up in thinking about it that he hadn't finished his water by the time they got to the front.

"What did I say?" one security guard asked Harrison, pointing at the bottle.

"No thermoses!" the other guard called, waving two couples pushing strollers inside.

"No hot-water bottles!"

"No jugs!"

Harrison could watch this show all day. He would pay money to see it. *Two People Shout Synonyms Against a Rainbow Background.* If this was Pride, he would come every year.

"Hello?" One of the guards was speaking to him again. Harrison came back to Earth. "What's the plan, my friend?"

"Oh!" Harrison yelped. He was holding a bottle! And it held water! Harrison fumbled with the cap on the bottle and took a big sip. He coughed roughly. It was his first day drinking water. He looked at the bottle. He'd barely made a dent. Everyone was looking at him. Linus's shoulders were shaking as he attempted to stifle his laughter. Harrison took another sip while staring right at the security guard. This was awkward. Harrison closed his eyes. This was more awkward. Harrison opened one eye. He took a break and breathed. How long had it been? An hour? He was getting a stomachache. Sports was hard. Wasn't it possible to die from drinking too much water? He wasn't sure that one twelve-ounce bottle of water would qualify as too much, but wouldn't this be an awkward moment to find out? Literally every queer person in Baltimore was standing around, judging him. Well, some were still walking through the gates, placing their Nalgenes and mini liquor bottles at the altar of Pride. But the Nalgenes were judging. Harrison took a breath and raised the bottle to his lips again. Water was spilling out the sides of his mouth. Finally, the last few drops of water came tumbling down, and Harrison gasped and bent over. The security guards applauded; Linus clapped him on the back. The human gates parted. He dropped his spent water bottle in the trash can. They walked through. Here he is, boys; here he is, world; ready or not, here comes Harrison Meredith, soaking wet, out of breath, and stumbling into his first Pride.

1:07 p.m.

The thing that surprised Harrison the most was how Black this Pride was. There were people who presented as all races and ethnicities, but he hadn't expected to see so many Black faces. It was a happy surprise. And then he felt surprise at his surprise. Black people were queer, too. I mean, hello. Here he was. And Linus. That was at least two. But when he'd tried to conjure images of what Pride might be, he'd always envisioned crowds that looked like so many other crowds that he saw and was sometimes a part of: crowds that were mostly white but dotted with people of color. He thought of the Pride he'd seen on TV or when he searched for images online—the clothes were always so colorful, but as a whole, the group seemed like his class picture at Plowshares or like the tourists often filing through the Harbor. *There seems to be two Baltimores in this way,* he thought. His neighborhood was almost all Black and Latinx; Linus's neighborhood was all Black; church was all Black; when they took the bus to the cemetery, the passengers were mostly Black, and most of the faces of the people they passed on North Avenue were as well. Harrison floated in and out of these different bubbles, sometimes even crossing over invisible lines on foot as he walked from his house to Aparna's in a neighborhood that was mostly white—the Aiyars excluded, of course. But he couldn't make sense of where one world started or ended. He couldn't decide if he was breaking some kind of rule by going to one place or another. Did he belong at Plowshares? Did he not belong in his neighborhood because he went to Plowshares? And did Linus have less of a claim to belonging because of where he lived or the fact that he went to Harper, which didn't seem to be mostly any one race but was across some other invisible line that separated public school from private, a city school from a county one?

There were places where he was sure he didn't belong. And there were places where he was sure he was invisible. And he didn't know which was worse. But what he did know was that at least at Pride, as his mother would sometimes say, "We outchere." He saw his features, his hair texture, his skin color in a rainbow of tones reflected back at him as they walked together down the middle of the street, taking it all in. There were people dressed in matching T-shirts touting their companies or their organizations, walking in groups after marching in the parade or breaking apart and creating a kind of "find the pattern" game. There were teenagers, some with multicolored track braided into their hair, some toting signs, some in all black (Aparna hive, rise up!). There were clumps of people who all looked alike and other groups who looked like they didn't all exist on the same planet and yet were cracking each other up and jostling each other and hugging and holding hands. There were so many little kids and more people on stilts than Harrison thought was likely in one space; there were a bunch of dogs and one guy with a parrot on his shoulder—which seemed like a lot of work to go through for a look, but whatever. There was a group of folks down the block, dancing and death-dropping and grinding to a live performance as Baltimore club pumped from the speakers, and a group of folks up the block were cheering and wining and clapping along with a dance-team performance to an old pop song. And there were so many people smooching. Harrison was astonished. Quick smooches as people walked. A smooch hello. A smooch goodbye. A smooch for a beer. A smooch for someone giving someone else their change after buying a beer. A couple full-on making out while sitting on a curb. Two people even smooched over the top of an ice cream cone and then went back to eating the cone. Efficient.

"I'm hungry," Harrison said. That was his big takeaway—there was ice cream available; smooch optional.

"Want to try the Mexican food?" Linus pointed out a food truck with a bedazzled rooster on the side. They got in line. "Do you think there's always a gay rooster on the side of the truck, or do you think it's just for Pride?" Linus asked.

"I feel like before this, I wouldn't have thought they'd go to the trouble just for one day, but . . ."

Everyone had gone to the trouble. The street, which Harrison had walked down hundreds of times, was transformed—vibrant and alive, and even the stores and shops and bars that sat behind the booths and stages and trucks seemed to take on a new dimension.

They both got burritos—Linus said he'd treat, but Harrison suggested they just each pay for their own—and then they realized that they did not know how to eat a burrito while walking in public. Lettuce and rice and tomatoes spilled down their arms.

"Are you trying to smooch someone at Pride?" Harrison said with a full mouth.

"You're dumb," Linus said, laughing. He struggled to keep a chunk of meat from falling out of the aluminum foil and ultimately failed. RIP, chunk of meat.

"You should!" Harrison said. He had sour cream smeared on his cheek. Linus reached over to wipe it off. "No, not me!" Harrison cried.

"I'm wiping your dirty face! Calm down."

"I wish they had a knife and a fork for this," Harrison said.

"You are too bougie for your own good."

"That is not even true. Corrine says I have no class whatsoever, so y'all need to figure it out and let me know."

"Bougie," Linus said, casting a final verdict.

"Okay. So, who are you gonna smooch?"

"I'm not kissing anyone!"

"What about that guy?" Harrison pointed at a shirtless Black boy who looked to be about their age. The boy looked back at them.

"Stop pointing!" Linus whispered. "Please ignore us," he called to the boy. "We got no home training."

The boy grinned and called, "Happy Pride!"

"And to you and yours," Linus said.

"He wants to smooch you," Harrison stage-whispered.

"You never said kissing was part of Ferris Day."

"I mean, it is and it isn't. It's up to you, of course. But I thought you wanted to sm—"

"Oh, hold up." Linus waved to two girls walking down the block toward them. "Fab! Phil!"

The girls lit up when they saw him and changed paths to reach them, slipping in and out of the stream of people effortlessly.

"Linus! Oh, my baby! I am going to miss you!" one of the girls said as she hugged him. She was taller than Linus and had a flash of magenta that peeked out of her long brown hair when she moved.

"Harrison, these are two of my friends from school. Fabiola Figueroa, she/her pronouns," he said of the hugger. "And Philadendra Truong, she/her. Y'all, this is my friend Harrison Meredith, he/him."

"The famous Harrison," Fab said. "Can I hug you? I hug."

Harrison looked stricken but said yes as he extended the hand holding the remains of the burrito away from himself to spare her.

"Are you having fun?" Linus asked.

"The minute I get someplace, I'm ready to leave," Phil said.

She had on a jersey and a pair of aviator sunglasses that did nothing to dim her eyes, which seemed to be taking everything in as she spoke. She pulled a white baseball cap from her back pocket and shoved it over her head. She looked like she was ready to coach a team. And Fabiola, majestic and decked out in a burnt-orange terry cloth shorts set, looked like the star player.

Phil continued. "But yes, fun. I like to walk around looking at all the decorations and everything and think, 'They made this for me.' Because, obviously, they did. I *am* the queer community." She looked Harrison in the eye. "Welcome to my party."

"Thanks for having me," he said.

"Are you sticking around?" Linus asked.

"You know me, I am down for whatever," Fab said. "I feel like it's my destiny to win one of those carnival games today, so that's what's up. But Phil is trying to bounce."

"Where?"

"If I knew, I'd be there," Phil said. "I'm not complaining. If I could think of an option, I would do that option. That just makes sense. All day long, I spend my time thinking of worse options than the present and not doing them."

Harrison hadn't spent much time thinking about Linus's school friends, but he definitely hadn't imagined this. Linus didn't talk about school that much. Harrison knew that he wasn't happy there, but it had less to do with the social scene and more to do with what Linus wanted to be focusing on. Nevertheless, very little about what Linus said about the few folks he hung out with in school suggested all this energy. *Is Linus different with his school friends?* Harrison wondered.

In the distance, the revving engine of motorbikes carried over the sounds of Pride. Harrison spotted two boys riding down a side street toward the festival and then making an elaborate loop and zooming away.

Phil saw it, too. "What I want to know is: Where do the motorbikes come from? I am very fascinated by this. I always see teenagers on them, and I'm like, is there a store I can go to? The motorbikes and the squeegees. I want to know about the supply chain." Baltimore had groups of boys who made money window washing at most busy intersections. Before he'd found the job at BaltiTours, Harrison had asked his parents how he could apply to be a Squeegee Boy. His mother said she'd look into it, but he was pretty sure she was just saying that to get him to move on.

"They don't do the motorbikes in New York," Phil said. "I've told you this: Nobody has a car in New York. That's why it's a city. If everybody has cars everywhere, it's not a city."

Fab was cackling, and Phil looked up at her, confused.

"Am I wrong?" Phil said.

"Yes!" Fab said. Phil pointed at Fab with a look of betrayal, which only made Fab laugh more. Phil had a blunt, rapid-fire way of talking that made her seem like the perfect combination of an old movie mafioso and a stand-up comedian. Harrison had no idea if she was serious or not.

"I'm not complaining," Phil said. "I'm just shocked you call this a city. It's a bunch of different amusement parks with deep economic and racial disparities."

This girl was full-on lecturing in the middle of Pride. Is this what people in New York were like?

"Are you from New York?" Harrison asked.

"No. Why?" Phil said.

"I like your shirt, Linus," Fab said, changing the subject.

"Mazz told me to buy it!"

"Of course they did! It's very much the dad aesthetic."

"I know! They totally know my aesthetic!" Linus said.

"Are you going to keep this aesthetic when you move to South Carolina?" Fab asked.

"I think so. I mean, dadcore works for me. Plus, you don't change your aesthetic just because you change locations."

Harrison wondered if they had some kind of class on aesthetics at Harper and also what an aesthetic was and why Linus was suddenly talking like an influencer.

"Look at us," said Phil, waggling her aviators, "a dad and a granddad out for the day." Harrison had heard Linus talk about himself dressing like a dad and others dressing "grandpa-ish" before, but he didn't approve of "dadcore" then, and he wasn't going to support it now. Linus did not dress like his own dad nor like Harrison's dad. Harrison's dad wore, like, jeans and shirts. He dressed like a person in person clothes. There was not a single defining characteristic about his dad's style of dress that Harrison could pull to mind. Sometimes there were hoodies. That was all he had; sorry. All these actual minors walking around talking about "I'm a middle-aged father of three, and that's why I wear baggy clothes." Ridiculous.

And no, Harrison wasn't salty because he had no idea what his own personal style was or how he was supposed to wear clothes that gave the impression that he was nearing retirement and going through a midlife crisis. People with body types like Phil's or like Linus's could throw on something a size larger, have it droop off them like they were human hangers, and somehow make it work. Clothes were made for people like them, Harrison decided. Harrison didn't feel like his body was so dramatically different, but that feeling went out the window the minute he stepped into a clothing store dressing room. When he bumped up a size, he felt like he was hiding himself. Or worse, that he was swimming in a tent of fabric. Why was it so hard for Harrison, with his non-clothes-hanger body, to find clothes that communicated to the world "I don't know what size I am, I don't really care how I look, and I will turn this car around if y'all kids don't stop bickering."

Harrison was ranting in his head, which usually meant he was hungry. But the remainder of the burrito in his hand proved that to be false. He'd had to chug water in some sort of new Olympics, so he wasn't thirsty. What was it? Was he actually mad about this? Phil, Linus, and Fab had continued clucking away, and Harrison had totally spaced out. There was nothing to be mad about. He was just . . . surprised to see this other group of Linus's friends, with their inside jokes and their Father's Day cosplay.

It was fine. He had friends, too. Aparna, for instance, who was probably at the library right now being an amazing friend and decoy. The best friendships are the ones where the other person pretends to be you and you don't speak to each other for hours, right? Aparna was a great friend. And Harrison imagined that when Linus got together with the rest of the Phalanx of Sad

Boys, it must have felt slightly disorienting, too. All of them save Linus spent their days at Plowshares talking, making up jokes, and building that library of incidental knowledge that houses a friendship. It had to have been weird sometimes.

Fab and Phil laughed uproariously at something Linus said that Harrison didn't get. He wandered over to a booth selling paper fans and picked up one that said DADDY on it. Okay, he was fairly certain that this was not about dadcore. But what did it mean? What did any of it mean? And how was he supposed to find out without embarrassing himself? He clacked the fan open and shut lightly, not wanting to draw attention and be accused of appropriating the culture of any dad, grandpa, stepfather, or wise old mentor.

Harrison's last living grandpa, Pop, was actually both a father figure and gay, but Harrison couldn't imagine him holding this fan, nor could he imagine him in a bowling shirt or a cardigan. The last time he'd seen Pop, on a trip to Virginia Beach with his cousins, Pop had been wearing a fitted polo and shorts that surprised Harrison with their, well, shortness. They were actually a normal length if you were playing tennis or, like, not seventy-five years old. Harrison didn't know why he'd had such a weird reaction to the shorts; it wasn't like it was embarrassing, really. Pop had a way of carrying himself that felt regal—lanky but sturdy, like a swan. Harrison had noticed it, really seen it for the first time, when Pop had strode through the visitors' center on the board-walk on their first day at the beach, his eyes alight with wonder, leading Harrison and his cousins like little ducklings in his wake.

Pop came here every year. He knew the visitors' center inside and out. But he still wanted them to see it through his eyes. And that was the compelling thing about Pop. He had made the special trip to point out the details of a quiet, rather unspectacular section of the beach to Harrison; his twin cousins, Melinda and Francis; his grumpy uncle Theo; and Melinda's friend from a camp, a boy named Rahul, because Pop was hosting them and wanted them to have the best possible time.

Speaking of the best possible time, Harrison luxuriated for a moment in the memory of how hot Rahul had been. And how surprising it had been when Rahul had decided he was interested in making out with Harrison on the third night of the trip. It was Rahul who'd changed Harrison's mind about the shorts, actually. The night after they made out, they were all walking through the visitors' center again (why couldn't they just go to the beach at the beach?), and Rahul had lightly bumped his hip against Harrison's. Harrison apologized for being. Rahul shook his head and bumped again to show that he'd meant it. They trudged through in silence for a while, not nearly as engaged as Pop was (and Francis, to be honest, but it was possibly just a bit). Pop leaned over a display case, miraculously not disturbing the hem of his polo, which was tucked into his shorts.

"Your grandfather dresses so well," Rahul had said.

Harrison had no response to that, so he said, "Oh. I don't know." Just brilliant; a sparkling wit. Rahul stooped down to look at a stuffed beaver in a case, posed with its hand-claw thing behind its ear like it was shyly flirting.

"Wasn't really a question." Rahul and the beaver were in deep communion. Harrison looked back at Pop, now standing straight-backed in the middle of the room, like a directional sign. His arms were folded across his chest, and he nodded enthusiastically as a visitors' center employee explained something Harrison couldn't hear. He thought his grandfather was magnetic, and the shorts were part of the whole thing.

Harrison explained his revelation to Rahul when they took a break from making out on the fourth night of the trip. They were sharing a room with Melinda and Francis, but the siblings had gone to call their mom, and Rahul and Harrison leapt at the opportunity. Literally. Rahul jumped onto Harrison's bed, which he shared with Francis, like a flying squirrel. It was a lot. Harrison, now sitting on the floor in the well between the two beds next to Rahul, his lips a little raw from kissing, tried to change the subject.

"I see what you're saying about Pop. His clothes. I guess he's just really into style. And it's not like he means anything by it."

"What do you mean 'means anything'?"

"He's not trying to look, like, sexy or something."

"How do you know?"

"Well," Harrison said. Ah, thoughts organizing themselves into words: his nemesis. "It would just be weird. I don't know."

Rahul waved his hand; he was over the conversation. Harrison's heart sank a little, and he realized he'd wanted to impress Rahul, even though he hadn't admitted it to himself.

"Harry," Rahul said. He'd called him Harry; it was awful. "Harry, how do you know your grandpa isn't sitting in his room with some other silver fox right now and the guy is like, 'I love your shorts, and—'"

"Okay, actually, I don't want to talk about this. It's gross."

Rahul made a face like Harrison was being ridiculous, which Harrison was certain he was not. He hitched himself up on his knees and then scooted back onto his bed. Harrison didn't have a lot of experience—or any—but he could tell that they had concluded their festivities. Harrison took off his glasses to clean the smudges that their faces had left on them. Rahul swept his hair out of his eyes and clicked the TV on with the remote. He then turned the remote to Harrison and used it to gesture as he made his closing argument. "I'm just saying. In general, it's not a good idea to slut-shame your grandfather."

STAGE MANAGER'S REPORT #4

SM: Aparna Aiyar

CAST: Harrison Meredith, Linus Munro, Aparna Ramamurthy, Aparna Aiyar?

SET: Central Branch of the Enoch Pratt Free Library (so gorgeous)

STAGE MANAGER'S NOTES:

All I needed to do was sit at the library until the time

when Harrison's sister was due at the hairdresser, then I'd drop off his bag at his house and I'd be done. This was, in concept, the home stretch. But in my planning, I hadn't anticipated having company.

Cool Aparna had gotten to the Harbor by car—her mother's—and she insisted on driving us to the library. Music came roaring to life as soon as she turned on the engine, and she made no attempts to turn it down again. She lowered the roof all the way, threw her sweatshirt in the back seat, and told me to put my stuff "literally anywhere." The car had an eggshell exterior with oxblood leather seats; it was spotless. I put the backpack on the floor behind my seat.

"Why does this look like a Versailles for books?" Cool Aparna said as we walked into the library. The Central Branch is a huge, block-long stone building with a light-filled O-shaped atrium in the middle. It did, I guess, look like a Versailles for books.

"Are you asking that or just saying?" I asked.

"Aparna. I've been in buildings before. I was just making a joke."

We sat down at the table near an older woman with a salt-and-pepper bob. She had a closed book in front of her and was crying quietly. Of course Cool Aparna approached her.

"Are you okay?" Cool Aparna asked. The woman

looked up and then smiled at Cool Aparna through her tears. She chuckled a little and wiped her eyes.

"Yes," the woman said. "It's just the book." She held up the cover. I'd read it before. I had also cried. "I just got to the most moving section and had to take a little breather."

"What's it about?" Cool Aparna asked. Very quickly, she and the woman became best friends, laughing about the book and the plot and crying over something that didn't happen. I guess it didn't matter that I had also read the book.

After the woman left, Cool Aparna hummed as she typed on her phone. She took a photo of the cover of the book. She scrolled through videos. She commented on many of them. Then she spoke to me without looking up. "So what now?"

"Oh, are you talking to me?" I said before I could stop myself. "Am I still here? Amazing."

Cool Aparna stopped typing and raised her eyes to meet mine. "You pissed?"

"Sorry. I'm just being a brat. I should eat the protein bar in my backpack."

Cool Aparna was quiet for a while, but she didn't take her eyes off me. What was annoying about her was that she was popular but not dumb.

"It's really nothing. I . . . I was annoyed because I

read the book you two were talking about. But I didn't want to intrude."

"Aparna. That's outrageous! I cannot believe this. We could have had a book club." She grabbed my hand. I gently removed it.

"Why are you hanging out with me?" I said.

"Do you not want me to?"

"Just answer the question, please."

"You invited me."

"I . . . What? I absolutely did not."

"You said you were going to the library and to your friend's house."

"That is not an invitation!" I said a little too loud.

"I feel like you're overthinking it. We ran into each other, which is totally random. And now I'm having so much fun," she said. "Why is this weird for you?"

"I don't know. We . . . never really speak. And we don't hang out."

"Oh my god, Aparna, we talk all the time at rehearsal," she said. She reached up and yanked at her ponytail to tighten it.

"Not the same," I said. "Plus, it just seems a little weird to be suddenly hanging out after years of being defined by our differences."

"I don't get it."

"You're Cool Aparna." Her smile dropped. I

continued. "And I am, by definition, Not-cool Aparna."

"I don't believe in hierarchies," she said.

"Well, that's good for you," I said.

We were both quiet for a while. I turned my focus to the life of the library. I usually try to watch things until I can come up with a way of understanding a place. I started doing it at the mall, on slow days at Potions. There is so much that goes unnoticed. I am trying to notice everything.

Cool Aparna spoke up beside me.

"Is there a reason you didn't say anything about what happened in the store?"

"What was I supposed to say?" I asked without looking.

"Aren't you curious?"

"I guess. But people don't like to be called out," I said.

"People do want to be seen, though," she said. "Aparna, don't you want to be seen?"

"Literally or figuratively?" I turned back to her.

"Does it matter?"

"Yes."

"Fine," she said. "Literally."

"No," I said. "I don't want to be seen literally."

"Aparna!" she stage-whispered. "That is not true! Oh my gosh."

Cool Aparna sat back down, and I suddenly

became aware of my mistake. She was going to try to help me. I had precious few seconds to construct a plan to keep this from happening.

She fixed me in her gaze. "You do not want to be invisible." She had a point there. But I would contend that it was accidental.

The thing about people like Cool Aparna and her friends at school is that they approached the world as if we were all the same while living in a world where they are clearly having a different experience. They all come from massive wealth, a difference that keeps showing up in small ways and large—the cars topped with bows their parents bring to school on their 16th birthdays; souvenirs from exotic vacation destinations; even the things they eat for lunch. Socializing with the few of them at Plowshares was like being a tourist in another kind of life that was Bigger and More Fun and for No One. Or, at the very least, not for me. And in that way, I was invisible. But that is not the way that Cool Aparna was thinking of things. Of that I was sure.

"What do you think 'invisible' means?" I asked her.

She fidgeted with her sleeve. She leaned forward across the table toward me. "Do you ever go to protests?" This was unexpected.

"Not really."

"Oh! I would have thought . . . Well! It's amazing,"

she said. "I've been going since before I was in high school. Like, during the racial reckoning, when we were all marching in masks. And I'm certainly not going to stop now. My parents don't really love it, but it's honestly the only thing I care about. Like, that's not true, but also it's kind of true. I wrote my college application about going to DC and marching and this thing that happens—Oh! That's why I'm telling you this. This thing that happens when you're in the streets with hundreds or thousands of people and, um, you're all saying the same thing and you can hear your voice as one voice echoing back off these huge, you know, fortresses of history or whatever. That's the opposite of invisible, and I never . . . I never feel that in my real life. And, like, I want to."

"But you—"

"Please don't say the words 'Cool Aparna.'"

"You're very visible at school," I said.

"For what, though? Like, school is fake."

"I don't think that's true."

"Okay! Anyway," she said. "I really love protesting, and there was this lawyer at this one protest who was handing out information sheets about what to do in all these different circumstances, and it talked about how she would represent us if we got arrested, and I just thought she was amazing. And so I took a flyer and I emailed her a while later and asked her if I could intern with her or something. And I was pretty proud of myself for taking the initiative. And my parents were like, 'If you want to work at a law firm, we can hook you up with our friends,' but I don't want to work at some big, fancy law firm downtown. I want to work with this lawyer from the protest who had on paint-splattered gaucho pants and had her own bullhorn and who could probably use some graphic design help, judging from the flyers.

"So," she continued, leaning back in her chair, "that's what I've been up to this summer, which, like, everyone thinks is weird. As you're aware, Cressida and everyone is at her parents' place in the Outer Banks." I was not aware. "The thing is, though, the lawyer, Katya . . . Like, it's a small office. There's only, like, seven of them, and since I'm not a lawyer or whatever, I can't really be helpful. So they have me in the copier room and I've been organizing their paper files and digitizing them and making copies of motions and stuff. And I just sit in that hot room all day and I don't hear anyone's voice, not even my own. And it just feels so different from what I expected."

"What did you expect?"

"I know that it's important work that no one had time to do before and I hope that I'm good at it and useful. But I just don't have any way of knowing. And . . . I don't know that I'm making a difference and it feels gross to say that because, like, that's not why you do things, but also it is. I just thought . . . I think I thought I would like myself more there. And I don't. Uh . . . Sorry. I didn't mean to, like . . ."

"No," I said. "I get it. I think that the work you're doing is thankless and maybe that's hard to deal with. But maybe what you're doing makes other things possible."

"I guess," she said. "I just. I thought I'd see Katya. Or . . . anyone at some point in the summer. And, well, that's a no."

I couldn't help myself. I didn't want to hurt her feelings, but I was struck by the irony and needed to share it. I said, "So you're not getting enough attention working for the law firm and as a result you decided to spend the day committing crimes?"

She looked at me with surprise and then laughed. "Okay, it is definitely not like that. You sound like my therapist. You should charge."

"Maybe." I paused. "I work at Potions, not the one we were in today. The one at the Towson Town Center. And it's sort of near this other lotion and soap place that always smells amazing and has little cartoons on the soaps to let you know who made them. And I think that's really interesting. Because it makes you think about how soap doesn't just happen. How there's somebody behind it."

"Exactly. Like when you use one of those bath bombs that covers your tub in glitter, somebody is going home from work also covered in glitter."

"Right," I said. "One time, my mom and I were driving through Dundalk and it smelled awful and I said something about it. And she said it was the soap factory down there. She told me soap doesn't smell good until it does. But, really, soap doesn't smell good until someone makes it smell good. So, you know, I feel like at the law firm, you're making soap."

"Yes! I'm making soap!"

"And maybe you've learned that you don't want to be a soap maker," I said.

"Wait, we're talking about being a lawyer, right?"

"Yes."

"Okay, yes, then yes. I still want to be a lawyer. I'm just tired of being an intern ghost! I just want to be noticed. Like . . . today, my mom told me I could take her car to get coffee and so I was like, well, I'll take it out and I won't come back until someone notices I'm still out. And here we are. Sitting in the library hours later."

"Why didn't you get your own car for your birthday?" I asked.

"Ugh." She rolled her eyes. "Because when I had my learner's permit, I took my mom's car out without asking and they were mad about it. Who cares?" Maybe after I was finished being a decoy for Harrison's and Linus's parents, Aparna could hire me to fill in for her with her folks.

"Let's do something," she said. "Let's get noticed. Do you want to—Oh! We should find a wall and graffiti our names on it."

There was actually something contagious about her energy. I could see why people were drawn to her. But also, I did not want any part in it.

"I think we should think that through," I said.

"You're right. Where would we get spray paint?"

"No, I meant we should think through whether this graffiti thing is a good idea for us."

"Oh. You think we should do less crimes," Cool Aparna said.

"I think you should do fewer crimes. I think I should do no crimes."

At that, my phone's alarm went off. It was time for me to go to Harrison's house to drop off his bag.

"I actually need to get going," I told her.

She grabbed her phone and her Mom Keys and stood up. "Okay. Let's go."

1:14 p.m.

Harrison felt Linus wrapping him in a bear hug, pulling him out of his reverie.

"How would you feel about a pool?" Linus was asking. How much time had passed? How many people had become fathers while Harrison was reminiscing about Rahul? Harrison wriggled out of Linus's grasp and turned to face him. Fab and Phil were standing on either side of him like backup singers.

"What pool?"

"We're going swimming," Fab replied, providing no answers to the question asked.

Harrison looked askance at Linus. *You don't know how to swim.*

It's a pool; we can hang out, Linus's raised eyebrows replied.

"There's a public pool in Druid Hill Park," Fab said. "It's walking distance. Phil goes there every day."

"I'm trying to live on a boat after graduation," Phil informed Harrison. "I have to get my sea legs."

Was she walking on the water?

"We just have other things we were going to do today," Harrison said.

"Well," said Linus, "we're mostly done, right? We can stop by the pool." After a moment, he added, "We said we were just going to do whatever we wanted. No agenda."

Suuurrre. Okay. But it did seem like Fab and Phil had a little plan going on. What one might call a schedule. A tiny touch of an agenda. *Une petite programme.*

"Okay, but I don't have my bathing suit. We'll have to stop by my house first."

"None of us have bathing suits," Fab said, spreading her arms wide, seemingly to display that she wasn't hiding a bikini up her sleeve like a magician. "We're gonna stop by our friend's store and thrift some shorts and towels. It's fine. The folks at Maybe This Time always hook us up."

Linus nudged Harrison. "My treat."

Fab and Phil went to go pee. Linus shimmied his shoulders to the beat of a song playing far away as he carved a path up the street to a pop-up run by a bookstore café. He plopped into a folding chair at a small table and drummed his hands on his thighs.

"This is everything," he said. He looked up at Harrison and grinned.

Harrison slid into the chair next to him. "You're having fun."

"Baby boy! When I said that this is everything, I meant that this is everything. Are you having fun?"

"Yeah," said Harrison.

"Good," Linus said. He drummed on his thighs again and

craned his neck to take in the scene. People were sitting at the other tables, eating, or talking, or drinking. Others browsed a long table holding stacks of used books.

"You're right," Linus said.

"About what? I mean, I know I'm right, but which thing are you talking about?"

"You're ridiculous. I mean about smooching. I should, right? Like, when I get to South Carolina, I'm not going to know *anyone*. I probably won't make any friends at school, and good luck getting Aunt Bird and my dad to let me leave the house. I don't even know if there's a bus that I can take. So I should smooch on Ferris Day."

"Yes!"

"What about you?"

"What about me?" Harrison asked.

"Isn't this day about both of us doing big things? Telling the future that it can't scare us? What's your thing?"

Harrison hadn't thought about that, about picking something for himself. This whole plan was overwhelming enough.

"You should kiss someone."

"Incorrect. Plus, Rahul—"

"Oh my god, here he go again talking about his vacation boy-friend," Linus said, playfully sticking a hand in Harrison's face.

"I'm just saying I've already done that."

"Yes, you made that very clear to me and all the un-smooched people," Linus said. "Also, I am going to kill you for getting me to start saying 'smooch.'"

"My impact!" Harrison said, grinning.

They sat for a while, scanning the crowd. Harrison felt so young all of a sudden. Not like a kid, but just brand-new, on the cusp of something, not there yet. To him, Linus seemed already there. Wherever 'there' was. Or at least closer. The far-off sounds of music were overpowered by a gospel choir making its way up the middle of the street, singing, stepping in time, and clapping. Each member had on a robe in a different color, making up a swaying, praising rainbow. The crowd parted as if this was expected. Maybe it was; Harrison didn't know. What he did know, however, from the one time there was a gospel choir at an assembly and the few times he'd gone with his mom when she sang in the church gospel choir at MLK Day events, was that people who didn't go to church treated gospel choirs like they were little baby Jesus Himself. Maybe it was because it felt so good—there was upbeat music and talking about Heaven and clapping; there was a way of expressing joy, and everything else, he guessed, that was bigger and bolder and Blacker than the way some people otherwise talked or sang. Gospel was another language. It was amazing to see Sheree up there singing. He could never make out her voice, but maybe that was better. She was a part of a body, and that whole body was more dynamic than anything else on Earth. He tried to conjure that sensation when he was, as always, in the chorus of a musical at school, but somehow it didn't feel the same. He wondered if he just wasn't the kind of person who could plug into that. But despite the fact that he would never shout or belt or march down the street in a rainbow of robes, he held on to the belief that it was inside him. Linus was swaying from side to side and clapping his hands together lightly. *Maybe Linus is a gospel-choir person,* Harrison thought. His body moved like it was operating on its own, but he wasn't engaged in the way that the people in the street were engaged. He wasn't calling out; he wasn't smiling or singing along. His eyes were unfocused. When he clapped his hands, his palms barely touched.

"This was a good day," Linus said. There was a distance to his voice that made Harrison nervous.

"There's so much more left! Oh! What about that guy in the choir?" Harrison pointed to a teenager with a mass of curly hair and a yellow robe.

"I'm not kissing a stranger," Linus said. But he kept watching the choir as they made their way past them and continued down the street, marching and singing and moving as one.

"You like him," Harrison teased.

Linus's tone was suddenly sharp. "I don't!"

He looked at Harrison then. *Sorry.*

"I just thought . . . It would be cute if you met a boy in a gospel choir, since you like gospel so much," Harrison said.

"I don't like gospel so much."

"You're literally always listening to it on your MP3 player."

"I just listen to one song."

"It's a gospel song, though," Harrison said. He had the

distinct sense that he was saying something wrong or rude, but he couldn't figure out what. It was disorienting. It really can't have been so disturbing for him to mention a crush on a boy to Linus, could it? They talked about this stuff. Was this part of the whole clean break? Linus would pack up his things and his MP3 player and his heart in the same box and move them all away from Harrison.

"It's a song from the concert they recorded at church," Linus said.

"What concert?"

"Remember, they made a CD?"

"I guess." Harrison did not know anything about this.

"Your mom is literally on the song. She's in the choir on the recording on the CD."

This was news. "*My* mom?" These are true facts: His mom was in the choir and had been for years. But beyond that? Breaking news. He did seem to recall, *possibly*, something about a concert years ago, but it really hadn't stuck out to him, and he didn't see why it would stick out to Linus. Also, who buys a CD?

Linus was watching the choir as it marched into the distance. The crowd filled the gap in their wake; the music from the DJ down the street rose back up. Ugh, "Press the Sky Higher." Again.

Harrison nudged Linus in the side. "It's your stupid song."

Linus turned suddenly. "It's not *my* song. It's my mom's song. I don't even know if she liked it. I'm trying to figure it out. Why are you being so weird about this?"

"About 'Press the Sky Higher'?!"

"What? No, about the gospel song on my MP3 player."

"I'm not talking about that. I'm talking about 'Press the Sky Higher.'" Harrison pointed up in the air at the sound waves helpfully. Linus tilted his ear up to listen.

"Oh."

"I'm sorry."

"No, I do like 'Press the Sky Higher.'"

"No, I mean, sorry for hitting a nerve," Harrison said. He had no idea what he'd waded into or how to get out. "Um. Your mom likes the gospel song?"

"Yeah."

Every time Linus talked about the period he spent living with Perfect Munro, his mood tanked. Harrison knew this. He wasn't sure if this gospel thing was part of it, but he couldn't afford the risk of asking more, as he normally would. Not on Ferris Day. He had to tread lightly. "Are you seeing your mom before you leave?" he said, absolutely failing to tread lightly.

"No," Linus said. "We haven't talked for a while. I guess I'll see her when I visit."

"When will you be coming back to visit?"

Linus was deflated. "I don't know."

And that was that. Harrison had asked his parents once about Linus's parents. He hadn't been able to find the words for his question, asking simply, "Are they okay?" This was after their divorce, after Linus moved from his mother's house to his dad's, after Mr. Munro and Linus stopped coming to church. There seemed to be a deep sadness that pervaded every mention of them, every part of that family, and Harrison didn't understand it. They seemed so similar to his own family. They'd all been friends once, from what he'd heard. They went to the same church. But something was wrong.

When he'd asked about them, his mother had been thoughtful. It wasn't that she didn't seem to know what to say, rather that she was trying to figure out which piece of it to release to Harrison. He hated that. He could see something was happening; it was affecting his friend. Why couldn't he know the truth?

Harrison's mom decided what to say. "I think that in big ways and in small ways, life has been hard for them."

"What does that mean?" he'd asked.

"It just . . . sometimes life is too much, baby. It just is." She'd gone on to tell him that they both loved Linus a lot and they were doing everything in their power to be good to him, but her assessment of life was the thing that hung in his head. "It just is." This was why he hated "Press the Sky Higher." The chorus said that hard times ain't coming round no more. But hard times don't just go away. They wait for you, out in that hazy future, down here on Earth. What was stopping his life from being too much? Especially when he was so powerless to change the things that mattered to him the most. Linus was leaving; Harrison could not reach the sky. It just was.

Linus spoke out of the blue, suddenly checked back in. "I am so glad you did this."

"Of course," Harrison said. It had been his turn to be in some far-off space.

"And it's not over," Linus said.

"Nope. We have the pool."

"And I'm so glad you got to meet Fab and Phil."

"I like them," Harrison offered. "Phil has so many opinions!" This sounded to Harrison like a read, but in truth he was impressed by anyone who was able to express themselves at an audible volume. Linus had that ability, too. Maybe that's why he and Phil were friends. Harrison could always depend on Linus to put words to what Harrison felt.

"Phil is a trip," Linus was saying.

"Is she going to be a sailor, or, like, what's the deal with her living on a boat?"

"Oh my god, that's my teacher!"

Harrison tried to determine who Linus was talking about. He wasn't sure how he'd figure out which one of them was a teacher. Nobody was carrying a smart board under their arm.

"Should I say something?"

"Which one is it?" Harrison asked, following Linus's gaze. Linus was already standing up behind his chair.

"It's Mr. Mirepoix. AP History."

Harrison did not tell Linus that this was not helpful information in locating said person.

"I'm going to go say hi," Linus said. "Are you okay if I leave you here for a second?"

Harrison nodded. Was it possible that Linus was nervous about this? Harrison wasn't looking forward to being left alone, and actually, as much as he'd heard about Mr. Mirepoix over the past two years, he kind of wanted to meet him. But then he thought better of it. He had no idea what to say to his own teachers on the rare occasions when they ran into each other outside of school. Some other person's teacher? Nightmare. He'd just sit on this folding chair and look for someone for Linus to smooch.

Linus approached the book table and then, oddly, picked up a book and started looking at it. He was stopping to shop? Linus was performing? Harrison stifled a giggle. There were times when Linus seemed far braver and more grounded and ready for the world than Harrison felt, and there were times like this that reminded Harrison of why they were friends. Linus could be awkward as hell. Look at that nerd dad, fidgeting with a copy of *Their Eyes Were Watching God*. Bless his heart.

Okay, but for real, where was this Mr. Mirepoix person? All he saw was—what would you call it?—regular Pride people milling around the table and filing past. Harrison decided that an older white man with a shaved head was Mr. Mirepoix. He was wearing a button-down. This all checked out. But the man with the button-down paid for his book and then left. Finally, Linus put his own book down and approached a young, dark-skinned Black man in a bright green crop top with shorts and shoes in the same color.

Linus tapped the man on the shoulder, the man turned, smiled widely, and called out Linus's name. This was Mr. Mirepoix? He was . . . well, he certainly didn't present himself like any teacher Harrison had, and that's all he was going to say about that, even in his head.

Harrison couldn't tear his gaze away, though. When Harrison saw guys in ads wearing crop tops, they usually had six-pack abs and the impossible bodies that all the fitness videos claimed came from just drinking a protein shake and doing a couple of crunches. The kinds of bodies Harrison saw piled high in human pyramids on the beach in those random Instagram accounts of happy strangers that he followed even though he knew that his life was nothing like theirs and probably never would be. But Mr. Mirepoix didn't look like those people. He didn't have a six-pack, for one. But, more importantly, Harrison thought, he looked comfortable. Yes, that was it. Mr. Mirepoix had looked totally at ease browsing for books, and he looked comfortable now, chatting it up with Linus. On one hand, this was perplexing. If somebody he knew from school caught him out in the street looking—okay, Harrison was going to say it—mighty good, he'd immediately evaporate from awkwardness. He would experience a total phase change and drift into the clouds, leaving behind a crop top and an apology for being. This did not seem to be happening. From what Harrison could tell, Mr. Mirepoix remained in a solid state.

On the other hand, though, Harrison wondered what there

was to feel awkward about. Everybody here—some dressed in more material, some dressed in less—had whole lives and people that they knew from all kinds of places, and it wasn't like Pride was some secret club with a password and a special knock. They were literally standing in the middle of Charles Street. The mayor was here. The jig was up.

Besides, a crop top was just practical. Who all wanted to be out here with a hot belly button? In this climate? Bayard Rustin didn't fight for our rights so we could stand around and be humid.

Harrison fiddled with the hem of his T-shirt. He bunched it up a little with his fingers. He pulled it together at the middle. Maybe he'd twist it up into a little knot like Corrine sometimes did when the family went to the beach. He was not so sure about this. Was there enough shirt to do it? What kind of knot? He didn't know any knots. This was why people joined the Boy Scouts.

He let his shirt drop back down to his waist. He plucked the fabric and fanned himself with it. It wasn't so hot yet. No need for all of that.

He felt a brisk tap on his shoulder. Fab and Phil must've returned. Phil seemed to be all business.

"So, the pool?" Harrison said, turning in his chair.

"What pool?"

Fab and Phil were nowhere to be seen. Instead, Harrison found the person with whom he shared two parents and a lifetime of annoyance, his archnemesis, the queen of space. It was Corrine, speaking in all italics, leaning her face into his. Harrison shrieked and jumped up, knocking over the chair.

Corrine jumped forward to meet him. "What are you doing here?" she asked, her voice syrupy.

Harrison shrieked again. "What are you doing here?" he cried, holding his hands up like he was in the middle a bank robbery.

"Look at you, hanging out at Pride, skipping work. Well, well, well." She righted the chair and sat on the edge of the table. She beckoned him forward with one finger. Corrine was clearly enjoying this. How did she find him? How was she here?

"Aren't you supposed to be getting your hair done?"

"I think it's very fascinating that you know my whole schedule for the day. Why is that, Harrison? Hmm?" She smirked. "My hair appointment isn't until two. Can you tell me what time it is, please?"

Harrison reached for the kitchen iPad in his tote bag but stopped short. Corrine's eyes followed his hand and then sprang back to look him in the face. There was a glint in her eye. What did she know and when did she know it?

"I don't have my phone," Harrison said.

"Oh? Where is it? Do you want me to use the app to find it?"

"No. It's fine."

"It's no trouble," Corrine said, pulling her phone from her pocket. "Let me just pull up Check In and see where my baby brother is."

Harrison ran through Aparna's schedule in his mind. He could hedge his bets and say that he left it at home and pray that Aparna was close enough for it to seem plausible. But it was already too complicated; he was thinking about ways to not get caught while actively in the process of being caught.

"Stop!" he said. "What do you want from me?"

Corrine puffed her chest out, haughty and dismissive. "*I* don't want anything from *you*." She stared at him then, a challenge. She was impossible! How could it be that his own sister had him feeling trapped in the middle of the street?

"Here's the rules," Corrine said suddenly. "No drinking."

"But I'm thirsty!"

"I mean alcohol, bighead!"

"Oh! Okay. Sure."

"Don't meet anybody," she said.

"When have I ever met anybody?"

"Well, today is not the day to spread your wings."

"Are you my chaperone now?"

"I have nine million better things to do," Corrine said. "I'm trying to enjoy my day. I'm trying to be at peace with the world. I'm not trying to hang out with you. This street festival ain't big enough fer the both uv us." She smiled, not unkindly.

"Definitely not," Harrison said. He let out a small chuckle.

"So whatever you're doing, wrap it up," she said, whipping a circle in the air with her finger. "You need to go right home after this."

Harrison nodded. He wondered if "after this" could technically be expanded to include this random visit to some pool. He thought to ask, but Corrine's expression said that wasn't going to go over well. It would be fine. She'd be getting her hair braided until late in the evening. They'd be home before she got home, and if she decided to tell on him, he could just say he was just walking back from work.

"Do Mom and Dad know you're here?" he asked.

"I am an adult. They don't track my whereabouts." Big talk from someone who was still on the Check In app just like everybody else.

"Why are *you* even at Pride?"

"Famously, I love Pride," Corrine said. "I've gone every year since I was fifteen."

"Wait, then why—"

"We're not talking about what I do. We're talking about what you're doing. Sneaking around all over creation. Not telling anyone what you're up do. What if something happened?"

"Nothing's going to happen."

"Exactly. Go home!" Corrine said. "Don't get into trouble. Don't have an adventure. I'm watching you." With that, she turned and plunged into the crowd, not looking back once before disappearing from view.

1:31 p.m.

"Is it okay that I said hi?" Linus asked Mr. Mirepoix. His teacher had been carrying a stack of books and a smoothie. Now he put them both down on the table and turned to Linus.

"Of course! I'm just browsing. Are you looking for anything in particular?"

"Not really. I just, actually, I came over to say hi. I, um, I'm glad to see you at Pride," Linus said.

"Well, you know. One must make an appearance. Have you been to Pride before?" Linus shook his head. "Oh! Congratulations. Okay, okay—I need to know your assessment."

"It's nice," Linus said.

"Excuse me?" he said. "Nice" was not allowed in Mr. Mirepoix's class. "Fine" was also forbidden. There was a whole list of words he kept on a poster on the wall that were the enemies of persuasive communication. The man had a whole dictionary of words that didn't mean anything.

"It's . . ." Linus searched for a word that would capture what he was feeling. An impossibility, despite the fact that Mr. Mirepoix always said that the words we need are always waiting for us to find them, if we put in the effort. Linus pushed himself—he rummaged through the pile of words in his head, trying them on against some internal version of himself like he was clothes-shopping. *The words are waiting for us,* Mr. Mirepoix had said. What would that mean if it were true? "It's dazzling," Linus said, finally.

Mr. Mirepoix leaned back, impressed. "Wow. Okay. Don't leave me hanging—tell me more. What's got you dazzled?"

Oh, great. A test. Why did he even bother to come over? Still, he was already rummaging through words. He might as well find some more.

"I just feel so free," Linus said. "Phil—Philadendra Truong?—she said, 'They made all this for me.' And I really felt that. I know it's for everybody, but it's, like, this thing that I feel inside, this thing that was a secret, is the thing that they're throwing a party for. I can't really . . . I can't describe it. It just feels like the opposite of lonely, if that makes sense."

"That's a wonderful way of thinking about it. I—" he stopped and chuckled ruefully. "It's been a minute since my first Pride. I hope it always feels like something for you. That reminds me of a Mary Oliver poem. I saw—" He scanned the table and plucked a book from a pile. "Here. Do you know Mary Oliver?"

"I don't."

"She was a lesbian poet. She wrote about nature a lot, but there was always a universal truthfulness. I don't know why it did, but . . ." Mr. Mirepoix flipped through the book. "What you said. Yes, okay. It reminded me of a line from a poem called 'Wild

Geese.' And . . ." He laughed at himself. "Well, now I'm feeling awkward. You didn't come over here for this. You're like, 'Why did I even say hi?'"

"I'm not!" Linus protested. He had been, but he wasn't thinking it anymore.

"Well, if you want, you should look this poem up. You can find it online, too. It's short. I actually—Linus, I highly recommend keeping this poem close as you go out into the world. It's about, well, sometimes it's about being overwhelmed, and there are other times I've felt it was about a family of choice. The kind you find at Pride, perhaps. And sometimes I just think it's about geese. . . . Well, you'll discover it. But the end, at the end, she writes"—Mr. Mirepoix held the book out so Linus could see while he read aloud—"'*Whoever you are, no matter how lonely / the world offers itself to your imagination.*'"

"Is that true?" Linus asked.

"What a wonderful question," Mr. Mirepoix said, which was not actually an answer.

"She really believed in herself."

"Do you think that's it, or do you think she was pushing at something true about the world? Don't answer. Sorry! You didn't come here for all . . ." Mr. Mirepoix laughed at himself. Linus stared back in awe. "Sorry! I got excited, and anyway, I hope that Pride expands to meet your imagination."

"I think it will," Linus said. He turned the words of the poem over in his head. "Oh! I wanted to tell you: We went to the

National Museum of African American History and Culture this morning."

"This morning? You've had a full day!"

"My best friend is doing a thing."

"Isn't it something?"

"It was amazing." Linus felt tears spring up in the corners of his eyes. He hadn't been anywhere near tears a second ago, and now here they were. He blinked them away, hoping Mr. Mirepoix wouldn't notice. Hoping the squint in the sunlight, the glint of a passing sequin would distract and disguise. He was suddenly aware of his body, how the disparate parts of it would give him away. The body tells the truth. "I just felt possible. Is that dumb? It was overwhelming. I couldn't handle it all. I got scared. All the history. I felt—I didn't even go to the history part. But . . . I don't know. I can't explain it." He was embarrassed to have failed to find the words. He realized in that moment how much he wanted Mr. Mirepoix to understand.

"The first time I went to that museum, I felt the top of the world open up above me. I cried, Linus. I did. This experience— life—can feel so small, and then to step into a space that feels big enough to hold you—as a Black person, as a Black young man. It is overwhelming."

"I want to go back. I want to move in," Linus said. He laughed. He was kidding . . . unless . . .

"I'll see if I can put together a field trip next year."

Linus shrunk. "That sounds great."

"Don't sound so enthused."

"My dad is moving us away. Tomorrow. So I'm not coming back to Harper."

"Oh. I'm sorry to hear that."

"But I really liked your class."

"I greatly enjoyed having you as a student, Linus. You're very thoughtful and very bright, and you always find the words. I hope you know that you're extraordinary."

In an ironic twist, Linus found himself speechless. Mr. Mirepoix fished some cash out of his shorts and paid the volunteer behind the book table.

"Here," Mr. Mirepoix said, handing Linus the book of poems. "A traveling gift."

"But I never gave you back your *Titanic* book."

"Yes, I have been stewing about that for months," Mr. Mirepoix said peevishly. Then he grinned. "It's fine. Enjoy it. Send me an email after you've read it, if you think of it. Or anytime. My door is always open. And watch the movie! Celine's song. Oh my god. She *shook the table*, Linus."

1:40 p.m.

"So we've been discussing," said Fab, appearing from behind a display rack of wigs that had captured Harrison's attention. She set Harrison in her sights. "We were wondering what your deal is."

"I don't know how to answer that."

"Are you mad? Are you okay? Are you sad? What's going on? Talk to us. I'm an empath."

"I'm fine."

"Do you want a tattoo?" Fab asked. Phil appeared beside her and held up a swatch of paper with an illustrated rainbow on it.

"Uh, sure," said Harrison. Phil grabbed his hand, doused it with a water bottle, and began vigorously pressing the temporary tattoo on it.

"Hold that there for two minutes," she said like she'd just given Harrison a booster shot.

"You seem like you're not really into all of this," said Fab, "and we were just curious."

"I'm into this!" Harrison cried, on the defense.

"You don't have to be," Fab said. She ran her fingers through one of the wigs on the stand. "We're just here to see my girlies on the dance team, and then we were planning to bounce. It's a thing. You come; you go. You know how it is." Harrison did not know how it was.

"You have a dance team?" he asked.

"No, she does not," Phil said.

"Don't put me out like this."

"She's obsessed with this dance team."

"See, now, why do we need to go down this road?" Fab exclaimed, laughing again. "You need to turn around. You got lost. You didn't listen to the directions, and now look at you."

"She follows this team around—"

"Lies! Untruths! Gossip!"

"—and runs a fan account for them."

"Which they appreciate."

"That remains to be seen."

"I support the arts," Fab said to Phil. "And it is a shame that you do not. Investigate that within yourself." They were grinning at each other widely; was it always like this between them? Linus's school days must have been like a vaudeville show.

"Anyway, they performed," said Fab. "They were great; I recorded it; they waved to me. Now we gotta go."

"My sea legs," Phil said.

"You don't have to come to the pool if you don't want to," Fab said to Harrison. "We just thought it would be fun. I mean, Pride can be a lot, and Linus said it was your first time and now you're over here moping around next to these struggle wigs."

"I'm not moping!"

Phil took Harrison's hand again and gingerly removed the backing from the tattoo. She looked at him with utter seriousness as she did it.

"Is Pride what you expected?" Phil asked.

"I don't know what I expected, actually."

"Is that a yes or a no, then?" Phil fanned Harrison's hand to dry it. The rainbow tat had a smattering of sparkles in it. "It's like this—this is a regular street, so you can treat it like a regular street and just walk through, or you can stop and enjoy yourself. They made all this for you. It's a lot of trouble to go through, and you ask yourself 'Why?' but then you think 'Oh, okay. I might as well.'"

"Be dazzled!" Fab added.

"Or something like it," Phil said. "It's very odd to me, the bigots who talk about how evil this lifestyle is. This? A food truck and a booth selling paper fans? We're just people. Basic. When I say that, though"—she glanced at Fab—"people think I'm being rude. I'm just saying. Sometimes you're just living. Even on Pride. It's allowed." Phil shrugged. She was still holding Harrison's hand, but she seemed to have forgotten this. It became an extension of her self-expression.

"I guess I could be dazzled," Harrison said.

"Don't do us any favors," Phil said. "Are you dazzled, or are you just living?"

"Are those my only choices?"

"I don't have time to haggle."

Harrison put aside the question of dazzlement for a moment—who could say? Who had the wherewithal to declare themselves dazzled? What he could say, however, was that he was surprised. He was surprised by how Black Pride was and how young and how open it felt. It was a street fair like any other. And on the surface, that was great, but there was a feeling—he hated it, but he couldn't help it—that this big street that was teeming with life was a preview of a world where everything was at a distance.

"I think I'm just tired," he said. "I thought I was going to have a different day with Linus, and when that didn't happen, I started feeling some kind of way. But I'm just going to not feel that way. No worries!"

Fab didn't look so convinced, but Phil nodded.

"Inside you are two wolves," Phil said. Harrison found this diagnosis alarming.

1:45 p.m.

Harrison had been left with a tattoo and instructions: Once
Linus was finished talking to Mr. Mirepoix, Harrison was to
bring him to meet up with Fab and Phil near one of the stages.
The dance team was on again. The two girls wound their way
into the crowd like a stream finding the ocean. Separating and
joining back together, they slipped through clusters of people
and slid past obstacles that wouldn't have been out of place on a
TV game show: the display rack of wigs, a ten-foot-tall blow-up
raven in a rainbow football jersey (where does one shop for
that?), the hand-fan booth, a cell-phone company's wooden
spinning prize wheel, a cupcake truck decked out in a mosaic
of pink and yellow glimmering shards of mylar. Soon they were
out of his sight, assumed by the crowd—expanded and broken
down into parts: the flash of magenta in Fab's hair, the white of
Phil's hat. They were a part of the collage. With Linus still occupied at the book table with Mr. Mirepoix, Harrison let himself
feel a little out of sorts despite what he'd vowed to Fab and Phil.
Let's just acknowledge: He hadn't thought it would be this hard.
Linus seemed to be having a blast, but Harrison feared fading

for good into this larger collage of far more shiny and appealing experiences and people and things.

He reminded himself that the overall plan was to show Linus a memorable time. He reminded himself that the goal was to loom large in Linus's memory, like a ten-foot queer raven or a rack of struggle wigs. But now Harrison worried that he'd lost his chance. There were too many wigs on this rack, as it were. He was the main wig! He was the . . . the whatever you call different hairstyles. He was the Tracy Turnblad hair in *Hairspray*. He was the Elsa wig in *Frozen*. He was . . . so distracted thinking about musicals with impressive hair designs that he didn't realize someone was trying to get his attention from across the street.

A white guy, maybe college-aged, with shaggy brown hair that fell into his face haphazardly like he'd come to a stop after a sprint, was waving at him and smiling. Okay . . . Harrison waved back and offered what he told himself was a smile, but what he knew, in his heart, looked pained at best. One thing he hadn't yet worked out was how to negotiate his desire to be a part of the gay happenings with his deep need to not be seen, acknowledged, or spoken to. Harrison wasn't a wallflower, heaven forfend! But in this decidedly grown-up, decidedly real-world environment, he realized that he didn't know his lines. He didn't know if he even had lines.

The shaggy-hair guy—less a Chalamet situation and more a Harry Styles after spending time on a desert island—was making his way over to Harrison, zipping and zopping through the crowd while contorting his body to keep from spilling a beer. He was so pumped to see Harrison, which was odd because he was a stranger. Maybe this was how queer people met in the real world. Enthusiastic consent involves enthusiasm, he reasoned.

"Jamal! Oh my god, man! What are you doing here?" The guy was right in front of Harrison now. He smelled incredibly good—not quite cologne-y, more like a minty lotion. "It's me," the guy said without bothering to elaborate. Harrison didn't respond. What was there to say? It was him.

The shaggy-haired boy threw an arm around Harrison; God, he smelled amazing. Okay, focus. What was happening? The guy was yelling at a friend of his—also white, slicked-back red hair, bright white polo, blue shorts—across the street. The friend looked like the main character in a movie about racing sailboats around the world.

"Jamal," Shaggy Hair said to Harrison again, incorrectly. "Boo, I am so excited to see you! I thought you'd never come out. You look so good!" He held Harrison at arm's length. "Look at this body, man!" He patted Harrison on his chest. This was a nightmare. The redhead had joined them. He winked at Harrison. Who were these people? The shaggy guy piped up. "This is Jamal, my good buddy from high school. I've told you about him," he said to the redhead. Oh! He thought Harrison was someone else. This was getting dangerously close to hijinks. This was the kind of thing that would definitely happen to Aparna. He wanted to text her immediately. And then, like an alarm had gone off, Linus appeared next to Harrison. And there they were, a trio of guys, all gathered around Fake Jamal, high school graduate.

"I'm sorry, I think—" Harrison started.

"Who're your friends?" Linus asked.

"They're not—"

The shaggy-hair guy grabbed Linus's arm. "Jamal and I were, like, so close. We haven't seen each other in *years*, Jamal! Oh my god! I can't believe this." He half-laughed and rolled his eyes. "I really thought you were one of those guys who would just make out with me at parties but never, like, actually come out. Oh my god, don't tell me you have a girlfriend or something here."

"No," Linus said. "Jamal does not have a girlfriend." Linus stole a glance at Harrison.

What are you doing? Harrison shot back with his tight smile.

Linus raised his eyebrows quickly and replied, *Hijinks* before turning back to the shaggy-haired guy.

"Oh, good. Okay. I mean, whatever; do you. I'm just saying. I'm sorry! I'm being so rude. I'm Triple Belk!" He shook Linus's hand and gestured to the redhead. "And this is my friend. Like, actual friend. Not a boyfriend."

The redhead stuck his hand out to Harrison. "Fitzhugh Quatch," he said, before adding conspiratorially, "no relation." No relation to whom?

Linus nudged Harrison. Harrison stuck out his hand and grabbed Fitzhugh's. "Uh, Jamal. And this is my friend—"

Linus interjected and stuck out his own hand. "Dizzy Gillespie," Linus said. "No relation."

"Oh," said Fitzhugh with a laugh. "I was about to ask!" What were these clowns talking about?

"I get that all the time," Linus was saying. He was smiling. No, grinning. His lanky body had angled itself so that one hip jutted out, and as he spoke, he looked up through his locks. This dizzy kid was flirting. Where did this come from?

"What've you been up to since high school, man?" Triple asked.

"I don't know," Harrison replied. "Um, working."

"No school?"

"No. I, uh, I dropped out. Because . . . I'm on Broadway."

"Oh my god!" Fitzhugh cried.

"Congrats, man, that's amazing. Wait, can you sing?" Triple cocked his head.

"Yes," Harrison said, literally and physically sticking his neck out.

"He's so good at singing! Sing for us!" Linus clapped his hands gleefully. "Do one of your numbers from the show!" He was looking right at Harrison and loving every minute of this. "Come on, *Jamal*! It's Pride!"

"Yeah! It's Pride!" Triple squeezed Harrison's shoulder with the arm that was still wrapped around him.

"I'd love to sing. But I can't. Because of contracts."

"Ohhh, yes, contracts," Linus said.

"Fair, fair!" Triple said, holding his hands up like he'd been caught sneaking a cookie. He chuckled to himself and drooped his head a little. It's possible that he was a little drunk. Harrison really had no idea. "I can't believe it's you, Jamal," he said. "Oh! Did you see Mr. Mirepoix?!"

"You know Mr. Mirepoix?" Linus asked.

"Sorry—that was a teacher at our school," Triple said. Linus looked at Triple more closely, trying to figure out if he recognized him. Triple didn't seem to notice. "I wonder if Mr. Mirepoix has a boyfriend," Triple said. Then he mumbled, "So hot."

"He wasn't with anybody," Linus offered.

"That's pretty weird. Wonder why. Maybe he sucks in real life." Triple shrugged. His focus had drifted from Harrison and was now somewhere between the raven and the wigs. "Oh! Jamal! I have a boyfriend now! I'll show you a picture! Actually, hold on, I should text him back. He's being so annoying." Triple laughed and then stopped, suddenly serious. He turned to Harrison but looked at some distant point over Harrison's shoulder. "I didn't think you wanted to be friends with me after high school. I thought you were, like, over me." His voice was hazy, its target indistinct. He looked back at Harrison. "I didn't want to be annoying."

Harrison was surprised at how much he was rooting for Triple and some guy named Jamal, who apparently looked like

Harrison. (Although, one never knows with these kinds of mix-ups. His first year at Plowshares, he was constantly called the name of the other Black boy in his class despite the fact that the other boy, Pharaoh, had white hair. White.) Wherever Jamal was, he hoped he could somehow feel how much Triple missed him. Harrison smiled at the shaggy-haired, slightly drunk guy. Triple smiled back. Then he started leaning forward like he was tipping over and came to rest with his forehead on Harrison's shoulder. He stayed like that, the two of them forming the letter *A*, with the bridge in the middle created by Triple's outstretched arms as he rapidly texted.

Fitzhugh brushed against Linus's shoulder and pointed to his hand. "You always bring a book to Pride?"

Linus looked stricken and then held up his hand, which was indeed holding a slim book, which Harrison hadn't noticed before. Was he going to do a reading at the pool? Was that part of his grand new plan, too? Linus laughed (a little too hard, if you asked Harrison).

"Yeah, in case I get bored," he said.

"Is that Mary Oliver?" Fitzhugh snatched the book from Linus and pressed it to his chest. "*Why I Wake Early* is my BIBLE!"

"What's the reason?" Harrison asked.

"What?"

"For waking early?"

"It's a collection. She was a lesbian poet. She lived this super-simple, beautiful life, and every thought she had was brilliant," said Fitzhugh. "I took this Mid-Century Poetry elective this year, just random, just to fill in the space, and I fell completely in love. She'd, like, walk for hours every day, just watching and writing and walking."

"I just know this one poem, 'Geese'-something," Linus said.

Fitzhugh beamed. "'*Whoever you are, no matter how lonely . . .*'"

"'*The world offers itself to your imagination*'*!*" Linus said, finishing his sentence excitedly.

"Do you know 'The Summer Day'?" Fitzhugh asked. Linus shook his head. "Ooh! You're in for a treat." Fitzhugh pressed the book into Linus's chest as if he could put the poems directly into his heart. It remained there.

"Where do you go to school?" Harrison asked, breaking the spell.

"Clemson. I'm a junior."

"South Carolina?" Linus said.

Fitzhugh nodded as he flipped through the book.

"I'm about to move down there," Linus said.

"Sweet, dude. Are you transferring?"

"Sort of. I'm staying with some folks in Charleston."

"Oh! That's so far away from me. I've actually never been."

Linus's shoulders inched up to his ears. Harrison could tell he was getting anxious. Whatever magic Dizzy possessed was threatening to ebb away. Fitzhugh had continued talking. "Maybe I should visit, though. I hear it's cute. Clemson is kind of a small town, and, like, I'm not really a partier, present appearances notwithstanding. I just go to school and then go home to Jersey at breaks."

"You're not from here?" Harrison asked.

"Naw. I'm just visiting. My sister Isobel goes to Towson. She just came out, and I want to support." Fitzhugh pointed and waved at a young woman in acid-washed overalls with rolled-up cuffs that revealed sharply pointed kitten heels. She sported red pigtails and was standing next to a mobile petting zoo, holding an impossibly small pig. She was giving *Anne of Green Gossip Girl* realness, and Harrison and Linus both gasped upon taking her in. I mean, how many times in life is one surprised by a glamorous person's pig? Fitzhugh beckoned her over, and she strode up next to him. She pointed at the pig in her hand.

"Can you believe this." She spoke with the kind of matter-of-fact inflection that leads one to believe that she could, in fact, believe this.

"This is Isobel," Fitzhugh said. "She's bi. We're partying."

She raised the pig's foot and made it wave to Harrison and Linus. "Isobel Quatch. No relation," she added apologetically.

"I thought you were sister and brother," Linus said.

"We are," Isobel said. "Oh! I mean no relation to *the* Quatches. We get it all the time." Did they? These Quatches had a really skewed understanding of how well-known their name was.

"Excuse me, can we have the pig back?" A volunteer in a purple T-shirt was hovering over Isobel.

"I am *so* sorry!" She kissed the pig on the snout and returned it to the volunteer. Isobel leaned into the group. "I thought I would adopt it. Can't you see me with a pig?"

"Can we not get kicked out of another apartment, Isobel?" Triple asked. He was somehow still texting, but he'd flipped himself around and was now leaning against Harrison.

"Our lease doesn't say anything about pigs!" she cried.

"It says no pets."

"Pigs are very intelligent; this would be more of a roommate. What's going on with brunch?"

"He says he's almost to the front of the line," Triple said. He craned his neck around and looked up at Harrison. "My boyfriend is waiting in line at Miss Shirley's."

"He's been waiting this whole time?"

"Yeah. Someone had to. They don't take reservations. Do you want him to add two more seats?" Triple asked Harrison.

"Don't tell him to do that," Fitzhugh said. "I'm sorry. I don't want to be rude, but it will take so much longer if we change the number in our party." He looked at Linus directly. "I feel so rude. I'm sorry. If I had my druthers, I'd be having a conversation about Mary Oliver rather than playing second fiddle to my kid sister, the Muppet."

"I heard that!" Isobel said. Somehow she had procured a silver wig.

"It's fine," Linus said, taking the book back. "It's her day. It's good of you to be such a good ally, though." His shoulders were sky-high again.

Isobel whipped her silver bob around. "Fitz is not an ally. He's so mean to me all the time. If he wasn't gay, it would be homophobic. I'd call the attorney general."

"I'm not mean. And I'm not really out at school, but you know." Fitzhugh nudged Linus as if Linus somehow did know about a) college, b) the South, c) life in general.

"Oh, totally!" Linus lied, his shoulders floating down from his ears like feathers.

Triple let out a groan and stood up. "We are apparently being 'rude' to my boyfriend and 'leaving him out of the fun.' So we have to go," he said.

"What fun?" Isobel said. "They took my pig! Worst coming-out party ever."

Fitzhugh leaned into Linus. "Give me your number. We can meet up afterward!"

Linus flicked a glance at Harrison that was probably mostly annoyance with a touch of panic. "I don't have my phone on me," Linus said.

"Ha, the madness of Pride, right?"

Isobel said, "Tell them to come to the party!"

"The car is here!" Triple called. He separated from Harrison and grabbed him by the shoulders. "It's been amazing seeing you, Jamal. Come to the party later."

"What party?"

Fitzhugh answered Harrison's question by continuing to address only Linus. "It's a Pride tea dance at this new lounge called the Evergreens. So chic. One of those restored old row homes. And they have this roof-deck that's breathtaking. A friend rented it out. So don't tell a bunch of people. But you can come."

"*My* friend rented it out," Isobel said.

"Isobel's friend."

"I met them at jury duty," she said. "Can you believe it. By the way, we acquitted."

"Come to the party? We'll be there, what, four-ish?"

"That's early for a party, isn't it?" Harrison said.

"It's a *tea dance*," Isobel said, as if that cleared anything up.

"We'll be there," Linus told Fitzhugh.

Isobel swept around her brother and grabbed Harrison and Linus by the hands. "I'm so sorry I didn't learn your names. But I look forward to finding them out. If not tonight, then in another life." She smiled meaningfully and let go. The siblings started walking away, following Triple, who was already halfway down the block and now arguing into his phone.

"See you later!" Linus called. He waved vigorously, like he was an old-timey person going down to the docks to see the *Titanic* set sail. He waved for so long that Harrison felt compelled to lift his hand and wave, too. That was, until the Quatches (not *the* Quatches) and Triple Belk got to the corner, checked the phone for the rideshare information, and approached a familiar blue (or was it gray?) car that was driven by Wallingford Munro, Linus's dad. Harrison gasped.

"Turn around!" he whispered to Linus, grabbing him by the shoulders and helping him on his way. Linus's dad was talking with Triple; Isobel had already gotten into the back seat. None of them seemed to be looking at Linus or Harrison.

"Put on a wig!" Harrison exclaimed, handing one of the display wigs to Linus and taking a rainbow-streaked one for himself.

"What are you doing?" Linus said. He turned back to look at the group and then let out a shriek and turned back around. "That's my dad!"

"I know! Stop acting suspicious!"

Linus shoved a long blonde wig on his head and held his breath. Harrison fixed some of the curls on it that had fallen inelegantly. They stood there for a long while, just in case. Not speaking, not moving, just staring forward in a pair of struggle wigs. Inconspicuous.

STAGE MANAGER'S REPORT #5

SM: Aparna Aiyar
CAST: Harrison M., Linus M., Aparna A., Aparna R.
PERFORMANCE NOTES: Happy closing!
STAGE MANAGER'S NOTES:

When I finally told Cool Aparna about what my mission was for the day and swore her to secrecy, she was very excited and then very disappointed to learn that my role would be over in minutes as soon as I dropped off Harrison's backpack. I was suddenly aware that we were hanging out. I can't say that I ever had a desire to hang out with Cool Aparna. But I didn't hate it.

"You never stop stage-managing, do you?" she said. "Do you remember during *Fiddler,* when you had to hook up my harness and then, like, throw me out the doors? You were, like, running the whole show while also making sure I didn't die from falling off the bungee fitness cords we were using. It was so serious! You wouldn't even let me talk."

"Why don't you understand that you can't talk when you're onstage."

"Talking onstage is literally what acting is," she said. She was technically correct, which was annoying and amusing in equal measure. "Okay!" she cried. She stopped walking on a street corner and pulled me to stop, too. "I get what you're saying, but you have got to see it from my side. I know you're all about that hiding-in-a-wardrobe-onstage life, but I think you would really like being in the spotlight."

"That is the opposite of what I would like," I said. She was definitely going to try to help me. I thought I'd escaped, but here we were again. I pulled out my phone. I needed to be at Harrison's in seven minutes;

more time than it would take to walk. I cursed myself for letting the performance get hijacked.

"Just, okay—" She pulled her phone out and put it on the ground, which didn't seem practical in the middle of Baltimore or anywhere. "Just do something for me. I want you to stand on this corner and I want you to sing a song. Like, just one verse. I want you to feel how it feels."

"I'm never going to do that," I said, incorrectly.

"It's amazing. I do it all the time. People love street entertainment! Sometimes people will give you money if you have a hat or something, but really it's just about—"

"Attention," I said.

"No. It's just about hearing your voice in the world. Or . . . we could do a protest chant together. Would you rather do that?"

"I have to go; can we please drop this?" I said.

"I will not drive you to Harrison's until you do this for me. Please?" She fiddled with her phone and "Press the Sky Higher" came on. She looked at me with wildness in her eyes. I had run out of time to debate. So I chose the only option available to me. On a random street corner a block from the library, I started to sing.

"LOUDER!" she called. She clapped her hands with glee and stood up.

I sang only marginally louder, but it was apparently all that Cool Aparna needed. She stuck her arms out and started spinning in a circle. Horribly, a random woman stopped to listen to me. Cool Aparna made a "keep going" motion. I kept going.

"We been down and we been broken, but we're pushing up and over . . . Something-something coming back no more . . ."

We got to the rap break and instead of freeing me from my torture, she jumped in and took the verse.

"And we back!" she rapped. "And we back and we back and we Black!" Just two Indian girls rapping on the street corner. Nothing to see here.

Finally, the song ended.

The random woman was still there, watching us. She spoke up. "Not great!" she said. Then she pointed at Cool Aparna. "Pretty good!" And she walked away.

"How do you feel?!" Cool Aparna asked.

"I don't want to burst your bubble, but that was the worst experience I've ever had."

"Okay, well, think about it."

We reached her car at last, climbed in, lowered the roof, and were off. She was buzzing from the terrible concert we gave. She didn't even turn the radio on. I fidgeted with the Moon Sounds gift set she'd purchased.

"Are you going back to work at the Potions at the Gallery?" she asked out of nowhere.

"Oh. I don't think so. It was just for the holidays."

"That manager woman was obsessed with you."

"I wouldn't say obsessed," I replied.

"She took the time out from arresting me to tell you how much she values you. You're not just useful; you have your own magnetism that pulls people to you." I started to interrupt, but she continued. "I mean, only one of us is welcome back in the store, so."

"That's very nice."

"I'm just saying."

We pulled up outside of Harrison's house with a minute to spare before 2 p.m. I didn't immediately jump out. We just sat there for a beat.

"The other thing about the wardrobe, though," she said, finally, "is that there was this shaft of light that came in through the slit in the door and usually hit your face and it was amazing to watch. Your concentration was so intense. It was so clear you knew everything that was happening outside of the wardrobe and all over the theater and everything that was going to happen and . . . everything. I know I'm probably going to get a great part in *Ragtime* next year, but honestly, *Fiddler* was my favorite show because I got to watch you do your thing every night and it was so cool. And I was excited to see you today because I was like, 'Oh, maybe I get to experience that again.' So, thanks. Just saying. While you're noticing everything about everybody, there are people who are noticing you. Not just me. But also me."

Once again, I didn't know what to say, so I just said, "Thanks, Aparna."

Aparna smiled.

"Okay, well. I'm around all summer," she said.

I nodded. "Cool."

"I'll see you later, then," Aparna said.

I got out of the car and started up Harrison's stairs. I stopped and turned. "Aparna! Thanks again. This was fun."

Aparna waved and drove off. I turned back to Harrison's door and pulled out my phone to look up the code, and it's then that I realized that at this performance, I was only appearing as myself: the backpack playing the role of Linus Munro and Harrison Meredith was still in Aparna's car, going slightly below the speed limit down the street and disappearing around a corner.

1:59 p.m.

The thing was, Fab and Phil's definition of walking distance was, frankly, out of touch with reality. After reuniting, returning their wigs to the struggle factory, and leaving Pride, they'd walked twenty minutes just to get to the thrift store. Who could say how far away this pool was. Maybe This Time, the thrift store, was tucked away in the neighborhood north of Harrison's home, sandwiched between a liquor store and a carryout place. The name had been painted in an elaborate mural that covered most of the glass of the front window. There were little clear portholes in the mural that let passersby window-shop.

"You're going to love this place," Linus told Harrison. "It's where I got this shirt, actually."

"This is the place where Mazz Reber works?" Harrison asked.

"Yeah!" Linus said brightly.

"We don't have time to socialize," Phil warned as they walked in. "We're on a schedule." *Oh, a schedule. Fascinating,* Harrison thought.

Maybe This Time was one of those stores that seemed to be organized by the principle "It's around here somewhere." With clothes and stray mannequin parts in bins and in piles, on shelves and on hangers, and even spilling out of an old piano, it looked like a cross between the costume closet at school and someone's grandparent's attic. It also looked just like Harrison's bedroom. This he understood. There was R&B music playing from . . . somewhere. Maybe it was like at amusement parks, where the speakers are hidden inside rocks. Harrison lifted up a fifties-style ball gown to check it for an aux cord. None of the clothes were organized by gender or size. As best Harrison could tell, the different zones of the store were just labeled by "vibe." He was standing currently in "Show up and show out," Linus was wandering over to "Zoom-conference-call realness," while Phil and Fab made their way to "Touch this skin, darling."

Harrison picked up a sequined tuxedo jacket with short sleeves and held it against his chest.

"Try it on," Linus called over a pile of jeans labeled "Stone-washed butch blues." Linus had found a cowboy hat and placed it on his head. He was twirling a feather boa around in the air. Harrison briefly entertained the fantasy of wearing the jacket to the pool, giving Aquatic Game Show Host realness. But he put it out of his mind. He would never. *"Try it on!"* Linus implored.

Fine. Harrison put his tote bag down and slid into the jacket. It was snug but not too tight, and the short sleeves cupped his arms perfectly.

"Baby boy," Linus called with a hoot, "that is you!"

"I have never worn anything that was less me," Harrison replied.

"You don't know," Linus said. "I think you should get it. My treat."

Harrison rolled his eyes.

Linus called over his shoulder. "Yo, Mazz, come look." Oh, good. An audience.

Mazz Reber poked their head around a rack labeled "Taking the bus to Chromatica." They had a low fade with lines shaved into it on the sides. It looked like they'd put some colored temporary dye in to accentuate some of the lines, and Harrison was immediately obsessed with the look. There was a surety to Mazz, like they were drawn in ink. They wore a white tank top that stood in both contrast and concert with their dark ebony skin tone. The tank top had a picture of a brick on it and the words HAPPY PRIDE.

"Oh, wow," Mazz said. "People sleep on that jacket, but it is a real find. Harrison, you need to get it."

"Oh, he's getting it," Linus said. "Don't you worry."

Mazz looked at Harrison again; it felt like they were sizing him up, and Harrison looked away, uncomfortable. Suddenly he was aware again of being in the presence of someone who was around Linus all day long. Maybe they knew a different side of him. Maybe they were his best friend also.

"You look comfortable," Mazz said. "That's it. I pass by that jacket all the time, and I keep thinking, 'What's the context?

What's it for?' I'm really obsessed with it. I have no idea why. But maybe it's not about where you'd wear it, but just how you feel. You should buy it."

Harrison briefly entertained the fantasy of coming down to next week's movie night in a sequined short-sleeved dinner jacket and gym shorts. Announcing to his family, "I'm comfortable!" This shop was dangerous.

Mazz tugged at Linus's sleeve. "You're wearing my shirt. You look great."

"Yeah, I thought I'd do you a favor."

"Oh, this is a favor for me?" Mazz laughed.

Fab slid through a cluster of barrels. "Mazz, we need towels. Do you have any towels? We're going to the pool."

"Sort of," Mazz replied. They disappeared into the back of the store. Harrison wondered what a "sort-of towel" was. He put the jacket back down on a pile and walked to the front of the store. He rummaged through a bin of T-shirts labeled "Sorry, not sorry—I kept these after the breakup." Some shirts had band names, others had political slogans, others illustrations. He found one that had the poster art for *Little Shop of Horrors* on it and let out a delighted little gasp. It wasn't his size, but . . . he held it against himself: Was this a good crop-top candidate? Or did shirts have to be made as crop tops? He didn't know, and he didn't want to find out the hard way. Harrison decided he was not ready for the crop-top aesthetic, whatever that meant. He put it back down.

The problem was that, in general, he didn't know what he was trying to communicate with a message tee, if anything. Maybe he was just like his father—a person wearing person clothes, never broadcasting a message. He noticed a cluster of mannequins positioned by one of the portholes in the front window. They were all dressed up in different Pride-themed outfits: a drag-queen mannequin, a mannequin in the trans-flag colors—pink, blue, and white—a shirtless mannequin in a harness and a leather jacket, and in the corner, a mannequin in a simple T-shirt with a familiar face on it. The text on the T-shirt said BAYARD. It was the man whose picture he saw in the museum—the Black, gay Civil Rights leader. This felt like something. It felt like a sign at the very least. The shirt looked like it was his size. He stepped up to the platform and started taking the shirt off the mannequin before realizing what he was doing. Was this even allowed? From the looks of the store, basically anything was allowed, but he wasn't sure. He stopped, the shirt bunched over one of the mannequin's shoulders. He searched in the back for a sight of Mazz but didn't see them. Over in the corner, Fab and Phil were testing out enormous sun hats. Linus caught his eye and trotted over.

"You find something?" Linus asked.

"Do you think Mazz will let me try this on?"

Linus hopped up on the platform next to Harrison and wrangled the shirt off the mannequin. He inspected it.

"You know who this is?" Harrison asked.

"I was going to ask you the same thing."

"I read about him at the museum today."

"Look at you, reading at a museum."

"I wanted to tell you about it," Harrison said. He paused before adding, "I'm sorry it was weird. I wanted you to have a good time."

"I had an amazing time. For real. I just... I don't know. I freaked out because the past seemed so big all of a sudden. It wasn't about you. But I'm glad you found out about Bayard Rustin."

"I wanted to know more. When we get our phones back, he's the first thing I'm going to google."

Linus laughed. "You know, it is so rude that I'm standing right here, the center of all information, and you're talking about 'I'm gonna google him.'"

"You're so salty all the time," Harrison said. "Fine, you want to tell me about him, feel free."

"You don't never listen, though."

"I'm listening now."

"Mm-hmm." Linus said. He jumped down off the platform. "I'll tell you about him at the pool. Come on, we gotta get some trunks or shorts or something."

Linus headed over to meet Fab and Phil. Harrison lingered on the platform among the mannequins. He examined the shirt. Maybe he would buy it. Maybe this did feel like him.

A movement by the window caught his eye. The sun-drenched outline of a familiar twist out passing by one of the portholes. Corrine! Why did he have the worst luck? Why was she everywhere? He froze, trying to blend in with his other manne-quin siblings and waiting until she passed.

"That was close," he said to the mannequin in the harness.

Harrison hopped off the platform and went to retrieve his tote bag from the pile. Linus screamed suddenly. Harrison hitched himself up to see Linus and then followed his gaze to the window. Corrine had doubled back and was peering in another porthole. She rapped on the glass.

"GO HOME," she said to Linus. Harrison crawled behind a bin labeled "But what would your Mothra say?!" and snuck around the back to watch. Fab, Phil, and Mazz crowded around Linus and stared back at Corrine.

"Who is that person?" Mazz said.

"Harrison's sister. Don't act suspicious."

Fab and Mazz froze with the garments they had in their hands. Phil removed her sun hat solemnly. Corrine pulled out her cell phone and held it up to the window. Linus waved his hands and said "No!" loudly. Corrine pointed at Linus and mouthed *home*. He nodded quickly.

"And tell Harrison!" Corrine shouted. "I know he's hiding in there!" Corrine's head dropped out of the porthole, and the group watched her shadow pass by the mural window. Nobody moved.

"I love her," Phil said.

"Do you think she's going to tell?" Linus asked Harrison, who was still cowering in the section marked "dadcore." He had found the source of all his ire.

"I think she's just being annoying," Harrison said.

"Are you not supposed to be out?" Mazz asked.

"We're free people who can do what we want," Linus said. "And also, technically, no. But we're going to the pool cuz it's my last day and what's she or anybody else going to do about it?"

Bold words from the boy who once told Harrison, "I think I'm more afraid of pissing off your sister than I am of pissing off my own father." Then again, Corrine didn't have the power to take him to South Carolina, so maybe he was just realizing the truth of the world. Harrison watched Linus and Mazz playfully folding shirts at a table called "Straight drag for your uncle's third wedding." *Maybe this doesn't have anything to do with Corrine,* he thought. Maybe it also didn't have anything to do with it being Linus's last day, despite what he had said. These were their last hours together, and Harrison was still discovering new parts of his friend.

Phil handed Harrison a pair of swimming trunks.

"These will work. I can go shorter. Just let me know."

Harrison held them up to his waist. They were bright red with a white stripe down each side. They went to the middle of his thigh, it looked like. Not too short. Not quite Pop-level. Linus was holding a pair that was green with palm trees all over. They were longer and cheerfully ugly. Dad status secured.

"Whatever. Let's go," Linus said. He turned to Mazz. "You approve?"

"Absolutely not," Mazz said.

"Are you coming with us?" Harrison asked.

"I told my manager I'd ring you all up first, but then, yes. I'm off."

"Let's go!" Linus cried, whipping his trunks around his head.

After paying, Harrison stuffed his trunks and the Bayard shirt and Linus's trunks and Linus's book and something that purported to be a towel but looked more like a quilt into his tote bag. It was bulging, a huge pillow bouncing against his thigh as they walked (twenty more minutes!), up the street, through a playground, and over a footbridge into Druid Hill Park en route to the pool.

🚃 🚃 🚃

Stuffed at the bottom of the tote, under a tangle of fabric, was the kitchen iPad. As the group, now ballooned to five people, walked into the pool, the vibrations of a series of texts coming into the iPad were too muffled for Harrison to hear or feel. If he had noticed them, he would have discovered they were all from Aparna.

Aparna: Hi. Don't worry. Small problem, though.

Aparna: Actually, a medium problem.

Aparna: Do you have a school directory at your house, and if so, where is it? I need to let myself in to get it.

Aparna: Never mind. I'm going to my house to get mine.

Aparna: I'm just going to come meet you. You have to call me. Big problem.

2:30 p.m.

"This?" Phil said. "Amusement park."

They'd arrived at the pool, which was not just "the" pool, singular, but a whole complex of water features that took up a plot of land the size of a city block. It was every pool. If it had a label from the thrift store it would have been "H2Oh My God." There was a kiddie pool, a lap pool, a pool with jets of water shooting out of it, a spot for aqua basketball, and then a huge central pool with a nest of slides in the middle. There was a DJ playing at the back of a field off to the side and a dance floor set up in front. Two people were selling sodas, ice cream, and hot dogs at a folding table. You could, if you wanted, never leave this place for the entire day. *This is a public pool, free for all, but also,* Harrison thought as he took it all in, *this is like a mini Six Flags Over Baltimore.*

Phil and Harrison set out to find a place to lay their stuff down as Linus, Fab, and Mazz went to change. The place was jumping. People on the dance floor, people on the decks, kids and adults and families and teens in each of the pools. And everywhere, the raucous white noise of delighted squeals and splashes and distant music. They chose a spot at the base of a hill, next to the main pool. Harrison began tugging on the tote bag to get the towel/ blanket out.

"You know what I don't get," Phil said, not waiting for an answer. "You gotta put your entire life on your back when you go to the pool. It's like you're packing for the Oregon Trail. Look at this. Look at your life. Think about this concept, Harrison: We go to the one place where you're allowed to wear as little as legally possible; we need nothing! And in response, what do we do? Load ourselves up like we're fleeing the apocalypse." She had nestled in the grass, leaning back on her elbows. Harrison continued to wrestle with his tote bag. Phil persisted, "Look at this bag! You've got shirts and blankets and a flashlight and road flares and six cans of tuna." A child shrieked as he cannonballed into the pool. "I'm just kidding," Phil said.

Harrison gave the bag one more tug, and the blanket came spilling out. He fell backward. Phil picked up Linus's book from the spent bag.

"The beach is even worse," she said. "My parents pack a small library and an entire set of patio furniture just so they can fall asleep. Why are we doing this? All you need is your body."

With one arm, she whipped off her jersey, and with it her hat and sunglasses, like she was doing a quick change in a production of *Cinderella*. She had a sports bra on underneath. She stuck her sunglasses back on her face.

She stood up. She dropped a wallet and a phone attached to a chain on the blanket.

"All right," Phil said.

She strode toward the lap pool, still in her shorts, sat on the edge, and slid in.

Mazz lay on the blanket, flipping through Linus's poetry book and giving impromptu readings aloud. Their voice was gravelly but bright, and it made the simple poems seem, to Harrison, even more curious. Like at the heart of each one about rivers and crabs and angels was wonder. Harrison wasn't really into poems if they weren't accompanied by music, riffing, and a chorus, but something about Mazz's reading made him want to listen for as long as they wanted to read. The Six Flags Over Baltimore experience apparently also included a live show.

Phil strolled over from the lap pool, dripping water. She snuck up behind Fab and shook the water out of her hair, dousing Fab like a human sprinkler. Fab shrieked, turned, and grabbed Phil around the knees, taking her down.

"You brute!" Fab cried.

"I'm helping," Phil said. She looked up, beyond the group. "Harrison, what would you think about introducing me to your sister?"

Harrison would not think of it at all. "Uh, I guess," he said.

"Stupendous," Phil said. "Shall we call her and invite her?"

Harrison looked at Linus. *What's going on with your friend?*

Linus responded, *You're the crazy person who said you'd introduce her.*

"Uh, no. I don't think that's a great idea. She's a jerk—"

"Love it," said Phil.

"And also, I'm not technically supposed to be here."

"Ooh, are you doing a caper?" Mazz asked. Harrison looked over and discovered that Mazz had shifted and now had their head resting on Linus's thigh as they flipped through the book of poems. That was new. Were they interested in smooching each other? It was exactly what Harrison had hoped to facilitate, and he knew in his mind that this was a good thing. But there was another part of him, let's say his heart, that felt some other kind of emotion. Let's say jealousy. But jealous of whom?

Mazz had gone back to reading when Harrison tuned back in, this time a poem that started out being about moths. *"'If you notice anything,'"* Mazz read aloud, *"'It leads you to notice/more/ and more.'"*

"A city doesn't care if you have fun," Phil was saying. The group had migrated to the largest pool, standing off to the side a bit to avoid the intermittent splashes from people coming down the slide. The water was up to Harrison's waist and the edges of his shirt, which he'd opted to keep on when he changed into his red trunks. The shirt floated up around him like a lily pad. Linus sat on the edge, dangling his feet. Harrison tapped him on the leg.

"You having a good time?"

"So good," Linus said. He grinned and flicked water at him with his toe.

Phil was still talking. "Do I wake up in the morning going, 'Oh, I wonder how the city will please me today'? No."

"You don't think a city has a responsibility to the people who live in it?" Mazz asked.

Fab sank low in the water until only her eyes remained.

"A responsibility? Sure, sure. Who said anything about that? Look, this amusement park? The city isn't required to do it. I'm saying, should they have to?"

"Are you against public pools?" Mazz asked incredulously.

Fab rose just enough to reveal her mouth. "Oh, no, she loves this."

"I love this! Can you believe this? For free? Incredible. Do they have these things in New York? Of course, yeah, bigger. But this is great."

"I'm saying you sound like you hate it," Mazz said.

"Well, that's my whole thing. What can you do? The point is"—she slapped the surface of the water—"at the end of the day, this is a hole in the ground filled with water. But they had to have meetings or whatever to get it done. Permits. I don't know how it works. Money. I guess. And they did it. And they put a slide in the middle of it. And we get to stand here and have a real human experience. We get to have fun. In the hole in the ground that the city made for us."

"I mean, yes, this is for us," said Mazz. "But I think the idea is to think of everything that way. Everything in a city, anywhere, is the product of some large decision-making process. Curation.

And what we need, you and me, nobody actually cares about. But I think—well, this is what my aunt says, but I agree—is that the only thing that makes an impact is the humans inside of the creation."

"How did this get started?" Linus asked.

"I mentioned that my dad spends all morning at the farmer's market near Hopkins," Mazz said.

"Yeah, it all connects," Phil claimed, absent of evidence.

This was all so much. Harrison turned the volume down for a minute. He shifted so he could see the geysering fountain in the distance. Little kids running underneath the spray, squeaking their delight. The world wasn't made for kids, but they took to it like daring explorers anyway. Around every corner, awe. The conversation in the pool had carried on, Mazz and Phil jousting with words. So many words. He wondered what it was about these intense classmates of Linus's that drew Linus to them. Is this what he was actually like? Would there be a Phil and a Mazz and a Fab in Charleston? Would there be a Harrison? Would he even need a Harrison? He turned to Linus.

"You want to go down the slide?" Harrison said.

Linus looked hesitant.

"You can hold on to me. I promise I won't let you drown."

"That would be one way to keep me from moving away," Linus said.

"Stop. As much as I want you to stay, I do have some limits."

"You could visit me in Baltimore Cemetery, though. That

would solve all our problems. What kind of statue should I get for my grave?"

"I don't want to talk about this!" Harrison said. He let out a nervous laugh.

"Come on! What kind of statue?"

Harrison hated these moments, rare though they were, when Linus swerved into darkness, seemingly on a lark. The thing that was hard was actually that he didn't mean anything by it. Now Harrison had to be creative and think of a fun statue while also thinking about Linus being dead and wondering what was really behind his obsession with hanging out at the cemetery. If it was so easy to switch into darkness, he wondered, would it always be so easy to switch back?

"You haven't lived enough to figure your statue out yet," Harrison said.

Linus considered this. "I guess I gotta get started." He jumped into the pool with a light splash and started toward the cluster of slides. "You coming?" he called.

Having climbed the steps up to the central platform from which all the slides spun into the pool, Harrison and Linus briefly considered that this was something meant for small children. Harrison bent down and looked at one purple slide; it did look like they would fit. That was a potentially good sign. Which would be more embarrassing: popping out of the slide in front of all of recreational Baltimore, or having to negotiate the process of climbing back down the steps, disrupting all the kids who seemed to have an endless capacity for scrambling up and tumbling into the pool?

Well? Harrison asked Linus.

Linus sat down at the mouth of the slide. *We're already here*, he told Harrison with an eyebrow wiggle.

"Are you going?!" a little kid demanded.

"Yeah," said Linus. "Just working up the nerve." The kid gave an annoyed groan, scowled at him and Harrison, and launched into another slide.

Harrison sat down behind Linus and squeezed his legs on either side of him.

"Wait," said Harrison, "I should be up front so you can hold on."

"Does it matter?" Linus asked.

"I mean, I guess not, but if I'm sliding down behind you, it'll be more difficult for you to get back up if I land on top of you."

"Well, don't land on top of me. Unless you're trying to turn me into a ghost and keep me around."

"You're so annoying." Harrison scooted back and stood up. "Move."

Linus slid out and elaborately spread his arms out to the opening of the slide in a mockery of a welcoming gesture. *After you, sir.* Harrison rolled his eyes and sat. Linus plopped himself behind and wriggled his legs into the tube on either side of Harrison. He latched his arms around Harrison's middle.

"You ready?" Harrison asked.

"No, I'm chickening out. You have to carry me down the stairs."

"Shut up."

They sat there. Harrison strained to look back. "Well?" he said.

"Well what, well?" Linus said.

"Are we going?"

"Am I driving?!" Linus said, legitimately confused.

"You have to push us off!" said Harrison.

"*I* do?"

"Oh my god," a kid muttered behind them.

"How am I supposed to push us off when I'm holding on to you?" Linus demanded.

"Ugh, fine." Harrison reached up and out of the tube to grip the edge.

"Don't do me any favors," Linus said, pulling an arm out and also placing it on the tube.

"I've got it now," Harrison said. He pulled Linus's arm down.

"No, no, I'll do it." Linus slipped his arm out again and pulled Harrison's down.

"Y'ALL." The babies were turning against them. Harrison and Linus jostled each other's arms, calling a truce, with each of them holding one side of the tube. They pulled back, heaved their bodies forward, and slipped into the slide. Linus let out a surprised yelp and wrapped his other arm back around Harrison. They tumbled downward much more quickly than Harrison had anticipated, tilting to the side at a curve. Linus's knee wedged itself into Harrison's stomach. Who thought this was a good idea? The blue-white light of the water at the end of the tube swung into view. They picked up speed as they reached the edge, bumped upward as they launched out of the slide, and landed in the water with a hard smack.

They sank to the bottom, still sitting like they were doing the ice luge at the Olympics. The water rushed in; it was shallow but enough to cover them. Harrison felt Linus's hands start to slip off, and he grabbed them and pulled them tight. The shock of hitting the water and then suddenly being underneath it was always a new surprise for Harrison. He remembered in this moment how disorienting it was and also how invigorating, how time moved slowly for a split second, even as everything else seemed to speed up around him. When he'd started swimming lessons, he'd dreaded this part. In many ways, he still did. What would it be like if this moment of weightlessness and timelessness felt powerful instead? What if the water could release all the binds that held him?

As quickly as it had receded, the world returned. Harrison gripped Linus's arms with one hand, and with the other he pressed down on the bottom of the pool and pushed up, standing in the pool and pulling Linus with him.

Linus coughed out water in a laugh and collapsed onto Harrison's shoulder. He tightened his grip on Harrison into a hug.

"You didn't tell me to hold my breath!" Linus cried.

"Oh no!" Harrison said. He loosened Linus's grip and turned to face him. Linus looked totally out of sorts but was also glowing with exhilaration. He shook glimmering beads of water from his locks. He slung his arms around Harrison's neck and buried his face in his shirt, still laughing.

"Woo!" he called out, half hoot and half breath.

"You okay?" Harrison asked.

"Never been better! But, baby boy, I gotta learn how to swim."

Linus looked back up, his face to Harrison's face.

"All right?" Linus said.

"All right."

Harrison pressed his forehead against Linus's.

"Were you scared?"

"Nah," said Linus. "I knew you knew better than to let me drown."

They lingered there like this, forehead to forehead, their exhausted arms a jumble on top of one another.

"This was a good day," Linus said.

"Was?"

"Yeah."

"It's not over, though," Harrison said.

"Well . . ." Linus pulled back and looked into Harrison's eyes. Light glinted off his face, his arms, his shoulders. The sun loved Linus's skin. "I don't know. We should probably—"

"There's still more things on the agenda. We have to ride a Ferris wheel. The convertible."

"Where we gonna do that?"

"I don't know yet, but . . ." Harrison turned his face skyward.

There was so much day left. Like, actual day. The sun would linger, and why couldn't they? "Let's just stay here. If we never leave the pool, then it doesn't have to end."

"I'm getting prunier than a raisin, though."

"Okay, well, let's stay in the general pool area. Just . . . don't say it's over yet. What about the rest of them?"

"What about them?" Linus asked.

"Don't you want to hang out with them some more? This is your goodbye party. You can't be the one to leave your goodbye party. Phil would have some words about it."

Linus chuckled.

Harrison felt the words come up and weighed them on his tongue. "And Mazz."

Harrison wouldn't look Linus in the eyes; Linus found him anyway. "What about Mazz?"

"Don't you want to hang out?"

"Is that okay?" Linus asked.

Harrison nodded. Linus squeezed him tight.

3:01 p.m.

Harrison watched Linus and Mazz hop out of the pool and trot back over to the blanket. Linus scooped up his bowling shirt and threw it on, leaving it hanging open. They briefly discussed their plan and then decided to head over to the food table. Linus gestured wildly to the slide and Mazz threw back their head, laughing. Well, what now? At the other end of the pool, Fab and Phil had joined another group of teens and were playing chicken, Fab on Phil's shoulders. Harrison hoisted himself up on the side of the pool and watched. The thing about pools, like everything else, it seemed, was that everybody knew what they were doing. Everybody had a plan. He stopped himself from getting too hung up about it. He had a plan, too. This was his plan. He hadn't set out to give his best friend a pool-party send-off—how weird would it be to host an aquatic goodbye for a nonswimmer? But here they were, and it was exactly what Linus seemed to want. Harrison looked over to the food table but couldn't spot Linus and Mazz. He searched the dance floor, the fountain pool, the kiddie pool. They weren't anywhere. Then he turned and spotted them trudging up the hill, in the direction of a set of tennis courts and, beyond that, the Reservoir. Harrison looked at the blanket; Linus's shorts were still there. They'd be back. It was fine. It was all fine. This was what they all wanted.

He drew his knees up to his chest, pulling his feet out of the water and onto the cement. Water streamed down from his shirt in steady rivulets and pooled around him. This was being a good friend, he decided. No matter how it felt.

He was brought back, suddenly, to the time last summer when he'd found himself hunched up next to another pool, at the hotel in Virginia Beach on vacation with Pop, and his twin cousins, and their friend from camp, Rahul. After he and Rahul had briefly but thrillingly made out and after Harrison had quickly and disastrously lost Rahul's interest by bringing up Pop's style of dress, Harrison had retreated to the pool. Rahul was watching a noisy cartoon, and though it was just the two of them in the room, it had suddenly felt overcrowded. Or rather, Harrison had suddenly felt out of place, extraneous, in the way. He told Rahul he'd be back. Rahul nodded without turning from the TV. And Harrison had let himself out and started wandering without a destination. He reached the end of a hallway, which emptied out into a courtyard that ringed the pool. He spotted Pop sitting in a deck chair, having a cocktail. He wondered why Pop had come this far and gone through this much trouble just to sit alone. Of course, Harrison was also currently on a journey to being alone.

He caught the elevator down, watching Pop through the glass wall the whole way. Pop didn't notice him. When he reached the bottom, he considered just hitting any button again and riding up so he could keep watching. He hadn't meant to make it seem like he was judging Pop for his short-shorts, or really anything about him. Instead it just all seemed like a mysterious image from another universe. How did one get to there from where Harrison was? Was it even possible?

The gold doors of the elevator opened, and he walked out. He approached Pop on the pool deck. Pop seemed lost in thought, and then, sensing someone near, looked at him. He took a second to process and then broke into a smile.

"Hey, honeybun," Pop said, his light southern accent and his cocktail conspiring to pull as many syllables out of his words as possible. Harrison gave a small wave.

"Am I bothering you?"

"No indeedy," Pop said, sitting up. "You want to join me?"

"I'll just sit here," he said. He settled at the edge of the pool and dangled one foot in. His back was to Pop, but he could feel his eyes on him. Harrison turned and smiled. "What are you doing?"

Pop rubbed his hand over his hair, cut close and flecked with white. "I sure don't know. I am *tired*. I hope I'm not boring you all."

"It's fun. We're having fun."

"Good, good. Where's everybody else?"

"Francis and Melinda are calling their mom. And Rahul is watching TV."

"You two seemed to hit it off," Pop said. *Oh no.* "Let me ask you something." *Here it comes.* If adults didn't linger on the worst possible subjects known to man—work, school, and college plans—they always zeroed in on the most awkward. He had no desire to talk about dating with his grandfather or with anyone, particularly because there was nothing to talk about. He had no desire to tell them there was nothing to talk about, either, because that made it seem like he was a failure. He had no desire to talk at all.

"So," Pop said, "if you and Rahul wanted to keep in contact after this vacation, would you use the phone? Or do y'all not talk on the phone anymore?"

Harrison scooted around to face his grandfather. Pop was sitting up, his cocktail in his hand. There didn't seem to be any mischief on his face, that weird way that adults get when talking about "So, you got a little *friend*?" He seemed to be genuinely asking.

"Do you mean how will we communicate?"

"Yes, yes, exactly. I'm very curious about this. Melinda and Francis, they FaceTime me now and again, but I don't expect they like it. I read these articles about new apps and platforms, and it seems to me that it's always changing, what young people use. I just don't have any desire to figure it out."

"I mean . . . I don't think Rahul and I will keep in contact. But if we did, we might follow each other's socials."

"Uh-huh. And then what?"

"I . . . I don't know. We might text? I don't think he's—"

He almost did it. He almost slipped up and talked about a boy with his grandfather. Tricky, tricky. Harrison redirected. "How . . . how did you keep up with friends?"

"The telephone. Which is what you're saying, but also very different. Letters. I send emails now and again, but I did enough of that at work. It doesn't feel like anything real. But no texts. No, thank you."

"I have this friend, Linus, who really doesn't like texting."

"Oh, I like him already. I cannot *stand* texting. Your father will text me all these messages and I have to tell him, 'I leave my cell phone in the glove compartment, so if you need to reach me, you need to figure yourself out.'"

"Why—Never mind. Anyway, Linus's phone is old and janky, and so we usually just call each other. But we started off sending emails back and forth. These long emails about . . . anything. School, our parents, what kind of stuff we liked."

"Really?" Pop leaned forward, resting his arms on his knees. "And this is different from your other friends?"

"I guess," Harrison said. "I mean . . . Linus is just, he's different."

"Because of the emails?"

"Yes. And because he's . . . he, we get each other. He's like a part of me that I've been looking for."

"He's your best friend."

Harrison nodded.

"You should invite him down next summer."

Harrison nodded again.

"Linus," Pop said with relish. He took a sip of his drink. "But you'll invite him on the phone."

"Because he doesn't like texting."

"Linus don't text, honey!"

Harrison scooted back around and looked at the water. "Do you have a best friend, Pop?"

Pop was quiet for a second. "I did at a time. It changes. Phyllis and I were best friends before she moved in, but now she got so woo-woo, I just can't take it. We love each other, but I tell you what! I'm glad you have a best friend, though, Harrison. Is he gay, too?"

"Yeah." Harrison held his breath, waiting for the nosy questions to start.

Pop just chuckled. "Oh, good. Good. That's important. You need somebody who sees you."

"So you don't have a best friend now?" Harrison asked.

"I suppose not. Things change. People, they, you know, they go on. They go live their lives."

"Well, what do you do with your time, then?"

Here his grandfather's eyes lit up, and he shifted onto his hip that he called his good hip, although it was really just his better hip and the pickings were slim. "I just live my life!" Pop said. And then he started talking animatedly about something he was part of called Soup Club. If Harrison had listened harder, he would have heard all about how this club was started by someone named Vincenzo Quatch—yes, honey, as in *the* Quatches—and how Pop and Vincenzo had had a whole rivalry but once upon a time they'd had a fling, and anyway, Pop would tell him about it when he was older. But Harrison drifted away a bit, thinking about Linus, thinking about himself, thinking about words sent out into the universe and returned to you warmer, wider, braver, more beautiful. He kicked at the water's edge, and waves scattered away from him and then came bouncing back.

He wondered if it was too late to go back to Rahul. He wondered if he even wanted to. He wondered what was next after that and how much time could pass before he had to move. He wondered whether he might be sitting poolside with some teenage grandchild of his at some point in the future, waxing rhapsodic about butternut squash and sage. He wondered how he'd even go about having a grandchild in the first place, as the truth was that his Pop wasn't actually his grandfather but really his great-uncle, who had no offspring of his own. But the truth was also that family finds a way to fit itself into whatever words we give it.

3:35 p.m.

It only took one comment from Mazz—"Harrison is so fun"—to get Linus going. He talked all the way up the hill, across the street, past the tennis courts, and up another small hill. He didn't stop until he and Mazz had reached the Reservoir at the top of the hill, where they had to briefly decide which way to walk around it. They chose left.

"And there was this time when Harrison was doing this play *Fiddler on the Roof* and he didn't have any lines or anything, he was just in the chorus. But he did get to bounce on a trampoline while playing a ghost in this one song where a girl flies out of a closet and he was really funny doing that. Anyways, we went out to a diner afterwards. I guess it's what they do. And he told me to come and it was nice but they were talking about stuff I didn't have any idea about, so I just spent time looking up what the play was really about, like, the historical background. But every time somebody made a joke, like, a theater joke or a joke about his school or anything, he'd lean over and he'd tell me what it meant. And I told him he didn't have to, because for real I was fine just reading about Russia in the 1800s, but he said he came to hang out with me and the jokes were just funnier to him if I knew what they were about, even if I didn't laugh. So then I start noticing that it wasn't Harrison who is making the jokes mostly. He's just sitting there, having French fries, laughing, and then leaning over to me to explain, and then laughing again. And I thought it was such a fun night. Even though I didn't say nothing to anyone, just about. But the fun was the connection, the connection he was making. He's really good at that."

Linus paused at last. They stepped onto the jogging path around the Reservoir and walked left.

"My aunt has this saying: You two are like a salt-and-pepper set. It's so annoying, but"—Mazz laughed at themself—"it's exactly what came to mind. It means like a salt-and-pepper-shaker set. I don't know where she got it. But it means you two are opposite but you're made for each other."

Linus laughed because that sounded dramatic and intense. But also, it was true. "He's my best friend. Which one is salt and which one is pepper, though?" he said. "This is important!"

"I don't know him well enough to tell you. I think you're—"

"Cinnamon," Linus said defiantly.

"Oh, you just have to be difficult."

"True. True. What are you?"

"You mean what spice, or am I difficult?" Mazz asked.

"Spice."

"Have you heard of the Spice Girls?"

"No," Linus said.

"Oh, never mind. I was going to make a joke, but you wouldn't get it."

"No, go ahead," said Linus.

"I'm Baby," said Mazz.

Linus stared at Mazz blankly. They were right, he had no idea what they were talking about. Linus wasn't even sure the joke had happened, so he just kept staring until Mazz cracked up and put their head in their hands.

"Oh no! I've totally ruined everything!" Mazz cried.

"There is no way," Linus said. "Seriously—so much of the time I spend with Harrison is me making bad jokes that he doesn't get or doesn't want to get. Not that what you said was a bad joke. I bet it's hilarious. You should tell Harrison. He probably won't get it, either, but I think it'd be funny to watch." Linus experienced a moment of crushing self-awareness. He turned to Mazz. "I'm talking about Harrison too much!"

Mazz laughed. "No! If you didn't talk about your best friend, who planned a whole day of adventure for you and also maybe a second ago saved you from drowning—"

"I was fine."

"—I'd be surprised."

"I'm glad that you're here, too," Linus said.

"When you texted me this morning, at first I was like, 'Who did I lend a shirt to?' and then I was like 'Oooh!' It made me so happy. And it looks so good."

"Really?"

"Yeah. Especially like that. All beach casual. You're all set for South Carolina."

"I don't think we're going to be close to the beach, but maybe."

"What are you most excited about?" Mazz asked.

Linus had thought about this move for weeks, from every possible angle, all of them terrible. And it had never occurred to him that he might be excited about some part of it. Now he felt like he'd shown up without doing his homework. Would Mazz be disappointed in him if he told the truth—that he just couldn't bring himself to see a bright side?

"I don't know," Linus said finally. "I like my aunt Bird. So. I guess that."

"Yeah, that's cool," said Mazz. "My aunt moved in with us last year, and I'm obsessed with her, so I definitely feel you on that. You probably know this, but Charleston is the most magical city. My aunt used to work at a gallery in the Low Country, and we went down to visit because she had put together a show as part of this thing called the Spoleto Festival. And it felt like I was in a different world. The trees and the horizon and the air and the art. The art, Linus. I'm telling you. I think my favorite thing, though—well, my favorite thing was the food. But my second-favorite thing was that all the buildings are so brightly colored and they're all built on stilts high above the ground. It just feels . . . strange and beautiful. Like a dream. All the buildings are flamingos and cranes. All the land is the sky. I'm so envious of your move, actually, Linus."

Linus was seized by the pang of an intricately mixed emotion. He was transported by everything Mazz was saying, by their voice and the way their face lit up as they talked about it. He was intrigued, maybe even excited to discover this new place. And he was sadder than ever that he couldn't experience it with Mazz, who saw it so vividly, or Harrison, who saw Linus so vividly.

He worried that if he tried to say anything about what he was feeling, he'd start to cry, so Linus changed the subject. "I love that tank top you've got on. Is it from Maybe This Time?"

"No, I made this." They pointed to the brick on the tank top. "This brick is supposed to be the first one that got thrown at the Stonewall Riot, the gay—"

"—gay rights protest in the sixties," Linus finished.

"Right. A trans activist named Marsha P. Johnson threw it—"

"—supposedly," Linus said. "But maybe Silvia Rivera, or—"

"—any number of people, but—"

"Yeah, I wasn't saying—"

"No, I know," said Mazz. "I think we're saying the same thing. It's largely—"

"—symbolic," Linus said.

"Exactly. Pride is a party and it's a protest. Always has been. Happy Pride."

"Happy Pride." He nudged Mazz's hand—maybe it was accidental, maybe he was saying hello. He didn't know for sure. Mazz smiled. They turned at the bend in the track, and Mazz climbed up on a low stone wall beside them, balancing. On the other side of the wall, a hillside of daffodils and tulips spilled down into an intersecting nest of curved highways. They were high enough that they could see most of the city, and the road noise barely reached them.

"I'm sorry we didn't get to hang out more before you left," Mazz said. "Are you coming back to visit?"

"I don't know. Right now I don't have enough saved to buy a plane ticket back, plus I gotta figure out how I'm going to pay for test fees and I don't know if I'm going to have a job down in Charleston . . ." Linus trailed off. The enormity of the future rose up all around him once again.

"Sorry, I didn't mean to—"

"There's the cemetery!" Linus exclaimed. He climbed up onto the stone wall behind Mazz and pointed. Beyond the looping, curving highways, down North Avenue, just between two high-rises, he spotted a patch of green. "Sorry, I didn't mean to interrupt. I just got excited. Do you see that thing in the distance that looks kind of like a castle?"

Mazz searched but couldn't find it. It was so far and so small, you had to know where you were looking. Linus tried to describe where to fix their gaze, but finally Mazz said, "Turn my head so I'm facing it." Linus gingerly tilted Mazz's head until it was just about the right spot. He ducked behind them to make sure, as if they were two parts of a telescope aimed at the heavens.

"You see the tall red apartment building?"

"Yes."

"Okay, now look down and you'll see something that looks like a castle. That's the front gate to the cemetery."

Mazz could see it. Perhaps it was the architecture or perhaps it was the journey to get there, but it felt like discovering a fairy-tale land.

"It's my favorite place in Baltimore," Linus said.

"A cemetery?"

"Is that weird?" Linus said.

"Everything is weird."

"Well, that's true. I just feel like, actually, everywhere feels awkward or strange or not where I want to be, but there, it's pretty and it's quiet and it's full of history and you can see the whole story, I mean city."

"Both, right? Story and city?"

"Sometimes. Although, some of these fancy grave markers? I tell you. I don't know what these folks were on. I go home and google some of these names, like, 'Who the hell did you think you were, with this twelve-foot angel on your grave?' But that's how I'm trying to be. Put a big ol' statue on my grave."

"No time soon, though, right?" Mazz said. They sat down on the wall and ran their hand over a tulip.

"No. I ain't in a rush." Linus sat down next to Mazz. "Truth is, the cemetery is where life makes the most sense to me. Everything just feels like being in the middle and not having any control over what's going on in your life. But at least in the cemetery, it's like, *'Well, all the questions got answered.'*"

Mazz laughed in spite of themself. "That's incredibly morbid."

"I think it's nice!"

The sound of two revving motorbike engines traveled up the hillside toward them. Down on the serpentine road, they saw two Black boys on bikes come roaring down an exit ramp and merge onto the highway. The road was essentially empty, and they took full advantage of it, each assuming ownership over a lane, revving their engines again, and speeding off southward down the highway.

"I feel like," Mazz said, "I know that feeling: *'Well, all the questions got answered.'* My parents used to spend so much time worrying about my aunt, trying to help her—she is incredible, but also . . . Well, my aunt likes to quote this one line by Langston Hughes—'Life for me ain't been no crystal stair.' It's like that. And when she finally came to live with us, it was like, not only was all the stuff that just never seemed to get solved got solved—well, not solved, but it wasn't weighing on our life in the same way. And with her around, I felt like I had new answers about who I was and what I was trying to be in life."

Linus tried to imagine Mazz's aunt—or someone he imagined was Mazz's aunt, since he had no idea what she looked like—standing on a crystal staircase. Maybe holding a teacup, like the painting in the museum. It made him smile to think about that, and he promised himself that one day he would find a way to describe what he saw to Mazz.

After a moment, Linus spoke up again. "I thought it was going to be like that when I moved in with my dad," Linus said. "My parents got divorced, and I went to live with my mom and things were okay, or I thought they were okay. But everything just felt so tense, and then I'd get tense and then we'd argue. This was like when I was a kid. Then in the pandemic, everything got worse. We were stuck at home and I had just gone to middle school and

I didn't have a computer, so I couldn't get to class, and I was angry at her about that and angry, angry at everything. And everything I was doing was making her unhappy. I just knew it. And I started to think that everything I'd done had always made her unhappy. There was this one time, before all that, when we went to a concert at church where they were recording an album. And the choir sang her favorite song. And when it started, she started crying so loud. And I could feel her crying, shaking in my hand. Because she was holding my hand. It was so loud, you can hear it on the recording, and I can't stop listening to it cuz I keep thinking that's where the answers are. I know that's not the case. But I don't have anything else.

"I just wish my mom liked me; it's always been hard between us. And when schools opened back up again, I got the idea that I would just leave. And I started telling her every day how much I wanted to live with my dad. And I called myself helping her by getting out of her hair, but I was mad, too. I was. And finally she said fine. She said, 'You and me, we need a clean break.' And so I went, but ain't nothing been clean about the break. And we kept arguing; I could never do right in her eyes, I felt like. And last summer, we had this argument over nothing. Over, well, she asked if I had a girlfriend even though she knows I'm gay, and I got mad. And she said it was just an honest mistake. Like . . . Anyways, I said I couldn't take it anymore. I told her, 'When something breaks, it's got to stay broke.' Because I didn't feel like I had another choice."

Linus ran out of words. Mazz slipped their pinkie around

Linus's pinkie and held it there. Linus wondered if he would get to be happy. Or whether he would have to settle for a piece of life that was a little less-than. He rolled it around in his mind, as he had many times before. He didn't let himself answer.

"Thank you for sharing that with me," Mazz said. "There's something really hopeful in the way you listen to that CD from the concert."

"You think?"

"You haven't given up on finding whatever you're looking for," Mazz said.

"Do you want to hear it?" Linus asked. He fished in his pocket for his MP3 player.

"No, thank you. If that's okay with you. I think that's yours. Is that okay?"

Linus nodded.

They watched cars go by on the highway for a while.

"Now that you've told me about it, I'm going to try to find that cemetery," Mazz said. "I'm going to go and try to imagine everyone who ever lived."

"And then what?"

"Well, I haven't done it yet. But I'll let you know."

"Send me a picture when you do."

They sat in silence again. Pinkies linked as their hands rested on the stone wall. On the far side of the highway, the two boys on motorbikes zoomed north.

3:36 p.m.

Harrison made his way across the pool deck to the folding table where two women were selling food. Behind them, it looked like the DJ had taken a break. The sound system played the radio— he could tell because the music was intercut with commercials. He assumed it was 92Q because there was a banner with the station's call letters hung up on the DJ booth, but he thought it would have been funny if the DJ was actually from the classical music station and decided to drop the beat all of a sudden. Harrison paid for a scoop of chocolate ice cream pulled from a huge cooler packed with ice and wondered how radio stations chose what to play. How did one station become hip-hop and R&B and another become country? He had never thought to ask his father, despite the fact that he worked in radio. Everyone he knew liked all kinds of music, and the artists who were popular were always releasing songs in different categories. In general this was good, but it was also how you got something like "Press the Sky Higher," which was performed by four of the judges of a TV singing competition, all of whom came from different styles of music, plus a children's choir and, on one remix, a cartoon.

Harrison asked where he could get sprinkles, and one of the

women pointed him to a table, which was currently being blocked by a man in jeans. Jeans at a pool? It takes all types. Harrison moved over to the table, still caught up on how radios chose their music and why there wasn't a Broadway radio station. Everybody likes Broadway. It's not called *Narrow*-way.

"Excuse me," he said to the man's back. The man looked up and then shifted over. Harrison started scooping sprinkles onto his ice cream.

"Harrison?" the man said. Harrison looked up at him. For a second he couldn't place him—this was just a person wearing person clothes.

A person wearing person clothes who looked like his father.

A person wearing person clothes who looked like his father, who worked for 92Q.

Now it clicked.

"Dad?" He loved seeing his parents out and about, it had to be said. Like when they came to visit him at work unexpectedly. He grinned at his father brightly, and then, seeing the confusion on Obed's face, Harrison came back to Earth and realized where he was, and what he was doing, and how much trouble he was in. "This isn't what it looks like," Harrison said.

"You already took your lactose pill?" Obed said. What? Oh, the ice cream! No, he also had not done that. In fact, he didn't have any pills with him.

"Um. No. Do you have some?"

Obed fished a foil-packaged pill out of his pocket and opened it for Harrison even though Harrison was capable of opening his own pills. "I would have invited you if I'd thought you'd be interested, but I know Linus doesn't swim." He gestured at the booth with the banner on it that, Harrison realized, really should have rung an alarm for him.

"We were . . . We . . ." Harrison could not figure out a way to explain himself, and he also could not figure out why his father wasn't asking him to explain himself. Harrison's mind raced as he tried to determine how to get information out of his father without revealing that he was very much not where he was supposed to be and nobody knew it. Well, nobody except Corrine and his father. He looked back at the food table to make sure that his mother hadn't been the one scooping the ice cream. Okay, no, that was actually a stranger. "Did you talk to Corrine?" Harrison asked.

"Not since this morning, why?" Obed said.

"No reason. It's okay that I'm here?"

"I'm not on app duty today, so I just didn't know. But if you've worked it out, fine with me."

"Well, this has been a treat," Harrison said. "I am loving the music. The vibe. The water. Everything you're doing here. It's great. Anyway, I gotta jet. It was great seeing you, and I look forward to seeing you at home."

"Love you, boy-o. Be careful in the pool. I'll try to keep an eye out."

Harrison turned and walked away as quickly as he could without arousing suspicion.

"Harrison! Wait a minute!"

Whatever spell he'd accidentally cast was broken. This was it. This was the end. He turned slowly.

"Yes?"

Obed cocked his head. "Whose shorts are you wearing?!"

"Um. Mine?"

His father clearly did not believe this, and yet it was the truth, finally.

▦ ▦ ▦

Harrison nervously shoveled ice cream into his mouth as he wound his way through packs of kids running along the pool deck long enough to be told to stop running. They needed to pack it up and get out of there. Or did they? As long as his dad thought that everything had been worked out, they could actually stay as long as they wanted. Then again, the minute his father figured out that Harrison hadn't told anyone in advance that he was going there, or, worse, that they'd been using Aparna as a decoy, everything would come tumbling down. The best solution was to finish up and leave, but that would also mean saying goodbye. And the desire to keep that moment at bay, to cement their friendship enough that maybe he could somehow keep it from happening altogether, was what made him to do all this in the first place. It was the thing that made him break all the rules he'd already broken, from calling Mondale in Arizona at 10 p.m. to leaving the state, without a care for what it would cost him down the road. He would pay any price. His parents wouldn't understand it, but in his heart he knew it was all worth it. And he'd already been caught by two-thirds of his family (perhaps a life of crime was not in the cards)—what did he have to lose? He was wild; he was out of control. This must have been how Elphaba felt! Ferris Day wasn't over, and he wasn't going home until he had squeezed every last drop of goodness and joy from his final moments with Linus. And if anyone else in his family cared to find him, they could look to the Western sky!

Or, actually, just the western side of the pool, where Phil had moved everyone's stuff so she could keep an eye on it while she swam more laps. But after that, maybe the sky!

Harrison pressed his toes into the pebbly concrete at the edge of the pool and watched Phil swim. He was struck by how much power she was harnessing. Each loop of her arm was tactical, each kick another jolt of force. She really did have sea legs. She hit the wall and pulled herself up for air. She slicked back her hair and spotted Harrison above her. She blew some stray water from her mouth and smiled.

"Wanna race?" she said.

"I'm not that great a swimmer."

"Well, then you'll lose," she said simply. "Someone has to."

Harrison chuckled at this, and then, a new thought: It was like Phil's voice echoed in his head, *Someone has to lose,* and then inside himself a voice replied, *Not me. Not today.*

He sat down on the edge of the pool and plopped into the water in the lane next to her.

"Now we're talking!" Phil said. Harrison hooked an arm onto the side and pressed his feet against the wall to keep himself up. "What do you think? Up and back? Simple," she said.

"Okay. What kind of stroke?"

"Who has time for all kinds of acrobatics? I do a forward crawl, one hand over the other. You do whatever you want." She flipped around to face the lane. "Ready?"

Oh! This was happening right now. Harrison, in his solo practices at school, had grown accustomed to doing the arms from the breaststroke—reaching out and splitting the water in two—but kicking as he would in a forward crawl. He briefly wondered if Phil or anyone else who was watching—no one else was watching—would find it weird, but then he remembered what she had *just* said. *Do whatever you want.* He raised his feet to the wall to kick himself off.

"Do you want to take off your shirt?" Phil said.

Did she mean in general or in this moment? Because the answer was no either way.

"I'm good," Harrison said.

"All right. Count of three," Phil said. She counted to three and then shoved off from the wall in a burst of limbs and water and noise. Harrison pushed off right behind her. He liked this part the best, the beginning. He liked the power that was hiding itself in his legs, waiting to send him sailing through the water. He lifted his arms up from his sides, then pitched them forward. He couldn't see Phil. His field of vision was all bubbles. He kicked his legs, trying to keep his feet underwater, as he'd been taught. He pulled his arms back down and then up the length of his body and then out. He felt air bubbles racing up the sides of his shirt. He reached the other end just before Phil. She flipped underwater and shot in the opposite direction, sending a blast of bubbles toward him. The flipping was always the hard part for him. He hit the wall with his hands, turned around, and launched himself off again with his feet. Phil was so far ahead of him. His hands kept getting caught on his shirt. He was aware of every part of his body as he moved through the water. His legs, his skin, his stomach, his breath, his heart pounding in his chest. He tried to concentrate on just moving his body, just being in the water, but his thoughts drifted. He heard the sound of blood pumping in his ears and thought how weird it was that people talked about their hearts when they talked about love. *"My heart is so full, it's bursting,"* they'd declare in a musical before breaking into song. He never thought about his actual heart, the thing that pressed against his rib cage, that sent blood racing through his veins, that vibrated inside him. This was the thing that was keeping him going, losing the race at this rate. What did it have to do with love? With a feeling that wasn't physical or maybe wasn't anything at all? *The heart,* he thought as he hit the wall and pulled himself up, gasping, *is a lumpy loaf sitting in our chests, minding its own business. It does not have an opinion on love.*

Phil was already bobbing in the water when Harrison crested. "Nice job," she said. "You're fast."

He pulled himself up to sit on the side. Water poured out of his shirt and dribbled into the pool. He tried to catch his breath.

"Thanks," he said. "Can I ask—why are you planning to live on a boat after high school?"

Phil looked puzzled. "Oh, sorry! I thought it was obvious. I want to be free."

Harrison twisted the end of his shirt to wring out the water. He felt so heavy with it soaked. It was dragging him down.

"You want to race again?" he said.

"Sure!" Phil said. "I could do this all day." She set herself up and waited for him.

Harrison pulled at the bottom edge of his shirt. He looked around the pool area again. No one was watching this very exciting race between two high schoolers. No one was just standing around waiting to offer their thoughts on his body, on what he should eat, on when he'd grow into it, on strategies for building muscle or burning fat or whatever, on whether somebody he didn't even know yet would like it or wouldn't like it. Nobody was noticing them at all, and this state of being was usually a comfort to Harrison, though he knew that he sometimes used it as a cavern to crawl inside and make himself smaller. He didn't want to do that. Not here. Not now. He'd spent the entire day trying to prove to Linus how much he meant to him; he thought he'd succeed. He wasn't sure. But if he had, it hadn't been by making himself less.

Harrison raised his shirt up and lifted it over his head. Because it was wet, it clung to him at various spots. A needy shirt. The air felt great on his skin. He dropped the shirt onto a pile on the cement. He was still just a person wearing person clothes, albeit fewer, in a pool full of people in person clothes, with bodies and lumpy loaves pumping blood in their chests, and, Harrison hoped, love bursting out of some strange and mysterious place.

He got back into the pool. "Ready?"

Harrison and Phil took off again. He didn't know if he was moving any faster, but the way that the water skimmed the contours of his body was new and electrifying. He felt the waves race from the tips of his fingers along his arms, his sides, his legs, kicking madly. He felt bubbles spinning wildly all around. He felt his own power.

How different this was. He didn't know if he'd changed or if the world had shifted around him to make more space for the fact of his being. He thought of how unyielding the water had seemed the time he'd almost drowned, how it was like the water had arms that held him and a will of its own. He thought of the swimming lessons that had taught him new things about his body but how even it had resisted him for a while. He thought of the solitary practices, the days when he just wanted to be alone, to be submerged, to be floating free.

He hit the wall and turned around, popping his head up to take in air before plunging back down. He thought of the smell of chlorine that singed his nose at school. He thought of the raining fountains at the Smithsonian in the Contemplative Court. He thought of his soul in the center of that water. Protected, encased, at peace. He reached, he kicked, his muscles drove him forward. It was like meeting his body anew for the first time, piece by piece. He thought of his grandfather's arm resting on his good hip; he thought of Corrine's hand reaching up to grab her hair. He thought of the way the sun delighted in Linus's skin. He thought of the waves flowing out from him as he moved, and the waves he made. He thought of the waves returning.

He thought of Linus again, his arms wrapped around Harrison's middle, his laugh, his silent communication. His fingers snapping into a V-shape at a graveyard. His eyes closed as he listened to his MP3 player. He thought of the version of Linus that existed away from him. The Linus in the future, the Linus before they met, even the Linus that was represented by the dot on a map made by a phone carried around by Aparna Aiyar.

They had done everything together. The only thing left to do then was to say goodbye and to say it well. He reached the wall and put a hand up to steady himself but didn't come up for air. Not yet. He let the water still around him and focused on the form to his left—black hair slicked back by movement, pale arms outstretched like an arrow, a blue sports bra, white shorts—it was Phil. She was coming down her lane, and she was just behind him. She hit the wall and burst through the surface, sending water spraying down. Little droplets hit the surface above him, breaking up the waves in her wake. Harrison raised himself up to the air and took a deep breath.

"Congratulations," Phil said, heaving. She reached out and gave him a high five.

"I didn't know I could do that," he wheezed. He flipped himself around to the edge of the pool and slapped his arms on the concrete. His heart was pounding; he'd pushed himself so hard that it actually hurt a little. But at least it worked. He drew in another breath and wiped the water from his eyes. He placed an arm back on the edge, and that's when he saw them: two black flats standing at his lane. He looked up at the legs they were attached to and discovered Aparna. She waved apologetically.

"Did you get my texts?" she said. "And hi."

"What? No. What's going on? What happened?"

"I may have had a small adventure."

4:15 p.m.

Harrison and Phil hoisted themselves out of the pool.

"So where are the phones now?" Harrison asked Aparna, panic creeping into his voice.

"The thing is that I don't have tracking on them," Aparna said. "But the last time Aparna texted back, she was in the county. She said she 'needed to nosh' and then she could come back down."

"I thought you were Aparna," Phil said.

"She *is* Aparna," Harrison said. "She's talking about Cool—"

"I'm talking about Aparna R. One of our classmates."

"Got it," Phil said. She picked up the pile of blankets and totes and books and the iPad with a bunch of unread messages and shoved it all into Harrison's arms. "Let's walk and talk," she said.

They moved toward the exit.

"The way I see it, this is fine," Aparna said. "I've thought about it from a lot of angles, and it's not convenient, but it's not a disaster."

Phil signaled to Fab, who started saying her goodbyes to the group she was hanging with.

"What if someone has been texting us and we haven't been responding?" Harrison said.

"That's the only unknown, unfortunately. But the good news is no one texted you all day before this."

Phil whistled to get the attention of Linus and Mazz, who were walking back down the hill. She gestured to them to wait right there, and they paused.

"All we need to do," Aparna said, "is get you home and wait for Aparna R. to swing by with the phones. You might want to do something that lets everyone know you're home and you've been home."

"Like what?" Harrison said.

"Make focaccia," Phil said. "It's gotta rise. That takes time. Can't fake it." She handed Fab a towel. Okay, so they would make focaccia, whatever that was. Harrison dug into his bag and pulled on his Bayard Rustin shirt. This wasn't as bad as it seemed. His dad had seen him, after all, and it hadn't caused a problem. They'd go home, they'd make fiyero or whatever . . . they'd keep doing Ferris Day. Somehow.

The group turned up the hill and linked up with Mazz and Linus.

"Harrison!" He knew that voice. Where did he know that voice from? Harrison turned. Oh. His father was rushing across the deck, his phone in his hands. "Is Linus with you?"

What was the right answer here? "Yes?"

"That's what I thought," Obed said. "Why is Wally texting me, telling me he's out in Baltimore County?"

"Oh! His phone is. It got left in Aparna's car."

Harrison's dad turned to Aparna Aiyar. "Where is your car now?"

She froze. Harrison knew that she did not like lying to parents, not her parents and certainly not someone else's parents, but he silently prayed that she'd decide that it wasn't lying, per se, in a manner speaking, if you looked at it in a certain light. "On an errand," Aparna blurted. "But the phones are being brought back to your house soon."

"All right," Obed said. "Oh, and hello, Aparna." He flicked his eyes up to Phil and Fab. "Hello, everyone."

Obed motioned for Harrison to step away and lowered his voice. "Harrison, did Linus's dad know that you all were coming to the pool?"

"I . . . I don't think so."

"Did *we* know you were coming to the pool?"

"Um . . ."

Obed sighed. "See, this is what messes me up. I explicitly asked you about this earlier. This is what I get for assuming, but . . . man! We don't ask you guys to keep us in the loop just to make your lives hard. We do it to make your lives better."

"Is Linus in trouble?" Harrison asked.

"Linus? You worried about Linus? You need to be worried

about yourself." But Harrison wasn't worried about himself. Harrison spent every moment of every day worrying about himself. He had made worrying about himself into an art. He was expecting a special Tony for Anxiety to come from Ms. Antoinette Perry any day now. He was only sixteen years old, but he deserved a lifetime achievement award for worrying. And what had it got him? It certainly hadn't stopped his fear about losing Linus from coming true. So, no offense to his dad, but Harrison was quite certain that he didn't need to be worrying about himself. All he knew in that moment was what he did need to do. He needed to make sure that Linus didn't end this day with a lecture from his father, who was always stressed and always concerned and was taking them to Charleston in the morning. He needed to make sure that he wasn't making tomorrow a nightmare for Linus because of what they'd done today. Ferris Day had become about being daring and braver in the present, but it wasn't about making the future worse.

"It's my fault," Harrison said. "Not Linus's. Linus shouldn't be in trouble. I surprised him with the pool."

"You know how Wally—" Obed started, but Harrison was working himself up and kept talking.

"And you were here. Which I didn't know, but it turned out to be okay anyway. But I just wanted to have one day with him before he left. And nothing even went wrong! We're sixteen years old! We have jobs! We don't do *anything* without you all saying so! But everybody talks to us about how we're supposed to be setting ourselves up for the future. If we can't be trusted to go to a pool together on a hot day without, like, destroying the world, then how are we supposed to be ready for the future?"

All those inside thoughts had just come tumbling out, and now he looked at them, sitting all around his feet on the pool deck, soaking up water in the sun.

"Well, you've been holding that in for a while, haven't you?" his dad said. "We can talk about this later, but you don't need to be upset." Harrison wondered if he should speak up more. *Eh, best not to push it,* he thought. One monologue a year, tops, like a beloved character actress. His dad continued, "Lemme—I gotta get back to work. Let me call Wally real quick. I'll tell him that I've been watching you all and that you're going to be at the house. Because you are going to be at the house, *right*?"

Harrison nodded. Obed dialed his phone and stepped away. He and Linus's dad spoke for all of thirty seconds, at most. He imagined trying to have that brief a conversation with Linus. Couldn't be done.

"Okay, man," Harrison's dad said into the phone, drifting back. "I got you . . . All right . . . You know it. All right . . . Love you, brother . . . Be well." He hung up. Harrison had no idea why his dad always said goodbye in twelve different ways on the phone. A peculiar marvel. "Crisis averted."

"Thank you!"

"Now, please go home. Cuz that's where I told Wally you'd be."

"We are! That's where we're going," Harrison said.

"All right, sounds good," Obed said.

"See you later," Harrison said.

"Be safe getting home," Obed said.

"Will do," Harrison said.

"All right," Obed said.

"Okay," Harrison said.

"Love you, boy-o," Obed said.

"Love you, too," Harrison said.

"All right."

"Bye, now."

The group, now six with the addition of Aparna, moved like one large mass of brown appendages and shirtsleeves and still-wet trunks and one flagging sort-of towel as they walked across the bridge from the park, making introductions, making conversation, and making a new plan.

"Are we all coming to your house?" ask Phil. "I need to get this straight because I'm hearing one thing from some people and other things from other people, and it's very confusing."

"How are you hearing multiple things?" Harrison said. "We're all talking to each other."

"I've heard some rumors," Fab said.

"There's a lot of conversation," said Mazz.

"So?" said Phil.

At the same time that Harrison said "Yes," Linus said "No." Phil threw up her hands in frustration. They crossed the street and through a busy intersection that led to the highway and beyond that the hill where Mazz and Linus had sat. With each passing block, the houses seemed to grow taller and more statuesque, going from homey squat builds with porches to narrow row homes and then to streets populated by tall old three-story mansions, most of which were now divided into apartments.

"What do you mean 'yes'?'" Linus asked.

"I mean, why not?" Harrison said. "We can just hang out in the backyard if we want."

"Uh, did you run this by your parents?"

"It's my house, too!" Harrison declared.

"I don't think we need to do all this."

"What if I want people to come over?" Harrison said. He was buzzing like he'd had a soda. "I think it will be fun. A little send-off."

Linus's voice got low. "Doesn't feel little," he said. "Feels like doing a lot."

Harrison looked at him seriously. "It's not too much. I promise you."

They crossed the street again, heading south. The block was lined with trees, most of which were as tall as the old mansions. It was cooler, calmer, quieter here, even though they were within walking distance of Pride and a little bit to the west of Linus's house. It was truly like the neighborhoods were encased in their own protective shells. How to get out, how to get in? They walked on. Here and there, a restaurant or a church broke up the line of looming brown buildings. People sat outside on steps or at café tables, arms, legs, knees, feet catching the sun. Harrison moved out in front of their group, walking fast.

"What are you doing?" Linus asked.

"The same thing I've been doing all day," Harrison said. "Ferris Day." He turned to the his friends and called out, "If anybody sees a Ferris wheel, let me know. It's important."

"Now you're doing too much," Linus said.

"Now I'm okay with that."

They crossed the street again onto another block with similar architecture. It made sense that this was where the rich people used to live, north of North Avenue, east of the park, close to everything. Harrison didn't understand why anyone would want to be far away.

"Who could hate this city?" he declared to no one in particular.

"That's what I've been saying!" said Phil.

Up ahead was a row home with huge swaths of fabric hanging down from the roof. The building was made up of two three-story mansions combined, with the door moved to the center. It was as tall as it was wide, a perfect square. The fabric was stretched tight, extending from the roof over a small cement yard and tied at a point along a black metal fence. As they got closer, they saw that the fabric made a rainbow, with one swath in each color— black, brown, red, orange, yellow, green, blue, and purple. It had the effect of making the building's yard seem like it was under a circus big top. The railings of the stone stairs leading to the double front doors had fabric in the colors of the trans flag looped through the bars on one side and magenta, yellow, and light blue fabric on the other.

"Looks like these people take Pride very seriously," Aparna said.

"What is the magenta, yellow, and blue flag for again?" Harrison asked.

"Pansexual Pride," Fab answered.

They approached the gate and took in the house behind the makeshift Pride tent. There was a checkerboard of windows across the face of the building, all frosted over in white with silhouettes of pine trees. The silhouettes looked like sketches, hasty and jagged and whimsical. Though the sun was still out, they could see the faint hint of colored lights moving behind windows on different floors. There was music coming from inside, a piano playing, and from up on the roof, the faint sounds of dance songs floating down like the smell of home cooking coming from a kitchen. It seemed alive and of another place. Harrison had never seen a house do drag before, but he thought that this house would get tens across the board. This house wasn't just a pretty face. This house had a rich interior life. In here, as the emcee in *Cabaret* says, life is beautiful. Harrison wished he could see that show again. Cool Aparna had been an amazing Sally Bowles.

Harrison stepped into the yard. Linus pulled his arm back.

Linus looked him in the eye. *We're supposed to be going home.*

We're supposed to be having an adventure, Harrison replied. He waggled his eyebrows in the way that Linus had done to him a million times. *This is a home.*

He ducked under the black fabric and walked to the base of the stairs. There were two doors, both glass, at the top. Each pane had the silhouette of a woman in a hoop skirt leaning in toward the middle like they were about to kiss.

"Should I knock?" Harrison asked.

"For what reason?" Linus replied.

Fab wandered down the block and disappeared around the side of the house.

"Do you think it's someone's house?" Mazz said.

"It's a lounge," said Aparna, looking at her phone. "It's called the Evergreens."

"This is the Evergreens?!" Harrison cried.

"You've heard of it?" Aparna asked.

"I've more than heard of it. I've been invited." He spoke directly to Linus then. "It's a sign!"

Linus turned to Mazz. "At Pride, we met this guy Fitzhugh Quatch—"

"You met a Quatch?!" Phil screamed, the most enthused Harrison had seen her all afternoon.

"No relation," said Harrison.

"Oh." Phil was crushed.

Linus continued, "He and his sister and his friends were coming here for a Pride party, and he told us we have to come. It was at some weird time. But he told us we have to come and here we are. So . . ."

"So?" Harrison said out loud, but giving his eyebrows a workout.

"I think it might be a sign," Mazz said.

"Did he say how to get in?" Aparna asked.

"He tried to give me his number." Linus offered unhelpfully.

"Did you take his number?" Aparna asked.

"No, Linus was being mad about not having his phone," Harrison said. "I'm just going to knock." He had not, however, moved any closer to the door.

"Wait. Who do you think is going to open the door?" Mazz asked.

"I guess the butler?"

"Just what are we supposed to do in some place that has a butler?" Aparna said.

"I don't know! Should I not do this?" Harrison said.

"Well . . ." said Linus. "They did invite us."

"Turning down the Quatches is social death," Phil said.

"It's not *the* Quatches," said Harrison.

Phil held her hands up. "I'm blocking that out. I can't deal with it."

Mazz piped up. "I think, whatever is going on inside, if we don't see it now, it's going to drive us nuts. Some things demand to be seen. That's the whole idea with Pride, right? Plus, it is Ferris Day after all."

Phil held up a finger. "I hate to interject, but I have to admit I'm a little confused about what Ferris Day is. I never really got clarity around what you're doing."

"We're doing anything we want. Together," Linus said, smiling.

"I'm going to knock on this door now, then," said Harrison, his bravado only slightly flagging.

Fab peeked her head around the corner. "Hey, folks, the entrance is actually around here. There's a line. So."

4:50 p.m.

They stood in front of a large wooden barn door that had been cut into the side of the building; it had the words OPEN ME CAREFULLY painted on it in white cursive. Linus imagined this was more than a simple safety precaution, but rather a message from the house to the world. He imagined that whatever was behind the door was somehow both more and less real than he was experiencing, like the vivid stilt houses that Mazz predicted awaited him down south. He imagined that to go in unawares would trip him up. He imagined that if the door was flung open, whatever magic that was alive inside would rush out into the streets and transform the world.

What then? Would he also be transformed? Would it be too much?

If it was, he decided, at least he knew what he wanted on his fancy gravestone at Baltimore Cemetery. He wanted a big pristine rock that read OPEN ME CAREFULLY.

The woman who was standing at the door, listening to Harrison chatter as Linus daydreamed, did not appear interested in opening the door, carefully or otherwise. Nevertheless, Harrison was lobbying her, displaying none of the usual awkwardness that both of them always felt around adults.

"Um, so I guess what I'm asking is," Harrison was saying, "is Fitzhugh Quatch on the list? We're with him."

"No," the woman at the door replied.

"Okay, because he told us to come here."

"For what?" she said. What did she mean, for what? For whatever was happening behind that door that she'd just let six people into. *Perhaps, madam, you can hear the piano playing "Home" from* The Wiz *behind you, so if we could hurry this part up, that would be great.* Harrison desperately needed to get there (wherever *there* was) before that roof-raising final note. It was his duty as a Black person and also someone who had a calling, and a cultural legacy, and a special Tony for Anxiety.

He tried to answer her riddles. "It was . . . well, it was a party. But it had a weird name."

"Yeah, it was a kind of drink and then a name for a party," Linus said.

Oh, hello, Linus; welcome to the door, thought Harrison. *Thanks for joining.* "You remember all that but you don't remember the name?" he said out loud.

"Do you?" Linus countered.

"Okay, fair." Harrison said.

Aparna had her phone out and was googling. "A drink and a word for 'party'?"

"Coffee klatch!" cried Phil.

"Soda shindig," said Mazz.

"Water blast," said Fab.

"I think the phrase you're looking for is tea party?" Aparna said.

Harrison shook his head. "No."

"But that is actually what you are describing. It is a drink and the name of a party. Tea party."

Harrison looked at her and gasped. "No! But! Wait... Dance! Tea dance! We're here for the tea dance."

"Okay," said the woman at the door. She had a ring on every finger. They clinked as she adjusted her hand on the door handle.

"So can we come in?" Harrison said. Is this how adult parties worked? You called it something ridiculous and if people could remember the name, a woman with teased hair and truly amazing floral-print boots would let them in? Who was this for? Also, was there a book he could study, because if this is how things operated, he had major concerns about his future social life. As usual.

The guard had questions, too. "Who invited you?"

"Fitzhugh! We told you!"

She pulled out a small black notebook. "He's not on the list."

"Triple Belk?"

"Sorry."

"Do you have someone named Triple Belk's boyfriend on there?"

"Why would I write that many words?" It was a good point. The notebook was miniscule.

"Isobel Quatch?" Linus said.

"ISOBEL! Why didn't you say so?! Oh my god, Isobel. Of course!"

The door rumbled shut behind them, and they were plunged into the darkness of a long vestibule. Neon lights in pink and blue and green sweat across their faces and arms. Each member of the group privately wondered what they'd gotten themselves into. They'd all seen the cartoon *Pinocchio* as kids. And also the news. You didn't just roll up into strange houses just because they had a Pride flag on the outside. And now what were they supposed to do? Push open the door in front of them? Continue walking? Go to the dance? Suspicious! No one spoke. The music crept in to fill the space. The barn door opened again, and a couple almost stumbled over the group as they crowded into the vestibule.

"This ain't the party!" the doorwoman called.

Carefully, they pushed open the door.

As Harrison stepped out of the vestibule and into the party, his skin, his Bayard Rustin shirt, and his trunks were all covered by geometric shapes in blue and red and yellow and white. Light. He looked up. He discovered that he was standing in the hollow of a great swirling staircase, rising up three tall levels, a flurry of right angles made of mahogany. And at the very top, in the center, sending lit triangles and squares raining down on them, was a giant rectangular stained-glass window. It glowed. It lit up the whole floor around them like they were all inside a gem.

Harrison turned to Linus and saw a version of himself. Linus's white bowling shirt was a pageant of light; the black birds stitched on the sides now flew off to a jeweled paradise. The light pushed in through the fabric, too, illuminating Linus's undershirt and neck in the same way that his arms and face were. It was like light wanted to take a physical form. They were vibrant new creatures standing in the middle of radiance itself.

And around them, other vibrant beings were suffused with light, lingering in doorways, coming and going. People moving up and down the stairs, glowing like sunrise and sunset. Folks in summer-casual and party dress gathered here by the bannister, there flirting against the ornate wallpaper of a hallway, or laughing behind a wooden column, just an arm and a flash of teeth visible. Posing for no one and for everyone, a hand hitched up the side. Careening through the entryway at odd angles, heels clacking, a glass dangling precariously from their hands. Peering down from the staircase like celestial hosts.

Harrison felt like they'd stepped back in time. No, not back, beside time. The inside of the Evergreens looked like it had been restored to the stately grandeur of its original 1800s form—all wood and brass and white light pouring in from huge square windows across velvet furniture. But that grandeur had been animated at some point by an energy that Harrison could only describe as queer. Harrison had never before described anything, particularly a physical space, as queer, but it was the word that came to mind. And as he judged his thought, he decided that perhaps the three-story inclusive rainbow on the outside might have been a clue. But there was something else, something molecular about it. There was a humor to everything; he would have thought a mansion with gleaming wood floors and a soaring stained-glass window and huge archways leading to bright rooms would be stuffy. But where there might have been a domineering portrait of some ancient general in the imposing entryway, there was instead a huge photograph of a Black woman with a low 'fro standing in front of a blackboard with WOMEN ARE POWERFUL AND DANGEROUS written on it. He broke off from the group to look closer. A sign said it was the poet Audre Lorde. Underneath, a turntable aimlessly spun a tray of succulents. The group moved deeper into the house and turned as one body through a doorway and found a great room, brightly lit and lined with books. Between the shelves there were framed signs from years of gay-rights protests. Above a doorway, there was a quote spray-painted on top of the wallpaper that read WE NEED, IN EVERY COMMUNITY, A GROUP OF ANGELIC TROUBLEMAKERS. And underneath the quote was the attribution: BAYARD RUSTIN. Harrison instinctively pressed his hand to his chest. He got the sense that this place had an infinite number of bustling rooms like this. Full of life. Full of the thing that he, again, could only describe as queer. It was . . . what was it? The sound, the tenor, the tone; the fixtures, the decor, the knickknacks secreted on a shelf that nobody would even see; the energy, the vibrance, the comfort.

Yes, that was it, too. It was comfortable. It had a busy comfort that he'd felt at Maybe This Time and also—he found this fascinating—at the museum. The hatpin in the display case. The elevator that time traveled. The paradox of liberty. All of time, a certain kind of time, lived here.

"Okay, whoops," said Fab quietly, "we up and went to gay Heaven."

"This is so much," Aparna said.

"It's too much," said Fab, her voice filled with awe. It was the highest compliment.

And with that, it was like a spell broke for Harrison. He wanted to see it all. Music rushed in from different rooms, beside him and above him, conversations overlapped in cascades, light danced with them. He started moving, and it was like you move in a dream. Here one minute, there another, with that dream insight that comes naturally because you're creating it yourself. They passed a bag-check station and checked the blanket-towel. The attendant gave them all the side-eye but stored it in a cubbyhole regardless. The group fell in line with the movement of the larger crowd, circling the first floor of the house. It seemed like rooms were all organized in a loop around the staircase, connected to each other through huge open doorways. Over the din, Harrison could make out a nearby instrument plucking out a familiar intense rhythm. Up ahead, he spotted it: a group of people crowded around a piano, singing along as the pianist played the opening number from *Ragtime*. Was someone going to hit the Audra McDonald high note at the end? Was Audra here?! Harrison held his arms out to stop the group. He waited. The end came. An attempt was made. Hmm. Audra was not in the building.

Now they were on the second floor, in a dark hallway outside a bathroom. Mazz waited in line. The doorway to the bathroom was accentuated with neon-pink bars. The door opened, and a man stepped out, face in his phone, his shaggy hair dipping down to almost touch the screen. Mazz slipped into the bathroom as the guy with the phone stepped aside and started walking down the hall.

"Triple!" Harrison called after him. Harrison was certainly not in the habit of being noticed on purpose, and he had never in his life drawn attention to himself by yelling someone's name out in a house full of strangers. But there was a new enthusiasm driving him. He hadn't envisioned this as the place to end Ferris Day, but now it felt right. He and Linus could make their clean break here if that's what Linus wanted, and maybe it would be different in the way that the light in the stairwell was different, the sounds were different, time itself was different. Triple Belk looked up, squinted into the darkness, and then broke out in a smile.

"JAMAL!" People squeezed past Triple to get to the bathroom, and he flattened himself against the wall. "Oh my god, so crowded. Meet me on the stairs! Fitzhugh's gonna freak!"

Harrison turned to the group as Triple made his way down the hall. "Okay, so the people who invited us here think that my name is Jamal and that Linus's name is Dizzy."

"Why do they think that?" Aparna asked.

"I have no idea."

"Well," said Linus, "I did tell them that my name was Dizzy."

"That would do it," said Aparna.

"Do they think you're different people?" Phil asked.

"I don't understand," Harrison said.

"Are they only confused about your names, or do they think you have different personalities?"

Well, that was the question. *Had* they been different in conversation with the Quatches? Had Linus, vibing with Fitzhugh about some book Harrison had never heard of, been a different version of himself? Had he, rooting for a rekindled friendship between Triple and Real Jamal, been someone other than himself? When he saw the way that Triple looked at him, did Harrison feel different, even though Triple was seeing Jamal? Harrison didn't have the script and he hadn't rehearsed and he wasn't the director's first choice, but he was playing the part anyway, and it was showtime again. It was baffling and delightful.

"I'm not sure what they think," Harrison said, "but they seem to like us. Oh, also—they think we're college students and that I'm on Broadway."

"Ah, good," Phil said. "We wouldn't want to end up in a strange house where there has yet to be any tea based on a complete lie."

"Should we all have fake names?" Fab asked, mischief in her eyes.

"I don't think that's necessary," Harrison said.

Fab was already scrolling through her phone. "It's no problem; I keep a list of possible aliases on my Notes app. I also have a list of drag-queen names. You just never know when you'll need one. Should I be a drag queen today? I think that's the vibe, actually." She closed her phone.

"Well?" said Phil.

Fab extended her hand to Phil, "Mirror, mirror on the wall, my name is Ferris Ofthemall." She turned to Harrison. "I just made that one up for you."

Phil took Fab's hand gallantly. "Nice to meet you, Ferris. I'm Frances Ellen Watkins Harper."

"I hear there's a school named after you," Fab said.

"I get that a lot," Phil said.

Aparna stepped up and extended her hand, a wide grin on her face. "I'm Lazar Wolf."

"Oh my god, yes!" cried Fab.

"I'm sorry, what exactly happened while I was in there?" Mazz asked, standing in the doorway.

"I'll explain on the stairs," Linus said.

Phil clapped her hands. "Let's walk and talk!"

There was cursive, in the same style as the writing on the door, painted in white over the wallpaper lining the staircase. As they climbed, following Triple Belk, Harrison read the words. On the first flight up: "HOPE" IS THE THING WITH FEATHERS—at the landing, it continued: THAT PERCHES IN THE SOUL—above them, the colored skylight radiated; a glass door rattled lightly from the sound of bass through a speaker. On the next flight came the phrase AND SINGS THE TUNE WITHOUT THE WORDS—they reached the top of the stairs, and the text ushered them through the doors with AND NEVER STOPS—AT ALL—.

The roof-deck was packed, and they had to squeeze through closely huddled groups of people to get to the bench by the edge where Isobel was holding court. At some point in the day, she'd procured an incredibly tiny top hat. Truly smaller than you would imagine. It was affixed to her hair somehow but fluttered in the breeze, threatening to go off on its own adventure across the city. She held a bouquet of gold roses in one hand, which she was using to gesticulate wildly. Freeing himself of the tangle of the crowd, Harrison saw the whole city beyond the edge of the building. Underneath them, the rainbow fabric rippled, a bridge down to the mansions and row homes, the office buildings, the park in the distance. He turned, and the Harbor came into view, the angular point of the aquarium piercing the sky. He felt like he was floating, raised up by the energy and the house itself and the pulsating bass that came from a DJ who was—he checked—not his father.

"Oh, at last!" Isobel cried.

"Is this your party?" Fab asked Isobel. They'd clustered

around her as Triple navigated the crowd to fetch his boyfriend and Fitzhugh.

"My darling, no!" Isobel said. "It's my friend's. Their name is Dazzle Gradually. We met at jury duty. We acquitted." She pointed to a figure across the deck—statuesque with bronze skin, jet-black hair, and a floor-length sleeveless white tunic—carrying a case of bottled water through the crowd above their head. "They rented this place for the tea dance."

"Okay, so that's my question," said Phil. "I get the dance part. But where is the tea?"

At that, a woman next to Isobel leaned in conspiratorially. "The tea is Dazzle didn't rent this place. They own it." The woman raised her eyebrows, waiting for a reaction that no one in the group provided. Undeterred, she continued, "It's that app money."

"Of course!" Isobel said.

Harrison resigned himself to never understanding anything that was said in the presence of a Quatch. "They made an app?"

"Where've you been?" the woman said. "Dazzle made that whole suite of apps. What's it called? With the location thing?"

"Check In," Isobel offered.

"Yes!" the woman cried.

"Dazzle invented the Check In app?" Linus asked incredulously. Harrison had always imagined he'd have a nemesis one day, but he never imagined they'd be so stunning.

Isobel nodded vigorously. "Can you believe it?"

"I have a couple of notes about possible improvements," Aparna said. "I'm intimately familiar with Check In."

The woman continued. "Well, tell them! They're a mogul in the making. Took that big money and plunked it down here. Of course, Baltimore real estate prices are another story altogether."

"I need to meet this person," Phil said, already diving into the crowd.

The woman raised her glass in affirmation and then squinted at them. She leaned forward. "Let me ask you something: Are you all children?"

"Dizzy, my favorite!" Fitzhugh and Triple were suddenly upon them. Fitzhugh lopped an arm over Linus's shoulder and pulled him in.

"Jamal," Triple said, "meet my boyfriend!" Triple excitedly pointed down to the bespectacled guy standing next to him. Triple's boyfriend (Harrison wondered if this person had a name) eyed Harrison/Jamal with no small amount of suspicion.

What would Real Jamal do in this situation? Harrison had no idea. For that matter, what would Harrison do? What was Harrison doing? He stepped forward and hugged the boyfriend. It seemed to take the boyfriend by surprise, which was ironic to Harrison because it was taking him by surprise, too. "I'm a hugger," Harrison claimed. He stepped back. "Um, hi, I'm Jamal."

"Me too," said the boyfriend.

"What?"

"My name is Jamal, too," the boyfriend (Jamal???) said.

A second Jamal? A *third* Jamal? Harrison looked at Triple, who was positively tickled by this Jamal symposium.

"I've really wanted to meet you," Harrison said. "Triple is so happy."

The other Jamal grinned. "He's been talking about you all day."

"I was going to say the same thing," Harrison said, laughing.

Harrison caught Linus's raised eyebrow over the boyfriend's shoulder. *Baby boy, what is this show you're putting on?*

Harrison responded, *I am just vamping!*

Harrison pointed to the rest of the group. "These are my friends: Dizzy, Ferris, Mazz Still Mazz, and Lazar Wolf." Everyone waved. "And over there is Francis Ellen Watkins Harper."

Lazar Wolf checked a message on her phone. "Harrison—sorry, I mean, Jermaine," she said, making an attempt. "Aparna is here with the phones."

The phones, the disguised Check In locations, the plan, the world, the reality of their situation—Harrison had forgotten all of it for a moment, but as he, Aparna, and Linus descended the stairs and back out the barn door, it all came back. Whatever this place was, it was temporary. Harrison had gotten happily distracted, but he realized now that he and Linus had hardly spoken since they'd gone inside. It had been a stunning whirlwind and he was newly aware of how little time they had left. He stole a grim look at Linus, as they stepped into the light. Harrison resolved to refocus. This was about the two of them. It was always about them.

Aparna R. was parked at the curb, deep in conversation about a book with the doorwoman with the floral boots.

"Well, naturally the mafia has a different relationship to patriotism," the doorwoman was saying. "I think that's what the chapter set on the train is meant to signify."

"Right, right, I've always thought that," said Aparna R. She spotted the trio on the curb. "Oh, there's my friends! We'll continue this later."

"You bet. You gotta finish the book."

"I'm trying! All these errands!" Aparna R. said. The doorwoman stepped back, and Harrison saw that Aparna R. was sitting in a convertible with the top down. She waved sunnily and held up the backpack. Harrison grabbed Linus's arm.

"Car Without Roof!" Harrison said. "It's on the Ferris Day list!"

Linus looked confused, and then it dawned on him. "Wait, did you plan it like this?! You're a genius!"

"No, I actually did not. Nothing has gone according to plan. It's been one disaster after another. But! I am learning to roll with it. And now we have our Ferris Day chariot!"

They approached the car.

"Hey, Harrison!" Aparna R. called. "I am so sorry I kidnapped your phones."

"It's no problem," Harrison said. "Thank you so much for bringing them back." She handed the bag across the seat.

"Sorry to bother you," Aparna A. said.

"Seriously, I do not mind at all! Would you believe that nobody has noticed that I'm not back yet? Still?!"

"So, listen," Harrison said, "this is going to sound a little weird, but my friend Linus and I have been doing this whole day of new experiences, and one of the things we were trying to do was ride in a car with the roof down. Like in the movies. And it totally feels like a sign that you're here with a car that has its roof down."

"Aww, that sounds so fun!" Aparna R. said.

"So can we ride around with you? Maybe down by the Harbor?"

"Oh!" Aparna R. said. "No. Thank you, though!" She turned to Aparna A. "See you next week, Aparna!" She waved, started the car, and drove off.

5:22 p.m.

As usual, Harrison had no notifications waiting for him on his phone. But as they hiked back up the stairs, Linus tapped him on the arm and showed him his own phone, which had three missed calls from his mother.

"Do you think she knows?" Harrison asked.

"She doesn't have the app," Linus said. "Should I call her back?" They lingered on the second-floor landing. Harrison and Aparna exchanged a glance.

"I'm going to see what's going on around that piano," she said. She trotted back downstairs and vanished into the house.

"I think you should call her back. I mean, it's your mom," Harrison said. "Does she know you're moving?"

"My dad said he told her. She was annoyed with him. You think she's annoyed with me?"

"But you don't even want to go!"

"I was always doing something wrong," Linus said. "I should've . . . Maybe I should've asked to live with her again."

"Is that what you want to do?" Harrison asked, a small hope fluttering in his chest.

339

Linus shook his head. "I don't know. It was . . . She doesn't want that."

"You should call her," Harrison said. The second floor was quieter, with two large rooms on one side of the stairs, one seemingly empty and the other playing lo-fi hip-hop to a smattering of folks. Harrison guided Linus into the empty room. The windows were reflected in the shining wood floors. Harrison and Linus stood side by side in the middle of the room, in front of a large gilded mirror that stretched to the ceiling. Linus snapped his fingers into a V and stuck his tongue out. Harrison gave a thumbs-up. Linus rolled his eyes and laughed. He leaned his head over and rested it on Harrison's shoulder. He caught Harrison's eyes in the reflection.

"Hey, thanks for telling me I should hang out with Mazz earlier."

"Dario, Fitzhugh, Mazz. You've been so popular today."

"Boy, if you don't stop . . ." Linus shoved him playfully.

"I'm just saying. I never knew you had so many boyfriends."

"Come on, now! Seriously, I am really not feeling you right now."

"Are you blushing?"

"How 'bout you mind your business?"

"This *is* my business," Harrison said. "I'm just happy for you."

"Like you were happy for Triple and Jamal."

"Wait, oh my god, what was that?"

"No lie, I thought they had caught us, for real," Linus said.

"Me too! And then I got mad. I was like, 'This can't be the Jamal from school because *I'm* the Jamal from school.'"

"New Jamal needs to fall back." Linus laughed. "But also, good for them."

"Oh yeah," Harrison said. "I'm very happy for them."

"Nothing makes you happier than when your fake friend from high school finds a boyfriend who is basically your twin."

They laughed, but an emptiness crept into it. It seemed like in such a big room their voices should echo off the walls and floor, but everything they'd said had been swallowed up. They stood as the beat from the lo-fi next door and the dance music upstairs competed against each other.

Harrison spoke first. "When you get a boyfriend in South Carolina, you have to let me know."

"Baby boy. First of all, that is not going to happen. And second of all, don't start that now. We're just hanging."

"If not now, when, though?" said Harrison.

"The sun is still out. We got till eight," said Linus. "We got our phones back; we're set. Lemme call my mom and then . . . you want to go back up and dance?"

Harrison absolutely did not want to dance. "Yes. I can't wait."

🚃🚃🚃

Harrison wandered back out of the room to give Linus his privacy, following the railing of the staircase. He peered down—people in constant motion, a blur of colors—and up, on a steady ascent toward the stained glass. He ducked into the room playing lo-fi. A couple people danced in small clusters throughout the room. A few more chilled on a sofa. Golden beams of light cutting through the yellow fabric outside made waves on the floor. On the far side of the room, a Black woman danced alone near a bricked-up fireplace covered with votives. She had her back to the room, seemingly in a world of her own. Harrison watched her sway and rock, her stretching shoulder muscles visible in a strapless jumpsuit. She lifted her hands skyward and let them fall across her shaved head. Harrison tried to conjure what it must feel like in one's body to walk into a room, set yourself up by the fireplace, and dance just because you want to. Harrison stepped inside, trying to be as inconspicuous as possible. Not that anyone was looking at him. He wondered what the rules of this room were. He wondered what would happen if he started dancing, too. Logically, he knew that nothing would happen. This was a tea dance. Whatever that meant. Since they seemed to be running low on tea, there was only one thing left to do.

Still, he didn't move. He couldn't bring himself to do it. He was here, wasn't he? He'd done a whole day. Wasn't that enough personal progress for the year? And he still had to, in some way, make sure Linus wouldn't leave him behind. So dancing would have to wait.

Harrison set his sights on a wingback chair in the corner of the room and headed for it. He would just sit here, in the hip-hop room, and manifest the *spirit* of dancing. In the dim light, he misjudged where the arm of the chair was and bumped into it. Of course, it let out a horrifying groan as it slid back. Harrison wished, yet again, to disappear. He was aware in a new way of the fact that this was definitely a party full of adults, and though most people didn't seem to be bothered by this, he had no idea how to behave or what to do or what he wanted. He had no idea where he wanted to be, actually. What place in the world was made for him? He scanned the room—no one was freaking out about the noise from the chair. Praise be to the chill vibes of lo-fi hip-hop. Harrison sat down. The chair made *another* squeak. The furniture was conspiring against him like a horror-movie version of *Beauty and the Beast*. The dancing woman with the shaved head turned at this new sound. Her face crossed into a beam of golden light. Harrison's jaw fell open.

"I absolutely cannot believe this," Corrine said.

5:35 p.m.

Linus paced in the empty ballroom. His reflection slipped in and out of the frame of the mirror. On the phone, his mother was asking him a question he didn't know how to answer.

"So what do you think about this move, huh?" He'd reached her at the nursing home where she worked and could hear a television playing in the background. It sounded like a game show. He had no idea what he could say about South Carolina that wouldn't sound surly, so instead he tried to focus on listening to the trivia question coming from the TV. He got that answer right.

"Honey?" his mom said after a bit. "You still there?"

"Yeah."

"Guess you don't think much of it, then?"

Linus shrugged even though he knew his mom couldn't see it.

"Well, I'm going to miss you."

"Really?"

He heard her breath catch through the receiver. "Yes, Linus. Very much. Your dad and I talked about trying to get you back up here to visit, but if we can't figure that out, I'll just drive down. Bird and I always got along—she'll let me sleep on the couch or something."

Linus couldn't figure out why the solutions that his parents came up with never seemed to make them any happier than the problems. The weariness—in their voices, in their bodies, in their beings—was the constant. And when the weariness wore out, then there was the tenseness. And that's all there was, it seemed. He felt it, too, now. Weary, tense, sharp. He didn't have an answer.

But he thought of what Mazz had said on the hillside in the park. Mazz thought that Linus hadn't given up on what he was looking for. Could that really be true? Linus didn't think of himself as someone who gave up, but beyond that, he felt like he was someone who knew when the story was over. And that wasn't giving up, was it? That was just being realistic. But what happens when you're wrong about the story being over? What then?

"I appreciate you taking my call," his mom said. "I, um. I thought you were avoiding me."

"No, I just left my phone. But I got it back."

"Well, good. Are you—Where are you?"

"I'm hanging out with Harrison."

"That's good," his mom said. "I guess you're going to miss—"

Linus interrupted. "Why would you come down to Aunt Bird's house?"

"Why . . . I don't know how to answer that. Because we can't afford a plane ticket right now but I want to know I'll see my son again in the near future."

"Even though you and dad don't get along?"

"We've tried to keep that from . . . changing things for you. As much as we can. I know we failed at that a lot. But we tried."

She paused. The sound of the game show overtook the call again. She spoke up, quieter now. "Do you not want me to come?"

"It's not about what I want."

"Well, I'm asking you."

"You'd be the first," he said.

"I'm sorry you don't want to move. I don't want you to move, either. I don't know why you wouldn't want me to come down, though. I don't know what I did wrong."

What she did wrong? Linus couldn't understand what conversation they were having. Even on the phone, it seemed like he was saying all the wrong things. Worsening her tension, wearing her down.

Finally, Linus just said it. He was so tired. He was so sad. He didn't think, deep down, that he'd find what he was looking for, because it didn't exist. But he didn't know what else to try, so he just spoke the truth. "You said you wanted a clean break. From me. I . . ." He felt the words get stuck in his throat. "I don't know how to be different. I'm sorry."

"Oh. Oh no." Perfect Munro sighed. "Hold on. I'm going to step outside." Linus listened to the *swish-swish* of her uniform pants, the passing voices, and beeps, and televisions. The *swoosh* of the sliding doors. And then a flat nothingness as she reached the still summer air. She made a small noise as she sat down. "I don't know why it always gets this way for us," she said. It almost

346

sounded like she was talking to herself. "When you were little, we were everything to each other. Maybe I was wrong."

Linus thought, *No, you're right*. But he couldn't bring himself to say it.

"When I said—When you moved to your father's house . . . that was a hard year. A hard year in the middle of a bunch of hard years. I had to figure out how to keep you from getting sick with me coming in and out of the nursing home every day, how to keep myself safe, how to get you fed, how to get you online to get to your classes. You're so bright, and I felt like I was failing. Failing you. And I could see it in your eyes. And you said it sometimes. I know you were frustrated. When things changed, I felt like, 'Okay, maybe that was just a moment.' But . . . we were just in the middle of a bunch of hard years. And you said—I'm not . . . I don't want it to seem like I'm blaming you—You said—Oh, please, please, don't let this be the only thing you remember about this conversation. Lord Jesus, please. I'm just trying to explain to you what happened inside me. You said that you wanted out, and I thought, 'It's been so hard; that's the exit sign.' That's what you want, that's what we're looking for, that's what we're supposed to do. I thought that it was the answer."

Linus sat down in the middle of the floor and held his head in one hand as he pressed his phone to his ear with the other.

His mother continued, "Linus, I never wanted you to be different. I love you so much exactly the way you are. I am so proud of you. You have to know that. I miss you every day. I kept waiting,

347

when we lived together, waiting on the right words to say that would make everything easier for the both of us. And I guess I shouldn't have waited. I should have just tried. And I'm sorry."

"I'm sorry, too," Linus said. Tears dripped off his face and landed on the shining floor.

"You don't have to be sorry. I have always hoped, I still hope, that the things that your father and I have to wrestle with in this life don't get passed down to you. I am still hoping for that."

"Do you remember that concert they had at church for the gospel choir's album recording?"

Linus could hear the smile in his mother's voice. "Oh yes! What a beautiful evening."

He didn't know what to make of that response. Is that how she really felt? If that was the case, then why . . . ?

He plunged on. "They sing that one song, on the recording, that you really like, and I found the CD at Dad's house and I made an MP3 because . . . because I knew you liked the song. And at the start of the song, I can hear you, in the audience."

Perfect drew a breath.

"Did you know that?" he said.

"Yes. I've listened to that track a lot."

"Me too."

"Why?" she asked.

"I . . . Why? I . . . It was like I found the beginning of all our troubles. Before that, you and Dad were married and things were fine between us and then after that, it was different. I thought if

I could go back to the beginning, if I could figure out what happened, I could figure out what went wrong. And then I could figure out what I did wrong."

Her breath came out a ragged sigh. "Oh, baby. I went to that concert to feel good. I went to be around people that loved me. Remember how tight I held your hand? I wanted to be there with you. With you, specifically. Things had already gotten hard between your dad and me. And we'd lost the business and he couldn't find work, and—that's all, that's all you need to know. That wasn't the beginning, though, Linus. That was the middle. And you didn't—you never did a thing wrong to me. Not ever. I hold that memory of that concert so close, even now. Because we were together. I wanted to be there in the middle of love. I held your hand so tight."

Linus pressed his hand to his mouth. The weight of her words threatened to crush him even as he felt something heavier being lifted off.

His mom spoke up again. "When I listen to the song, I think of how much joy you bring me. I hope that one day you can remember it like I do. Life is not always easy. Your father and I, we've had a rough go of it. I know you have, too. But I just want it to be different for you. I know this move is not what you want. But . . . you're in the middle of your story. And so am I. That's what I've learned. After all these years. That woman I was on the album didn't know how she was going to make it through to the next day, let alone to now. But here we are talking. Here I am. I

349

love you, son. I thank you, so much, for returning my call. I—I don't want to be broken from you."

"I don't want to be broken from you, either." He wiped his face with the bottom of his shirt and breathed out slowly to calm down. "I love you."

"Thank you for saying that. You will have a whole history; that's my hope. This is just the middle. The middle has a lot of stuff in it, but what I've learned—I'm learning—is to hold on to joy. We need it."

5:36 p.m.

On the other side of the mirror, Harrison leapt up from the wing-back chair as Corrine, with a newly shaved head, stared at him, shocked. Harrison stepped forward as Corrine stepped to the side; they began to circle each other like gunslingers in the Wild West, crossing into and out of the yellow light beams.

"How are you following me?" Harrison whispered.

"How am *I*?" Corrine shot back. "You came in here. You're following me!"

"That can't possibly be true!"

Corrine stopped moving. "Harrison, be reasonable. How would I have followed you here when I didn't know you were coming here and I'm just trying to mind my own business and dance to this boring playlist?"

"I don't know! The same way you followed me to the thrift store and to Pride!"

Corrine smiled at that and flung herself into the wingback chair. She crossed her legs and tapped the foot dangling in the air.

"Well?" Harrison said.

"Don't hover over me. Sheesh. Pull up a chair, brother of mine."

Harrison sighed, exasperated, and searched the room for

another chair. He spotted a wingback in the corner and dragged it over, this time not caring one bit about the noise. He set himself up opposite Corrine.

"Oh my goodness," she said. "The drama." She rolled her eyes. "You thought you were being so sneaky today."

"I didn't!"

Corrine gave him a look that said, *Oh, really, now?*

"Fine. I thought I was being a little sneaky."

"Your face will always tell the truth, Harrison. When you and me were in the kitchen this morning, you kept looking from me to the tote bag, and I said to myself, 'He's up to something.' So shifty! And, lo and behold, I looked and you were stealing the kitchen iPad."

"Borrowing." He reached for the tote bag, forgetting that Aparna had taken it.

"Mm-hmm. I was curious about what all was going on, so after you got out of my car, I used Find My Phone on the kitchen iPad."

Harrison gasped.

"Little did I know how useful it would be! You went all over creation!"

"It's Ferris Day!" Harrison cried.

"I don't know what that means. You know, you're lucky I did decide to check in on you. This city isn't a playground! You could have gotten into trouble, you could have gotten hurt, you could have been stopped by the police, and who would have known?"

"But I didn't! Nothing happened."

"A man chased you through the commuter train like you were in *Snowpiercer*, Harrison. If the conductor hadn't gotten there, I would have had to fight him."

Harrison remembered now the glimpse of a twist out he'd seen riding down to DC. "I *knew* that was you on the train."

"Of course it was me! I am trying to keep you alive. You think you're so grown."

"I don't!" He did a little.

"Clearly not, since you purposefully went to a pool where our father was working. How'd that go over?"

"He caught us!"

"Wow. A real shock," said Corrine dryly. "I thought about trying to warn you, but by that time I was at the barber and had to deal with my own life."

"Wait, what happened to your twist out? Did I make you miss your hair appointment?"

At that, Corrine laughed. "You are deranged, but you're also really thoughtful." She ran her hands over her head. "I cut it off because hair holds pain and it holds trauma and I needed to let it go."

She'd said it so matter-of-factly, but Harrison felt gutted by it. The truth of being sometimes revealed itself so casually and cruelly that it left him empty.

"Are you okay?" he said.

Now she looked at him more closely. She bit her lip lightly in thought. "Yes. Thank you for asking."

"Do Mom and Dad know about your hair?"

"Yeah. I went to Dad's barber. I just forgot to change the appointment on the family calendar. But people don't need to be in my business anyway."

"Exactly my thought."

"You and I," she said, "are on different trains, buddy."

Were they, though? He couldn't take his eyes off her head—it looked wonderful, but at what cost? Was whatever prompted this change waiting for him? How would he know? That was what he decided to ask. That felt safe.

"How did you know you wanted to shave your head?"

"Truth be told, I didn't." She stared out the window for a moment at the yellow fabric waving in the breeze. "I talked about it with Mom. I don't think she wanted me to do it. I just told her that I was going to go to the barber to talk to him about it."

"Just a chat with the barber," Harrison said.

"I was just wandering around, looking for a place to sit."

"You were on a treasure hunt for some *Sports Illustrated*s from 2001."

Corrine laughed again. "Exactly. My haircut was the last thing on my mind. A total shock, actually!"

"Do you like Dad's barber?"

"He's fine, I guess," she said. "Do you?"

"Not really."

"Well, if you don't like him, you should go to a different barber.

You deserve to be comfortable." She fixed him in her gaze. "I'm serious."

"Okay." Great, now he had homework.

Corrine leaned forward then. "The minute I sat in that chair, I knew. I knew it had to go." She considered what she was going to say and then continued. "Some of these kids at school—in college—these white kids in my dorm would just stick their hands right in it. Like it was a petting zoo."

"Oh my god." This had happened to Harrison before, too, at school, years earlier. He'd never told anyone—what was there to say? But the way that Corrine said it made it sharp for him all over again.

"I knew there were plenty of folks who've never been in close living quarters with a Black person before," she said. "You give them a pass because not being around Black people makes them underprivileged. But, everything . . . everything started to feel like fingers in my hair. The words that people used on me, the questions they put on me, the energy they placed on me. The way they made it seem like my presence, my body, was a problem. All of it, everywhere. In the classroom, in the dorm. These were my friends."

She paused. Her eyes flicked away from him, and Harrison saw the pain of the memories flash across them for just a moment before she locked them away in whatever place she kept them stored.

"We've been taught to stick up for ourselves, right? To say when something isn't fair?"

Harrison nodded.

"I did that," Corrine said. "I held a space for myself. And people started telling me I was being too sensitive. My feelings were also an inconvenience. I couldn't take it. Someone told me, 'Maybe you're not cut out for college.' My friend. My friend said that."

"But you're so smart," Harrison said.

"I know." Corrine said fiercely, beating back the echo of her friend's past comment. "I know," she said, back in the room, across from her brother. "But I forgot. I told myself I was feeling too much. I had too many feelings. I was a problem. I thought—" She stopped abruptly. She looked at Harrison plainly. He reached across and grabbed her hand.

"I'm glad you cut your hair off," he said.

"I didn't want whatever it was holding because that wasn't mine. I had thought, before I dropped out, that it would be better to not feel anything at all. To not . . . Just to not. To not feel, to not exist. But I want to feel everything." She raised her hands up and squeezed her head, shutting her eyes tight. After a moment, she opened them again and smiled. "I want to feel everything."

"Do you think that's going to happen to me? When I get to college?"

"I hope not. But if it does, you better call me, okay? I'm serious. I spent my entire day chasing you all over the greater

Baltimore-DC metro area; I will do anything for you. Do you understand that?"

"Yeah."

"Do you?"

"Yes."

"Anything," Corrine said again.

"I'm sorry I made you waste your day, though."

"Harrison," she said with surprise. "I had a wonderful day! I always enjoy myself. And your face every time you saw me! Ooh, priceless." She cackled and then made a face like a terrified mouse.

"You should be pursue a career as a CIA assassin."

"That is *terrible* karma. No, thanks. Hold up, you got me all distracted. We never established why you followed me here. What are you doing?"

"I didn't follow you. This girl Isobel that I met at Pride invited me."

"Isobel Quatch?" Corrine asked.

"Seriously?!"

"She was on the jury that I was on with Dazzle Gradually. We acquitted. Obviously."

"Smalltimore."

"Let me tell you, Harrison Meredith, you can't do a *thing* secret in this town."

Linus appeared in the doorway of the room and made his way over to Harrison. He looked like he'd been crying. He opened his mouth to speak to Harrison and then recognized Corrine. He screamed. Everybody in the lo-fi room was over this crew.

"It's okay," Harrison said. "She's just here on her own."

"Your hair looks so good," Linus said.

"Thank you, Linus. Are you okay?"

"Yeah. I'm good. Yeah. Harrison, you want to go back up to the roof?"

"Okay."

"Linus," Corrine said, "I didn't hear an invitation for me in there."

Linus got awkward and stammer-y. "I didn't know you wanted to come. But yeah. You can—"

Corrine was already on her feet and headed out the door. "We've been hanging out together all day long. No sense in stopping now."

5:45 p.m.

They found the group clustered in the middle of the roof-deck, a de facto dance floor slowly forming around them. Phil was shouting up to Fab's ear excitedly; Mazz and Aparna had their faces close together, attempting a conversation at a regular volume. As Harrison, Linus, and Corrine made their way across the floor, Harrison watched smaller groups close to the DJ start to dance to an old song recently remixed. Then, on the other side, a huddle by the building's edge started squealing and rushed to the middle. In front of them, a couple went seamlessly from animatedly talking, their fingers waggling in each other's faces, to dancing low, their fingers still busting a move. All around Harrison's friends, more and more people seemed to catch the spirit of the music and commit to dancing. It was like the party was a living thing, waking up at all sides, pulling them in, beckoning them to join.

Corrine got to the group first. She tapped Aparna on the shoulder. Aparna shrieked; Fab shouted, "It's the woman from the window!"

Phil turned and grinned. She tipped an invisible cowboy hat. "Howdy."

"Howdy!" Corrine shouted over the music. After a beat, she tipped her invisible cowboy hat back.

And then the spirit was upon them. Harrison and Linus linked up with the group, and when they all touched, it was like a current ran through them. The music caught them, and they all swirled into a tangle of arms and legs, moving to the beat, or some just attempting to move to the beat. It didn't matter. And then the whole roof was *living*. Unguarded and flushed. Every body moving. The remix bled into a newer song, and the whole crowd started screaming. Harrison was screaming, too. He had never even heard the song, but here he was, yelling at the top of his lungs, his mind short-circuiting with glee. Could whatever was coming also be like this? It felt like as the party came to life, it spread a secret knowledge to everyone there. Harrison tried to figure it out so he could remember it and get back to it. They were all plugged into the music, and the motion, and the history, and the soul of something bigger, wilder, freer. Corrine stretched her arms like she was trying to grab a piece of paradise itself. Harrison belted out the chorus he'd just heard for the first time seconds earlier, and it was as if it had become a part of his person in that moment. He turned, and there was Linus, belting the words out at the same time. They grabbed each other's hands and sang into each other's faces. Linus spun him around, and Harrison threw back his head, gasping with laughter. Aparna was fist-pumping and twisting. Mazz was body-rolling for the gawds.

Phil dropped it low and Fab shimmied gloriously. Something had broken and something had come together in its place all at once. He didn't have the words, but in this moment, it didn't matter. The words were already there, rushing from the speakers to their bodies, out of their mouths and their outstretched arms and their bouncing feet, making meaning out of feeling.

And now another song, bass-heavy and gritty. A Baltimore club remix: shouted refrains over old-school samples, all to a relentless beat. Harrison felt it like electricity in his bones. Jubilant cries went up all around them. The people were going *in*. Linus joined them, howling. Harrison followed his lead. He shook his whole body with joyous wailing. Wait, he knew the song that was being sampled. Was the DJ playing a Baltimore club song with bits and snatches of a song from *South Pacific*? What in Gay Heaven? Harrison stuck his head up to try to hear more clearly. A femme voice sang over the crunchy beat: *"High as a flag on the Fourth of July."* The mix circled back on itself, and here she was again, *"High as a flag, high as a flag, high as a flag."* Then, it was like the song exploded from the inside out. A shrieking horn came in, echoing the beat; the shouting refrain stopped. The singer's voice, isolated, declared to the whole roof, the whole city, *"I'm in love, I'm in love, I'm in love, I'm in love, I'm in love."* Over and over and over again. Harrison felt himself toppling over the edge of some boundless joy. He shouted into the air "DJ! Turn it up!" and shot a finger skyward. Linus, across from him, was a mirror, his hand aloft, his smile huge. They were both jumping up and down, sweating, singing at the top of their lungs. Everyone was. The whole roof a reflection of their glee.

The music kept going, and they couldn't find it in them to stop dancing. They moved into a circle, they paired off, they swirled around each other. Harrison danced with Aparna; he tried to have a body roll–off with Phil (Phil won). He clasped hands with Mazz, and they pranced around the group. The two of them tumbled into Linus, and they all began to dance together. Harrison turned to Linus, eyes wild.

Smooch! Harrison told Linus with a dramatic wink and a far too obvious head nod toward Mazz.

You're too much! Linus replied.

Kiss! Harrison implored him. He turned to Mazz and tried to communicate the same thing. That electric connection that he and Linus had didn't quite translate, but Mazz seemed to get the gist nonetheless. Harrison skipped away. Linus made a face at Mazz, and then he and Mazz kept dancing. Inching closer, laughing the whole time. The DJ switched it up mid song, and Harrison whipped his head around to the booth, as if the changing of the track indicated some grand happening. There was no such happening, although a drag queen and a drag king were engaged in a walk-off near the booth and the crowd had parted to give deference to royalty.

He looked back at his friends. Mazz leaned in to say something to Linus. Linus's mouth ticked up into a smile. Mazz threw their arm over Linus's shoulder. They kept dancing. Linus leaned in. Mazz leaned in. And then they were kissing. Their dancing slowed to a sway, their forms illuminated by the sky behind them. Harrison felt exhilaration spring up in his heart. He stared at them while also telling himself to stop staring. He clutched his hands together and gasped, emitting an audible "Aww." It was so much. It was everything.

Corrine looped her arm around him and pulled his head in close to her playfully. He gazed at her and grinned. "They're smooching!" he cried.

"Oh my god," she said, laughing, hugging him.

A record-scratch sound effect ripped through the speakers.

There was a moment of silence; the whole roof held their breath in anticipation.

Then the needle dropped into a familiar holler across a spare banjo.

"PRESS. THE. SKY." Oh no. *"HIIIIIIIGHER."*

The roof went wild; people were delirious with rapture. *"HAAAAAARD. TIMES. AIN'T COMING BACK NO MORE."* The beat dropped, and the crowd whipped themselves into a frenzy. Corrine looked like she was going to burst out of her skin, like she was levitating.

"Your favorite song!" she shouted in his ear. She pulled back and grabbed his arms, dancing with him. He played at resisting for a moment and then dropped the act.

"Why do people like this terrible song?" he shouted at her.

"No one thinks it's terrible except you!" she shouted back. "Interrogate your taste!" She laughed.

She looked so new then, with her freshly shorn locks and her glamorous jumpsuit and the power of the party and the song and some other mysterious life force pulsing through her.

"It doesn't mean anything!" Harrison shouted.

Corrine rolled her eyes and continued dancing. Then she leaned into him, wrapping him in a hug as they swayed. "It means the world will try to crush you, but you can make a bigger world," she said. She held him at arm's length. He saw the song play out in her eyes. Press the sky higher. It was an intention. An intention so big, it was hard to speak. But when you can't speak, you sing.

The rap verse came on, and Corrine let out a sky-shaking whoop. She released Harrison and started jumping up and down, singing along. *"AND WE BACK!"* she shouted triumphantly. *"AND WE BACK AND WE BACK AND WE BLACK!"*

The wave of triumph flowed off her and onto her brother, and he found himself leaping, too. He threw back his head and sang along. *"AND WE BACK AND WE BACK AND WE BLACK!"* Linus was at his side with Mazz. They were all leaping, higher and higher and higher. Shouting with everything in them to everything that surrounded them. Lifting their intention beyond their reach. He felt strong enough in that moment to push the sky up a little bit higher, and he raised his arms to try. For hope is the strongest thing in the universe.

6:30 p.m.

They danced until their legs felt like water. They scream-shouted lyrics and held each other, their faces upturned, open, shining for as long as they could. Finally, Harrison and Linus broke off from the group, in search of those bottles of water Dazzle had been carrying. Grabbing two from a table, they planted themselves at the edge of the deck. The sun felt like a resurrection. The day, so long, so near to ending, was beginning again for them. The city stretched out without borders in every direction. They would, in some ways, always be here. Harrison looked up to the cloudless sky. It was astounding to him how the same blue could be different every season, every hour, every time you looked at it. The color of the sky was like the future: less a fact than a promise. Linus slumped against Harrison happily. He followed Harrison's upturned face. Harrison wondered if he saw the same sky. He wondered if the world looked the same to anyone. Linus drew a small breath, preparing to talk. Harrison looked at him. The sun framed them both. They could see each other's faces in all their detail so clearly, but anyone else who might have been watching from the roof would only have seen two silhouettes, leaning in close, sharing the magic of the moment.

Linus opened his mouth to speak.

The whine of brakes pulled Harrison's attention down to the street. A car pulled up to the curb and double-parked, blinkers on. A blue—or was it gray?—car with a rideshare logo in the window. Linus's dad got out, looked around, and walked quickly under the rainbow fabric and up to the front door.

Linus must have seen it, too, because when Harrison looked back, he was already gone, pushing through the crowd trying to get to the exit.

Harrison caught up with him at the top of the grand staircase. He grabbed Linus's hand, and they raced downward in that jagged spiral. The glow from the stained glass skylight cast them in blue and in yellow and in green and in red as they descended, throwing squares and triangles across their skin as a canvas. They were going against the crowd, a steady stream of people rising, following the music and the light. They tumbled through arms and hands, color and noise, laughter and conversation, the aroma of sweat and warm perfume radiating off bodies that had spent the day getting their fill of sunshine. They raced past the flash of sequins, the whoosh of Lycra, and the errant feather on a leisurely descent; the faces they passed were all tipped up as if pulled by some greater force, a blurred collage of lips and teeth and eyes and scars and shades with features that spoke of many roads, a thousand stories all converging in this place. They were all drawn skyward by pure anticipation. The vivid world of the Evergreens unfurled like steam above them and then floated away.

Harrison and Linus reached the ground floor and didn't stop as they pushed back through the vestibule door, plunged into darkness again, the neon bars on the walls casting them as animated figures traveling through nowhere. They never let go of each other's hands. Linus pulled open the barn door, and they were thrust into the street, with its bright flat light and its quiet and the slow cooling of a long summer day. They rounded the corner to find Mr. Munro emerging from the tent of the front yard. He looked at them like he couldn't make sense of what he was seeing.

"What is this?" he demanded of Linus.

"We just went to a party."

"What business do you have being at a party?"

The Quatch clique burst through the barn door, a noisy jumble, and started walking up the street. Fitzhugh spotted Linus and called out. "Dizzy! Come hang out! We're going to the Crow!"

Mr. Munro's eyes got large; he leaned in close to Linus. "Have you been drinking?"

"No! We were just hanging out on the roof! It's all-ages. It's nothing!"

Aparna was behind them now, the tote bag slung over her arm. She and Harrison exchanged a glance.

"You wanted to see the world," Linus's dad said. An accusation. A barb.

Harrison stepped forward to say something, anything, but

then another car pulled up behind Mr. Munro's. A pristine white sedan. His mother got out of the car.

"Harrison Meredith!"

How to communicate to her that it all came so close to not slipping away, that it had all been at his fingertips. Where were the words? He looked at her, panicked, and then swung his head back to Linus. He was already in the car. Mr. Munro got in the other side. Linus looked out his window. He waved goodbye. Harrison hadn't even felt Linus let go of his hand.

6:50 p.m.

It was a small mercy that Aparna was good enough with adults to keep Harrison's mom engaged in light conversation (school, work, college—the trifecta) the entire ride to Aparna's house. Harrison, in the back seat, was silent. He was numb. That was their end? A frantic wave and then nothing. After all of that, after the whole day, after the years they'd spent together, now they were people who used to be best friends. Two boys who had seen each other every day once upon a time. Two more strangers in the world.

They dropped Aparna off at her house. The exterior was lit up from below and glowed against the sky, now a deeper shade of blue.

"Good night, Mrs. Meredith, thank you. See you later, Harrison," she called. Catching Harrison's eye, Aparna pulled her face into an expression that said both *This is so awkward* and *I hope your parents unground you in time for college.*

They watched as she let herself into her house.

"Well?" said Sheree. Harrison looked up at her in the rearview mirror. "Are you moving up, or am I chauffeuring you around?"

Harrison scrambled out of the back seat and got up front.

He closed the passenger door and met his mother's gaze. The temperature in the car seemed to drop twenty degrees. Call the government; there was a new solution to global warming in town. Sheree switched on her blinker and pulled out into traffic.

He knew she was waiting for him to explain himself. But he also knew that there were no words to explain any of what happened or what was happening inside him now. So he sat. He waited. He hated this part of being in trouble. The stewing, Corrine called it. He wondered if, in these moments, his parents were finding their own words or tamping down their frustration, or worse, ratcheting it up so that their children knew they were serious. He wished that they could just say the truth to each other, whatever that was. He hadn't done anything terrible. He'd felt helpless and he'd done something about it and wasn't that how they encouraged him to act?

The road they usually took to get back from Aparna's was closed off, the discovery of which only seemed to further encase his mother's car in ice. She sighed and made a U-turn, taking them the long way around and then down.

They came to a point where the large, expensive houses gave way to more squat homes and apartment buildings. The streets were teeming with people. The sky was only hinting at the fact that it would at some point get dark; this was one of the longest days of the year. It seemed that all of Baltimore was just heading out, just perking up, just getting started. Here and there, he saw people in rainbow clothes or bright wigs or branded company

Pride shirts, the flotsam and jetsam of the dissolving day. His mother's car idled at a light. A group of college students was sitting outside a restaurant, talking loudly. One of them brandished a plastic sword triumphantly.

Sheree drew a breath. Here it was. She turned to Harrison.

"So, it sounds like you had *big fun* all over Baltimore," she said sternly.

Harrison burst into tears.

Sheree's face said she had not been expecting this. The light turned green, and she inched forward. "Oh my Lord, why are you crying?"

Harrison tried to speak but only snuffled louder.

"Okay, well, I had a whole thing prepared, but I have to admit this is throwing me off a little bit. Are you okay?"

Harrison nodded pitifully.

Sheree inhaled and started again, a few degrees warmer.

"One of my coworkers texted me and said she'd seen my son at Pride. I said, 'Not *my* son.' She's white, and in my mind I thought, 'Here she goes thinking we all look alike.'" Sheree chuckled; Harrison let out a sob.

Sheree reached down to give his hand a squeeze at a stop sign and then returned her hands to the wheel.

"Harrison, baby, it's doesn't need to be all this." She screwed up her lips in thought and then continued. "The thing with Katya, my coworker, it just reminded me of the thing I always worry about: that people won't see you in your specificity. How many

Black boys, Black men just 'match the description'? That's why I need to know where you are; that's why we use Check In. If I don't know what you're up to, I can't keep you safe."

Harrison felt himself getting hysterical. It was all too much. The world at large, the bubble that his parents put around him, the tether that connected him and Linus—a universe of connections drawing close and flying apart. He felt himself splinter. He could not hold it together, literally, figuratively, and any other way that he didn't know about. He buried his face in his hands.

"Harrison! What is it?!" His mother's eyes darted from his face to the mirror beyond his window as she swerved out of the lane and pulled over to the curb without signaling. This was how Harrison knew it was serious. A new thought entered his head— he was suddenly self-conscious. Embarrassed by this display. He was afraid that perhaps he was doing too much, but he couldn't stop himself. The feeling was overwhelming; it was bottomless. His mother shifted into park and wrenched her body around to face him. He couldn't look at her. He just felt her full attention like something physical. Another tether, this one between them, pulled taut suddenly.

Up ahead, there was a group of people sitting on the white marble steps of a house. A woman with cornrows had turned from the group to face the car as it pulled up to the curb. She met Harrison's gaze. What must he have looked like, his face pulled at odd angles like the sad side of the comedy/drama theater mask? Sitting in the car with his mom, sobbing like he'd just been eliminated from a TV dating show. The woman with the cornrows held him in her sights for longer, frankly, than Harrison would have liked. It wasn't hostile or even particularly judgy. She was just watching. Wouldn't you? Finally, she turned back to the group. Her face changed as she slipped back into the stream of their conversation. She cracked a smile as the rest of them threw their heads back in laughter. She tapped the person next to her on the shoulder, pointed at someone across the group from them, and said something that was inaudible to Harrison. The group laughed harder.

"Baby, you have to talk to me," Sheree was saying. "You have to say something." On one hand, Harrison knew this was true. But on the other, he thought, wasn't it Linus who always had the words to put inside thoughts outside without sounding foolish? Saying something without him was a risk. But wasn't everything true a risk?

Harrison wiped his nose and held his hand there, wrist pressed into his cheekbone hard to staunch the flow. Harrison thought then of the water in the museum that never stopped. He thought of the way it could be tears but also something that cleansed you, renewed you, like a baptism. It could also be the thing that moved you along.

When he spoke, at last, his voice was thick and muddled. "Why did I do it?" He looked at his mother. "What did it get me? I thought that Ferris Day could fix this. And I was so nervous all day that I'd mess up, or that Linus didn't actually want to be fixed, or . . . everything would go wrong. But then everything did go wrong, over and over again. I got caught! By everybody in the family. I'm caught right now! But somewhere in the day, I stopped being nervous. I got comfortable, Mom, and it was wonderful. I knew that I couldn't fix this. I couldn't stop Mr. Munro from moving them. I just wanna hang out with Linus every day. I wanna go on dumb adventures. I want to talk to him. In person. All the time. He is my best friend. And I did all this to remind him, to remind us both, of that. Even though things will change. Even if he goes off and has a new life. I will, too. I know. That's what happens. But he'll remember this and know that I cared. That he mattered to me. I did it for him, but I also did it for me. For me. For me." He paused, realizing that another inside thought, one he hadn't even fully understood, was about to come sailing past his lips. Sheree was quiet, listening. Harrison thought, *Why stop now?* He looked her in the face. "I know I didn't do things the way you wanted me to do them, but I'm so proud of myself." Suddenly he was crying again, out of nowhere. He pressed his hands to his face and then started laughing that he was crying, which only made him cry harder. Chaotic. "I'm so proud of myself. I worked so hard. And I did it. I did all the things that scared me. And I'm so frustrated! I'm proud and I'm frustrated. And I'm disappointed, actually."

"Disappointed?" Sheree said.

Harrison spoke through tears. "I'm disappointed in myself for crying, because I'm so proud." He let out a sob.

"Oh my goodness."

"This is so much!" And then, suddenly serious. "I think my heart is breaking."

Sheree nodded like she could hear the myriad sentences running through Harrison's head. She didn't look away. She reached over and grabbed his hand. "Harrison, I know your heart is broken, and I wish there was a way I could take it and put it back together, hold it in my hands until it heals. I wish . . . I'll tell you what I told Corrine one of those many long nights while she was away. Your heart will break in this life, but when it does break, I hope every crack makes more space inside for love."

Tears streamed down his face. He thought about how strange it was that tears kind of just did their own thing. You could work yourself up to starting, sure, but they really had their own independent agenda. Just falling out of his face, pulling sadness out of the heart and putting it into the world. Evaporating. Off to do some other sad business somewhere.

Sheree took the keys out of the ignition and looked out through the windshield at the people on the steps, at the world beyond.

"So what now?" Harrison asked.

6:51 p.m.

Linus and his father had been talking over each other since they left the Evergreens, and neither showed any intention of relenting. They'd gotten caught up in traffic that was detoured from Pride street closures and were now at a standstill, boxed in, arguing.

"And what did you think I was going to do?" Linus was saying. "What did you think I did? You're acting brand-new, like you don't know me."

Meanwhile, his father, Wally, was saying, "A tea dance! Like you're the first person to try to slide by with some made-up words for a house party. Man, come on!"

Then Linus: "Why can't I just have this? What's so wrong? It's Harrison! You know Harrison! And you still—even after all this—need to embarrass me. For what? For who?"

And Wally: "I've seen this game before! I lived this before. People crammed in there, shoulder to shoulder. DJ pumping so loud, you can hear it on the street. And you talking about somebody's *tea party*? Linus, why do you always treat me like I'm dumb?" He banged his hand on the steering wheel and let out an exasperated grunt. He looked away. For the first time in twenty minutes, Linus stopped talking. This was weird, he thought, and then he revised it, imagining the voice of Mr. Mirepoix in his head, encouraging him to be more specific. He didn't just think it was weird; he was stunned. He didn't think his father was dumb. If he had thought that, Harrison wouldn't have had to go through all the trouble that he did and the two boys could've been living it up all over the city for months. Dumb? Where was this coming from? Why was he always at crossed purposes with his parents? Why couldn't they ever see each other in reality?

If not now, then when?

"I don't think you're dumb," Linus muttered. "It's not about you."

The cars around them inched forward, and Wally shifted into gear and inched along with them.

"We said we were going to be a team," Wally said. His eyes stayed on the road even though they'd come to a stop again.

"I thought so until you moved us away."

"What choice? What choice did I have?" Linus's dad's voice was coming out raspy and dry. Tired. Linus was tired, too. They were both silent for a while. A space opened up one lane over, and Wally signaled, checked his mirrors again, waved a thank-you in the air, and carefully navigated into it. Linus had always wondered why his dad was so precise in the car, so polite, so careful. It wasn't that he acted some other way in real life, but there was a delicateness to the way he drove his car that didn't carry over anywhere else. He'd check and re-check and ask permission and say thank you before changing lanes, but, Linus thought, when it came to uprooting his own son's entire life, all Linus got was a shrimp and grits after all the decisions were made and it was too late. Linus knew that the driving habits had come from Brother Aldo at church, who had taught his dad to drive years ago. He had no idea where the life habits came from. Maybe Brother Aldo, too. Linus had only taken one lesson from him and gotten so terrified by the talk about preparing for police stops that he'd never gone back.

Wally turned a corner, heading north and away from the traffic. The road was clearing up now. They swooped around the Baltimore version of the Washington Monument—shorter and rounder than DC's, but still imposing.

"What do you want from me?" Linus's dad asked finally.

Linus felt his anger flash up all over again. He wasn't going to waste his time having the same old conversation, especially if his dad didn't care or didn't listen. He threw his hands up and shrugged.

"No. Don't do that. Tell me what you want."

"I want to stay in Baltimore, obviously!" Linus snapped.

"That's not possible right now. You know it's not possible. Maybe it will be. I'm working hard to figure it out, but right now, I got no choice, and you know this. So, son, tell me: What do you want?"

The notecard on which Linus had written what he thought was going to be his day's schedule fluttered on the dashboard under the cool air from the vents. **WORK, LUNCH, LIBRARY, HARRISON'S HOUSE AS USUAL.** That was what he wanted.

Well, no. That was fine. But what he wanted was ... whatever that ridiculous list that Harrison had shown him on the train said. Or, no, not even that. Because that had been a plan that quickly went awry. He thought back through the day as if scrubbing a video in reverse—dancing on the rooftop with Mazz and Harrison and all of Baltimore, sailing down the waterslide in tandem, getting a goodbye gift from Mr. Mirepoix, the cat who did not want to give them change at the ATM, and the self-portraits—the sight of himself, a version of himself, a dream of himself, on the walls of the museum. It all seemed to belong to some other person, some other life, but it was his. He'd lived it. Harrison had given it to him. His eyes started to burn with tears, and that, too, stunned him. Linus felt like he was losing control. But of what? What did he really control?

"Let me put it this way," Wally was saying. "What do you need? To make this okay? You need to say what you need."

"I need to stay in his life. And I need to keep a part of my life, this life. Even at a distance. I don't want to lose my friend." Now Linus was crying, and he didn't do anything to stop it. Wally reached over and popped open the glove compartment; an avalanche of tissue packets came tumbling out, each with a sticker that read PLEASE RATE ME 5 STARS! He picked one up and handed it to Linus.

7:09 p.m.

"Thank you for being honest with me," Sheree said finally. "I really appreciate it. I . . ." She paused like she was choosing her words carefully. "I am very grateful and I know this is hard. I also have a lot of questions about some very minor things. But mostly I'm grateful."

"What kind of questions?"

"Well, I guess the first is: What's Ferris Day?"

Harrison laughed. "It's just what I called our day of activities. Just, like, a day of adventures." He thought and then blurted the next part. "That you're not supposed to do."

"'Ferris' as in *Ferris Bueller*?" Sheree asked.

"Yes. I got the idea from movie night. Dad's a bad influence on me."

"Apparently." She squinted at him for a second and then shook her head, amused. "All right. Ferris Day." She handed him the car keys and unbuckled her seat belt.

"What do you want me to do with these?"

"Drive us home. You have your learner's on you, right?"

"Yes, but, Mom, I don't think I can handle this right now. I've had a long day."

"Me too! Good, but long. We'll take the scenic route home. No need to rush. I'll tell you where to go." She looked at Harrison, who hadn't moved. "Come on. Unbuckle your seat belt."

Harrison had no idea what was going on with his mother or why she suddenly wanted to circle back to their driving lessons. At such a time as this? His parents were mysteries. Was this part of the punishment? He couldn't drive! Everybody knew that. At least, he thought he couldn't drive. It hadn't gone well when he'd tried, let's leave it at that. Harrison realized his mother was still looking at him expectantly, and she hadn't taken back the keys. Okay, so this *was* punishment. Fine.

"This isn't a punishment," Sheree said. Was his face *that* readable? "We keep you so close because we don't want the worst of the world to get you. But in so doing, we may have been keeping some of the best of the world from you, too. So. Let's start to fix that. Let's see the world."

Harrison unbuckled his seat belt. Sheree moved to open her door and then stopped.

"Wait a minute. You said everybody in the family caught you today? I know about you crashing Dad's pool party, but—"

"Corrine is at the tea dance, where you picked me up."

"Oh! She is? Why didn't—? Who all is she with?"

"Just some people," Harrison said.

Sheree looked at him askance. "You two . . . Come on, out of the car." She opened her door.

7:10 p.m.

Wally and Linus waited at the light next to the train station where Linus and Harrison had begun their day. Linus blew his nose into one of his father's complimentary rideshare tissues.

Then Wally spoke out of the blue. "Linus, are you two in love with each other? Is that it?"

Linus caught his father's eyes. There was nothing reflected back in them but the surface of the question. Maybe he was willing his expression to commit to neutrality, or maybe the question was all it was. Maybe he just wanted information. And what is love but information about the soul and the future and the place in the universe where you feel complete? Love is information like the address of your home is information. Like the color of the sky is information.

Linus studied the information he was getting from his own heart. It was insufficient to say he loved Harrison like a friend, because that made it seem less than another kind of love, when really, it felt huge. Dazzling. Extraordinary. This was the destination, wasn't it? That was the place that resisted a clean break. The center of joy. This friendship that made the whole city seem a welcome adventure. How was it possible that love could feel so many different ways? How was it possible that a friend felt like an appendage? No, even more than that. Was it too much to say that a friend, this friend, felt like a part of his heart? A chamber that he was losing.

Linus cried harder, his head lolling against the window. "I've been so lonely. And he's been my friend."

Linus's father reached over and squeezed his shoulder, leaving his hand there. It was such a deep comfort. Linus hadn't understood how much he'd wanted to just stop and be held safe and feel seen. The light changed, and Wally crept forward, never moving his hand.

"We're going do whatever we need to do to keep y'all two in each other's lives, okay?" Wally said. "Why don't—Why don't you call him? If I know Sheree and Obed, he's probably in big trouble, but . . . I think it'll be okay to call."

Linus picked up his phone. Of course it was dead after a day of riding around doing nothing in the back of Aparna R.'s car. And of course his dad didn't have a charger for Linus's type of phone in the car.

"Do you want to call him from my phone?"

Was he crazy? If Harrison saw a call coming straight to him from Wally's phone, Harrison would wet his pants in fear. Linus shook his head. *It's fine.*

Wally moved his hand then and woke up his own phone on the

dashboard. He went to Favorites in his contacts and tapped the button for "Obed Meredith." After one ring, Obed's voice came out of the car speakers.

"What's up, man?"

"How you doing?"

"All right, all right. How are you?"

"Can't complain, brother. You know."

"Yeah, I know."

"Right?"

"Right."

Linus was amazed that these two men were apparently friends, possibly good friends, judging by Harrison's dad's placement in Wally's phone, and yet they seemed to have nothing to say.

"Listen, I got Linus here. You mind putting Harrison on the phone right quick?"

"I, uh—Hold on." Obed's voice got far from the receiver as he called into the house. "Man, ain't nobody in this house. I think..." His voice got distant again. "Yeah, he's still with Sheree. On the Check In app, it looks like they're driving in a circle. Around Druid Hill Park. I don't know. I just live here."

"I know that's right."

"Tell me about it."

Both men laughed. Incredible.

"All right," said Wally. "Thanks. And thanks again for your help with everything, Obed."

"'Course. Absolutely. Y'all drive safe, okay? We'll see you soon."

"All right."

"Okay."

"Take care."

This went on for a while. Linus tuned out slightly. He wondered what kind of help the Merediths had given his dad. He wondered about the constellation of the friendship between his family and Harrison's. Finally, Wally hung up. He switched on his blinker and made a U-turn.

"What are you doing?" Linus asked.

"Can't get to Druid Hill Park this way. We'll get stuck in Pride traffic. Gotta go down to go up."

7:45 p.m.

In his head, Harrison could hear the voice of Brother Aldo of Jesus Is Lord Driving School bellowing, *Ten and two! Hands on ten and two!* But Brother Aldo was not there; it was just him and his mom as he drove down an empty road near the pool, going ten miles per hour and yet sweating profusely. Ten. Two. Ten. Two. He knew his mom was trying her best to keep him from spiraling, but he was really on the edge with this whole driving thing. He'd lost track of how many times Sheree had gently said, "It's a stop sign, not a red light" as they made their way slowly but surely around Druid Hill Park. Harrison felt it was safer to wait a full minute at each intersection. Brother Aldo would be proud. He had no intentions of ever driving more than fifteen miles per hour, and if he'd seen another moving car, he would have immediately pulled over and curled up into a ball. But he was getting the hang of it!

Sheree seemed to be happy with his driving, too, from what he could tell from stolen glances during minute two of a stop-sign rest. Her hand was definitely gripping the door handle like it owed her money, but everything else about her was chill, and she'd kept up a monologue as circuitous and unending as their trip around the park in a performance that rivaled Motormouth Maybelle in *Hairspray* for stamina. Harrison was happy for the company and that his mother didn't seem to be pissed anymore, but also, as a new, safety-focused driver, he had recently decided that all cars should be operated in complete silence, at very low speeds.

"When I was a kid, I wasn't allowed to watch *The Simpsons*," she was saying. Where did this come from? He thought about hazarding another glance at her, but then he noticed someone walking across the grass about 500 feet away and decided he need to double down on his concentration in case they sprinted onto the road randomly. "You know, you're lucky. We let you all watch all kinds of things," Sheree continued. Debatable, but sure. "Grandma and Grandpa thought *The Simpsons* was a bad influence. They didn't like that little Bart Simpson. They thought he was rude. He had this phrase, 'Eat my shorts,' and, baby, when I tell you those folks got *upset* about it in the eighties—they lost their minds. Now, I was in middle school when the show came out, I think. But Grandma and Grandpa, they ruled that remote with an iron fist. Wasn't nothing getting past them." Harrison guided the car around a corner and proceeded up a hill he'd climbed half a dozen times now. "But I still know all the little phrases. They get inside you. Like, he says this one thing that I think of all the time: 'Smell ya later!' I thought that was so funny. I used to—when your father and I were dating, I used to tell him 'Smell ya later!' instead of 'I love you' when we got off the phone. Because he was in Newark working at the station at the time, and I was in Charlottesville at school. Because I didn't want to say goodbye. So I think you ought to think of today as you telling Linus, 'Smell ya later!'" She turned to Harrison, a smile playing on her lips. "Profound talks from Mom," she said. Because they were sitting at a stop sign, and had been for about ninety seconds, Harrison felt free to just stare back. It felt like, in the movies, parents always figured out something wise to say, but sure, let's keep talking about *The Simpsons*. Sheree, perhaps sensing how underwhelmed her son was, plunged on. "There's so much more of life, is what I'm saying." She laughed at herself. "I was about to say there's so much more road ahead, but I went ahead and gave it a quick edit. You get the point."

After a beat, Harrison burst out laughing. His mother was weirdly funny sometimes.

"What do you think," Sheree said, "you ready to pack it in?"

"I think so."

"Sounds good. Take me home, Jeeves!"

Harrison turned on his signal, looked, looked again, checked his mirror, and turned right onto an empty road, heading toward the city.

Leaving the park, the white sedan turned east onto the wide, brightly lit corridor of North Avenue. Up ahead, Harrison caught the top of Baltimore Cemetery rising into view: credits at the end of a film.

"You know why this is called North Avenue?" Sheree asked. Harrison did not. Harrison didn't know the history of the name of any alley, road, street, boulevard, or avenue except "The Great White Way," thank you very much. Sheree continued. "This used to be the northern boundary of Baltimore. Everything in the city was below this street. But, of course, the city kept expanding. Baltimore kept growing. We live above North; Linus lives below North; all of us in the same city." They pulled up to a red light beside a souped-up car with a rumble that threatened to drown out her voice. But Sheree, and truly all of the Merediths, was used to projecting. "I think it's interesting how they—some people, some time ago—decided that this was all there was. Well, they didn't decide—they just acknowledged. But then, later, there was more. I guess it can be useful to have geographic lines so that we can tell each other where we are and how to reach each other. But we're always bigger than boundaries."

7:50 p.m.

The knot of traffic was so tangled that Linus and his dad had to go all the way over to Broadway before they could turn back up and start heading west on North Avenue toward the park. Baltimore Cemetery swung into view behind them, and Linus twisted around to get one last look. The sky had started to darken behind it; the castle gates were lit from below. Linus's first thought was that it looked like Disney World. He chuckled to himself. *Now this is vacationing.*

Linus made a note to tell Harrison about this joke, knowing full well that he would not appreciate it. Linus was depending on that, actually. He looked forward to it. Then the anticipation was met with a wave of anxiety. Linus started to wonder what he was supposed to say to his friend when he found him in the park. "Hey, so I chased you across town using the Check In app so I could say 'Thank you and I won't lose you.' This message brought to you by local millionaire Dazzle Gradually." Not their best talk. He'd spent all day saying to other people what he should have been saying to Harrison about what their friendship meant and what the day had meant. Linus feared that he'd failed at every chance he'd had to secure their future and was about to fail again.

The traffic lights were in their favor as they coasted down North, passing the street where you'd turn if you were going to Harrison's house, past the street where Pride was still going strong, closer and closer to the park. And at each intersection, Linus's anxiety grew.

Finally, a light ahead of them turned red and Wally slowed down as they approached it. Behind them, Linus heard the tenor growl of motorbikes start to rise. Then they were upon them: two Black boys, shirtless, about his age, maybe a little older, standing up on their bikes. One on either side of the car, coasting. The boys sped up, revving their engines and grinning at each other over the hood of the car. They floated out in front of the car and stretched out their arms, somehow always staying just ahead of Linus and Wally, held in the running lights like a tractor beam. One of the boys had locs, and the wind and the force of his movement pulled them up and back, like the sky itself was tousling his hair. The other boy wheeled his head around, scanning the road in front of them, eyes wide, mouth open, chest out. As if pulled by the same tether, the boys hunched forward, grabbed the handlebars of their motorbikes, and zipped in front of the car, crisscrossing and changing places. Two sentinels rotating their stations. Wally hissed quietly. This wasn't safe, obviously, especially since they weren't even in lanes, but Linus privately thought that they looked glorious. These works of art.

The boys sat back up and spread their arms out again. The streetlights came on and played across the surface of their skin, creating abstract pools of depth on their bodies. The light and the road and the city, the heat and the noise and the energy, it all found a home here. Their depth was limitless. Indeed, the boys sat perched at the back of their motorbike seats like rulers of everything they surveyed, all they sped past, everything under their whirring wheels. They were not bound by gravity or circumstance, physics or form. They were air itself.

The light ahead turned yellow, the boys caught each other's eyes, and through some private, unspoken exchange, they cracked each other up. Their grins were electric. Lips, and teeth, and tongue, and air, and moisture. Even their laughter was expansive. And then, with that same unfathomable silent communion, the boy with locs reached two hands down; the other boy reached one hand down; they steadied themselves; they sped up; and they sailed off into the night, weaving in and out of lanes, as if all of it—the traffic, the city, the world at large, was just water to be traversed. They crested a hill ahead and disappeared.

When the light turned green again, Wally pulled out into the intersection. As they passed through, Linus pulled his gaze from the wake of the two sentinels and looked out his side window. There was one car waiting at the light in the cross street, a white sedan with its blinker on. And in the driver's seat: Harrison

Meredith, gripping the steering wheel like it was a life preserver. Linus looked and turned forward without processing. Just Harrison Meredith, his unlicensed best friend, looking like a terrified Henry Ford on his first jaunt in a Model T. Harrison Meredith, who got nervous boarding a *bus*, inching into the intersection. Harrison Meredith, with his mother in the passenger seat, creeping slowly into a turn and driving down North Avenue in the opposite direction.

Linus suddenly reached a hand out and gripped the dashboard. "We need to turn around!"

7:58 p.m.

Harrison was undone. Nobody told you that turning a corner from one empty street onto another nearly empty street was more difficult than landing a spaceship on the moon! He had to be constantly moving his hands, one over the other, while pressing his feet and looking, like, everywhere? What in the Fosse choreography was all this!

"Baby," Sheree said calmly, "don't do it now, but you're going to need to turn left coming up. So start thinking about changing lanes." Um, what?! Changing lanes and a turn? No. Out of the question, unfortunately. They lived here now.

At the next intersection, he found himself next to a loud red pickup that kept revving its engine. All that noise and for what? *Hurry up and wait,* as Pop would say.

"Edge out just a little," Sheree said.

"Into the crosswalk?! Illegal!" Harrison cried.

"Just so you can get his attention. In the truck."

"And then what?"

"Ask him to let you in."

This was, frankly, an impossible suggestion. But, after momentarily deliberating, Harrison realized that he had no choice but to break the law and appeal to the kindness of this stranger in a truck. He edged the car into the paint and, mercifully, Sheree leaned out into the windshield to get the driver of the truck's attention. She mouthed *Can we get in?* and pointed in front of him. He looked down at them from his noisy throne and shook his head no. He had refused them! What did it harm him to let them in? And yet! Harrison was spiraling; humanity was a mistake!

Sheree muttered, "This son of a gun." Oh, she was *pissed* pissed. Everybody in the car was furious. The opposite light switched to red, and the pickup started to move. Did this person think Harrison was going to try to race him? Baby, no. No, indeedy! The pickup revved its engine again, squealed to life, and roared away. "Honestly . . ." Sheree said. In the truck's wake was a line of cars equally as impatient and equally as invested in ruining Sheree's and Harrison's lives. Had no one heard of public transportation? This was why the Earth was dying.

Finally, Harrison caught a break and inched his way over to the left turn lane just as the light was changing back to red. And even though he'd done everything right, as he calmed himself down, he became aware that someone was honking, a lot, from somewhere behind him, and getting closer. Everyone's a critic.

7:59 p.m.

"There's Harrison!" Linus cried, pointing out the back window. The Merediths' car had crept through the intersection and was now plodding down the avenue in the opposite direction. Wally squinted into the rearview.

"You sure?"

"Yes, obviously! It's them."

"Oh, good!" Wally said with the kind of nonchalance used for finding a movie you like on TV or discovering there was still leftover pasta in the fridge. *Oh, good?* This was everything. They'd found them. This was what they'd come to do! There'd been a part of Linus's mind that had imagined he and his father were already down on some foreign South Carolina road, away from the familiar world of chance encounters. Time and space were a mystery. But here they were! Still in Baltimore, making a U-turn to pursue his friend down the street after tracking him using an app and trying to intercept him at a public park. Human connection was wonderful! Linus stared at his father expectantly as he puttered down the street, doing the speed limit, like he didn't have anywhere to be.

"Can you catch up to them, please?" Linus asked.

"What do you think I'm doing?"

Linus had enough sense to swallow his sarcastic retort. He didn't know what his father thought he was doing but, man, whatever this was, it was not it.

"Do you think you want to go faster, maybe?"

"Why?"

Why? Linus was going to lose his mind. He spotted Harrison ahead—they were three car-lengths away from them, crawling through an intersection on a yellow light. Wally coasted to a stop on the red.

"DAD!"

"Linus, do not yell at me. I ain't about to get pulled over by the police talking about 'I'm sorry, officer. I'm in a car chase because my son and his best friend have unfinished business.'"

"We are barely even moving! The speed limit is twenty-five!"

"Oh, now you know the rules of the road?"

"It says it right on the dashboard!" It's true; it did. The light changed, and Wally crept forward behind a red pickup. Linus let out an exasperated sigh.

"What am I supposed to do?" Wally said. "The truck is making all that noise and not going anywhere. Don't make no sense. But I can't control the other cars." Wally cast a look his son's way. His demeanor dropped into a more serious place. "Linus, if we don't catch up with them, we'll just meet them at the house. It's not hard to figure out where they're going."

"I need to say it now." Linus declared suddenly, before he'd even fully formed the thought. "I need to say it now. I need to talk to him now. I need to make sure he knows that I'm not going anywhere. I spent all day not saying it, and if I don't say it now, I'm afraid I won't." Linus looked at his father. "Please."

Wally nodded. He got it. "All right, man. Let's go."

The light turned green, and they were off. A block ahead of them, the red pickup was gunning its engine and peeling out of the intersection. A few car lengths behind it, a white sedan was gingerly turning into the lane. Wally started honking wildly as he sped up to catch them. Okay, so *this* was dramatics, Linus decided.

Harrison's car turned the corner and proceeded up his street. Wally caught the light just in time and followed them, still honking intermittently. How was Harrison not aware of this? Or was he aware of it and totally freaked out by the car that was chasing and honking at him? Linus's father seemed to have had the same realization that Linus did in that moment, because he pulled his hand off the horn suddenly, signaled, and pulled into the next lane.

They coasted up next to Harrison, which wasn't hard, as he was going so slow, pedestrians on the sidewalk were passing him. Linus rolled down his window and started waving. Harrison looked over briefly, did a double-take, seemed to scream, had a brief back-and-forth with his mother, and then slowed down almost to a stop despite the fact that they were in the middle of the street. Harrison rolled down his window.

Linus shouted out across the cars, "Hi! Can you pull over?"

Harrison looked panicked. "I don't think I know how!"

Sheree leaned forward, past Harrison. "We'll figure it out," she called. "Hi, Wally!"

"All right!" Wally called back.

Harrison and his mother jointly maneuvered their car to the curb.

Linus was already unbuckling his seat belt.

"Where are you going?!" Wally cried. "Wait till I get to the curb."

They pulled over behind the sedan.

Harrison was already running around the back of his car.

"Get out of the street!" Linus's dad yelled out the door. "On the sidewalk!"

They met on the curb. Cars zipped by them up the street, roaring, honking, blasting music. There was a restaurant a few doors up, and people were gathered around tables, laughing and shouting at each other. In the distance, the ice cream truck was playing its creepy song. The sounds of the rude world did not stop just because Linus needed to make a declaration.

For a moment, they just stood together in the pool of a street-light.

Harrison's face, shining with sweat, was etched out in blue and purple and golden blocks. It was stained glass installed in the house of Linus's soul. He imagined that he perhaps looked the same to Harrison. The two of them a beautiful set. Salt and pepper shakers, as Mazz's aunt would say while sipping her tea in South Carolina.

Harrison spoke first, before Linus could. "I'm not saying goodbye to you!"

"I'm not saying goodbye to you, either. I was wrong."

Linus wondered if that was all that needed to be said. But he knew that the thing that held them together was more than that. There was a universe inside of Harrison that would surprise and amaze and delight. He'd seen it all day long. Even though Linus usually found the words to say almost everything that was on his mind, Harrison lifted the words up, gave them life and music. Harrison was a song.

"Tomorrow I won't be here," Linus said, "but I'm never going to stop being in your life. I don't want to stop talking to you every day. I don't want to not know you. I can't not know you, Harrison." The ice cream truck turned down the block, blasting music. Harrison leaned in like he was having trouble hearing. Linus continued. "You're a part of me. You're a part of my heart. You are my best friend. And I love you. It's the brightest thing I have ever felt." One of the tables at the restaurant burst into the chorus of "Press the Sky Higher," screaming and singing with abandon. Harrison looked over and rolled his eyes at them. Linus plunged on. "When you're up, I'm up. When you're down, I'm down. I hear you when you don't have anything to say. I hear you when you raise your eyebrow and catch my eye. I hear you when you're not even there. And you hear me, too. You hear me when no one else hears me. You did this whole day for me, and it was so fun and so . . . I don't know. I've never experienced anything like being your friend. And I won't, I can't, live like this without you." The words were tripping over themselves, but Linus couldn't stop. A group of boys on motorbikes, a dozen or so, roared up the street beside them. Linus raised his voice to yelling. "I feel silly standing out in the middle of the street, like one block from your house, begging you to be my friend, but I don't care!"

"Let's be friends forever!" Harrison shouted. He started to say something else but then stopped and just grinned. He raised his eyebrows. *This is so much*, they said.

Baby boy! Linus said in return. *This is everything.*

And it was. And it was beautiful. They let the words take a break for a moment as the music and the singing and the motorbikes and the honking and what seemed like the entire city bustled around them. They talked through exchanged looks, standing there on that street corner in the middle of Baltimore. This space, between their two faces, was where their friendship lived. It was where they lived. Free and vibrant and magical together in this connection they made. In that electric space in the middle of the two of them, anything was possible. Everything was possible. And nothing could tear it apart.

"I know things will change," Harrison started. Linus grabbed his arms and looked at him intensely.

"We will always be in each other's lives, Harrison. Things are going to change. *We're* going to change. But we'll meet each other new every day. Believe that."

They hugged then, both squeezing so tight.

"Have the best time," Harrison said.

"Not without you," Linus said. "But I'll try. Harrison, you're extraordinary! Thank you." He climbed back into his car. "I'll talk to you tomorrow!" His dad started to pull away from the curb. Linus turned and waved.

Epilogue

8:00 p.m.

Harrison waved back. He kept waving as the light turned green, as the car turned the corner, and as the Munros disappeared from view. He climbed back into his car. In the passenger seat this time.

Harrison would tell Linus anything, everything over the course of their friendship, but he decided he would probably never mention that it was too loud to actually hear him on the street corner when they were yelling about their feelings while a group of college kids belted "Press the Sky Higher." Harrison had caught bits and pieces. He got the gist. It wasn't ideal—he'd put it that way. But also, he wouldn't have changed a thing. Sometimes they heard each other; sometimes they didn't. But they always saw each other. They always understood.

The first blush of night was finally creeping over the Baltimore skyline as Harrison and his mother pulled up to their house. Sheree had decided that the evening was too beautiful to give up and the day was too long to end, and had taken them on another drive through the streets, past singers and motorbikers and everyone who ever lived.

Obed was sitting on the couch watching a movie when they got in. "Everybody's out partying except for me, I see." Harrison paused, waiting for him to turn and for the grounding or phone confiscation or whatever other punishment to come down. Instead, his mom just joined his dad on the couch.

"We'll talk tomorrow. I'm glad you're safe," she said. Harrison waited like the information didn't compute. Then he turned toward the stairs. "Oh," Sheree called. *Here it comes.* "I like your shirt, by the way."

Harrison's phone was dead, as usual. He plugged it in and lay across the bed. He was still buzzing from the day. His skin felt electric; he heard the sounds of every place they'd been ringing in his ears. His phone came to life and dinged with a new message. And then dinged again. And again. And a fourth time. To say this was unusual would be an understatement.

He opened up what looked like a group chat, but he didn't recognize any of the numbers except Linus's. He scrolled to the top and started reading.

Linus: Hello

Linus: We had such a good time, I thought y'all should be friends.

Linus: But also I don't want to miss out. So now we can all talk.

And then, from an unknown number: THIS IS FAB! Hi Harrison!!

And another unknown number: Mazz. I was so sad when you left. Glad we can hang!

And another: Philadendra Truong. We're still at the party. Your sister says howdy.

Linus: Y'all know I don't text. But . . .

Linus: You can use this group chat to plan a visit to Charleston. So get on it.

Linus: Also, check your email, Harrison.

This was more online communication than he'd received all year. It was overwhelming. He opened his email.

FROM: LINUS MUNRO
SUBJECT: Hello

I know I just saw you, but I wasn't finished talking. And I don't think I'll ever finish talking to you, so here's an email. When we left the Evergreens, I was thinking about this thing I read I wanted to tell you about. I thought about telling you just now, but it was so loud and I got nervous and I'd have to show you anyway. So I didn't. It works better with the picture and the whole backstory.

Harrison stopped reading and opened the attachment. It was a picture of a small white gravestone. Okay. What a thrilling gift. He went back to the email.

Don't go looking at the picture first. Read the description.

Too late.

> So, this is John Laurens's grave. Alexander
> Hamilton's best friend. We saw him in the musical
> *Hamilton*.

Okay, so what Linus didn't need to do was try to act like Harrison didn't know what musical Alexander Hamilton of the musical *Hamilton* was in. However, Harrison did not know that Laurens was buried in South Carolina.

> Did you know that Laurens was buried in South
> Carolina?

He did not!

> It's in a place called Mepkin Abbey. I downloaded
> this picture from the internet. I was looking up some
> information about their friendship because I was
> thinking about all the times we watched the musical
> together.

Nine. Nine times.

> So when I found out he was near where I'm moving,
> I got so excited. You know we have to go together.

A leisurely and ordinary day of cemetery tourism with Linus Munro. Harrison couldn't wait.

I promise I won't go until we can go together. I wanted to send you a picture of the grave to tell you about it. And also so I could send you this quote I found. Alexander Hamilton once wrote to John Laurens:

"Cold in my professions, warm in friendships, I wish, my Dear Laurens, it might be in my power, by action rather than words, to convince you that I love you. I shall only tell you that 'till you bade us Adieu, I hardly knew the value you had taught my heart to set upon you."

I couldn't find all the words to tell you how much you mean to me, but maybe these will work until we get to see each other again.

Thank you for finding me in that random Zoom room and following me through graveyards and taking me all around the city on the greatest day I've ever had.

Harrison opened the photo again. It was just a simple, time-worn gravestone, not fanciful or ornate like the ones in the cemetery where they'd spent so many afternoons talking and wondering and worrying and hoping and living. It was odd, but also so lovely, the loveliest gift Harrison had ever received.

Wasn't that what drew them close to each other? Wasn't it what they saw in each other's faces and silent expressions? Wasn't it the thing they treasured about each other?

And, Harrison thought, *isn't that exactly what we are together?* Strange and beautiful and magical and dazzling.

Acknowledgments

First of all, I think we should acknowledge Audra McDonald doing a high kick during the *Shuffle Along* Tony Awards performance, don't you?

I read a tweet this year that said instead of blurbs, book jackets should tell you what kind of wild, intense stuff the author was living through while they wrote the book. It's like showing your work on a math equation, but instead of formulas scratched out on the side of a page, it's, like . . . strife and emotional labor. I'm not going to list all the things that went down in my life and in the world while I was writing this book (but call my therapist and tell him he has my permission to tell you). What I will say is that I hope this book is a place of joy for you. For me, that joy was hard-won and often elusive. But possible! So I want to acknowledge us for getting through whatever we got through to arrive here together.

My incredible agent, Anna Sproul-Latimer of Neon Literary, and her co-founder, Kent Wolf, are miracle workers, soothsayers, geniuses, and treasure hunters. I'm so grateful to work with you.

This book's extraordinary editor, Joanna Cárdenas, has been a dream collaborator, thinking partner, and visionary since our first conversation. We have never met in person because, well, see above. I have no idea how tall she is. None!

But it has been a delight and a respite to make a human connection and create something beautiful despite the distances.

The whole team at Kokila is so wonderfully collaborative, so smart, so generous. It's been an honor to work with them. Thanks to Namrata Tripathi, the endlessly creative and indefatigable Lathea Mondesir, Caitlin Taylor, Jasmin Rubero, Theresa Evangelista, who designed the stunning cover and jacket, Natalie Vielkind, Ariela Rudy Zaltzman, Debra DeFord-Minerva (I LOVE COPY EDITORS!), Alison Throckmorton, and Margo Winton Parodi. Thanks also to LaMar Timmons-Long and Dr. Kim Parker for their invaluable reads.

I was *so thrilled* when the great Alexis Franklin agreed to illustrate the cover! The first time I saw Harrison and Linus in the flesh, I gasped. What a gift!

Thanks to friends and writers (and writer friends and friendly writers) who read early drafts, or talked me down from a ledge, or inspired me. Thanks to John Fram, Tina Canady, Jarrod Markman, Chris Newcomer, Sean Simon, Philip Ellis, Kristen Norine, Abraham Johnson, Rebecca Adelsheim, Steven Gross, and more. I owe a huge debt of gratitude to the great Alena Smith, creator of the AppleTV+ show *Dickinson*, for hiring me to write for it and giving me an excuse to reignite my Emily Dickinson love.

Thanks to the National Museum of African American History and Culture for being the most incredible place on Earth. And to the real-life Ms. Doreen for a transportive first visit.

My wonderful husband, David, taught me to see Baltimore in a new light and encouraged me through the writing process of this book. And my parents, Bob and Judi Thomas, sacrificed a lot to send me to a school *a tiny bit* like Plowshares (but NOT Plowshares; this is fiction). They showed me what love is and bridged gaps for me and made this city—this life—limitless.